]

Bo

In memory of Stormy Stuart.
A very special lady, gone far too soon

With love to John and Ben
as always

ECHOES OF DREAMS

Book 8 of "Circles of Light"

———

E M Sinclair

Echoes of Dreams – Book 8 of *Circles of Light*
First published 2015

Typeset by John Owen Smith

Cover photo by D Conyers

Published by Murrell Press

E M Sinclair can be contacted via the **Circles of Light** Facebook page.

ISBN 978-09554135-8-2

Printed by CreateSpace

Chapter One

The upheaval and fear of the last year had finally ended. Lives were gradually settling once more to ordinary, everyday concerns. A great deal of work needed to be done in many parts of the world. Two thirds of the population in the north of the continent of Drogoya had perished, and the survivors were struggling to restore some form of organised society.

Here, on the great land mass of Sapphrea, the southern lands of Malesh under the leadership of Harbour Master Chevra, were slowly being rebuilt after the earthquake which had devastated large areas. In north western Sapphrea there had been less damage. The fortress towns were smaller and more scattered, but the inhabitants had been badly frightened and looked to their Lords for help and reassurance.

In Return, the town where the mage Tika had been born into slavery, the people were confused and uncertain. Their Lord, Hargon, had been possessed, so the rumours went, by an evil demon and had led a troop of armsmen westward to the coast. He'd said he was in pursuit of the runaway slave Tika, that she was the cause of the terrible events that had taken place.

Over half a year had passed since Hargon and his men had departed. His two young sons were dead, in mysterious circumstances, so said the whispers, and there was no one to take Hargon's place. Finally the Lords of the allied towns arrived to hold open council. The doors of Hargon's great hall were flung wide, letting all citizens who wanted, hear what the Lords decided.

When Lord Raben of Tagria had finished explaining what he knew of the fate of Return's Lord (which wasn't a great deal,) he glanced at his two companions. The Lord Seboth of Far rose to his feet.

'We believe it will be best if we leave Captain Fryss and Officer Mallit in charge of your town. You all know them both and they know most of you. Being close to Lord Hargon before these troubles, they understand the running of things here.' Seboth spread his hands towards his large audience. 'If there are any objections we would hear them now?'

A murmur rustled through the crowded hall but no one spoke up in response to Lord Seboth. He gazed over the people crammed before him.

'There is one matter to make clear. Lord Hargon still held slavery to be an acceptable thing. You all know that none of us,' he gestured to his two companions. 'None of us have had slaves in our towns for many years. Therefore we decree that any who have been counted slaves here, are slaves no longer. We expect Captain Fryss and Officer Mallit to arrange for paid employment for all such people and to let no one of them be cast out and made destitute. I know most slaves here have been born slaves within Hargon's own household. They will be treated with respect and with dignity.'

Lords Raben and Zalom nodded as Seboth resumed his seat. Zalom leaned in to speak softly to him while the packed hall slowly emptied. The two men the Lords had named to take charge of Return waited until there were very few stragglers left in the hall. Seboth waved them to draw chairs up to the table.

'You have spent some considerable time in my town.' Seboth said. 'You have also visited Tagria and Andla. You know how we rule our people. Hargon was a bitter man who lived by a set of very narrow and rigid opinions. We want Return to become a good place to live in, without fear of sudden cruelties.'

The two men were nodding while Seboth spoke.

'It got bad in the last two, three years sir, and everything went crazy last year. Hargon was a strict Lord, but he didn't use to be as nasty as he got then.'

'I know Captain,' Seboth agreed. 'But it ends now. No more slaves and no arbitrary killings, floggings or any other vicious punishments for petty sins. Anything you feel you can't handle, you send to one of us.'

Officer Mallit cleared his throat. 'What about that circle thing sir? Do we put a guard on it, or will it be – er – used?'

Zalom scratched his bearded chin. 'I think a couple of men could keep watch to start with. You were shown how to use it were you not? Then use it for urgent messages for now and let stories spread slowly through the town – about mages and suchlike.'

Seboth hid a grin: "mages and suchlike" indeed.

Officer Mallit shifted in his chair. 'There are a number of slaves sir, who are too old to be sent out to earn their livings.'

Lord Raben answered him. 'Then let them choose, either to stay within Hargon's household which you will now have charge of, or find them small houses of their own and pay them a modest pension. They deserve no less.' He scowled at a memory. 'They suffered, especially in these last years, under Hargon's madness.'

'It will be as you say sir.' Mallit sounded relieved and Seboth was glad Hargon's old officer had survived the events of the last year.

The three Lords were finally left alone and Seboth stood, stretching his back.

'I still find it all nearly impossible to believe,' Zalom grumbled.

Raben of Tagria climbed to his feet beside Seboth. 'I am convinced of the truth of all the reports we've received.' He slapped Zalom's shoulder. 'It's all too fantastical *not* to be true. Who could invent such tales?'

Seboth clasped first Raben's wrist, then Zalom's.

'I know you've chosen to wait until dawn, but I will take my leave now I think.'

Zalom laughed. 'Give our deepest respects to your lovely lady then, and safe journey.'

Just before dusk four days later, Seboth and his escort of ten armsmen arrived back in Far, his steward bowing in welcome in front of the great doors of the hall. Seboth dismissed his armsmen and ran up the broad steps to where Meran waited.

'All is well?' he asked the elderly steward.

'Yes my lord. Lady Lallia is in the library. Shall I bring a meal to you there sir?'

'Yes please.' Seboth stopped halfway down the side staircase leading to his private quarters and turned to regard Meran. 'Tell me,' he demanded.

Meran spread his hands, his eyes wide and innocent. 'A visitor or three, that's all my lord. Your brother and Lady Lallia have been a touch over excited. I'm sure they'll tell you all my lord.'

'Visitors,' Seboth repeated.

'Hmmm, yes sir. they came by way of what they called a gateway.' He regarded Lord Seboth solemnly. 'There are still two here – they are with Lady Lallia and Olam – in the library, as I said.'

Seboth muttered something that his steward chose to ignore, and hurried to the stairs. Meran moved off to the kitchens to fetch a meal for his lord.

Seboth paused outside the library door: he could hear nothing. He extended his senses, as that child woman Tika had shown him, and was startled to discover the library was shielded. He could probably penetrate the shield quite easily – it felt more like a simple warding than a proper defensive shield, but it would be immediately obvious to whoever had set it in place. And it held no hint of his wife's mind signature. He knocked lightly on the door as he lifted the latch and felt a faint tingle as the ward dissolved around him.

The lamps were lit and he found his wife, brother and two strangers seated on the heaps of pillows near the further window. Lallia smiled and rose gracefully to greet her husband. Seboth saw the latest infant was sleeping close to where Lallia had been sitting. His brother Olam grinned.

'All went well in Return then?' he asked.

'Yes indeed,' Seboth replied distractedly, his arm around his wife, his eyes fixed on the strangers who stared straight back at him. Seboth thanked the stars that he had received detailed reports from the mage Tika, or more accurately, from one of her company. He was therefore able to keep a welcoming smile on his face when the male stranger rose and bowed. The grey skinned, hairless head lifted and slightly tilted leaf green eyes met Seboth's gaze.

'I am Kern, of the bloodline of Darallax, Second Son of Mother Dark.

The man's voice was soft, with the slightest of accents.

The woman also rose. 'And I am Jian, sister of Shivan, Grandson of Mother Dark. Tika told us of you.'

Seboth stared at the thin face, dominated by eyes of brilliant

8

gold, and clutched at his wits. He bowed in his turn. 'Please, seat yourselves. I am glad to meet you.' He shot a quick glare at his brother who chuckled unrepentantly. Seboth sat beside Lallia and gave the baby a poke in its stomach.

'Do leave her alone Seboth, she's only just gone to sleep.' Lallia caught his hand and waved the other hand at their guests. 'Kern and Jian have interesting news.'

Seboth scowled. 'Interesting? In a nice or nasty way?'

Closer inspection suggested Jian was much younger than he'd first thought: he found it impossible to guess Kern's age but sensed he was also relatively young. Kern gave a sweet smile and looked at Jian. The girl from the Dark Realm took a deep breath.

'We have heard that Lord Cyrek's sister, Seola, is gaining strength. she is nearly insane with rage and grief at the death of Cyrek and she has vowed to continue his cause.'

'His cause being?' Seboth asked mildly.

'Well, to destroy everything of course.' Jian's youth was all too apparent in her indignant reply.

'Of course,' agreed Seboth. 'And you heard this where precisely?'

Faint colour stained the girl's pale face. 'I heard my brother speak of it. He is deeply worried.'

Seboth smiled and raised his brows. His lady wife slapped his arm. 'Don't be difficult Seboth. I believe that Jian indeed heard her brother voicing great concern.'

'I'm sure she did, my dear. Listening at doors no doubt.'

'Oh really Seboth, you know full well it's the only sensible thing to do when men start trying to keep secrets to protect us poor women from the truth.'

Lallia gave her husband a dazzling smile just as a rap at the door indicated Meran's arrival with a bevy of maids bearing trays of food and drink. Once they were alone again and Seboth eating, Olam poured himself a goblet of small beer.

'Seriously Seboth, Shivan is still trying to reorganise his Realm and he is terrified someone might tell Tika that Seola is alive and promising great problems for the world. Tika needs much more time to recover her strength before she can get involved in more trouble.'

'It's been nearly a year,' Seboth mumbled through a mouthful of pastry.

Although both Olam and Jian glared at him, it was Olam who got in first.

'And have you forgotten brother? We were told it took the First Daughter far longer to regain her strength years ago? You never saw Tika after she'd used a lot of power. The flesh fell from her. She was skeletal. A breath would have knocked her off her feet. She has done so much, so much at such cost to herself, none of us want her to risk more anytime soon.'

Jian gave him a grateful smile.

'And what makes you think you, or we, could deal with this Seola ourselves?' Seboth wiped his fingers on a damp towel. 'When Tika visited us briefly, she showed us how we could use power we didn't know we possessed. But my strength is as nothing – how could we deal with someone like Seola? She is from your Dark Realm Jian, and more powerful than her brother Cyrek, or so the reports suggest.' He stared at Jian thoughtfully. 'How strong are you actually?'

Jian knotted her fingers together then cleared her throat. 'Were you told about Shivan?'

Seboth shrugged. 'He came into his powers very early. His mind works somehow differently from most of your people. He has a great deal of, as yet, untapped strength. Is that about right?'

Jian sighed. 'I am very like Shivan.' Her golden eyes met Seboth's steadily. 'But *I* am much stronger.'

Seboth suspected the girl spoke only the truth, and felt completely out of his depth in this situation. Kern spoke into the silence.

'Jian came to visit Skaratay and told us of her fears. Shivan had already alerted us to beware if Seola should appear. I asked to travel with Jian to seek further information and to perhaps try to combat whatever evil Seola might plan. We have visited Gaharn and spoken with Lady Emla and her advisors. She has offered two of her people to help us track down Seola. The Vagrantians too have said that they will assist in any possible way. Their leader, the Lady Thryssa, has strongly advised we seek the ruins of their ancient cities.'

Olam grinned and Seboth rolled his eyes. 'Just what you hoped for I'm sure Olam.'

He leaned back on the heaped pillows, thinking over the information he'd received in many scrolls sent from who knew where over the last year. 'I understand that Tika asked for help from various gods? Has anyone thought of asking any of them? Or are they all still – recovering? I confess the ideas of Places Between and different Planes of Existence are difficult for me to comprehend, but I do believe they are real. Would any god be able to perhaps *see* where this troublesome woman is?'

Jian frowned and chewed her lower lip.

'The Lord Darallax asked his Shadows that very thing, but they were unable to locate her,' said Kern.

Seboth considered that remark, could make no sense of it so put it firmly from his mind. For now.

Olam stretched his arms over his head. 'We could ask your Mistress of Death,' he suggested.

Jian looked aghast.

'Oh for stars' sake. Tika thought she was lonely, like that hideous great raven, and she was right, wasn't she? Your Mistress of Death looked after Tika for days when she needed total rest. Yes. Let's ask her – if she can hear us from here.'

Jian's mouth opened but Olam had already called a name: 'Ferag!' He added quietly: 'If she turns up Seboth, your very best manners would be safest.'

Seboth stared at his brother in some alarm as a chill breeze riffled through the library. Five heads snapped round towards the rear of the long room and they saw a slender woman advancing on them.

Seboth struggled out of his nest of cushions and offered a hand to his wife. They stared. The woman had long, long, dark red hair and wore a dress of a similar colour which seemed woven of cobwebs. Her dress and her hair moved softly around her although she was now standing quite still and there was no draught in the room. Her face was beautiful beyond compare and Seboth found himself short of breath. He swallowed hard and bowed low.

'We are most honoured by your presence lady.'

Dress and hair settled about Ferag and a devastating smile lit her face. 'How wonderful to meet a man who understands courtesy. 'Her gaze rested on Olam, who also bowed, hand on his heart.

'I remember you,' she said. 'You travelled with the dear child Tika did you not?'

'Indeed lady, and I know how greatly she treasured your generous care of her.'

Ferag's gaze settled on Jian and her smile diminished. 'You are Shivan's little sister I think.'

Jian could barely nod.

'Oh my goodness, you believe all those cruel stories of me do you not? You all seem to think you are so very special that I must only appear among you to take you off to my Realm. It makes a nice change for me to have the occasional chat with the living, you know.'

Ferag's hair was twisting and curling about her shoulders and back again.

'I am Kern, of Shadow,' he smiled at Ferag.

She inclined her head slightly but said nothing because Lady Lallia had taken a step forward and dropped into a deep obeisance.

'Lallia, my lady wife,' Seboth informed Ferag.

There was a piercing wail from behind him and he closed his eyes for a brief moment. 'Excuse my daughter's rude interruption,' he began as he saw Ferag's frown.

Lallia reached gracefully behind Seboth's legs, plucking their now squawking baby from the scattered pillows. She glanced up at Ferag, an apology forming on her lips, but that lady was already sinking elegantly to the pillows beside her.

'A baby!' she breathed, looking at the small scarlet face in wonder.

Lallia didn't think twice. She held out the shrieking bundle and Ferag's arms closed around the baby.

'She is gorgeous,' Ferag murmured, her long, cold finger stroking the flushed cheek.

Tightly closed eyes opened and stared up at the woman. A final shuddering sob and a wide gummy smile was offered. Lallia was watching Ferag and saw she was near tears.

'Her name is Pella, my lady.'

'Hello little Pella. What an amazing creature you are.'

A huge yawn greeted that remark, a thumb was jammed into

her mouth and Pella's lids fluttered briefly before closing.

'So few children are born to the Dark Ones now,' Ferag told Lallia. 'And they are all so very precious.'

She held the baby gently, in a manner which told Lallia that Ferag had held many other children.

Olam coughed discreetly. 'I dared to call you, my lady, because I wondered if you might know the whereabouts of Seola?'

Still gazing at the child in her arms, Ferag answered vaguely. 'She was always such a dreadful creature. Far worse than that brother of hers. His conceit made him laughably stupid. 'She looked up and frowned. 'Why do you want *her*?'

'We don't,' replied Olam. 'But she's planning trouble and we thought we'd try to stop her, rather than letting Tika get involved.'

Ferag's frown deepened and the temperature in the room dropped noticeably.

'Tika? she must do nothing but rest and relax and enjoy her new home.' The room warmed a little. 'I shall see what I can do and then I'll come and tell you.'

With obvious reluctance, Ferag passed the sleeping baby to Lallia and rose. She brushed a hand lightly over Lallia's hair. 'I would very much like to visit again.'

Seboth took a deep breath but his wife spoke first.

'You would be most welcome Lady Ferag. Perhaps you might like to meet our other children too?'

Ferag clasped her hands together under her chin. 'Other children?'

'The oldest is six, a boy. Then two more boys, a girl of just four, another boy and Pella here.'

'And you would let me see them?' Ferag whispered.

'Of course. You are most welcome.'

Seboth closed his eyes.

Ferag stooped and kissed Lallia's brow. 'I shall see what I can discover for you and return as soon as I can.' And she was gone.

Seboth let out the breath he hadn't realised he'd been holding and slumped back on the cushions next to his wife.

'Did you *have* to invite her back?' he asked.

'Well of course I did. Tika was right. The poor lady is dreadfully lonely – did you not see how she behaved with Pella?'

Jian shuddered. 'I think you are right Lallia, but it is very hard to treat her "normally" when all my life I have heard how unpleasant she is. She is said to appear only to take people into death.'

'Oh pooh,' retorted Olam. 'She's a lovely woman.'

Seboth and Jian looked unconvinced but Kern nodded.

'Many people reacted with fear and horror when she appeared in Skaratay last year. But Chancellor Konrik said much the same as Tika – that Ferag adopted the strange, teasing manner she has just to conceal her own pain.'

'So.' Olam rubbed his hands together. 'Shall I make arrangements for a trip to the coast?'

Seboth scowled. 'You've been trying to find a good reason to let me send a group there ever since you got back.'

'We would like to travel with you,' Jian put in quickly, and Seboth glared at her.

'Does your brother know where you are, or what your plans are?'

'Not *exactly*, but. . .'

'I thought not. It will take fourteen or fifteen days to get to the coast. I don't know how long you're thinking of poking around the ruins. What am I supposed to tell your brother – who is, let us not forget, the *ruler* of your Realm, if he demands to know where his baby sister's gone?'

Seboth realised belatedly that Jian's golden eyes were blazing, and she *had* told him her powers were greater than Shivan's.

'We can probably sort something out,' he added and grinned at her.

Her eyes lost their dangerous glitter and her fists unclenched on her lap. Seboth reached for his goblet.

'Seriously, I don't see how much information on anything you might get if you do get inside those ruins. You told me things crumbled to dust as soon as you touched them.'

Olam nodded. 'That's been worrying me a lot, but Kern and Jian both have ideas about that.'

Seboth raised a brow at Kern.

'Shadows may be able to help.'

'How do you mean?'

'It is hard to explain about Shadows,' Kern said with an

apologetic smile. 'There are times when they seem to *change* time itself. Among other things. We have scholars who have dedicated their lives to studying Shadows.'

'And I have been studying time,' said Jian. 'Shivan was always interested in how time works. I've followed his experiments but I've also investigated different aspects of time, which I believe Shivan neglected to do.'

'And fascinating it all sounds,' agreed Seboth. 'But I fear it means very little to me.'

'There's no danger now,' Olam began.

Seboth snorted.

'No. Not like before, when Hargon was charging after us,' Olam insisted. 'I think we'd only need two or three men to accompany us and one wagon for supplies.'

'I wish I could come.' Lallia caught Seboth's expression and gave a gurgle of laughter. 'I know I cannot go now, but one day, husband, I *will* travel where I choose.'

Wisely, Seboth made no reply, watching when Lallia gathered the baby and a couple of stray shawls. 'I will leave you to your plans.' Lallia smiled at Kern and Jian. 'This child needs its cradle and I need my bed.'

'Good night Lallia, and thank you for your kindness.' Jian moved to open the door for Seboth's wife.

'And thank you for the honey cakes,' Kern smiled. 'They are wonderful.'

'Her name will be praised throughout the world for those honey cakes,' said Seboth, getting to his feet with a groan. 'After four days riding, I need a bath and my bed.'

'Age catching up with you, brother?'

'Indeed it is.' Seboth cuffed Olam's head good naturedly as he made his way out.

There was a brief silence before Kern offered: 'Another would join us in this search.

Jian narrowed her eyes. 'You didn't tell me that. Who?'

'I don't think you met her, but she is a cousin of mine. She spends her time buried in the archives but her knowledge, consequently, is considerable in many areas. Her name is Dellian and although she is younger, she is a great friend of Subaken.'

Olam remembered Subaken, the heiress to the Shadow Realm.

He also remembered Tika saying the woman was over three hundred years old although she had looked the same as the sixteen year old Tika. Olam knew that Jian was *really* only seventeen but now, staring at Kern, he wondered just what age the man might be.

Seboth clearly thought they were crazy. For the first time, the thought flitted through Olam's head, that perhaps they were.

Chapter Two

Once Olam had retired to bed, Jian and Kern spent some time composing messages. They sent one to the Lady Emla in Gaharn, and one to the Shadow Realm on the island of Skaratay. Satisfied, they too sought their beds for the brief time left before dawn.

Most of the day was spent collecting items Olam thought necessary for exploring the city buried in the sands. He also chose two armsmen to travel with them – Tursig and Riff. Riff had travelled with Olam last year. he had been restless since they'd been home and was delighted at the chance to go wandering again.

Barrels were checked and double checked before being filled with fresh water and secured on a wagon. The year was warming and waterholes were rarities in the blighted land they would have to cross to reach the coast. Olam hope the freshwater pool behind the cliffs was still there but chose not to burden the others with undue worry on this point.

Most of the day passed with Olam packing and unpacking various items until Jian was no longer speaking to him and Seboth was weak with laughter. Lallia came to the stables to suggest they all came inside for a peaceful evening meal. Taking in the situation at a glance, she suggested Jian and Kern might like a brief stroll in her courtyard garden before the ate.

Lallia and Kern chatted amiably while Jian simmered. Kern stopped suddenly and a heartbeat later they heard a groan. They hurried round a clump of newly budding shrubs and found a woman huddled on the path, a large pack beside her. Kern was appalled.

'I forgot – Dellian hates gateways. And I have no healing powers.'

'Nor me.' Jian knelt beside the woman.

'Well for stars' sake, let's get her inside. I can help a little but it will be with more mundane medicine than magical powers.'

Kern lifted the woman easily and Lallia saw the same oval, grey skinned head, quite hairless but yet strangely beautiful. She led the way quickly to a small chamber, obviously a room she used when she needed peace and quiet, close to her garden.

'Put her on the couch,' Lallia instructed. She opened an inner door and called for a maid who she then sent running to fetch Meran. Lallia soaked a cloth in a bowl of scented water, wrung it and gently wiped the woman's face.

Dellian's uptilted eyes were scrunched shut in pain and Lallia cursed the fact that she'd had no chance to learn any healing skills. Without turning, Lallia knew Meran had arrived.

'She came through a gateway, Meran. Kern says she gets sick when she travels thus. Will you make a herb tea,' she glanced up at the man who had watched over her since her babyhood. 'The tea you used to make when I got sick on papa's horse?'

The elderly steward touched her shoulder lightly. 'At once lady. It will take very little time.'

Dellian moaned and tried to curl into a tighter ball. Lallia soothed her, looking at Jian.

'Do you really know nothing of healing?'

Jian coloured slightly. 'Sorry, not a thing.'

Meran was already back with a teapot steaming on a tray. 'Get her to take small sips lady, until it is all gone. let it cool a little.'

He poured a small amount of liquid into a shallow dish, various mellow herbal scents rising as he swirled it to hurry the cooling. 'I can tend her while you go to dine with Lord Seboth.'

'And I will stay, said Kern firmly. He helped Lallia to her feet and then took her place beside the couch.

Jian was already at the door.

'Sorry if I sounded cross my dear.' Lallia slid her hand under Jia's elbow. 'It is just so frustrating, having these powers and yet being unable to do the smallest healings.'

At the meal with Seboth and Olam, Lallia explained Dellian's – unexpected – arrival. Olam scowled.

'Let's hope the woman's recovered enough for us to leave in the morning.'

Jian kept her eyes on her plate when Lallia glared at Olam

18

before delivering a scathing speech about unfeeling men. It seemed politic for Olam and Jian to agree that an early night would be beneficial before starting their journey on the morrow.

Olam, Tursig and Riff were in the stables at dawn and horses stamped restlessly as two were hitched to a wagon. Four other animals were led out and loaded with personal packs. Kern and Jian emerged from the main building, the newcomer striding between them, and introductions were made. Olam noted that Dellian's face had a slightly greenish tinge but her hazel eyes were clear and she assured him she was quite fit enough to travel.

Lallia and Seboth came to see them off and wish them safe travelling. Riff, Olam and Jian swung onto three of the horses, Riff leading the fourth. Tursig drove the wagon with Kern and Dellian perched alongside him.

It was still early and few people were about in the small town. The party was soon moving beyond the fields to the west. Although it was not yet the hot season, by midday Kern and Dellian had retreated under the wagon's canopy. Olam produced woven straw hats which Jian regarded with some doubt but she very quickly discovered the benefits a straw cone could confer.

Each day took them deeper into nearly barren landscapes. Occasionally a wind sprang up from nowhere, blowing dust and sand into their eyes, and would then drop just as inexplicably. On their tenth uneventful day out from Far, the wind began to rise just as they'd decided to make camp for the night.

Olam had packed several large sheets of canvas, remembering from his previous time in this area, just how devastating some dry storms could be. Now, he lashed them to the wagon and made a large secure room on its leeward side, big enough for the horses too, to be sheltered from the stinging sand and grit hurled against them. This time the wind did not drop; instead it built until it was a howling gale pounding the wagon and the frail canvas tenting.

When it finally ceased, the sun appeared – the air had been so thick with dirt the travellers had been unaware dawn had arrived. It took a while to clear the wagon of debris and fold and pack the canvas sheets, so it was close to midday before they could get on their way.

'There should be a waterhole ahead,' Olam told the others. He had been following a map made by Navan and sent to him from Tika's new home.

'After a storm like last night, how can you imagine it will still be there?' Jian asked him.

He shrugged. 'What the wind hides one day, it can reveal the next,' he began, but was interrupted by a bugling cry from high overhead.

The horses, who had stayed relatively calm during the night, now rolled their eyes and became hysterical. Olam tossed his reins to Riff, slid off his horse and hurried to grab the heads of the two animals pulling the wagon. Even as he soothed and murmured to them, the horses calmed and a huge crimson Dragon landed gracefully before them. Olam abandoned the horses and rushed to the Dragon, hurling his arms as far round the massive neck and shoulders as he could reach. He felt affection pour into his mind and stepped back, his hand stroking the long jaw above his head.

'It's wonderful to see you Brin,' he finally managed. 'But what are you doing here? Did you know we were here? How are you? Have you come from Tika?'

Brin's laugh rang through the minds of all the travellers, his eyes whirring in hues of pink and rose.

'We came to visit. Yes, we heard you were on the way to the coast. We are all well. No, we have not come from Iskallia.'

'Iskallia?' Olam frowned.

'That is the name Tika has given to the land she was given.' Brin's voice in the minds of the humans was deep and warm. 'Greetings to you Riff,' he added when he recognised the armsman who was grinning wildly at him.

Jian dismounted and came towards the Dragon. She put her left thumb to her brow, her lips and her heart, then spread her hand towards Brin. 'May the Dark be with you,' she said softly.

Brin studied the slender girl for a moment. 'And may the stars guide your path,' he replied.

Olam introduced Tursig who could only gape. He'd heard all the stories but this was his first encounter with a Dragon.

Dellian and Kern had both seen Brin on Skaratay but had not been introduced. Olam suddenly noticed the two smaller Dragons had hidden behind Brin's bulk.

'You have brought your children?' he asked.

Brin seemed a little embarrassed. 'They are my youngest children. Their mother wished to go travelling and – er – left them in my care. This is Skay, she is named for my mother.'

The Dragon, black as night, dipped her long face shyly. They all heard a soft feminine voice whisper in their minds: 'May the stars guide your paths.'

Brin nodded to the other young Dragon whose scales were like butter glowing in the sunlight. 'And this is Flyn.'

The voice in their heads was polite, male and sounded as shy as his sister's when he too gave formal greetings to the humans.

'I thought I would bring them and spend some time with you.' Brin explained, specks of scarlet flashing briefly in his large eyes.

Olam was puzzled, then suspicion dawned. 'Trouble?' he asked with sympathy.

'Well I saw nothing wrong but Tika got rather – agitated. A small matter, involving a donkey, I believe.'

Olam snorted. 'I seem to remember Storm met a donkey once.'

The eyes of all three Dragons whirred rapidly and a sense of discomfort flowed from them. Olam smothered a smile.

'If you've come to visit a while, perhaps you could tell us if there's a waterhole close enough for us to reach before dark?'

With a flurry of leather wings, the two young Dragons were in the air, arrowing westwards. Brin huffed.

'I will escort you, if you are ready to travel on,' he said, lifting into the air with effortless ease.

The land had appeared deceptively flat ever since they'd left the boundaries of Far. In fact, it undulated, in places quite steeply, and the flat stretches were a welcome relief. Brin drifted above the wagon and riders, telling the company what had been happening with Tika and her friends. He interrupted himself to relay the information that there was a waterhole not too far ahead. Olam had been fooled by a Dragon's estimate of "not too far" on previous occasions and questioned Brin more closely until he was satisfied that they would really reach water before dark.

They came to a gully torn straight across the ground in front of them, which extended north to south as far as they could see.

Tursig climbed down from the wagon to peer down the steep slope. Olam joined him and they finally chose a route down. Olam led two of the riding horses, followed by Tursig and Riff at the heads of the two animals drawing the wagon. Jian followed with the remaining two.

Brin was settled on the opposite side of the gully, the two young Dragons with him, perhaps half a mile distant. It took longer than Olam would have wished to negotiate the slope but the horses stayed steady thanks to Brin sending waves of calmness from his mind to theirs.

By the time they'd clambered up the further side the sky directly ahead resembled a huge furnace and Olam was relieved that the gully had been traversed before darkness engulfed them. The three Dragons had settled to one side of a small pool, which, at first, Olam feared would be insufficient for their needs. Then he realised a spring bubbled in the rocks nearby, feeding the pool constantly.

Camp was quickly set up and food prepared while the two young Dragons watched proceedings with deep interest. The night darkened and settled over them and Brin kept the company entertained with tales of his travels. Olam and Riff exchanged glances occasionally: they'd both heard many of Brin's tall stories last time they'd journeyed with him.

Another two uneventful days and the group reached the ocean. Tursig was the only one not to have seen the vast expanse of water before and he sat on the wagon seat gazing open-mouthed at the view before him. Olam and Riff were delighted to find they recognised where they were and explained to the others that one more day's travel south would bring them to the caves they'd sheltered in before.

Brin stayed with them, drifting above the cliffs, sometimes swerving out over the water a short distance. He explained that his children had flown on, hoping to find the Sea Dragons. Olam had the foresight to keep the wagon on the inland side of the cliffs for the last half mile. He remembered trying to persuade the horses through such a narrow gap from the beach.

Jian and the two from the Shadow Realm exclaimed when they reached Olam's goal. A broad swathe of new green grass surrounded by huge boulders gave the sense of a garden deliberately planted, behind the wall of granite cliff. Brin settled comfortably on one such large, flat topped rock still flooded with late evening sunshine.

'Skay says they have flown further south. They have not yet seen any sign of the Sea Kindred.'

Olam paused in unloading supplies and frowned, but before he could express any concern, Brin continued.

'The Sea Kindred travel far up and down this coast. There is nothing unusual about their absence.'

Tursig and Kern had made a fire in the hearth built by Pallin and Sket last year and organised the usual meal of dried foods. Olam grinned.

'We'll have fresh fish soon – fish such as you've never seen Tursig!'

The armsman smiled doubtfully. 'Yes sir.'

Riff let the fire die quickly once their food was cooked. He remembered searching for scrubby bushes for the fire and knew better than to use their supply of fuel blocks too fast now. Their eyes grew accustomed to the dazzle of starlight, uncountable lights jewelling the sky.

'I know why *I* want to see the ruins again,' said Olam, 'but tell me exactly why *you* think they're important. And how they can have any connection with Seola.'

Jian drew a breath. 'I told you I was interested in time?' When Olam nodded, she went on. 'I'm sure there is some way we could – alter – time. I find it hard to explain my ideas to anyone, but I have thought about it since I was very young. There are a few reports of experiments that I found in our Academy. And I'm sure Seola must have been working on something very similar.' She raised her hands helplessly.

Olam frowned. Something nagged at him. Jian caught his expression. 'What? Do you know anything of the manipulation or alteration of time?'

'I'm sure I've heard some talk of it, but I can't remember by whom. Let me think on it. What about you Kern, Dellian? Why are you so interested in these old ruins?'

'We are both historians,' Kern replied. 'But Dellian is also a map maker and planner.'

'Planner?'

'I understand how towns should be laid out, among other things,' Dellian's voice was soft.

'Drains and bridges, roads and open spaces,' Kern explained. 'Hopefully, Dellian might be able to work out the way this city once looked and where the important buildings might lie.'

Riff and the other four went off to the caves they'd chosen, leaving Olam with Brin. Olam scrambled up the side of the boulder on which Brin still reclined. He rested a palm against a scaled shoulder, just able to see starlight dancing on water beyond the low cliffs.

'It seems a lifetime ago since we were here last,' Olam murmured. 'Yet it is barely a year.'

Brin's rumbling laugh sounded in Olam's head. 'You humans have such short lives.' He lowered his head so that one huge eye was close to Olam's face. Stars were reflected in that eye as Olam returned the Dragon's gaze. 'I was listening to your talk. I am sure Captain Sefri spoke of time when Tika healed Sefri's poor ship.'

Olam nearly overbalanced off the boulder. 'Of course! Now, all I have to do is recall the exact words.'

Brin lifted his head to study the ocean again. 'I do not remember I'm afraid, but I'm sure Tika would. I could return to Iskallia and ask?'

'No, no,' said Olam quickly. 'Tika's still supposed to be recovering in peace. We would much rather she didn't know about this trip.'

'Aah. Then perhaps you should sleep. Skay bespoke me that they'd seen the Dragons of the Northern Flight. They may be here tomorrow.'

Kern, Brin and Riff escorted Tursig to the beach the next morning. Kern was familiar with the seashore, living as he had on the island of Skaratay, and was able to offer some explanation on the working of tides, ocean currents and the immeasurable depth of water in some parts. Brin reclined at the top of the beach, listening with amusement, his eyes glinting with pink flashes. Riff pulled off his boots and persuaded Tursig to do so and then to stand with him at the edge of the water. Small waves broke over their feet, surging nearly to their knees.

Kern abandoned his attempts to explain why the water was salty, and wandered back towards Brin. The crimson Dragon suddenly pushed himself up onto his haunches and five humans appeared in a heap in front of him. His eyes whirred and flashed in momentary alarm until one, a female, disentangled herself from the pile and spoke to his mind.

'Brin! Brin! It is I, Reema. From Gaharn. I met you when you visited us on your way back from Vagrantia.'

Brin's eyes calmed their wild spinning and he settled back on the sand. 'Indeed,' he agreed. 'But I was not expecting you here, and not in such a manner.' His eyes flickered again. 'I believe Shadows brought you?' There was a very cautious note in his mindtone.

Reema gave a laugh that hinted at near hysteria. 'The Son of Shadow kindly instructed his own Shadows to convey us here. They don't seem to think any warnings necessary.'

A short stocky man staggered forward, clutching his middle. 'Appalling! Utterly appalling way to travel!' He sank to the sand under Brin's nose.

Reema brushed her fingers across the man's forehead and he groaned, faint colour appearing in his cheeks. He opened dark brown eyes and dragged in a deep breath. 'I am most grateful for your attention Reema, most grateful.'

Two more men and a woman were slowly getting to their feet amid a jumble of packs and cloaks. The two men, like Reema, were very tall, thin and dark haired. Brin vaguely recognised one of them and inclined his head slightly in his direction.

'We met at Lady Emla's house I think. You are called Jenzi?'

The man thus addressed grinned. 'We did. Very briefly though.'

'You are a healer.'

Jenzi bowed. When he straightened his grey eyes were alight with excitement. He turned on the spot, taking in the cliffs, the sandy beach and the endless water. Reema's brows drew down in a frown. 'Perhaps you could make sure our friends are unharmed Jenzi?'

'Huh? Oh. Yes, of course.' Jenzi turned towards the two people who had sunk back to the sand again, looking ill.

Reema nodded at Kern. 'I am glad to see you again Kern. I presume Jiais with you?'

'Yes,' Kern replied, 'and another of my people – Dellian.' He studied the three who were still looking far from happy. 'Perhaps a bowl of tea would help?' He waved at the narrow gap in the cliff behind Brin. 'Our camp is just through there.'

Riff dragged Tursig from the water's edge and joined everyone at the camp. The newcomers were soon revived with copious bowls of tea and Jenzi's ministrations. The other very tall man, also from Gaharn, was introduced as Shuli. The much smaller woman was Kara from Kedara Circle in Vagrantia and the stocky man was Reshik of Segra Circle.

By the time they had inspected the caves and sorted out their possessions, it was past midday. Brin had reclined on his chosen boulder but suddenly lifted into the air. He rose high and fast, his bugling cry roaring around the company. Olam and Riff grinned at the startled faces turning to them.

'Visitors,' Olam announced and hurried back through the gap to the beach.

'Whatever now,' muttered the still shaken Reshik, but he followed everyone from the camp.

Brin was dropping now, slowly and gracefully. He landed in front of the group of travellers, rearing erect, his wings outstretched. Olam saw the two young Dragons racing towards them to land either side of their father. Behind them came a large number of Dragons, all calling aloud, their voices high and piercing.

Olam shivered when a grey green Sea Dragon settled in front of Brin. He saw the scars all along her left side and the empty eye socket. This was Mist. A much bigger dark slate coloured Dragon landed beside her and Olam recognised Salt, Eldest of the Northern Flight. Cloud, palest ivory, Mother of the Flight, settled on Mist's other side and the three exchanged formal greetings with Brin.

At a quick glance, Olam estimated there were more than twenty Sea Dragons crowding behind the three leaders. Brin introduced the humans who were closely inspected by the whole Flight. It was Cloud who chose to let her mindvoice be heard by them all, and there was a teasing note in her words.

'Perhaps the humans would enjoy some fresh fish to eat?'

Riff dug his elbow sharply into Tursig's ribs and grinned. 'You just watch, my friend.'

Olam bowed to Cloud and agreed fresh fish would be most welcome. Instantly half a dozen much smaller Sea Dragons rose, arrowing out over the water and diving below the surface. Within heartbeats, they were back and enormous fish dropped on the beach until Olam raised his hands laughing.

'Enough,' he called. 'We are most grateful.' He saw the eager youngsters were disappointed not to be able to show more of their proficiency. 'We are all most impressed with your skills and hope you will provide more fish another day.'

'If you fetch stones,' Brin murmured, 'I will heat them for you here. I still don't understand why they must be cooked,' he added, 'but there is more room for everyone out here.'

As the sun sank, flaming, into the waters, eleven people enjoyed a meal of baked fish and settled back to spend the evening chatting and exchanging news with a Flight of Sea Dragons.

Seola had been alone for a full turn of the seasons, slowly regaining her power. When her brother Cyrek had been destroyed, Seola had fled north, far north. She had taken Dragon form and flown high and fast, her grief and rage giving strength to her mighty wings.

She flew from her home in the Dark Realm, following the eastern coastline ever northward. On, over the Kelshan Confederacy lands, and then over ocean for a full day. Finally, even her Dark strength weakened and she glided down to land on the high cliffs she was then approaching. The scent of burnt cinnamon rose as her huge Dragon form shimmered and faded, leaving a slender woman in its stead. Seola took a few stumbling paces before slumping to the ground. She had just enough physical strength left to roll towards a low clump of bushes before losing all awareness.

Hard pellets of rain roused her eventually and she blinked water from her lashes. She bit back a groan when she tried to move; every part of her hurt. Crawling deeper into the bushes, she drew her knees up to her chest, staring out at greyness.

Somewhere, she *would* find sanctuary, a place to gather her enormously depleted powers. She *would* regain her strength and find the ruined cities. Valsheba *would* rise again to control the world. Then, she would confront that misbegotten brat who had destroyed her beloved Cyrek. And she would kill her. Slowly.

Chapter Three

Brin and Skay left Flyn playing with the younger Sea Dragons and flew high, Brin relaying pictures of the land beneath them to the company below.

'I'm sure I recognise that area,' Riff muttered.

Olam shrugged. 'I'm sure I don't, but why don't you go and check it? I'd expect the entrance we dug out to be filled again after all this time, but you should be able to see some sign we were there.'

Riff didn't need telling twice. Pausing only long enough to grab a small shovel and a coil of rope, he vanished amid the boulders.

'Why are there no birds in these cliffs?' asked Kara.

'Sea Dragons are not fond of them,' Olam smiled at her. 'The birds move on when the Dragons arrive.'

'Do they have plavats here?' Kara asked curiously, then jumped. Cloud and Mist had floated down to settle on a boulder beside the woman and were hissing vigorously. Cloud's eyes flashed.

'We do *not* have plavats near us.'

Kara swallowed, then she smiled. 'I'm glad to hear that. I can't imagine much worse than a plavat as a neighbour.'

Cloud calmed herself, radiating approval. 'We sometimes see these.' She sent a mind picture to Kara's head.

'Goats?'

'We have no name for them. They don't use their minds to speak to others. They're very good at climbing.'

Kara's smile broadened. She perched on the rock just below Cloud. The Sea Dragon reminded her strongly of the old grannies, gossiping in Kedara market, but she kept that thought firmly blocked away in her head. Kara settled in for a good gossip with Cloud and Mist, keeping an eye on what the others were doing.

Dellian sat cross-legged, sheets of paper on a board on her lap, scribbling notes and shapes as she watched the view from Brin's eyes. Olam led Reshik, Shuli and Tursig out among the boulders, Jian following more slowly. Occasionally, glancing back, Olam saw Jian had clambered up onto a boulder to stare in every direction before sliding down and wandering on.

The sun had begun its descent when they all regathered. Papers, secured by handfuls of pebbles lay all around Dellian and Kern suggested she explain what she thought to begin with. Dellian rooted round for one particular sheet and held it up.

'All the blocks fell in the same direction,' she began.

Riff nodded. He was still annoyed that he'd been unable to find their previous excavation site. 'We knew that from before,' he grunted.

Dellian smiled faintly. 'I'm sure you did,' she agreed. 'But I asked Brin to do a wider sweep and some miles south and east, they fall in another direction.'

Silence greeted her words.

'And that means?' Olam prompted.

'If I can find the point where the directions change, I'd guess that's probably near the centre of the city.'

Kara nodded. 'Our histories tell us the people who lived here – our ancestors – were strong in power. They were nearly all mageborn, even labourers, farmers and artisans were gifted with a little talent. The truly powerful were greatly revered and lived in splendid houses in the centre of cities, places called Siertsey. That is where we are sure the explosions occurred, which caused such utter devastation.'

'But surely that's the place that will be completely destroyed,' Olam objected. 'What could you hope to find there?'

Reshik cleared his throat. 'I am an earth mage. I should be able to sense much more.'

'Much more of what?' Shuli asked with interest.

'How the building stood.' Reshik paused. 'I should also still be able to have some hint of what they were trying to do.'

'Do we really need to know that?' asked Reema.

Reshik looked nonplussed. 'Surely we should want to learn all we can?'

Olam sighed. 'And this helps us find Seola how exactly?'

Reshik stared at him blankly then turned to Kern.

'Jian visited our Realm,' Kern explained. 'She told us she had found evidence that Seola had heard of Shadows, and also that she had sought information on these very cities, so long lost to dust and sand.'

'She came to Vagrantia,' Kara interrupted. 'I did not see her but my uncle, Orsim, is Speaker for Kedara Circle, and he met her once. He said the council were uncomfortable with her questions and her very presence, so they told her very little. They also concealed many of our archives. He said she did not bother to hide her contemptuous opinion that Vagrantians were unworthy heirs to the might that had been Valsheba.

'The questions Seola asked worried our High Speaker enough that she sent messages to Lord Shivan and Lady Emla. And so we find ourselves here.' She smiled ruefully round the company.

'So do you know where the centre of the city was now Dellian?' asked Olam.

'It was roughly two miles south and half a mile inland,' she replied.

'Then Riff and I will go and check tomorrow. Perhaps the Sea Dragons will know if there's fresh water nearby, otherwise we'll have a long walk there and back each day with water skins to carry while we search the area.'

Olam and Riff set off early next day, while the air behind the cliffs was still cool. Jenzi, Kern and Jian chose to go with them. Brin and Skay flew overhead. Flyn and two young Sea Dragons chased each other back and forth. Olam saw a rare smile curve Jian's mouth when she watched the antics of the butter coloured Dragon and his two new friends.

Riff was watching them too. 'I wonder why the Sea Dragons are a different shape from *our* Dragons,' he mused.

Brin's chuckle rumbled through their minds. 'Sea Dragons are a more slender shape so they can move better in the water.

At that moment, one of Flyn's friends plunged into the sea for several heartbeats before surging up into the air in a glittering spray of water droplets.

'I have met other Dragons,' Brin added. 'In the lands that Jemin now rules.'

31

'How different were they?' Jian demanded at once. 'And where exactly did you see them?'

The five humans felt a brief agitation from Brin's mind. 'Quite different. A long way from here.' Brin's reply was short. 'Oh look, I see a pool ahead.' And he moved quickly on before any more might be asked of him.

Olam laughed at Jian's scowl. 'You'll get no more from him! But I wonder why he's so mysterious?'

Jenzi led them between and round the apparently endless boulders and they found there was indeed a fresh water pool. It curled in a narrow line along the base of the cliff which was much lower here.

'I'm not sure that cliff is natural,' said Olam.

He began to work his way up the side and after only a short climb, he called down. 'This is made of the same stone as the boulders. And it has definitely been cut and shaped.'

Kern scrambled up beside Olam. 'You're right,' he agreed. 'These must have been from huge buildings.' He gazed around. 'The destructive power needed to move such blocks,' he murmured.

'Do we *really* want anything to do with uncovering such things?' Olam asked, looking directly into Kern's leaf green eyes.

Kern leaned closer. 'That is why the Lord of Shadow sent us.' He paused, then pushed his sleeve back, revealing a black bracelet circled above his wrist.

Olam nodded. Tika had what appeared to be a black ring on her hand. Kern let his sleeve drop again. 'They are the Lord Darallax's personal Shadows. More powerful than any I could summon. Olam, I was told I could trust you, and I have reached the same opinion myself. Kara, too, is trustworthy but Reshik is another matter.'

Olam's memory conjured a brief vision of Ren Salar, a man Tika had trusted on their earlier journey and who had proved quite otherwise. Kern nodded, watching the play of expressions across Olam's face.

'We must be very cautious my friend. There is no question about Jian's loyalties. She adores her brother Lord Shivan – although she'll never admit that of course. She has enormous respect for Lady Tika and loathes the very thought of Seola.'

'Dellian?' Olam asked, following Kern back down to ground level.

Kern looked startled. 'There are no doubts around Dellian. They are definitely blocks used for buildings,' he continued more loudly as they joined the others.

'But they are all jumbled,' objected Jian. 'They haven't all fallen the same way.'

Kern smiled. 'Which suggests Dellian is correct and the explosion began close by.'

'Dellian said two miles inland.'

Kern's smile vanished. 'Exactly so.'

Jian paled slightly. 'I take your point.'

Brin appeared with his escort of three young Dragons.

'Where are you going now?' he enquired.

'We need to go perhaps two miles eastwards.'

Brin huffed, still not entirely sure about human ideas of distance. 'I will fly in that direction until you tell me you have reached the place.'

Very soon Olam and his companions found themselves walking, not between great blocks but over shattered rubble. Flyn suddenly flew ahead faster. They could see him circling before he returned more slowly. The ground rose slightly in front of Riff who was in the lead. He stopped while the others drew level.

They stared in silence into the crater before them. It wasn't deep, centuries of weathering had smoothed the edges and filled it with debris and sand so it resembled a shallow dish. But it was its extent that held them silent. It was huge.

'Stars above, how do we ever start to find anything here?' Riff muttered.

Brin and his son settled near the humans, the Sea Dragons continuing to circle above, clearly not willing to get any closer.

Jenzi stared at the crater. 'Kara is an air mage, is she not? Perhaps she will be able to sense something. Reshik too, if he is gifted with earth magic he may know where we might begin.'

Olam caught Kern's eye and left it to the man from the Shadow Realm to reply. 'Both Kara and Reshik will be of help,' he agreed. He glanced at Jian but said no more.

Olam clapped his hands, making everyone jump. 'Let's have a quick look round and then get back to camp. I think we should leave a couple of people with the horses. We'd never get the wagon out here anyway. We can bring supplies for a few days serious searching before we'd need to go back to them.'

'Depending on who stays, they could resupply us and save us the walk,' Jenzi suggested.

'Good idea. Right, let's begin along this side. Just see if there are any particularly odd looking dips or hollows.'

They didn't spend long, all of them quietly daunted by the idea of anything able to cause so much damage.

Tursig was quite happy to stay with the horses. He was delighted with the Sea Dragons' tales of storms and fishing and of the other creatures who lived in all that salt water. Dellian said she preferred to stay and continue with her attempts at mapping the ruins. Flyn offered to fly above and send pictures to her mind to help her: obviously he would rather stay with the Sea Dragons than watch the humans scraping about in the ground.

Two of the tall Gaharnians also decided to stay – Reema and Shuli. Both of them were interested in the plants that grew around the freshwater pool behind the cliffs. They began sorting what they would take besides food – ropes, shovels, two picks, and two of the big canvas sheets.

Early next day they set off, leaving only Dellian behind. Olam had decided Tursig at least had to know their location and Reema and Shuli went as well to help carry the equipment. Skay flew with her father and the pair settled some distance back from the crater, Skay's eyes whirring with agitation. She calmed herself and watched as Olam set about making a camp.

He spread one of his canvas sheets from the top of a block, securing it with smaller rocks. Their possessions were stored beneath, along with two barrels of fresh water Shuli and Tursig had filled at the second pool.

'Gives me the shivers,' Tursig commented when he set off with Shuli and Reema on the walk back to their original camp.

Olam organised the search as methodically as he could. No one had any real idea what they were looking for, or if they would recognise anything if they saw it.

Three days after they'd begun, they had worked about half a mile along the northern side of the crater and stopped for a rest at midday. Kern was sitting beside Olam and he nudged him. Olam followed Kern's gaze, seeing Jian frown. She, in turn, was watching Reshik who was still prowling along the edge. He turned suddenly towards the group, a triumphant smile on his face.

'Have you found something Reshik?' called Kern.

'So much power beneath the ground,' Reshik answered. 'And I can feel a doorway very close by.'

Brin and Skay, both reclining behind Olam, pushed up onto their haunches, both pairs of eyes whirring wildly. Olam opened his mouth, there was a blinding flash, an ear-splitting roar, then darkness.

He heard a muffled groan. Olam realised it came from himself. He lay on his face, on grass, with someone's elbow digging in to his thigh. He bit back another groan and tried to climb to his feet. His head ached abysmally, he was badly dizzy and he felt as if he'd been pummelled from shoulders to feet. He chose to abandon the attempt to stand, just sat back on his heels, and forced his eyes open again. Still dizzy, but not quite so bad, he decided.

He heard other groans and someone was sick behind him. Olam just knelt there, trying to breathe deeply and steadily. Slowly the dizziness faded and he blinked, focusing on his surroundings. Ahead and curving to his left, was a small clump of trees. To his right, rough grass sloped down towards a fence beyond which cattle grazed. Past the cattle, was a small house with a wisp of smoke rising into an evening sky.

Olam tried to send a mindprobe towards the house but the appalling stab of pain suggested that was not a good idea. He waited until the pain ebbed then turned his head carefully to survey the bodies sprawled around him. Riff was nearest and lay on his back, looking at Olam with an outraged expression. Jenzi crouched by Riff's feet and was still looking ill. Kara and Jian were a short distance away, both now sitting holding their heads. Olam checked again. No, there was no sign of Reshik anywhere near them.

The sky had darkened considerably before they managed to stumble to the shelter of the trees where they slumped to the ground again.

'What happened?' Riff croaked finally.

'I *think*,' Jian replied, 'that we've moved through time.'

Kara nodded, then winced.

'I'm so sorry. I should be able to help you all more. I feel so ill myself I can't reach for the power to heal.' Jenzi's dark hair accentuated the pallor of his skin.

'Where would Reshik be do you think?' Olam looked at Jian and Kern.

'He used some sort of summoning power. It was only meant to apply to him but somehow it – sprayed. And we got dragged in. To be honest, I'm surprised we're still alive.'

Kern grunted at Jian's words. 'The Shadows protected us as best they could. If they hadn't, we would be scattered in small pieces, stars know where.'

'Thank you Kern. I'm sure we all feel much better now.' Jenzi stretched carefully. 'I feel as though I'd been thoroughly beaten. I'm glad your Shadows protected us from anything worse. But *where* are we? How do you move through time?'

'"Time is water. It flows and eddies and will not be held,"' Kara intoned.

'Who said that?' asked Jian.

'According to one of my teachers it was a famous thinker named Sapek the Bewildered.'

Jian snorted and the tense atmosphere among the group eased a little.

'Have we gone backwards or forwards?' Riff demanded. 'And are we in the same place we were in before?'

'The Shadows say we are a little further west – nearer the coast again, but not by much. And we have gone back.'

Jenzi rubbed his forehead. 'I think all of us know of the Shadows, but how are they going to help us now? Can they get us back? And *where* is Reshik?'

'It is not easy to explain but I think somehow – no, I have no idea *how* – he must have touched a susceptible mind here, in this time. That could have been enough for him to be pulled into proximity with the other person. Especially if that other mind was more powerful than Reshik's.'

'So Reshik could even now be telling his new friend all about us?' Riff sounded indignant.

'That was it!' Olam exclaimed. 'The Ship Tika healed. Captain Sefri said they had "coordinates" which they could use to move through the fabric of time.'

They all pondered Olam's words before Jian sighed. 'That makes no sense to me. There was no such thing described in any of the researches I've made. We'll just have to try to survive here.'

'Obviously we've moved far back in time. This land is fertile, this is a farm, so we are perhaps lucky not to have ended up in an alley in some town or city.'

'The Shadows say they are not strong enough now to get us away from here, certainly not back through time.' Kern fell silent before continuing. 'They have decided to divide, and some will accompany each of you. In case we are separated.'

'Have you all got a knife? Any sort of weapon?' Olam asked.

Everyone had an eating knife and a much sturdier dagger. Riff and Olam each had three businesslike knives.

'I have already told you Olam, I am stronger in the use of power than my brother Shivan. I believe Jenzi of Gaharn is also a strong mage?'

'Yes Jian,' replied Jenzi. 'My powers are strong, but first and foremost I am a healer. Needing to mend people's hurts means I am slow to use my power to injure them in the first place.'

'And I am an air mage,' said Kara. 'There are some things I can do, manipulate weather for instance, but other than the combat training we all had at school, I will be of little use in a fight where power is used.'

'There is a considerable amount I, and the Shadows, could do against an enemy,' Kern said quietly. 'So. We cannot depend on magery to defend ourselves.'

Olam chewed his lip and tried to think past the dull ache still pounding in his head.

'We need to sleep,' Kern said firmly. 'In the morning we will just walk until we find a town. I think we can only present ourselves as travellers, lost in this land. Maybe runaways from a ship? Let's sleep and hope we all feel better tomorrow.'

It was fortunate the weather was warm and dry. They made themselves as comfortable on the ground as they could and slept within heartbeats. Except for Kern.

Shadows murmured when he lay down: 'Dragons caught too.'

Kern's eyes snapped open, staring up at a multitude of stars. '*What?*'

'Red one. Black one.'

'Are they safe?'

'Not happy. By the sea.'

'Can you tell them to keep away, keep out of sight, until we can work something out?'

The Shadows sniggered. 'Could. Will.'

And by the emptiness in the back of his head, Kern presumed, *hoped*, the Shadows would communicate with Brin. Kern closed his eyes again. Stars forefend anything befell the Dragons.

Seola had found a few families along the coast. She used them to replenish her strength more quickly and not for a moment did she stop planning her revenge. Once her powers returned, she moved to the Sapphrean lands across the sea, hunting through the hundreds of islands scattered in the southern waters. At last she found the one she sought. She appeared as an innocent traveller, a slender woman, still slightly frail, as if she was recovering from a long illness. Short dark hair, muddy brown eyes instead of the gold of her people.

Seola was welcomed and offered hospitality. On her first evening there, she heard the name Namolos. It was spoken sadly and Seola enquired further. Later, after she'd killed all in the complex, she began to search.

She found the Ship far below the dwellings, in a cave which opened to the sea. The Ship was mad. It was not possible to converse, only for Seola to sit and listen to its rantings and grief. When Seola had gleaned all she could from Star Dancer, she left the cavern. She could probably have destroyed it, but it amused her to leave it to its insane ravings. Her arrogance suggested no one else would venture here again. She stayed on that island for a few more days, considering what she'd learned. Deciding there was only one way to do so, she followed some of the information from the Ship combined with information she'd gathered elsewhere.

Seola had always detested travelling through the gateways used by the mageborn of the Dark Realm so she was prepared for a headache and a feeling of nausea. It was a thousand times worse. Seola's mind was shielded, a trick her brother had taught her when they were still small children. Unconscious or ill, still no one could invade her thoughts or rummage through her memories.

The man who watched her was Astian. He was held in the very highest esteem throughout Valsheba for his prowess in both healing and in the understanding of geology. Unknown to any others, he had also studied time in its many aspects for most of his long life. He had discovered time could behave much like water, ebbing and flowing with quiet phases and violent fluxes.

Unlike the water in the ocean, time was never predictable. He had been made aware of some – tampering – with the normal flows of time, a sudden churning. Astian leaned forward to wipe the sweat from the woman's face with a cool, wet cloth. He sat back. Time was perhaps more like air, he mused. He had experimented with air as well as time. He'd learnt how to push a breeze here, smooth a gust there.

He seemed to enjoy watching armsmen of Segra City practice their archery, but no one guessed it was High Mage Astian who was doing the practising. A twitch of air and an arrow, from a master bowman, could plummet to earth or whisk to one side. Astian studied the woman on the bed.

She had arrived, in his garden, three days before and had not roused since. Two elderly maids, long in Astian's service, were given care of her. They had been told not to gossip outside the household about this unexpected guest. Astian's healer's eyes could tell this woman was far older than the mid thirties she looked. Therefore, he concluded, she was of mage blood.

But try as he might, he had not been able to breach her mental shields, even in her present state. She was much improved physically since her arrival. Astian had stabilised her body which had been ravaged by her passage through a time vortex. He believed she came from the future and wondered idly if she was Valsheban.

A descendant of one of Astian's colleagues perhaps. He had no family himself: no siblings, no cousins, no wife or children. This woman's hair was dark but her skin was extremely pale. Not just through sickness, Astian thought, but her normal colour. The man who had also materialised in Astian's garden had merely screamed for half a day before he died.

He had been fair haired with a ruddy complexion. Sturdily built, nothing like this woman. So High Mage Astian sat and waited. He was a very patient man.

Chapter Four

It was not long after sunrise when Olam and his five companions scrambled down the slope on the other side of the group of trees which had sheltered them through the night. They could see that they had arrived very close to a city. Perhaps a mile or two towards the rising sun, buildings rose. And so very many. Olam and Riff had seen the enormity of Harbour City and this was far more modest. Yet it was an impressive size. Buildings rose to different heights but the very tallest seemed clustered towards the centre. The group had paused briefly to stare at the city then started walking onward. They soon saw a road wound close to the fields edge and early as it was it already seemed busy with people.

Wagon after wagon, intermingled with handcarts, men and women with poles over their shoulders from which swung great baskets of fruits and vegetables. Olam was pleased to note the people's clothes were not much different from his own. Most folk seemed to wear trousers and loose shirts, a few wore robes, and a very few women wore dresses.

Olam listened to the chatter of the people around and could just recognise an occasional word, but it was mostly incomprehensible. Kern moved alongside.

'I'm sure they will have guards at the gates,' he murmured. 'Probably not powerful mage born, just gifted enough to spot wrongdoers – cheats and tricksters and so on. But they may be able to identify other mage born, so I think we should all shield our minds – just in case they don't like mages entering unannounced.'

Riff grinned sideways at his Armschief. He knew Olam had certain talents, awakened by Tika last year, and he was grateful that he had no need for shielding or subterfuge. Riff was happy to know he had about as much mage talent as a stone in the road.

Even so early the heat was growing and dust rose from the

road to form a gritty cloud through which they walked. People slowed in front and Olam's group joined the end of a line waiting to be passed through a wide archway. Olam watched as the line shortened. There were three men standing on a raised step just within the arch. Two wore brown uniforms with yellow flashes on their shoulders. The third man was much younger and wore black trousers and a grey shirt. Olam glanced back at his companions and shrugged.

'Don't cause trouble anyone. Just do whatever they say – if we can understand them.' He had been deeply relieved to find Jian's golden eyes had become a dark warm brown when they began their walk to the city.

Jian had smiled at him. 'It's one of the very first tricks we learn as children,' she'd told him. He was glad it was, now that they were under close scrutiny from gate guards, one of whom was a mage.

It was their turn. The younger man asked them something. Olam shrugged, spread his hands helplessly and smiled. The young man frowned, looking at them more closely and pausing for several heartbeats on Kern. With Kern's hairless head and grey skin, tilted green eyes, he definitely looked unusual. The young man spoke again. Clearly he was trying different languages but each time, Olam shook his head apologetically.

The older of the two uniformed guards said something and Olam nearly recognised his words. The man spoke again, slowly. Olam smiled and nodded. The man had asked where he was from and the language was close to the common tongue of Sapphrea, although heavily accented.

He replied slowly and clearly. He said he was from the far north and east, and he and his companions had become lost, separated from those with whom they'd been travelling. He had to repeat his words several times before the guard nodded. Words flew between the guard and the young man before the guard turned back to Olam.

'Go with,' he said, waving at two more guards who had appeared from a room within the arch.

Olam smiled widely and kept nodding. The two new guards led them through winding streets. Shops were just opening, awnings pulled out and a great variety of wares set out on the stalls beneath. It grew ever hotter as they marched on through the city. Olam noted they were heading inwards, towards the tallest buildings, to the area Kara had called the Siertsey.

At last the guards halted before a solid looking gate with a grill near the top. An old man was peering out and he at once swung the gate open. Olam and his companions followed the guards through and into a lush courtyard garden. A white haired woman in dark green trousers and a cream shirt stood beside a fountain. The older guard saluted her with a clenched fist to his forehead. He spoke, indicating the six strangers now waiting patiently to see what happened next.

The woman listened, smiled and replied. Both guards saluted and marched back the way they'd come. The woman studied the six people before her for a short while. Finally she smiled again. 'You look weary.' She spoke the common tongue with scarcely any accent. 'I am the High Mage Rajini. This is my home. Come inside and have some refreshments and we can talk more comfortably.'

Rajini led the way through a cool stone hall into a large room. Windows overlooked the garden and the varied green tones made the room seem even cooler. There were several couches and low tables around the room and some large paintings hung on the wall furthest from the window. Olam itched to get a closer look at them, remembering the paintings they'd found deep under the sand last year.

He waited until Rajini had seated herself in an armchair to the side of the window then sat on a couch. Olam looked up, over the garden, and saw a needle thin spire rising beyond. Yes, he'd seen spires like that in those other paintings.

An older man entered, carrying a tray on which a teapot steamed, and two girls also brought trays. One held tall glasses and a glass pitcher filled with something pale lemon, the other carried cakes and pastries. The man placed the tea tray beside Mage Rajini. She smiled her thanks. 'If any of you would prefer tea to the fruit juice, please join me.'

Kara and Kern immediately chose tea as Jenzi filled four glasses with the green juice. Rajini nodded to her steward who left the room with the maids, returning almost at once with trays far more heavily laden with food. Kara smiled at the High Mage.

'Thank you Lady Rajini. We have not eaten for a day or so. Your hospitality is much appreciated.'

Rajini inclined her head. 'You are most welcome. Perhaps you could tell me your names now?'

Kara blushed and named her companions.

'The gate guard understood you to be travellers who had become lost?'

Kara glanced at Olam. 'Yes Lady Rajini. We were on board ship and somehow found ourselves here. After a storm you know.'

Rajini stared rather pointedly at their clothes, which showed no signs of serious travel damage.

'I see,' she said. 'And where were you travelling *from*, might one ask?'

'We were travelling from my home island.' Kern's soft voice intervened. He smiled sweetly and took a sip of tea.

'Your home island. And wherever your home might be, I imagine the people all look as you do?'

Kern nodded. Rajini sighed. 'I have guest rooms here for occasions such as this,' she began.

'Occasions such as this?' Jian repeated sceptically. 'You mean you interrogate other visitors to your city here?'

Rajini laughed. 'No child. Not in the way you imply. I will have you shown to the guest rooms where you may rest and wash. I dislike eating in the evenings so my main meal is taken at the third bell.'

As if on cue, bells suddenly clanged, dinged and carilloned throughout the city. For several heartbeats the sound was nearly deafening. 'Second bell,' Rajini explained.

The steward appeared and held open the door. Olam rose with the others, bowed to Rajini and followed the steward. They were led up four flights of stone stairs until they reached a long, well lit corridor passage. The steward, who told them he was named Mavar, indicated the doors lining the corridor.

'You may choose any rooms you wish. There are no other guests here at present. There is a bell pull beside each door. Do not hesitate to use it to summon me if there is anything you require.' Mavar opened the nearest door and showed them a good sized room with a bed, table and couch. He opened an inner door and they saw a small wash room, towels piled on a bench against the wall.

'I will leave you to settle in,' said Mavar. 'Please pull the bell cord should you want for anything.' He half turned away then turned back. 'I notice you have no baggage with you. Perhaps you would not think it rude if I have some clothing sent for your convenience?'

'A very good thought,' Kara agreed quickly.

Mavar bowed and departed.

They chose rooms, showered and met again in the first room, which Olam had picked as his. The sun was high and they had no idea when the third bell might ring. Mavar had sent fresh clothes as promised and they'd sorted out garments for themselves. Now, they sprawled around Olam's room.

'The Shadows say there are wards throughout this building but no one is listening to us.' Kern smiled at Olam. 'We really should have worked out a bit more detail about where we're from.'

Olam grunted. 'I know. But it was the best I could come up with, with a headache worse than any after one of Seboth's wine tasting sessions.'

'Oh sorry.' Jenzi got to his feet. 'I'm recovered enough to help you now.'

Olam, Riff and Kara were most grateful for the brief touch of the healer's fingers across their brows. Olam looked across at Kern. 'The Dragons?' he said softly.

'They are safe. For now. They were very confused and frightened. Brin is angry, although he understands it was not our doing.'

Olam had a mental picture of facing an enraged Tika if he got back without Brin and Skay, and he shuddered.

'This mage Rajini is strong,' Kern went on. 'And she is confident of her powers. She has made no attempt to read any of us.'

'So far,' Jian finished.

'We must not believe she would mean us harm if she learns where we are really from Jian. She could help us. And I suspect she *would* be more likely to help rather than harm.'

The clangour of bells burst out and a tap on the door

45

announced Mavar's arrival. 'I will take you to the dining room if you please.'

They were led to a room across from where they'd sat with Rajini. She stood now at the head of a long dark wood table, and a girl stood beside her. 'My grandchild, Mitali, will be joining us. Please seat yourselves.'

Much later, Olam and his companions retired for the night, first gathering in his room.

'That was an interesting evening,' said Jenzi, settling on the straight backed chair beside the small table.

Olam scowled. 'In what way? I thought Mage Rajini was very polite – as if it was just a normal meal with normal chatter. She asked us no questions. Nor did the child.'

Jian snorted. Kara smiled. 'That "child" is already a most powerful mage. She was well shielded but still, it was discernible.' Kara laughed at Olam's expression. 'Yes, she seemed a pleasant child but still, be wary if you speak with her, as you would with her grandmother.'

Olam shook his head while the others made their way to their own rooms. Stars, what a mess they were in! And where was Reshik? What about Seola – could she *really* be here too? The Armschief of Far bit back a groan and went to his bed.

Breakfast was served shortly after the first bell, the clamour of which was enough to wake the dead, as Riff pointed out sourly. When they'd finished the meal, Rajini stood.

'We will talk in my study today. Mitali would like to attend, if you wouldn't mind?'

'Of course,' Olam agreed. What else could he say?

Jian scowled but said nothing, for which Olam was grateful.

Rajini's study was a room towards the rear of the house. It was big enough for eight people to sit without seeming overcrowded, but it also had a cosy air. Bookshelves covered the walls, a modest desk stood under a window and a long table, covered in papers, ink pots and books, stretched the width of the room. Rajini waved them to stools round the long table. She swung a chair from the desk and sat facing them. Mitali perched on a windowsill.

'You appear to be the leader,' Rajini began, smiling at Olam.

'Could you tell me who you really are – other than "a traveller"?'

Olam stared into steady grey eyes. 'I am just Olam.'

'Not "just" Olam surely? You and your man Riff, you are both armsmen I think. And you are an officer.'

Olam paused, then spread his hands. 'I am Armschief to my brother, who is a Lord in our lands. Riff is under my command.'

'And your island Kern, is far from here. I have never seen any such as you in Valsheba.'

Kern nodded. 'Indeed Lady. Far from here and – hidden. My people suffered in battle long ago and retreated to our island to recover.'

Rajini was silent for some time before turning her attention to Jenzi. 'You too are of a people I have not met or even heard of.'

Jenzi smiled. 'That is probably so Lady, but I do come from a place far north east of this land, and these are my friends, not chance met travelling companions.' Although Jenzi's tone was light there was the faintest hint of warning in his voice. Rajini again paused before looking to Kara.

Kara smiled too, but slightly nervously. 'I am from a place a long way to the east Lady.'

Rajini's attention finally rested on Jian. 'And lastly there is you, suspicious child. Where will you tell me you are from?'

'From a distant land, across the sea,' Jian replied calmly.

'From such scattered places,' Rajini mused. 'And yet you are friends. So you must have met somewhere familiar to you all. And why would you then come to Valsheba?'

Kern cleared his throat. 'Is it permissible to ask what area you specialise in Lady Rajini? Where I come from, mages usually have great expertise and interest in one or two facets of power in particular.'

Rajini smiled broadly. 'Now we approach the heart of things, do we not? Yes, you may ask. Perhaps you in return, will tell me of your particular talent? I am interested in several aspects of power. There are now few among us who can speak mind to mind. I am one who can do so. I am also a dreamwalker, but that is far less generally known. My abilities to truth read is why some visitors are sent to me by the gate guards. I can tell very easily if they are untrustworthy or offer any threat to the security of Segra City.'

Kara gasped, then quickly looked down at her hands, knotted in her lap. Rajini's eyes narrowed but she said nothing, merely turned her gaze to Kern for his reply.

'I am mageborn. I suspect my people use power in different ways to you, but I can mindspeak. I spend most of my time as a historian and recorder.'

Jenzi stretched his long legs out in front of him. 'I too am mageborn. I am a healer.'

'What of you Riff? Olam? Are you mages too?'

Riff snorted. 'Certainly not,' he snapped.

Olam punched his arm. 'I have some talent, which I learned of only recently. I can use mindspeech and I can sense other minds at some distance.'

'Something disturbed you just now Kara. Can you tell me what?'

'I am an air mage,' Kara whispered, still staring into her lap.

'We have air mages here in Valsheba. They live mostly further north, in the city of Kedara.'

Kara's hands clenched into fists. Rajini waited a heartbeat but Kara remained silent and rigid. Rajini turned to Jiam.

'Jian, from a land across the sea. Are you, too, a mage?'

Jian seemed utterly relaxed, sitting on a stool beside Olam. She smiled gently, gazing directly at Rajini. 'Oh yes Lady. I am most definitely a mage.' As she spoke, her dark brown eyes changed to the most brilliant gold. She had been seated but now she stood. A breeze fluttered her shoulder length dark hair – so like Tika's, Olam suddenly realised. Then, the breeze faded, golden eyes became dark brown, and a slim girl sat quietly facing Rajini. The High Mage sat perfectly still.

'You are of the Dark.'

Jian inclined her head. 'I am granddaughter of Mother Dark. My brother is the Lord Shivan, Grandson of Dark.'

'We know of you only through tales, legends from long past.'

Jian gave the faintest smile. 'We hid, after terrible battles, needing much time to recover.' Her smile broadened. 'Like our cousins of Shadow.'

Rajini's gaze moved to Kern then back to Jian, but it was the girl Mitali who spoke.

'Why are you here? Why now?'

Jian answered the question with one of her own. 'Who among you studies time?'

Rajini's hands tightened on the wooden arms of her chair and her grey eyes closed. Mitali glanced at her and then answered Jian's question.

'No one is supposed to know, but Babu and some of her closest friends learned that High Mage Astian has been doing experiments with time. And also with air. One of Babu's school friends is an air mage from Kedara City and she confirmed Babu's suspicions when she visited us a while ago. Astian is a famous healer, and a geologist. He teaches the senior students and is said to be writing a history of how the world was made, from all he's discovered from his study of rocks. Babu? Babu?'

Jenzi was already kneeling at Rajini's side, his fingers against her neck. He looked up at Mitali. 'How long has she been this ill?'

'A year. Perhaps nearer two.'

'And no one has healed her? This famous healer Astian could do nothing for her?'

'She would never allow him to touch her.' Tears trembled on Mitali's eyelids.

'There are no other healers?' Jenzi sounded angry. 'Show me to her room. I will carry her and then do what I can.'

Mitali opened her mouth, closed it and hurried to the door. 'Babu's rooms are at the top of the house. Should I call Mavar – he always cares for her when she's ill.'

'Whatever.' Jenzi strode up the stairs, Rajini's body limp in his arms, as if he walked a flat road.

Everyone else followed, trying to keep pace with his long strides but puffing by the time they'd reached the third floor. They slowed, letting Mitali and Jenzi race on to the fifth, and top, floor of the house. When Olam and his friends staggered into Rajini's bedroom, they found Jenzi sitting on the bed by the High Mage's slight form. Jenzi's head was bowed, eyes closed, holding her left hand loosely in both of his.

Mavar arrived, not breathless Olam noted resentfully, and immediately seemed to understand the situation. For the briefest moment, Olam feared the steward would order them all from the room, but obviously Mavar decided against such a suggestion.

He stood at the foot of the bed.

'Can this man heal her Mitali?' he murmured.

Tears sparkling on her cheeks, Mitali never took her eyes from her grandmother's face. 'He can, if anyone can,' she whispered.

Mavar nodded. He looked at the six strangers again but still said nothing about their presence in Lady Rajini's bedroom. Olam took pity on the man.

'We wait Mavar. If the healer needs more strength, he knows he can take it from any of us.'

The steward's eyes widened. Then he bowed. 'I thank you for your kindness and willingness to help my dear Lady. Please tell me if there is anything you, or the healer, might need. It will be brought at once.'

The morning crept by. Olam wondered when the next outburst of bells would break the deep silence within the room. Then he realised there was no sound from without, no bird calls, no footfalls – nothing. Glancing round, he saw Kara's eyes were slightly unfocussed: as an air mage, she must somehow be blocking sounds trying to move into the room. At one point, Mavar left the room, returning with a supply of the fruit juice.

When Jenzi straightened at last, they all saw how ashen he was. Clearly he had needed a great deal of strength to hold Rajini to life. Olam pushed a glass of juice into the healer's hands and he drank thirstily. He rolled his shoulders and stretched his back while Olam hurriedly fetched more juice. Jenzi looked round at the concerned faces.

'She lives. It was a close thing. There was much damage to her heart but I have repaired most of it.'

'Most?' Mitali squeaked. 'I am sorry. I am so grateful for what you have done, but do you mean she will still be ill?'

Jenzi yawned. 'The worst is mended. I am too tired to work safely at the moment child. I must rest for a time before I can complete the healing. Is there somewhere close by where I could sleep? Don't hesitate to wake me if you have any concern for her, but she will sleep now until I rouse her.'

'My room is next door. Please use that, and I thank you sir, more than I can say.'

Jenzi left Rajini's room and people got to their feet to follow him out just as the bells began outside.

'That is the third bell.' Mavar frowned. 'I didn't hear the second. Please, there will be a meal set in the dining hall for you. I must stay here for now.'

There was nothing Olam's company could do but wait. They wandered through the courtyard garden and spoke quietly together, but they all felt that until Rajini was recovered enough to talk, they must just wait.

It was the second day after Rajini's collapse and healing, shortly after the third bell, when Mavar summoned them to her private rooms.

'Quite agree with Tika and Sket about bloody stairs,' Riff muttered.

Jian laughed. 'Shivan told me about that. I have to say, they had a point.'

Mavar opened a door to reveal a small sitting room. High Mage Rajini sat in a comfortable armchair, her feet on a cushioned stool. She looked pale but rested, and smiled when they entered.

'Please sit where you will. I'm sorry our conversation came to such an abrupt halt. Mitali was telling you of Astian and our belief that he has studied time very closely. Before I say more, I would ask what your interest is in that subject?'

After a quick exchange of glances between the group, Kern spoke.

'Lady Rajini, I'm afraid I have to tell you that we come from the future. The quite distant future I suspect.' He smiled his sweet smile. 'We most certainly did not intend such a thing and we have no idea how we might reverse our position.'

Mitali's expression was of stunned disbelief, but High Mage Rajini nodded slowly.

'I was beginning to wonder if, insane as it sounds, it might be something like that.'

'There was another with us, a man named Reshik. He had just told us that he felt there was a – doorway – close by. He is an earth mage, but we had our doubts about his intentions.'

'And what were you all doing when this man found his "doorway"?'

Kern drew a breath. 'We were investigating the ruins of an

51

ancient city, not far from this very place, which Olam had discovered, with some other friends last year.'

'The name of this lost city? Was it known?'

'Oh yes Lady Rajini. It was Segra City.'

Chapter Five

It was Mitali who broke the silence following Kern's soft words.

'This city? *This* city? How can it be ruined? These buildings will last forever!'

Rajini smiled, reaching to catch the girl's hand. 'No my dearest child. Nothing lasts forever. May I ask how this city fell to ruin?'

Again, it was Kern who spoke. 'We believe a mage, or perhaps a group of mages, was experimenting. We do not know with what, or why. It is recorded in histories that there was a vast explosion of both physical and mental powers. It was not just this city Lady, it was all of Valsheba.'

'And who holds these histories?' asked Rajini quietly. 'Are you so sure they speak truly?'

Kara stared at the High Mage, her hazel eyes glassy with tears. 'They are my histories. Because I was born, far to the east, where my people found refuge after the disaster that overtook Valsheba. I was born in Kedara Circle, in Vagrantia. We named our land Vagrantia because we were outcast, vagrants wandering and hiding from all the other peoples of Sapphrea.'

'And that will go no further than this room.' Suddenly there was a depth in Kern's voice which held the strongest command.

'But we could make sure such a terrible thing never happens,' Mitali protested.

Rajini squeezed the girl's hand. 'And suppose this catastrophe does not happen, dear heart? Perhaps Kara will not be born? Perhaps many, who are wiser than us, will never exist? No Kern. Your words will go no further, although they are indeed terrifying words to hear.' She suddenly looked tired again. 'Is there more, or can we leave further talk until the morrow?'

Kern nodded at Olam. Olam attempted a smile but it was more of a grimace. 'I'm afraid two Great Dragons were pulled through with us. They are hiding, along the coast, but they are dear friends of ours and we will not have them hurt. Also, there is a woman who we believe has got here. Her name is Seola and she is most dangerous. We had our suspicions that she was meddling with time and that is why we too sought the ruined city.'

'You have given me much to think on,' said Rajini ruefully. 'I fear you must let me rest now but please come tomorrow, after you have eaten.'

When they gathered next day, Rajini appeared stronger, with colour in her cheeks once more. Jenzi was continuing to check on her at regular intervals but had informed his companions that he was most pleased with Rajini's progress.

'I sent Mitali to visit two friends yesterday – you may remember I told you of others who have concerns regarding Astian? He has not been seen for five or six days. This is most unusual. He is always to be found at the archery grounds just after the third bell. He rarely misses watching the bowmen at their practise.'

Rajini paused to take a sip from the tea bowl beside her. 'Astian has some power – nowhere near as much as he likes everyone to believe. He can push his way into another's mind but it is clumsy, he has to use force rather than finesse.'

Kern smiled. 'Whereas you can slide into another's thoughts without them being aware of your presence I would guess?'

'And I trust you did no such thing?' Jenzi interrupted sternly. 'I told you to make no attempt to reach for power for a few more days.'

'I have obeyed you healer. But one of my friends was able to trace a different mind within Astian's house. She showed Mitali the mind signature.'

Jian sat up. 'Can you show us Mitali?'

Mitali looked at her grandmother in confusion.

'Let me see into your mind child.'

Mitali closed her eyes.

'Which of you will look into my mind?' Rajini asked a heartbeat later.

'I will.' Jian's eyes were brown again. She nodded and turned to her friends. 'Look. It is Seola. There is no doubt at all.'

Kern settled his back against the wall. 'We must assume Seola discovered something which let her connect with Astian. I do wonder who might have given her such information but that is a distraction for now. Regardless of how, we know she is here.' He smiled at Rajini. 'I am so sorry Lady, but I have to tell you this woman *must* be destroyed.'

'I had assumed that, young man.' Rajini was quite sharp. 'The problem as I see it, is how? There is no way you could get inside Astian's house without his knowledge. The houses of High Mages and indeed, of lesser mages, are well warded.'

Shadows sniggered in the backs of the companions' heads, although they all kept their expressions blank.

'I believe your wards are not strong enough to stop us if we so chose,' Kern replied mildly.

'Wards – nothing,' Shadows muttered in his head.

Rajini seemed startled by Kern's comment but chose not to dispute his words. 'The Dragons you spoke of. I have worried about them during the night. There are Sea Dragons known to migrate along the coast here and occasionally hunts are organised for all the people of the city to enjoy.'

'Enjoy? *Enjoy?*' Riff spluttered furiously. 'Don't you even know how much more intelligent Dragons are compared with most humans?'

'Enough,' Olam growled at his armsman. Riff subsided, still muttering. 'You were talking of hunts,' Olam added to Rajini. 'Is one about to happen?'

Rajini and Mitali both looked shaken. 'Not that we've heard of,' Rajini replied. 'I was about to suggest that I take you all to my home on the coast. It is much more modest than this house but we prefer it there to be honest. It would not be thought unusual if I travelled there now – having been unwell. It is, as I say, an unpretentious old place but there is a large estate, and it is secluded. If you have a means of contacting your Dragons, they would be safer there.'

Riff exploded again. 'They are not *our* Dragons. They don't belong to us like some pampered pets.'

Once more Olam gripped Riff's arm. 'We do have a means of communicating with them so we could tell them to meet us there. Is it far from here?'

Rajini shook her head. 'If we left at midday we'd be there by the fourth bell.'

Olam looked round at the others who all nodded. 'I think that would be best Lady. Can we assist in the preparations for departure in any way? We have seen only a few maids and Mavar. Do you have stables?'

Mitali got to her feet. 'I'll show you. They are hidden from the house.'

Rajini laughed. 'My mother hated horses so my father rearranged the stable block.'

Riff's face suggested he was preparing a further outburst but Olam glared him to silence. 'Then let us make ready Lady. I, for one, will breathe easier away from here.'

They all rose and filed from the room but Kern paused. 'Can you picture your house by the sea Lady Rajini? We can show the Dragons, then they will know where we will meet them.'

Rajini sank back into her chair. 'Do you mean that you can mindspeak the Dragons?' she whispered. 'Such powers you must have.'

Kern smiled his sweet smile. 'The Dragons mindspeak us Lady. My people believe they have used mindspeech far longer than we have.' He bowed politely and followed his friends.

A very ordinary looking wagon left the residence of High Mage Rajini when the sun was highest, drawn by two dark brown horses. Riff sat on the driver's bench with Mavar. Mitali rode a pale grey horse alongside while everyone else sat inside out of sight. They heard Mitali speaking occasionally and Rajini explained the girl was telling acquaintances that she was escorting her grandmother to their seaside estate to recover from illness.

There was a brief halt at the gate but Rajini's seal was clearly marked on the wagon sides. The guards also recognised Mavar and Mitali and the wagon was quickly waved on. After some time, Mitali called to Rajini. The High Mage turned to Olam. 'You can fold the shutters back now. We are well clear of the city. There are three farms to pass before we reach my holding.'

It was a relief to have fresh air blowing through the wagon and the companions saw they were moving between fields neatly planted with a variety of crops. A few figures could be seen, in the fields or around small farm houses, but as they passed the third farm the road rose quite steeply. Cresting the rise, the smell of the salt sea gusted into their faces.

'A few miles more,' Rajini told them.

The well organised farm fields gave way to rough grassland and as the wagon rolled down the slope, they saw a deep valley, increasingly wooded the further it stretched back inland.

'This is my holding,' Rajini said. 'As I said earlier, it is a large area and the nearest hamlet is over five miles further north.'

'How many servants do you have here?' Kern asked.

'A married couple who have been with my family for most of their lives. They have a son who is simpleminded. He is a sweet boy. Well, he is a man really – he is past forty years. A big, strong man who loves to work, but he will live his life safe here. He would not survive in a town.'

'Will they be able to understand us?' Kara asked. 'I had no idea my people speak such a different language to our ancestors.'

Rajini smiled. 'Where do you think I learned what you call the common tongue? Oxsana and Burak fled from the northern Sapphrean lands because of fighting between the little lords.'

Olam bit back a comment and waited for Rajini to continue.

'They managed to get round the city of Kedara but, not speaking our language, fell foul of some traders on the road. My father was the one who found them in the forest quite close to our house. Both were badly injured. Father had them brought in and we nursed them to health. Oxsana was carrying a child who was born very soon after my father found them. He always wondered if it was the hardships and injuries which damaged Enki's brain.' She smiled. 'I had a gift for languages and learnt their speech while teaching *them* Valsheban.'

The wagon entered the first of the trees, jolting along what was no longer a road, more a rutted trackway.

Huge oaks, ancient but freshly green, stood as solid guardians along the track which twisted and wound between them. Mitali rode ahead and Rajini visibly relaxed when the track opened into a wide clearing. A stone built house sat comfortably at the northern edge, and a large fenced vegetable plot extended from one side of the house out into the open space.

A man came out of the garden, closing a gate behind him.

Olam and his companions noted the greying hair and beard, and also the walking stick on which the man leaned heavily as he hurried forward. Mitali slid off her horse and hugged him when he drew level. Rajini climbed carefully from the wagon and kissed his cheek. He frowned and spoke in Valsheban. Rajini laughed, waving towards her guests.

'My visitors speak only your common tongue Burak, so that is what we will use whilst they are with us.'

Burak nodded although he couldn't hide his surprise at the High Mage's words. Mitali had run up the short flight of steps and pushed open the door while Rajini spoke to Burak. Now, a very short, very round woman appeared, smiling at the High Mage. Rajini repeated her words to Oxsana about the need to use the common tongue with these guests. Olam saw a brief wariness flicker in the woman's blue eyes, then it was gone.

The companions were ushered in and shown three large bedrooms they would share, and then taken off to a huge kitchen. Pastries, cold meats, cheese and fruits were appearing on the table, Oxsana bustling from cupboard to pantry to cellar. They had eaten hungrily and were listening to Burak reporting some fallen trees some distance from the house when there was a joyful bellow from without.

The door from the kitchen to the backyard burst open and a big man stood there, beaming. He reached for the High Mage and lifted her in a hug, twirling her round. Rajini laughed even as Oxsana scolded.

'Put me down this instant you rogue. We have guests.'

'I know.' The man's voice was surprisingly light and higher pitched than might have been expected.

'Did you see us arrive then?' Rajini sat down again, letting Enki keep hold of her hand. He looked puzzled. Rajini nodded round the table. Enki followed her gaze, frowned and shook his head.

'Not *them*. The beautiful, beautiful flying ones who spoke to me.'

Olam was on his feet beside Enki. 'Greetings Enki. My name is Olam. Can you tell me where you saw these beautiful flying ones?'

Enki's smile returned. 'They told me your name.' He nodded

happily. 'They said they'd come soon.'

Olam looked up into bright blue eyes under a thatch of golden blond hair, in a face as innocent as a four year old child's. He patted Enki's arm. 'I am glad you think they're so beautiful. They are very dear friends of ours and I promise they would never harm you.'

The frown returned. 'Hurt Enki? No, no. They said I would be their special friend too.' The smile lit his face again. 'The big red one's name is Brin and the black one is his little girl. Her name is Skay.'

Olam nodded.

'They talked to me just like the other creatures do. I'll wait outside for them to visit.' Enki's gaze fixed on the table. He shot a mischievous look at his mother, made a grab for two meat pies and was out the back door, chuckling.

Rajini had her hand to her mouth, staring up at Olam. Olam shrugged. 'I'd guess you never bothered to check him for any mage talent?'

Mute, Rajini shook her head. Oxsana looked to the High Mage.

'Now what nonsense is this Lady? Our poor Enki having mage talent? You know he's told tales since he could talk, about all those conversations he's had with the horses, and the crows and all. Made it all up in his poor head.'

'No,' Mitali whispered. 'I remember when he made such a fuss about one of the horses feeling ill. Don't *you* remember Burak – your best plough horse? And she was, wasn't she?'

'I would certainly not recommend you start trying to probe his mind now.' Jian spoke for the first time. 'I suspect he is an utterly natural talent.' She studied Burak. 'Does he lift heavy things too easily?'

Burak shrugged. 'Nature, or the gods, have compensated his slow wits with great physical strength.'

Jian laughed. 'I don't believe that for a heartbeat. But he should be left for now, no probing or testing.' Her brown eyes locked with Rajini's grey ones.

The High Mage nodded. 'It shall be as you say.'

Oxsana began clearing plates and bowls, keeping her head down.

'I'd best finish settling your horses Lady.' Burak made a hurried exit.

'I'll help,' and Mitali followed him.

Kara began to assist Oxsana while Rajini suggested the rest of her guests go outside. She took them to the right once through the back door, where they discovered a large walled garden. There were stone benches near the house in the shade and an irregular shaped pond filled with lilies in bloom. Kern asked questions about various plants and Riff wandered off in search of the stables.

The afternoon drowsed by. Rajini fell asleep first, closely followed by Jenzi. Kern, Olam and Jian ventured further down the garden towards the pond. Fish poked their heads out of the water when Jian knelt and dabbled her fingers.

'What are Kara and Riff up to?' Olam asked.

Kern had sat down beside Jian. 'Kara is talking to Oxsana. She comes from a fortress town called Andla.'

Olam groaned. 'And there is still a fortress town of Andla how many years on?'

Kern grimaced. 'I don't even want to guess. Many hundreds of years at the least, and that thought just makes my head ache.'

Jian watched the fish darting under the flat lily pads. She glanced up, her eyes brightest gold. '*Will* we get back, do you think? Or will we die here?'

Kern brushed his fingers across Jian's cheek. 'If we travelled one way through time, I have to believe we can travel the opposite way too.'

His leaf green eyes met Olam's over Jian's dark head, and Olam knew Kern harboured serious doubts about the accuracy of the statement he'd just made so confidently.

Suddenly Olam spun on the spot, head back, scanning the sky. Two dark shapes were spiralling downwards and Olam cast a hasty look around to be sure there was space for two Dragons to settle. Jian and Kern rose to stand beside him as first Brin and then Skay settled gently on the other side of the pond. Olam sprinted round, trying to touch crimson scales and black at the same time. The eyes of both Dragons were flashing and whirring. Olam was near to tears as he felt the fear and alarm within the two.

'Oh my dears. I am so sorry you were caught up in this mess. We have no idea how we might get ourselves back through time.' He could sense both Dragons calming and leaned back, holding Skay's long beautiful face between his palms. 'I am *so* sorry,' he repeated.

Brin's deep voice rumbled through Olam's head. 'We know it was no fault of yours. It was the Vagrantian, Reshik, was it not?'

'It was. With a mage here meddling with time we think.'

Before more could be said, a happy shout came from the entrance to the walled garden. Olam turned, knowing he'd see Enki hurrying towards them, a radiant smile on his face. Olam was fascinated to note how both Dragons relaxed completely as Enki reached them. The big man plumped himself down to sit cross-legged before them.

He spoke aloud: 'You found your friend Olam then?'

Skay let her soft voice be heard by all in the garden. 'We did indeed Enki. And we are glad to find him and our other friends all safe in your house.'

Enki laughed in delight. 'No, no, no! This is Lady Rajini's house. My mama and dada work here.'

Brin lowered his head to Enki who immediately stretched a hand up to stroke the Dragon's nose.

Out of the corner of his eye, Olam saw Rajini slowly approaching beside Jenzi. She was plainly shocked, both by the size of the Dragons and by the fact that she could quite clearly hear their speech in her mind. Enki turned to watch her and held his free hand towards her.

'Come and see Lady.' He climbed to his feet and hustled over to grab her hand. He tugged her gently closer to the reclining Dragons. High Mage Rajini started to bow but Enki crowed with laughter.

'No, no Lady. Only *people* bow themselves down. Others don't.'

'My daughter and I are grateful Lady Rajini, for your care of our friends. And for allowing us to stay here.' Brin's tone was gentle. 'Please sit with us and tell us of your lands.'

Enki tugged Rajini down to the ground, keeping hold of her hand. 'Brin has wonderful tales to tell Lady.'

Olam smiled when Brin's eyes flickered slightly. Everyone

loved Brin's stories, even if they weren't all strictly based on fact.

In the house of High Mage Astian, his visitor was beginning to rouse. The shielding web, behind which Seola's mind twisted in agony, held firm against any attempt by Astian to infiltrate her thoughts or memories. But, he was patient. Wherever in this world the woman came from, he was complacent in his belief in his own superior powers. The two elderly maids spent most time with the woman, Astian spending the days concentrating on his time experiments more earnestly than ever before. He sat with the woman in the evenings and quite long into the nights.

He presumed she was an investigator into time, as he was. He also presumed she had arrived, literally on his doorstep, due to his summoning power combined with the accuracy of his time predictions. Astian concluded that the woman had returned through time from a period perhaps one hundred years in his future. Not for one heartbeat did he consider the possibility of how very much further she might have travelled.

There had recently been reports of Valsheban travel circles being found outside of Valsheban lands. Astian had reviewed the archives on the matter and had been astonished to find there was no record of any Valsheban mage actually inventing them. Surely such an achievement would have been recorded for posterity? But no. There were learned discourses by several mages on *how* the mosaic circles might be used, which had shocked Astian to the core. He had grown up in the belief that the circles were of Valsheban invention, yet these dusty old records quite clearly indicated they were not.

He enquired among some of his colleagues and it was soon apparent that they happily accepted the opinion that ancient Valsheban mages had constructed the circles. A string of such circles ran through Valsheba. This land was a really fairly narrow land, lying north to south on the west coast of the Sapphrean continent. Astian's colleagues could see no point in needing further circles sited anywhere beyond this comparatively small country of theirs.

Astian now wondered, far more seriously, just who had made the circles. Were there more, not just in Sapphrea, but across the sea in the mysterious lands they knew existed but as yet had no contact with? Only one mage had asked Astian why he was suddenly interested in the origin of the travel circles. That was Annella.

He had never had much to do with Annella. She was slightly older than he was, a powerful earth mage. She had once made the grave mistake of laughing at Astian in Council. That was something Astian would never forgive. When he'd made casual inquiries about the circles, someone mentioned that Annella was the acknowledged expert. She had apparently done extensive research on the subject, although she'd published very little.

Astian would never demean himself to speak to her, or her close friends, although he occasionally passed a few words with Mage Rajini. Rajini had not joined in the laughter against him so Astian felt able to speak to her, albeit always briefly. The fact that Rajini had not attended that particular Council session, Astian chose to ignore.

Now, he leaned forward. The woman in the bed said something without opening her eyes, then was silent again. But Astian had not recognised the words. She'd spoken several words, quite clearly, but in no language Astian was familiar with. He wiped away the fresh sweat that had popped out on her forehead and sat back. He'd been sure she was Valsheban.

He spoke the formal Valsheban language which was used among the High Mages and at formal occasions and Council sessions. He spoke the everyday Valsheban which was considerably different from the formal version. Also, he could speak several dialects, learned from the barbaric tribes' people he'd met during his geological expeditions east and south.

Astian smiled to himself. A conundrum no less! *Where* could this woman be from? He settled more comfortably in his chair and continued to watch his intriguing guest. He had no qualms at all about his ability to solve this riddle by the time the woman awoke. It never even entered his head that she might be far beyond his strength to control.

Chapter Six

The first morning after reaching Rajini's holding, Olam looked from the window of the room he shared with Riff. He could see into the walled garden where Brin lay, half curled around Skay. He could also see Enki, still sitting cross legged in front of the two Dragons. He thought it more than likely Enki had sat there all night. Olam was hugely relieved to have the Dragons close by, although Brin had told him he had no idea how to alter time to get them home. Olam found great comfort in just knowing the crimson Dragon was near.

Turning from the window, Olam wondered what he was supposed to do now. Rajini's friend, who had found Seola's mind signature within Astian's house, was due to arrive here later this day. Perhaps she would have some helpful ideas. He made his way downstairs, passing a dining room which was rarely used. Mitali had told them Rajini preferred to eat in the kitchen with no fuss or formalities.

Oxsana nodded as Olam appeared. 'Could you fetch that boy of ours in sir? Out there all night he was.'

Oxsana and Burak had met the Dragons the previous evening. Neither of them appeared worried or afraid of the two great creatures, which puzzled Olam. Now, he paused by the open back-door.

'Have you seen Dragonkind before Oxsana?' he asked.

He thought perhaps she wasn't going to answer, then she sighed.

'We saw them when we were children in the north, near the Ancient Mountains. The Wiseman of my village spoke with them when the Dragons came at harvest times.'

Olam smiled. 'These two are from the Ancient Mountains too.'

The slightest smile touched the corner of Oxsana's mouth. 'I always loved to see them, they are so very beautiful.'

'I'll go and drag Enki in for you!'

Annella arrived on horseback soon after midday and Rajini greeted her with a hug. Burak took her horse while Mitali carried her saddlebags into the house. Rajini showed Annella to her room, where the two women remained for some time. Mitali joined Olam and his companions in the walled garden and sat on the ground beside Jian. The two girls were around the same age but Jian seemed far older to Olam's eyes.

'Babu has been friends with Nel forever,' Mitali explained. 'She's probably telling her all about you. And these two friends.' She grinned at Skay and Brin.

Skay appeared calm and relaxed, but Olam knew Brin was very worried about the situation in which they found themselves.

'I believe Oxsana has food for you all,' Brin announced. 'We will fly to the north. There are no humans there,' he added, forestalling Olam's concern.

It was cool in the kitchen although Kara and Oxsana had baked bread and pastries earlier. Olam checked but saw no sign of Riff or Enki. Burak sat down at the far end of the table.

'Your man went off with Enki early on,' he said, seeing Olam's glance round. 'Stars know where they are but he'll be safe enough with our boy.'

Olam nodded then stood up again as Rajini entered with another woman. The new arrival was also elderly, as thin as a stick, with enormous blue green eyes in a sharp bony face. Those eyes rested longest on Kern, who bowed slightly, before they passed on to Jian.

'Food please. I am starving.' Annella dropped onto a stool beside Rajini. 'Sorry. Food first, talk second.'

Olam was astonished by just how much Annella ate. And she was still so thin? He hoped he would have the opportunity to tease his brother Seboth with such a tale. When Annella finally finished eating, she sighed.

'Thank you for the food Oxsana. You saved me from certain death from hunger.'

Oksana flapped her apron at Annella. 'Get on with you Lady. You and your jests.'

Annella ran a hand through her hair. It must once have been

beautiful. There were still streaks of dark copper showing among the white even now. 'Jini has told me all about you.' Her glance encompassed the whole group about the table. 'Now I have news for you. The woman you seek, the one whose mind signature you recognised, is no longer in Astian's house. Both she and Astian *were* there yesterday evening, but they were not there this morning. Astian also has a small property, east of the city, which he visits perhaps a dozen times a year, sometimes for only a day or two, occasionally for longer. I have not yet checked, but I would wager that is where he has taken the woman.'

She paused. 'He did take a full squad of guards with him. We might expect him to take one or two, but a full squad? Either he expects trouble or he feels he needs protection.'

'Did the woman – her name is Seola – seem conscious or rational, when you touched her mind?' Kern asked.

'No to both. But she may well have *become* conscious last night.'

Kern nodded. 'And we have to decide if she was aware enough to control Astian or is simply doing as he wishes until she *is* strong enough.'

Annella's eyebrows shot up her forehead. 'Control Astian? Surely not?'

Jian laughed. 'Lady Annella, Astian would hardly be considered a mage by my people, or Kern's I think.'

Kern nodded in agreement.

'But child, you've never even met him. How could you know this?'

'Forgive us,' Kern spoke before Jian. 'I think your use of power is quite simple. I believe it will be some years before your people reach the heights they will be known for.'

Annella lost all colour from her face, staring at Kern.

'I'm sorry Lady, I have no intention of offering insult to you. I simply speak the truth.' Kern bowed his head.

Annella stared at him before turning to Rajini. 'Did you know this Jini?'

Rajini spread her hands helplessly. 'No Nel, I didn't *know* but I had begun to wonder.' She looked towards Jian and raised her brow.

Jian smiled, the dark brown vanishing from her eyes to be

replaced by molten gold. A breeze ruffled her hair and a deep stillness permeated the kitchen.

Annella stared. 'You are of the Dark?' She could scarcely get the words out.

Jian simply nodded.

'But. . . '

High Mage Rajini patted her friend's hand. 'I know,' she said with sympathy. 'I felt the same after believing they were merely legends.'

'You must think us pretentious children,' Annella began but Jian frowned.

'We would never think such a thing Lady. Lady Rajini told you we have somehow travelled a great distance from your future. We have learned much in all those years ahead of you and we will continue to learn as will you.'

Annella gave a humourless laugh. 'Jini told me you were in a ruined city when you fell through time. It was once *this* city, was it not?'

'All things come to dust,' Kern said softly.

'The land is, the stars are.' Jenzi spoke equally quietly. 'That is the belief of my people.'

'Is it all for nought then? Do we study and work and care for people and things, all for nothing?' Annella looked sick.

'There is always purpose,' Jenzi replied but Annella shook her head and stood up.

'I need to think. Excuse me Jini, let me think for a while.'

'She will come to understand.' Rajini didn't sound wholly convinced.

'Where is Astian's country house?' Olam enquired.

'Hmm? Oh, it's about twelve miles from here I think. Maybe a little more.' Rajini gave him a sharp stare. 'Why? He has a full squad with him, that is twenty guards and their officer. You can't just rush off and try and break in. Please tell me you were *not* considering any such action Olam?'

Olam grinned. 'No harm in having a look. Is his house as isolated as this one?'

It was Burak who replied . 'No neighbours for half a mile in any direction. Had to go past his house on business for you Lady, years past,' he added defensively.

Rajini merely glared.

'So if we could borrow two horses Lady, Riff and I could check out the situation.'

Jian snorted. 'And you could send your mind into his house unnoticed? I think not Olam. *I* will go with you. Where is Riff anyway?'

Burak shrugged. 'Went off with Enki, straight after breakfast.' He left the kitchen, just in case he was questioned further by these strangers. He thought they seemed nice enough people, but Burak was very content, living hidden away here with his wife and son, and occasional visits from Mage Rajini and her granddaughter. Six extra people in the house was a crowd, and Burak did not like crowds.

Jenzi studied Rajini, noting her drawn face and bruised looking eyes. 'Come,' he said. 'Show me some of the walks you spoke of yesterday.' There was the faintest compulsion laced in his words and Jian nodded when Rajini rose obediently and followed Jenzi outside.

Olam had felt the compulsion but clearly Rajini had not been aware of it.

'You could be much stronger than you believe you are, with a little practice,' Jian murmured.

'And when has there been *time* to practice?' Olam snapped back.

'We have time now. Let's find a nice shady tree to sit under and you'll see.'

When they'd left, Kara caught Kern's eye and sputtered with laughter. 'Poor Olam,' she said before sobering. 'Are we going to get out of here Kern? Your honest opinion if you please.'

Kern stretched across the table and touched her hand. 'Honestly my dear, I have no idea. We arrived here, there must be a means of going back, but there is the dilemma. Did Reshik know what he was doing? Was it mere chance he made some sort of mental connection with Astian? How did Seola manage to travel through time to this very moment and place?'

Kara smiled. 'My conclusions are the same. Reshik was an earth mage. I have no affinity whatsoever with earth magics so I am no help there. As far as I know, Seola has no specific powers aligned to earth or air, as we do.'

Kern's uptilted leaf green eyes were watching Kara closely as she spoke.

'Astian?' he asked.

'Yes, Astian. Can he really be so powerful when Rajini and Annella are not? And Jian said Mitali had the potential to be a powerful mage, so there *is* power here. I really have to wonder if it was Seola who found the means to move through time and somehow caught all of us quite by chance. I'm not sure that she would be aware of us here either.'

'And I think that is our only advantage. She does not know of our presence.'

Astian had moved Seola to his property beyond the city limits on a whim. He suddenly decided he would have far more privacy there than in his town house, well warded though it was. He had no suspicion of another mage trying to spy on him – such an idea was too ridiculous to even occur to Astian. But something impelled him to have the woman moved to his carriage, extra city guards peremptorily summoned, and to move himself and a few of his household out of Segra.

Whether it was the jolting of the carriage or simply the moving of her body from one bed and, much later into another, but Seola was nearly awake. Astian, unusually, retired to his own bed rather than sit with the woman, leaving one of the maids who had tended her these last days.

Now Seola was aware. She carefully probed her immediate surroundings without opening her eyes. One other person was present, a woman who was on the edge of sleep. Seola finally opened her eyes, seeing a dimly lit wooden ceiling above her. Cautiously, so cautiously, she turned her head towards the other person in the room. She saw a slightly plump woman, past middle age, curled in an armchair. Her head was propped on her fist and her mouth slightly open.

Seola slid into the woman's thoughts with ease. After a time, she withdrew and quested further through the house. Aah! There it was! The mind that had tickled at the edges of her awareness while she lay physically helpless. As the High Mage slept, Seola excavated his mind of every detail. It didn't take long, but it left her with a throbbing headache yet again. She lay, perfectly still, knowing she must bide her time a little longer before she could begin to search these lands for the one who could truly manipulate time.

On the long eastern border of the Valsheban land, empty grasslands stretched endlessly in every direction. A few nomadic tribesmen travelled those lands with their herds and their families. They knew their lands intimately and most of them avoided contact with Valsheba. Very occasionally, tribesmen encountered a Valsheban farmer tracking his lost livestock. Sometimes they'd help him, sometimes they vanished before the farmer ever guessed they were nearby. Some three days ride from that border a range of hills broke the smooth roll of the plains. The tribes avoided one area of the higher land and whispered that it was cursed.

The man who had made his home there was unknown in Valsheba, for he came from far beyond the visible stars. He had fallen through the same rip in time's fabric that a group of enemy ships had torn open. His only advantage then was that he was fractionally ahead of their position in time. His ship, Rational Hope, popped into existence high above this barely mapped planet. Knowing his enemies were close behind, Captain Karlek sent his ship plummeting down to land among this line of hills.

Then he shut down all the ship's systems so there was no chance his enemies would pick up any trace from his ship. For two days he kept within his silent ship, expecting to be attacked at every moment when one of the following ships located him. But nothing happened. Nothing at all. The third day he re energised a very few of the ship's systems and risked a low level scan of the skies. And he found them. Nine enemy ships in holding orbits high above.

Another day passed and he was able to pick up communication chatter. His laughter bordered on hysteria when he realised only four of the ships still had a living captain within them. The others were empty shells, drifting on automatic controls. From the information he gleaned through the comm channels, something catastrophic had occurred during the time jump, causing the deaths of five ships and five captains. The remaining four were now preparing to die themselves as they had insufficient power to either land or attempt to return to their home star system.

Karlek never realised that although the captains died, the ships continued to live. The Conglomeration Forces had not understood exactly what the bio ships were, so the five in orbit continued to communicate with another four that had, unknown to Karlek, descended to the planet.

Six days after his emergency landing, Captain Karlek left his ship for the first time. The outside air was cold and snow lay in patches and crevices among the rocks around him. Grass carpeted the ground he stood on and the tops of what looked like evergreen trees waved beyond a ridge to his left. He heard water rustling somewhere nearby. It was difficult to guess if it was autumn or spring but bending to pluck at the grass, Karlek decided it was more likely to be spring.

The tribes had first regarded this stranger as a god, and laboured to move rock and stone for him, until he had a solid house which encompassed his ship with its solar powered systems. They gave him crop seeds, and a few of their herd animals, and in return, he healed some of their illnesses and injuries. But by the time the second spring arrived, the tribes shunned the stranger god and his hills. They did not understand how they had angered him, but one day he had pointed a tube of metal towards them, and fifteen fell dead. The rest of the tribespeople fled, never to return.

Now, all these centuries had passed and Karlek was no longer the Conglomeration Combat Officer he had been. The regeneration pod within the ship had been used far more than it had been designed for, and no longer functioned so precisely. Karlek had concentrated all his energies to the manipulation of time. Occasionally, he accepted that he was working on a ridiculous idea, but mostly he convinced himself that he *would* find a way to return to a moment just prior to meeting those enemy ships.

Then, this would be just an appalling dream, his life would continue as before. The ship's Computer had run so much data, so many simulations, until the day he'd made a pile of stones disappear. The Computer told him that the stones had moved back in time.

More years went by, more experiments, more data to check

and double check.   Then, the Computer recorded a great fluctuation in the time vortex and Karlek knew he had drawn a group of people – perhaps nine or ten he thought – back into this time.   Somehow he would have to find them, to use their time patterns to construct a formula to finally move himself out of this nightmare.

Riff and Enki appeared in time for supper.

'It's a solid house, walled grounds, and guards on watch,' Riff announced.

'What house?' demanded Jian.

'The house Astian's supposed to have taken Seola to of course,' Riff retorted, spraying pastry crumbs and making Enki giggle.

'You can't have found the right house,' Olam frowned. 'Burak said it was twelve miles or so from here.'

Riff looked confused. 'Twelve miles?' he repeated. 'I would have said four, maybe five.'

'Well it *must* have been the wrong place,' Olam insisted.

'No,' said Enki. 'Mage Astian's house. I was there with Dada before.'   Enki continued piling food on his plate until Oxsana rapped the back of his hand with a ladle.

Four pairs of eyes fixed on Enki just as Rajini, Annella and Mitali joined them.   Rajini smiled as she sat down and poured tea for herself and Annella.

'Did Enki show you right through our forest, Riff?'

Riff glanced uncomfortably at his companions.   'Erm, yes indeed Lady.   Most interesting.   Beautiful trees.'

Enki giggled again, swallowed the wrong way and choked while his father thumped his back.   Riff appeared to have lost his appetite, but Enki mopped his eyes and worked steadily through his overloaded plate.

'I must apologise for my abrupt departure earlier,' Mage Annella offered.   'All that you spoke of – it took me a while to get my mind clear.'

'No need for apologies Lady,' Kern replied.   'We certainly had no intention of either shocking or offending you.'

'I know,' Annella nodded.   'But you must concede that your news was rather – bewildering?'

Riff slid off his stool and made for the door.   Olam rose

quickly. 'Please excuse us.' And he hurried after Riff, cornering him as the armsman was vanishing into the stables. 'Stop right there.' Olam ordered. 'What, in the name of the stars, happened today Riff? Did you really walk twelve miles there and twelve back? Yet you don't seem as exhausted as I would expect. Come on man, what happened?'

Riff shrugged and perched on the stone wall alongside the paddock. 'Honestly sir, it just seemed four or five miles, and Enki said it was Astian's house. There were guards, very obviously placed around the house. The gardens were just narrow strips to each side and stone walls perhaps this high.' He patted the wall on which he was sitting. 'I didn't know it was twelve miles distant. Sorry if I've done wrong sir.'

Olam thought back and realised Riff and Enki had already gone when Rajini had described where Astian's country house actually was. Olam joined Riff on the wall. 'No, you did nothing wrong, but there's far more to Enki than seems likely.'

Riff grinned. 'He's a good fellow sir. Knows more about trees and plants than I ever thought there was to know. I did notice none of the animals we saw seemed bothered by us. Enki called out to some deer and they all just stood and stared back – no panic or anything. And he can copy every bird song we heard.' He shrugged. 'Other than that, I didn't notice anything odd about the walk. Sometimes, when he talks, he sounds like a very little boy but other times, like when he spoke of the trees, he sounded like a scholar.'

Just then Enki emerged from the house, ambling towards them. He smiled his beaming smile. 'Nice walk today Riff.'

'It certainly was,' Riff agreed warmly. 'Where are you off to now?'

'Got to say goodnight to the horses then put the hens to bed. They like me to sing to them. Then I'm going to talk with Brin and his little girl.'

Riff and Olam watched the big man duck his head as he entered the stables. Olam sighed.

'I'm sure Kern and Jian will want to know all about your "walk" with Enki. Come on.'

Riff groaned but followed Olam back to the house. Before they reached the back door, Jian, Kern and Kara emerged, turning towards the walled garden and the Dragons.

'Where's Jenzi?' Olam enquired.

'He's concerned about Lady Rajini,' Kern told him. 'And Lady Annella. They are both much older than they seem and he's not happy with their health at all.'

Olam frowned. 'I thought Jenzi healed her, back in the city?'

'He did what he could, but there was too much damage, done over too long a time.' Kern smiled sadly. 'Jenzi exhausted himself if you remember, and yet he could only just stabilise her. It won't last too much longer I fear.'

'And the other Lady?'

'Jenzi said much the same of her. They have extended their lifespans by some means he didn't understand, but it has left them very vulnerable now.'

They had entered the walled garden and moved to the further end where Brin and Skay reclined soaking in the early evening sun. Olam went to Brin, stroking his long beautiful face, then greeted Skay in the same fashion.

'Brin, I need to ask you what you know of Enki's powers. He will be here shortly I'm sure. We want to know how he took Riff twelve miles to see a house we believe Seola has been moved to, and back again, when Riff only thought they walked but four miles each way.'

The companions tossed ideas between them until Enki arrived. Then the talk became general. Kara got to her feet.

'I'm going to see if your mama is sitting down,' she smiled at Enki. 'Do you know just how hard she works?'

Enki laughed. 'Oh yes. Sometimes her hands and feet hurt really bad, until I kiss them better.'

Five humans and two Dragons considered Enki thoughtfully.

Jian was next to leave. 'I think I'll walk for a while,' she said.

Kern watched her stroll off but Brin began a story about one of his adventures and Kern turned his attention back to the crimson Dragon. Suddenly Skay pushed herself up onto her haunches as Brin's eyes started to whirr. The faintest smell of burnt cinnamon wafted through the garden. Olam was first on his feet.

'What, in the name of the stars, is that dratted girl up to now?' he asked furiously.

'Calm yourself Olam,' said Kern. 'She is not yours to

command, neither is she stupid. Leave her be. She will not take unnecessary risks.'

'I could follow her,' Skay's gentle voice murmured in their minds.

'Certainly not,' Brin retorted, his eyes flashing with scarlet and gold. 'As Kern has said, we must let her be.'

Jian had walked a short distance along a narrow trail into the surrounding woodland to a clearing she'd found the previous day. She moved to the centre of the open space and raised her face to the evening sky where the earliest stars were prickling through. Her slender body shimmered and lost shape, reforming into an enormous Dragon with wings seeming frail as gossamer. A strong scent of burnt cinnamon gusted through the clearing and Jian's Dragon form floated gracefully skyward.

Chapter Seven

Jian gained height very swiftly. Anyone glancing up would perhaps notice a speck in the sky and think it might be a hunting bird slowly circling in search of prey. Spiralling ever higher, Jian saw the city of Segra spread like a child's plaything, the centre laid out in a more formal, deliberate pattern, the outer buildings haphazardly clustered within the walls. She saw the many small farms radiating around the city.

Drifting east, Jian searched for Seola's mind signature. She was extremely cautious, letting only a tiny thread of her mind sweep over the buildings below. The instant she felt a trace of that signature, she withdrew her own thought, simply studying the house from whence it came. Riff had described it accurately: a solid stone built house, low walls around its small gardens, but definitely containing Seola within.

Seola's mind had felt quiescent; either the woman slept, or was still unconscious. Jian drifted further east, seeing farms still spreading outwards until empty grassland began to appear. She pushed herself ever higher, aware of the air's sudden chill despite the setting sun still glittering along her wings. In the furthest distance, she saw hills rising. Nothing like the northern mountains of her homeland, nor those of Gaharn. Mere hills. But something called to her from those hills. Something niggled.

Jian was tiring and reluctantly she turned away, curving back to the west and Rajini's wooded lands and a small clearing where Enki waited.

Seola opened muddy brown eyes and stared at the ceiling again. Someone had reached for her mind with the faintest feather of a touch. Not the man sitting beside the bed, and now leaning forward eagerly. No. Seola recognised the mind's touch as being from one of her own people – a Dark Mage.

Who? Surely Shivan couldn't know how to follow her back

through time? But the man was talking at her and she relinquished her own questioning thoughts to concentrate on his words. Rummaging through his mind the previous night, she'd realised he did not speak the common tongue. She could understand his thoughts but not his actual spoken words.

Seola just stared at Astian while deciding what her reaction should be. She had a use for the man, for now, and she needed to keep him cooperative. She sighed. It was such a bore. All her life, dealing with such lesser minds than her own and her beloved brother. Having to bend to the wishes of inferior people. Not for much longer, Seola vowed to herself. She gave Astian a tremulous smile.

Jian landed in the clearing just as a new moon peeped shyly over the treetops. Her vast Dragon shape shimmered, the burnt cinnamon smell filling the glade and the girl stood there, swaying slightly. Enki walked towards her and his huge hands engulfed hers. He frowned, blond brows meeting in a line across his forehead.

'Are you always so cold when you do that?' he asked.

Jian leaned against him, feeling warmth spreading from his hands on hers, throughout her body. Warmth, and strength. Slowly Jian straightened, looking up into Enki's face. His eyes shone such a brilliant blue even in the fading light within the clearing. Jian let the gold of her eyes shine up at him and his smile widened in delight.

'Who are you Enki?'

He chuckled. 'I am Enki.'

Jian scowled. 'I'm sure you know what I'm really asking you.'

Enki released her hands. 'You are so very beautiful in your Dragon shape. Are you still Jian when you're a Dragon?'

'Of course I am.' She paused, studying him carefully. 'Are you still Enki, in all your shapes?'

She held her breath, wondering if he'd understand her question or if he'd even answer.

He pushed Jian gently towards the trail back to High Mage Rajini's house. 'I am always Enki,' he said softly.

Jian sighed and kept walking. She was too tired to think right now, but there was certainly a very great deal to think about.

Jian had to smile next morning when the companions gathered for breakfast. It had so obviously been decided that she was not to be questioned. Olam in particular, was near bursting with curiosity but restrained himself heroically. Jenzi was even quieter than usual and Jian guessed he was worried about Rajini and her friend. Mitali looked tired and Jian suspected she had been caring for her grandmother during the night along with Jenzi. Jian had just sat down when Olam asked Mitali about the city guards.

'Are they arms trained? he pressed. 'Do they live in barracks or in their own homes?'

Mitali shook her head in confusion. 'They live at home I think. They take turns doing night patrols. There are only a few around at night, more in the day.'

Olam continued with his questions. 'Do they march through the city? Are they smart, disciplined?'

'They train most afternoons. Anyone can go and watch. The bowmen go to Archers Field and swordsmen train at the Iron Park.'

'Is it the same men every time in the Archers place or do they change about, all practising different weapons?'

'Oh no,' Mitali was definite now. 'I know they only train with one or the other. Everyone watches both lots of training and at the midsummer games, huge wagers are made on certain guards. People who've watched, know which will do best in the contests.'

Olam nodded. Unlike his own armsmen who were made to learn the use of all weapons in his armoury, the Valsheban guards seemed to specialise in one form only. Very unwise in Olam's view. He wanted men who, when their arrows were spent, could wield a sword with strength and ability.

'How is the city governed?' Kara's gentle voice took over from Olam's brusque questioning.

Mitali frowned. 'The five great cities of Valsheba rule themselves in most matters. There are eleven Councillors in each city and if there is something of great import to all of us, a Speaker is chosen from among the Councillors. The Speaker then goes to Parima for discussions with the others.'

'Who pays the city guards?' Kara asked.

Mitali shrugged. 'The Council I suppose. There is a tariff everyone has to pay and that money goes towards paying the road menders, the drain cleaners, the scribes in the Council offices. Is this really useful for you to know? I know little of such things truly.'

And clearly, Mitali had little interest in such things either.

Olam forced a cheerful smile. 'All information is useful. Thank you for your help.'

Mitali's answering smile held more than a little doubt but she nodded and rose. 'I must return to Babu. She is not feeling so well again, and Annella is more tired than I've known her.'

Jenzi also rose. 'I will accompany you.'

Oxsana began clearing dishes from the table. 'My Lady is very sick, isn't she?'

Kara nodded. 'I fear so. Jenzi is a strong healer, but even so, there is only so much he is able to do.' She stood, helping Oxsana with the dishes.

Olam tilted his head towards the door and the others followed him out. Brin and Skay were not in the garden, neither was Enki.

'I saw Enki going down that trail earlier when I looked out,' Riff offered.

'He was still sitting with the Dragons when we went to bed last night.' Olam glared at Jian. 'Before you came back.'

Jian laughed, took pity on Olam, and described what she'd seen and sensed. Kern was most interested in the hills she'd barely glimpsed, and the "niggle" that she'd felt. It was with some hesitation that Jian spoke of Enki while Olam, Kern and Riff listened in silence.

'I think Enki is a great rarity,' said Kern at last. 'My people have found records of such mages, scattered throughout history. In several instances, the mage was regarded as a simple minded fool.'

'What could those mages do?' asked Riff. 'And what happened to them?'

'Could any of them travel in time?' added Olam.

'I think one of them claimed to, but the reports mocked him, called him a fool. Most of them seem to have died very young. Perhaps they could not control their powers and the power itself destroyed them.'

'But what sort of mages *were* they?' Riff persisted.

Kern lifted his shoulders. 'All kinds. They could apparently do many things well – one could heal but also be a weapons crafter, a weather mage – all forms of power concentrated in a single individual.'

Jian nodded slowly. Her eyes, dark brown this morning, met the leaf green of Kern's. 'That is Enki.'

'Does he know, do you think?' Olam asked.

'Oh yes,' said Jian softly. 'I think he knows far more than we could imagine.'

Olam began to pace around the lily pond. 'We should head east,' he announced. 'Let's see what's in those hills that gave Jian a nasty feeling.'

'What about Seola?' Jian objected.

Olam paced another circuit. 'She doesn't know we're here. If Jian thinks there's the chance of a mage hiding out in those hills, I'd wager it wouldn't take Seola long to sniff him (or her) out too.'

'But then she'd be behind us,' Riff sounded dubious.

'But *I* will be with you.' Enki stood behind Jian.

No one had seen or heard him approach but no one felt inclined to question him.

Kern cleared his throat. 'We appreciate your thought Enki, but we go into danger, I fear. It would be best for you to remain. Your parents would be upset if you left surely.'

Enki's beaming smile faded a little, then he shook his blond head. 'I've been their little boy for forty years. And I've been a *good* boy. Now I must leave. I'll go and tell them.'

They watched the big man march out of the garden, then looked at each other wordlessly. Brin and Skay drifted down to settle in the sunshine and Olam was glad to feel they were both calm and relaxed.

'We went along the coast,' Brin's deep rumble sounded in their minds. 'We met some of the Sea Kindred.'

'They were most interested to meet us,' Skay added.

Olam explained that they were planning to travel east but would need to find horses for transport.

Brin's eyes started to whirr in excitement. 'You won't need horses,' he said. 'We can carry you with no bother.'

Olam considered the suggestion. Four grown men and two women. Kern was much the smallest of the men and Jenzi was of very slight build despite his height. Kara and Jian were both slender. He caught Jian rolling her eyes at him and remembered she could take Dragon form.

'What about Enki?' he said aloud.

'Enki will keep up.' Brin's words were a confident statement,

Olam chose not to ask how that might be possible. He and Riff began to consider

what might be needed on this journey, both of them much more cheerful at the prospect of actually doing something positive at last.

When Olam and his companions re-entered the house, they wondered how Burak and Oxsana would treat them. Oxsana made a large pot of tea and opened a box of biscuits. There was no sign of Enki. Olam opened his mouth but caught Kara's quick head shake and closed it without saying anything. It was Oxsana who spoke. Her voice trembled at first then firmed.

'We knew he would leave us one day. We're lucky he's stayed so long.' She sat down beside Kara. 'Forty years and more. Lady Rajini never paid any attention and we never said, but his father and me, we knew very early on.'

'Knew what Oxsana?' Kara asked, her hand on the woman's shoulder.

'That he was like the Wisemen of our old villages. Only much more so. When I put his cradle outside when he was a tiny babe, birds would perch there and sing to make him laugh. Oh too many things to tell of. He told us when he was but four years, that he would stay as long as he could but one day, he would have to leave us.' Oxsana's tears slid down her face. 'He's been such a good boy. You'll take care of him won't you?'

Kara folded her arms round the woman's plump body. 'You know we will.'

'When will you go?'

Kara looked to Olam to reply.

'We'll need a few things, if you can spare them. Tomorrow, early I would hope.'

Oxsana gently freed herself from Kara's arms. 'There is far too much in this house. Put away for years. I'll find you blankets, clothes, whatever I think of.'

'Thank you Oxsana.'

Oxsana glared at Kara. 'I need no thanks child. Just you look after our boy. Come on now, you can tell me what might be of use to you.'

'Do you think there might be swords lying around?' Riff ventured. 'Water skins?'

'Let's take a look.' Olam led the way deeper into the house.

Jian and Kern stayed sitting quietly at the kitchen table, both deep in thought.

Sometime after midday, Rajini entered the kitchen on Mitali's arm. Olam thanked the stars that Oxsana had shown them an unused room beyond the kitchen. It might once have been an office or a study but it had an air of being long forgotten. Oxsana told them to sort out the things she piled in there while she went to prepare the meal for the third bell.

Rajini looked quite shockingly ill. Her white hair had dulled like a tarnish overlaying silver, and lines had deepened in her cheeks. She lowered herself onto a stool with a sigh but forced a smile for her guests.

'I have neglected you most rudely,' she said. 'My dearest friend is sick and I would spend my time with her.'

'Nonsense dear Lady,' replied Kern. 'We are more than content with your gardens and Oxsana's cooking.'

Rajini picked at the food on her plate before pushing it away. 'I have no appetite Oxsana, I'm sorry.'

There was a distant look in Rajini's grey eyes as she rose unsteadily and left the room with her granddaughter supporting her.

The companions ate their meal in silence until Jenzi appeared. He drank two glasses of juice without pause then rubbed his hands over his face.

'Not good?' Kara asked.

'Annella is close to death, Rajini not far behind her.'

'Has it happened so fast because of what she's heard from us?'

Jenzi smiled. 'No Kara. Well, perhaps partly. I told you, they have extended their lifespans but they didn't really know what they were doing. Yes, they have lived far longer than would be usual but they have also done much damage to themselves.'

Kara lowered her voice. 'What about Mitali? Olam told you we're leaving tomorrow?'

Jenzi nodded. 'There is no more I can do for the old ones. Mitali. . . '

'Jian said she felt the girl had the potential to be a strong mage, but she is so young to be left alone.'

Jenzi leaned closer. 'There is the potential within the girl but there is also something wrong – twisted. She is not trustworthy.'

Kara was shocked. 'Surely not?

Jenzi closed his eyes briefly and smothered a yawn. 'I'm fairly sure it is Mitali who has brought about such a rapid deterioration in the two old ones.'

'What do we do?' Another thought struck Kara. 'She won't hurt Oxsana or Burak will she?'

Jian had been listening to the quiet conversation. Now she snorted. 'You think Enki is unaware of Mitali? You think he will allow *anything* to hurt his parents?'

Kara continued to look worried. Jenzi smiled at her. 'From the bits I've heard about Enki, I imagine Jian is quite correct. Now I am going to get some sleep. When I wake, I'll spend some time with the High Mages but there is no more I can do for them.' He brushed crumbs from his shirt-front and got to his feet. 'I'll see you later.'

Olam and Riff had gone back to sorting the heap of equipment Oxsana had retrieved from who knew where, but Jian was still at the table, sipping tea.

'Kara, don't fret. I'm positive Enki's had a long time to think how to protect his parents. And I think Jenzi is right about Mitali. I've not felt – comfortable – whenever she's around us. I also know that Skay doesn't like her near.'

Kara sighed. 'I have been in the garden for a while. No one was there except Skay. She thinks the Sea Kindred she met with Brin were too wild, so she chose not to visit them again today. I am a weather mage.'

Jian grinned. 'Did you see the hills I told you of?'

Kara smiled back. 'Yes. And there is definitely something there, something different. There was a place where sunlight seemed to be concentrated. My mind was very high above and I thought it best not to go lower. But I'll check again when we're closer.'

'Can you let me see?' Jian asked. She touched Kara's mind lightly and at first saw only the infinite grass. Then she saw what Kara had seen; a tight focus of sunlight in one specific area of higher ground. 'Thank you.' Jian withdrew from Kara's mind, her own thoughts racing. It was obviously the same place where she'd sensed that "niggle" but there was also a familiarity about it. What did it remind her of? She wandered off in search of Olam and Riff, deciding she *would* remain calm, even if Olam was being as difficult with packing as he'd been in Far.

Oxsana prepared a much more substantial meal for supper, and Kara told them travel food was cooked and packed in the larder. Burak produced some beer which Olam and Riff accepted with delight, Kern more warily. The inner door suddenly crashed open and Mitali confronted them, her fists clenched at her sides.

'So much for your great healer.' She spat the words towards Jian. 'Annella has died, and Babu's grief will take her, too, before dawn. I don't believe he helped either of them. More likely sped their deaths.'

Olam and Kern had both got to their feet, watching Mitali closely, but it was Jian who replied to the girl.

'You know perfectly well, *Jenzi* did nothing of the kind.' Her tone was cool and she appeared completely calm as she sat and watched High Mage Rajini's granddaughter.

Spots of colour flared on the girl's cheeks. Oxsana gave a gasp and clutched Burak's shoulder. 'And what do you mean by that?' Mitali retorted with a sneer. 'You think we believed your lies? Changing the colour of your eyes is a simple trick for anyone with the slightest talent. I've been able to do it since I was scarce five years.'

'Really?' Jian purred. 'Like this?' Her eyes flared sun gold and a wind raged round her body. Mitali took an involuntary step back, but her chin still jutted aggressively.

'Go to your room, stupid child. Lie down and sleep until tomorrow.'

Jian's voice was ice, slicing through the space between her and Mitali. Mitali's hands relaxed, her eyes vague. Without another word, she turned away and left the kitchen.

Oxsana sat down with a thump, fanning herself with her hand. 'Delighted to see that lady put in her place at last.'

Jian regarded her in astonishment. 'Really?'

Oxsana nodded. 'Enki said, since she was brought here as a toddling child, that she was a bad girl. He always tried to keep away from her. She was spiteful, blaming Enki if *she* broke something. As she got older, there were nasty comments. Lady Rajini always corrected her if she heard anything but we,' she nodded towards her husband, 'we knew Enki was right and she was a bad one.'

'You said she was brought here as a small child,' Kern asked. 'Did Lady Rajini have a son or daughter who could not care for the child then?'

Oxsana sniffed. 'Lady Rajini never married and she never bore a child. We never knew where she got that girl. She just arrived from the city one day and said Mitali was her grandchild from that moment on. But my Lady Rajini has been a good mistress to work for, and her father – well, he was the sweetest man – he took us in and saved our lives. We know she was doing something, she and that Lady Annella, since the girl came here.

'Enki said it was bad. He said Lady Rajini was too old to start changing herself. We didn't know what he meant but now, from your words, I guess he knew she was trying to live longer? She was never a particularly strong or healthy woman.' Oxsana glanced at her husband.

'That Lady Annella. She started visiting much more often when our Lady brought that girl. Never liked her. No kindness in her. Never bothered if her horse was fit or cared for.' Burak nodded as if no more needed saying.

Kern bit back a smile, just nodded, but Burak obviously felt Kern didn't understand the seriousness of his words.

'Woman can neglect a horse she expects to carry her here and there – well, stands to reason, she'd not waste her time or care on much else neither.' He grunted and pushed up from the table. 'I'll go and see if I can find that boy of ours.'

Oxsana busied herself with the dishes and Kara moved to help her.

'I wonder if even Mitali knows from whence she came?'

85

'Is it important Kern?' Jian asked. 'I can check. While she's asleep?'

'No. It is not important. We only met Lady Rajini and this girl by chance. If they had been part of the magic dragging us through time, we would surely have arrived much closer to them. We traced Seola to Astian's house. I would suggest there was a deliberate link there, drawing her in. I also believe Reshik did not survive the transfer from our time to this.'

'Reshik was an earth mage,' Jian mused.

'Yes, but *only* an earth mage. I am beginning to wonder if a single talent is enough to get through time.'

Jian considered Kern's words. 'Or perhaps none?'

Kern looked puzzled.

'Riff. He has no talent whatsoever, yet he came through with us.'

'I see what you mean. More to think on!'

Rajini died just after sunset. Jenzi met the others as they made their way to bed and told them the news.

'I did not try to wake Mitali.' He smiled at Jian. 'I thought it best to just leave her.'

Jian returned his smile. 'We will be long gone by the time she wakes,' she told him.

Everyone slept at once, except for Kern. The Shadows murmured in his head and he listened closely. 'Let me see,' he commanded them.

He watched, inside his mind, as Enki drifted up the stairs and along a corridor on the other side of the house. He opened a door and slid into a room. Kern was amazed at how smoothly and silently such a very big man could move. The Shadows made no attempt to show Kern anything beyond the door, but it was mere heartbeats before Enki emerged. He shut the door noiselessly behind him and retraced his steps down the corridor. But he paused, glanced over his shoulder directly to where the Shadows must be gathered. He smiled his huge smile, waggled his fingers in a wave, and went on his way.

Well before dawn, Olam woke everyone. Oxsana had outdone herself with breakfast and they thanked her profusely. There was no sign of either Burak or Enki when they made their farewells to Oxsana. She had tears in her eyes as Kara hugged her tight but shooed them all off as though she would surely be seeing them later in the day.

Kara and Kern took three of the heavier food packs and climbed onto Skay's back. Both were slightly nervous, never having flown with Dragons before. Olam and Riff sat behind Brin's great shoulders with Jenzi in between. The rest of their baggage was firmly roped together and spread among them.

Kara gave a faint squeak of surprise when she realised Skay had lifted effortlessly into the air. Skay circled once above the house then headed east where a pearly glow indicated sunrise on the distant horizon.

Chapter Eight

Brin, Skay and Jian flew steadily towards the ever brightening east. They flew high but not so high as Jian had gone. Brin and Skay were both happy to be moving away from the city with its crowds of humans. Jian was constantly checking for any mind probe but she detected nothing. She was relieved they'd arrived in the city of Segra rather than Kedara. Kedara was the city of air mages and that would mean many minds searching the skies and the weather patterns and surely finding three Dragons above their city would cause considerable agitation.

Kern was finding the heat uncomfortable by mid morning and the group came down to settle perhaps twenty miles beyond Segra, on the long grasses of the plains. Jenzi dug out a pot of salve from his own pack which he offered to Kern. Olam tossed him a pale green cap – one of the many inexplicable items Oxsana had thought might be of use to them.

They stretched their legs, drank some cold tea and rested while the sun reached its peak and began to slip down to the west. Brin and Skay sprawled, their wings extended to absorb all the warmth they could.

'I've seen the place you spoke of Kern,' Brin rumbled. 'It reminded me of something.' His enormous eyes opened, blinked and closed again. 'I do not remember of what.'

'It seemed familiar to me too.' Jian sounded a little worried.

'We'll stop for the night before we quite reach the hills I think,' Olam said. 'No point trying to find that place when it's getting dark.'

They loaded themselves back onto Brin and Skay and set off once more.

'Do you know where Enki is?' Jian sent the thought to Brin's mind.

His long face turned to look at her briefly then he looked ahead again. 'No. I have no sense of his presence. Do you?'

'Unfortunately no.'

Jian and Brin found a place to camp for the night. It was some distance to the north of where the "niggle" had been found. While the camp was quiet, Kern sent his Shadows forth to see what might be seen. It was after dawn before they returned. Kern listened for a while as Kara and Riff lit a small fire and made a meal. Kern rolled his sleeping mat and strapped it to his pack before joining his companions round the fire.

'I will command the Shadows to tell you what they have found,' he announced. 'You will all be able to hear and see what they have to show. I told you I asked some of them to stay with each of you so do not fear their voice within your minds.'

'Kern sent. To find.'

Jian rolled her eyes. The others just looked slightly startled.

'Found this.'

A picture filled their minds, of a solid house, built with irregular stone blocks.

'And this.'

Olam and Riff both gasped. 'But that's a ship! A star ship!' Riff exclaimed. 'Like Singer and Flower.'

'No,' Olam corrected him slowly. 'It's different.'

The Shadows sniggered. 'Much different.'

'How?' Jenzi demanded.

'Not alive.'

Jenzi, Kern and Kara had all *heard* of the bio ships that Tika and her company had met but only Olam and Riff had been in that company and witnessed them for themselves. Jian was studying the picture in her mind closely. She had visited Wendla and she too had spoken with Star Singer and Star Flower. Olam was right. This ship looked quite similar in shape and size but there was an emptiness about it.

'It's too dark to see it properly,' Riff complained.

The Shadows snarled. 'Night *is* dark.'

Riff subsided, somewhat flustered.

'Found this.

They could just make out a narrow bed on which a man lay sleeping. A dim lamp, such as they'd never seen, stood on a table across the room, giving just enough light for them to see it *was* a man, his white hair and beard ghostly in the gloom.

'Karlek.'

'What does "Karlek" mean?' asked Jenzi aloud.

'Name.'

'How do you know that's his name?'

'Ship say.'

'So the ship speaks – like Star Dancer.'

'No.' The Shadows sounded exasperated. '*Not* like.'

They all felt an emptiness just at the back of their heads. Kern sighed. 'I'm sorry. They are not the easiest to talk to, except of course for the Son of Shadow.'

'Apart from apparently scouting for us, what exactly will Shadows do?' Olam asked crossly.

'Kill.'

The single word hissed through every head and five people froze. Kern shrugged and said nothing.

Brin and Skay had gone hunting before dawn and now settled back near the group. Brin's eyes whirred and sparkled.

'There is a place you could make your camp, quite near a house. The house must be where the one you seek lives – it's the only place for a great distance with any living person. We saw a man outside. He walked about then went inside again.' His mind voice carried a tone of great satisfaction at his own helpfulness.

'Any sign of Enki?' asked Riff.

Brin raised his head high and appeared to find the very few clouds of great interest. 'He was at the place I thought you'd like to make your camp.'

Kara giggled and Jian's mouth twitched.

'Why don't we go and find this amazing camp site?' Jenzi suggested brightly, making Kara giggle harder.

The scent of burnt cinnamon gusted across the plain and three Dragons quickly gained height. Jian stayed higher, spiralling gently when Brin led Skay through a region of tumbling hills and narrow valleys. Trees might fill one such valley, then the next few held only rock, scree and short, tired looking grass. They saw a handful of goats scrambling across precipitous rock faces and, Jian noted, a few crows.

Brin took them north and then east before dropping to fly very close to the ground. As the huge crimson Dragon swerved between rocky pillars to avoid a sheer rock wall, even Olam and Riff tightened their grip on his back. Jenzi simply closed his eyes. Skay followed her father. On her back, Kara and Kern had copied Jenzi's example and refused to look, hearing Skay's soft laughter in their minds.

The Dragons set down and their riders slid from their backs, grateful to be on solid ground again. They were in one of the tiny valleys, or gullies, and found there was a small grove of evergreen trees tucked along one side. A few tiny bright flowers speckled a strip of short grass alongside a thread of water. The smallness of the stream was made up for by its vigorous rushing and splashing. Jian joined them, the smell of cinnamon fading around her.

She turned slowly on the spot, surveying their camp site. She smiled. 'Hello Enki. Have you been waiting long?'

The others had been sorting out their packs and now turned to follow Jian's gaze. The big blond man sat in the shade of one of the trees and some small furry creature dashed away from him as he waved to them. He half climbed, half slid down to join them, reaching to touch first Skay's face, then Brin's.

'I found a place, just down there.' He pointed past the trees. 'I'll show you.' He grabbed up most of the packs and stumped on down the almost enclosed gully. Enki took them to a broad flat area under an overhang of rock. Riff walked under the rock and disappeared into the darkness. Enki dropped the packs and beamed at everyone.

'It goes a long way back, into a tunnel. I expect it will go right to the strange man's house.' He laughed at the looks of alarm from Olam and Kara. 'The man doesn't know of any tunnels. He's been here so long and he's never found any tunnels. Never *looked* for any tunnels. Never goes far from his house.'

'How long has he been there?' Kern asked.

Enki's blond hair flew in all directions as he shook his head. 'Long and long. Long before Enki.'' With a final "long", Enki showed them a firepit he'd built and where he thought each of them should put their bedrolls. 'Room for Brin and little Skay if it gets cold or nasty,' he finished proudly.

Olam and Riff grabbed some food and a water skin each. 'We'll go on through the tunnel Enki spoke of,' Olam said.

Riff took a small lantern although he knew Olam could conjure small glow lights.

'Don't get lost,' Kara called after them.

Enki chuckled. 'They won't. Anyway, I'd find them, easy, if they did.'

'Are your parents safe Enki?' Kern spoke softly.

The big man looked sad for a heartbeat, then he gave a gusting sigh. 'My mama and dada are safe now.'

'What happened when Mitali woke yesterday?'

'My dada dug a good place for Lady Rajini to sleep in the earth. Mama put a flower bush to grow there.'

Kern nodded. 'A very kind thing to do indeed. And Lady Annella and Mitali?' he pressed.

Huge blue eyes stared straight back at him. 'They were gone.'

'Gone?'

'Hmmm. Shall I show you where there are some onions growing?'

'That would be a good idea.' Kara held a hand out to pull Enki up with her.

'Will Mitali cause any trouble – to your parents or for us?'

Enki looked vague. 'Mitali's gone.'

'Gone where?' Kern's usually gentle tone sharpened.

'Just gone.' Enki followed Kara back out into the afternoon heat.

Jenzi grunted. The healer from Gaharn sat with his back against the rock and his long legs stretched towards the shelter's opening. 'Very far from simple minded is Enki.'

Kern looked alarmed. 'You haven't tried to test his mind?'

'Stars above, of course I haven't. He has enough power to fry us to dust without blinking.' He laughed at Kern's expression, settled more comfortably and closed his eyes.

Riff and Olam had no idea how far they'd walked. The tunnel they followed had no confusing side openings, just ran mostly straight. Occasionally they found the ground rising, then dipping away. Olam had made two glow lights and they each carried one, illuminating their way for several feet ahead.

'Wonder who dug this tunnel,' Riff said. 'And why.'

Olam peered closer at a stretch of wall. 'Look,' he said. 'Tool marks. So it was not caused by water. As to why, who knows.'

Light began to glitter back at them when they rounded a gentle curve and they both stopped. Slowly they walked closer and saw their glow lights were reflecting back from hundreds upon hundreds of shards of crystal. The closer they got, the colour changed to a brilliant green, winking and flashing at them.

Riff whistled. 'They look like jewels – do you think they really are?'

Olam dug one of the shards free, scraping his nail round the jagged shape. Riff copied him and they rubbed dust away from the pieces they held.

'Perhaps that was why the tunnel was made? They are no use to us.' But he pocketed the piece he'd pulled from the wall.

Riff glanced at Olam, walking on along the tunnel. He hurriedly dug out more pieces and tucked them carefully away. Half running after Olam, Riff grinned to himself. Perhaps he'd be a rich man when they got back to Far.

They reached the end of the tunnel more abruptly than Olam had expected. One last sweeping turn and there was daylight ahead of them. Olam snapped the glow lights out and crouched low. He worked his way forward, Riff close behind. The sky was darkening, so their walk through the tunnel had taken much longer than Olam had anticipated.

Reaching the opening they saw they were at a much higher level from the valley floor than the cave they had entered earlier. Creeping towards small boulders heaped just in front of the entrance, Olam and Riff peered out and down. A long low house stood perhaps a quarter of a mile across and to their left. The house looked solid but was not expertly built. The roof seemed less steeply pitched than might be expected but it was covered in strange blocks of a black material.

'Catch sunlight,' the Shadows informed them.

Riff and Olam exchanged glances. Shrugging, Olam peered over the boulders, checking the slope for a possible route down. Realising what Olam had in mind, Riff touched his shoulder. He shook his head vigorously when Olam turned to him.

Olam grinned. 'You stay here. If I don't return, you go back to the others.'

Riff was still shaking his head when Olam slipped silently passed him. 'I sent a glow light along the tunnel in case you have to go back alone. Just say my name at it and it will move as you command.' Olam's teeth flashed in a last grin and he was gone, crouched low, down to another pile of boulders.

Riff cursed steadily to himself, watching as Olam moved from rock to rock ever lower down the valley side. He bit his lip as Olam froze, flattening himself against the stony ground. The one door visible from Riff's position had opened and a man walked out.

The man held a stick of some kind across his body and he turned slowly in each direction. A slight breeze ruffled white hair which was raggedly cut at shoulder level and tangled with a wispy white beard. The distance was too great for Riff to make out more detail other than the blocky shape of the man. Medium height with broad shoulders, the man began to walk further from his door, away from where Olam lay.

Riff suddenly remembered the Shadows supposedly tucked away in their heads. 'Erm, Shadows?' he thought.

'Yes.'

'Could you tell Olam not to move please?'

He had no idea if the Shadows had done as he asked but at least Olam didn't move.

The man wandered around for a while as if he knew there was an intruder close by but after what felt like half a day to Riff but really could not have been too long, he went back to the house. One last look round and the door shut behind him. Riff almost groaned with relief when he saw Olam beginning to worm his way back up towards him. A light appeared at one of two long windows in the front of the building.

Riff saw a figure move across and knew the man would not see Olam if he should glance out. A foolish man, Riff thought, letting the light spoil his night vision, especially if he suspected an intruder near his house.

'Weapon sees.'

Riff frowned. What did the Shadows mean by that? How could a weapon see anything?

'Very different weapon.' The Shadows sounded grudgingly impressed.

Riff ignored them as Olam arrived next to him. 'The Shadows said I should leave him. That stick he carries was some sort of weapon.'

'Star Flower might know what it is,' Riff suggested helpfully and got a thump on his back from Olam.

'And how exactly would we ask Star Flower given our present situation?

Riff didn't bother to answer, following Olam back into the tunnel where a small glow light hovered by the wall.

'What now?' Olam scowled, sliding down to sit on the floor. 'I'd like to wait until full dark and then try again. If I could get close to a window, I might get some idea of who he is.'

Riff could see several dangers in that idea but wisely kept his mouth shut.

The Shadows sniggered. 'Not go.'

Olam snarled in frustration. Obviously the Shadows had spoken to both men and Olam did not like their comment.

'We need to know about this man,' he argued aloud, 'what kind of mage he might be.'

'Not mage.'

'Very well, he's not a mage. If I could find out what his weapon does I could. . . '

'Be dead.'

That seemed to quieten Olam, Riff was glad to see. He handed over the small pack he'd carried. 'Eat something, then we can start back.'

Olam gave one last glare and sighed.

'Enki might know something about this man,' Riff suggested while Olam chewed on a strip of dried meat.

'Do you think Enki knows him?'

'No.' Riff was definite. 'Enki's a good fellow, knows more than any of us I'd guess, but he keeps to himself. Can't see he'd have come out here and met that man before.'

'That's another thing. *How,* precisely, did Enki get here?'

'One of them gateway things? Everyone else seems to use them. I wonder why none of our people ever thought to invent them?'

Karlek was scanning the area around his house. Again. 'There must have been an error,' he said aloud.

'No Captain. Sensors picked up body heat, to the south west.'

95

'Surely you can recognise an animal wandering about after all this time, Computer?'

'Size was commensurate with humanoid, Captain.'

'Well, keep checking. I have work to do.'

'There is something else Captain.' The metallic voice sounded unusually hesitant.

Karlek turned back to the monitor, frowning. 'What?'

'I cannot calibrate it sufficiently clearly. Some kind of creature, life form, has been within this building sir.'

Karlek thought for a while. All the systems within his ship had deteriorated slowly but inexorably. The ship's automatic repairs had shut down increasing numbers of functions and he now feared this might be a symptom of yet further breakdown of equipment that was nearly a millennia old. 'What kind of life form?'

The machinery hummed and buzzed. 'It is simple energy Captain, but a knowing energy. An intelligence.'

'See if you can refine the reading and let me know.'

'Your command Captain.'

What intelligence could there be on this misbegotten planet that the Computer, with all its stored data banks recording every known life form in so many galaxies, could not identify? Karlek left the remnants of his ship and went back to his worktable in the room that also served as his bedroom and kitchen.

Piles of tattered composite notebooks held all his theories and experiments and he settled down to what he hoped would be the final calculations. The person he had brought back through time must be made to travel here, to him – he had no intention at all of attempting land travel himself. He rarely ventured out of sight of this house.

He was fully aware of how much more vulnerable he would be if he was separated from his weakening ship. Karlek had hoarded certain parts of the ship, sacrificing most of its flight capabilities along with the life support system. He had failed completely to take into account what might happen if he actually did manage to reverse time to return him to the point when he fell through the tear in time's fabric. He forgot he would need a ship around him, to have any hope at all of surviving in the sector of deep space where this had all begun.

Olam and Riff decided to stop and sleep briefly when they reached the section of tunnel where the crystals protruded from the rock. Olam idly picked at some shards from beside him as he sat with his back to the wall but quickly fell asleep. He was able to sleep wherever he found himself, a habit much resented by those who could not do the same. Such as Riff. Riff wriggled and twisted, but could not get comfortable. He stood up and wandered along the short stretch of wall that held the sparkling stones.

By the time Olam woke, as abruptly as he'd slept, Riff had a large quantity of the stones in his pack. If they ever got back to Far, he'd find out if he had a bagful of plain stones or would be a wealthy man. Lost in thought, Riff walked behind Olam down a tunnel that seemed infinitely longer than it had on their previous walk.

When they finally emerged, blinking in bright sunlight, only Jian was in the rock shelter. She glanced up questioningly when the two men dropped onto their bedrolls. Riff closed his eyes while Olam described what they'd seen. 'Where are the others,' he asked when he finished.

Jian smiled. 'Enki insisted they had to go fishing. There's a pool further down there,' she waved to the left. 'You know Jenzi and Kara are always plant hunting so they went along. Kern is with Brin and Skay. They're basking higher up. There's some shade apparently so that's where Kern is sitting and listening to Brin's stories.' She grinned.

'Most of them have *some* truth in them,' Olam defended Brin. 'Why are you still here?'

'I found these.'

Olam looked at the objects spread on the ground in front of her. She passed one to him. A lump of rock but shaped like a teardrop with half moons chipped down towards the pointed end. It fitted comfortable in his hand as he examined it.

'I've seen others like this. We believe they are the first attempts at tool making by humans.'

Olam frowned. 'How long ago?'

Jian laughed. 'Beyond any measuring our scholars have worked out. This is a lamp.' Another piece of stone, flat on the bottom with a shallow dip chipped out of the upper part. Looking more closely, Olam saw lines scratched all around, making a regular pattern.

'Oil or fat would go in there, a thread of some sort dipped in for a wick and there you are.'

'Were these made by our ancestors?'

'Ancestors we would not recognise.' Jian handed him two beautifully fashioned black arrow heads, one damaged along one side. 'They were much different from us. Shivan once talked to me about Ancient Ones. He said Tika had spoken of them. Do you recall her mentioning them?'

Olam shook his head, passing the stones back to her.

Jian drew in a slow breath. 'Shadows? I'm sure you've looked inside that house you told us of. What is within?'

For several heartbeats it seemed likely the Shadows would not choose to answer.

'Ship nearly dead.'

'But you said it wasn't alive, not like Flower or Singer.'

'*Not* like. Karlek makes bits work.'

'What is Karlek doing?'

'Trying to turn time.' The snigger echoed eerily in their heads.

'Will he be able to?'

'Course not.'

Olam's fists clenched. Oh to be able to get hold of one of these Shadows and throttle it.

'Not hold Shadow.' That comment was horribly smug.

Jian rolled her eyes. 'Can you turn time?'

The silence this time extended much longer. 'Not sure.' Another pause. 'Ancients can.'

'*What?*' Jian sat up straight, the stones rolling off her lap. But this time there was no answer.

Olam scratched his head and yawned. 'Ancient Ones? You said they were long gone.'

Jian stared at him blankly. 'I did didn't I? But Olam, they said "Ancients *can*", not "Ancients *could*". That suggests there must still be Ancient Ones existing now, in this time.'

'I see what you mean, but have you any idea how we might find such people, speak to them, and ask them to send us back?'

There was a glint of gold in the glare Jian turned on him. 'I need to think,' she snarled.

'I'll catch up on some sleep then.' Olam retreated to his bedroll again and was asleep almost instantly.

Jian scooped up the stones and put them in her pack, carefully wrapped in a spare shirt. She kept the tiny broken arrowhead out, turning it over and over between her fingers. She flinched and saw blood pooling in her palm. So very sharp, these little flakes of stone. A metal blade would long since have rusted and gone to dust but this stone was as lethal now as when it was first crafted.

Jian carefully wiped the smear of blood off the arrowhead with a fingertip and tucked the stone in her shirt pocket. She studied the small straight cut in her palm. It was much deeper than she might have expected and blood welled slowly but steadily from it. She picked up a waterskin, stepped out into the sunlight and poured water into her hand, rinsing away the blood. While she tended her cut, her mind turned to Shivan. Not for the first time, Jian fervently wished her brother was here.

Chapter Nine

Seola had let Astian believe she was extremely confused by being pulled back through time. High Mage Astian explained, enunciating slowly and carefully as though she was an idiot. She nodded occasionally but said nothing in reply. She understood the gist of his words from seeing within his mind, but was gradually making sense of his spoken words.

It took another full day before she was confident enough of the language to reply to one of Astian's questions. He appeared overjoyed that she could actually speak. She answered him hesitantly, even a little nervously, giving the impression she was in awe of being in the presence of such a powerful High Mage.

Seola tired of his inanities extremely quickly, pleading exhaustion so that he would leave her to rest. Once he'd gone from the room, she searched in a widening area for the mind that had previously touched hers. To no avail. East. She knew she had to travel east to find the real source of the power that, combined with her own, had drawn her here.

Astian had explained that she'd arrived in the garden of his house in Segra City but he had brought her out of that city to his country property. He told her he had considered being among peaceful farmlands far more suitable for her recovery than the noise and bustle of Segra's streets.

Next day, Seola casually asked what lands lay to the east. Astian was dismissive: grasslands stretched indefinitely, inhabited by barbaric tribes who trailed endlessly with their herds. 'Nothing of interest,' he told her.

In the morning Seola rose and dressed in clothes she found in a chest under the window. Grey trousers and a grey shirt that fitted her tolerably well. She wondered what had happened to her own clothes for no more than a heartbeat. One of the elderly maids who'd cared for her, entered and gasped when she saw Seola standing, dressed by the bed. Very carefully, Seola tried out her grasp of the Valsheban language, asking if the woman knew where she might find her boots.

Belatedly the woman bobbed a curtsey, then opened a narrow cupboard in the corner. She lifted out Seola's own boots, of a soft black leather. Boots she'd taken from Namolos's settlement, in fact. Seola sat on the bed to pull them on, then smiled at the maid. 'I am well now. Can you show me where I will find the High Mage?'

By the time Seola walked down two flights of stairs and along a passageway, she was annoyed to find herself light-headed and with trembling legs. The maid showed her into a medium sized room, clearly a study. Seola was more than glad to drop into an armchair facing a desk. The maid said something Seola didn't grasp and left her in the empty room.

Shortly the door opened again and High Mage Astian came in. He sat behind the desk and beamed at Seola. 'You are still extremely pale my dear. Are you quite sure you should be out of bed so soon?'

Seola managed a smile. 'I am much recovered thank you. I wondered if you had perhaps any idea of the distance the grasslands extend?'

Astian looked completely bemused by the question. 'But I told you my dear. There is nothing beyond Valsheba's border which is of any interest at all. There is no such thing as civilisation once you enter the plains.'

Seola stared at the High Mage for a while and he continued to look perplexed. 'What is your evaluation of me Astian?' she asked finally. 'Oh come now, you tried to invade my mind whilst I slept. What is your opinion?'

The switch in topic clearly confused Astian even more. 'I was not able to see into your mind, dear lady, which suggests you have a strong talent for shielding. Obviously, I could discern little else of your strength.'

'But you suspect I would offer little challenge to *your* strength, do you not?' Seola smiled gently, inwardly increasingly annoyed by his persistently patronising endearments.

Astian spread his open hands above his desk and smiled with false modesty. 'I believe there are few in these lands who could challenge my abilities my dear.'

101

Seola's smile widened and her muddy brown eyes changed slowly to a dull gold. Astian's expression would have seemed comical if Seola had possessed a sense of humour. 'You are a pathetic pretence of a mage Astian, and the one who has the real power to manipulate time lives somewhere in those grasslands you so easily denigrate. Never mind, *dear man*, you need fret yourself no more.'

The shield Astian tried to throw around himself was shredded before it was fully formed. Seola ripped into his mind and shredded that, too. By the time Seola withdrew her power, the man in front of her was no longer the High Mage Astian. He gazed at her vacantly as she leaned her head back on the armchair. Her eyes were muddy brown once more and she was irritated that her head was pounding again. How much longer before she fully regained her strength?

She remained where she was for a while, until the pain in her head subsided. Astian mumbled unintelligibly now and then and studied his fingers with a deep fascination. Seola took a breath, then wrinkled her nose. Oh dear! Poor Astian! She left the study and saw another maid along the passageway.

'I fear your master has been taken ill,' Seola said. 'Some kind of seizure I believe, You should tend him and perhaps summon a healer.'

The maid rushed past and entered the study, only to re-emerge white faced. 'My lady, whatever happened?' The woman was tugging on a bell rope beside the study door as she spoke.

Seola shook her head sadly. 'We were speaking, the High Mage raised his hands to his head and then – he was as you see him.'

The maid nodded as though she'd witnessed such a thing before. Perhaps someone in her family, Seola mused before giving herself a mental shake. What did it matter? Astian was neutralised and she must be on her way. 'I found his sudden illness quite distressing,' she told the maid. 'I will walk for a while, out in the fields.'

The maid nodded again, distracted by the appearance of another woman and two older male servants. All four rushed into Astian's study. Seola grinned and went in search of an exit.

Guards stood along the walls and at a gate in the rear wall of the garden. Seola sent the lightest touch of a compulsion and they returned her smile, opening the gate and saluting her through. Seola strode towards an area of orchard, passing through them so they stood between her and any who might be watching from the house.

The scent of sour cinnamon blew through the small trees and a Dragon lifted high and fast into the clear sky.

Kara and Jenzi returned with a triumphant Enki bearing three good sized fish and a large cloth filled with small shelled creatures which Enki swore were wonderfully tasty. Kara had an armful of various leafy plants and all three seemed very pleased with themselves.

Olam had woken and gone to see Brin and Skay while Riff still snored on his bedroll. Enki put the fish in the shade and turned to Jian. He smiled and reached for her hand. She hesitated but his huge fingers covered hers so gently she offered no resistance. Heat flowed from him, and the cut on Jian's palm burned hot as fire. Enki released her, turning to the others and demanding the biggest cooking pot they'd brought from Rajini's house.

Riff was dragged upright and, protesting furiously, sent to fill the pot from the stream. Jian remained where she was and while Kara and Jenzi listened to Enki's instructions on how their fish would be cooked, she turned her hand over to look at her palm. She exhaled softly. As she'd guessed, the cut was now merely a white thread of a scar.

Enki was proved right. His fish and shelly things, green leaves and shoots , made a meal all of them thoroughly enjoyed. Brin and Skay flew down to join them as the sun sank, and Olam repeated all he and Riff had seen at the stranger's house. Kern had been even quieter than usual but when everyone had discussed Olam's news from every possible angle, he spoke.

'The Shadows told me they have been within the house.' He glanced at the faces now watching him closely. 'There is indeed a ship inside, but nothing like the ones we know of. It has no true life. It is what Star Flower's Captain called a machine. Karlek was the captain and when he came to this world, he thought the other ships were chasing him. That's why he hid here, so they would not find him with their devices.'

Olam and Riff were nodding, remembering the strange things they'd seen in the City of the Domes on their journey with Tika.

'The Shadows said the machine knew they were there. It could not tell what they were but it told Karlek it had detected some form of life within his house.'

'Can Shadows be killed?' Jenzi asked thoughtfully.

Enki chortled. 'Course they can't. They can get very cross though.'

Jian laughed. Oh if only she could understand what Enki was! That he was sweet tempered was an important point, in her estimation. He held so much power in him she didn't dare think what he might do if he was a bad tempered soul. Enki caught her eye across the embers of the fire and he gave the smallest nod.

'Enki is quite correct. The Shadows can indeed get rather cross. Not with the Son of Shadow himself of course, but definitely with anyone else,' Kern continued. 'I am at a loss to know what we can do. If this man *is* the one who can turn time, we cannot have him killed.'

'Is it likely he would even attempt to return us to our time?' Kara asked.

'That is a most excellent point,' Kern smiled at her. 'I wonder if he would try to kill us rather than talk to us? Perhaps we are just lowly toys to be moved or destroyed – as he pleases?'

'Could we find out if he would talk to us?' asked Olam. He frowned, considering his idea further. 'Could the Shadows speak to his machine, rather than risk alerting him?'

'And if he agreed for us to meet him, which of us should go? All of us is not a good idea.'

Kern nodded in agreement with Jenzi's words.

'Maybe Jian and I should meet him – two women would surely offer little threat?' Kara smiled at Kern. 'You look too different I would suggest, and Jenzi is far too tall to be a native of these lands.'

'I could take you.' Brin joined the discussion for the first time. 'I have noticed many humans are quite impressed when they see you carried by Dragon Kin.'

Olam chewed his lip. He would like nothing better than to have Brin at his side but he feared more for the Dragon's safety than he cared for his own comfort. 'I think, if Karlek will meet with us, we should go through the tunnel. You could watch us Brin, from high above.'

Brin's eyes flashed while he considered the idea. He gusted a sigh, making the embers in the fire flare back to sudden life. 'It shall be as you say. We could be with you in heartbeats should you need us.'

Olam was sitting against Skay's black scaled shoulder and he leaned forward to stroke his fingers along Brin's neck. 'That would give us great comfort,' he said. 'Will you send Shadows now Kern?'

Leaf green eyes crinkled in a smile. 'They are speaking to the machine even now,' he admitted.

In the silence following his words, Jenzi spoke. 'Enki, do you know where the woman Seola is now?'

Enki's blue eyes closed, then blinked open. 'South.' He thought a bit more. 'She might be here tomorrow. Or the day after. She's not very nice.'

Everyone laughed.

'She is most definitely not very nice Enki,' said Jian. 'You do know she is one of my people? That she can take Dragon form?'

'Oh yes. But you are beautiful. She is ugly.'

'How do you know that Enki? Have you seen Seola as woman or Dragon?' Jian asked.

'Course.' Enki beamed at them all. 'My dada always said you should know what you're about.'

Not for the last time, six pairs of eyes regarded Enki very thoughtfully.

There was a disturbed air about the Council Chambers in Segra City. Mavar, long serving steward of the High Mage Rajini's household had brought worrying reports. The Council sent guards to check the accuracy of the man's story and were now in deep debate.

After leaving Rajini, her grandchild and the six mysterious strangers at the High Mage's country holding, Mavar had returned to Segra. He was to organise the twice yearly cleaning of the city house, visiting the country house every few days with any messages or papers directed to Rajini.

When he'd arrived on the fourth morning after he'd left the High Mage, it was to find the place deserted. He'd gone into every room in the house and he found no one. There was no sign of Oxsana, Burak, or their halfwit son. Mavar went outside and eventually he found a freshly dug grave, the earth still dark and damp on the surface. He recognised the small bush planted at one end as one of High Mage Rajini's favourites, and he knew who was buried here.

She had told him she was expecting a visit from her great friend High Mage Annella when he'd departed back to Segra, but of her or the granddaughter Mitali, he could find no trace. There were no horses in the stables, no hens cackling in the yard, no goats in their pen. The place felt peaceful enough with no sign of violent disturbance within the house. But there was an air of desolation, as though it had been empty a very long time rather than a mere day or two.

Mavar had carefully secured the doors and windows and ridden hard back to Segra. He went directly to High Mage Annella's house and was dismayed to learn that her steward believed her to be staying in the country with Rajini. From there, Mavar went to the Council Offices and repeated his tale to High Mage Samir, the mage charged with all matters concerning safety and security in Segra.

Samir called in his deputy, Tenzin, who excelled as a truth reader, and had Mavar go through his story once again. He was eventually sent to wait in an adjoining room while Samir called a Council meeting. At such short notice, the Summoning Scribes managed to locate only four of the eleven Councillors. With Samir and Tenzin, six Mage Councillors were enough to hold formal Council.

They met in the Small Chamber and no witnesses or recording scribes were admitted. Samir gave a quick summary of his concerns and then called for Mavar to be sent in. Yet again, Mavar repeated his tale. When he finished, Samir thanked him.

'I know you have already waited a considerable time, Steward Mavar, but if you would wait just a little longer in case my colleagues need clarification of any points. Refreshments will be brought to you.'

Mavar bowed to Samir, to the other Councillors, and left the

Chamber.

'Tenzin?' A Mage, bowed with age called the name.

'He spoke true Calin,' Tenzin replied.

Before more was said there was a knock at the door.

'Come,' snapped Samir.

A scribe entered and handed over a piece of parchment. Reading it, Samir frowned. 'Send him in.'

The scribe backed away and waved another man inside.

'And you are?' Samir barked.

'Vikas, Steward to High Mage Astian, Great Sirs.' The man, of middle years, was dusty from travel and had an air of distracted worry.

'Speak then Vikas.'

'Sirs, my master ordered us to remove from the city to his outlying house near four days past. He had a guest, a woman. The maids said she was unconscious, very ill.' He shrugged. 'No one saw her arrive Great Sirs, and Mage Astian had her moved in his own carriage. A maid summoned me this morning, to Mage Astian's study. Sirs, he is as a year old child. The maid told me that the woman had woken and sought High Mage Astian. She came from his study and told the maid to fetch help as my master was taken sick. She went outside, to walk she said, because she was distressed. But Great Sirs, we have found no trace of her since.'

The younger of the only two women present, Orissa, asked for a description of Astian's guest, which she scribbled down as Vikas spoke.

'If there are no more questions you may leave Steward, but we may need to speak with you again.' Samir nodded a dismissal at the man. 'Well?' he asked, turning to his fellow High Mages.

The younger woman spoke. 'The descriptions are strange Samir. Two men and one of the women, sound like us, but two of the men are definitely from another land and two of the women also.'

'I agree. The man described as hairless and grey skinned bothers me. I'm sure I've heard a similar description.'

'You've read of it Remi.' The ancient Calin gave a laugh which turned into a hacking cough. 'Children's tales, boy. You must remember the story of The Shadow Folk and The Dragon?'

The middle aged man referred to as "boy" stared blankly at Calin before nodding. 'That's right. So does that mean those tales are true?'

Old Calin spluttered, whether due to cough or laughter was unclear. 'They all hold some truth. Sometimes the merest grain, others tell all the truth in such bold words everyone thinks it must be made up!'

The second woman laughed. 'I remember you making us study all those old tales for homework you old rogue.'

'And you were the only one of my idiot students who actually read them were you not, Daria?'

Her smile faded. 'I went over and over them,' she admitted. 'I felt sure there must be something of amazing importance in them.'

'Enough of this,' Samir interrupted her. 'You think the strange little grey skinned man is one of the Shadow Folk?' His scepticism was obvious. 'What of the giant?'

Calin shrugged. 'We know nothing of people living far distant from Valsheba.'

'And the two pale women?'

'The same argument holds for them.'

Samir sneered, turning to the other four Councillors. 'Your opinions please.'

'I think it is quite clear that some of these strangers at least are mages. What happened to Astian so suddenly was surely caused by the woman who has now disappeared.'

'Thank you Orissa. Remi?'

'I'm inclined to agree. The disappearance of Rajini, Annella and the young girl also indicates magecraft.'

'But Steward Mavar spoke of a grave that was made with care, with Rajini's favourite flower planted on it. And there are also her three slaves unaccounted for.' Tenzin put in mildly.

'Which only shows how dangerous these strangers must be,' retorted Remi.

'I propose that we search the city at once. There are a dozen mages strong enough in seeking, to find them within the day,' Samir announced.

'As long as they *are* in the city,' Daria commented.

'Where else would they go?' asked Orissa.

'The plains?' suggested Tenzin. 'Along the coast either north or south?'

That thought had obviously not occurred to High Mage Samir. 'Then we will pursue them. It is more than time we made our presence felt among the savage tribes. There has been an increasing number of cattle thefts reported from farmers along the border.'

Daria raised a brow at Tenzin who replied with the tiniest shake of his head.

Samir and Remi began listing names of mages to be called in to start scanning for the strangers through the city. Orissa offered names too and it was she who left to send for the mages. Calin heaved himself upright and teetered gently before Daria hurried to help him.

'I wish you luck Samir. I can be of little assistance I fear.'

Samir looked at the wizened figure, the white beard like a tangled nest and the food stains decorating the shirt front. 'As you say,' he agreed. He and Remi rose to leave the Small Chamber.

'There are some matters I must deal with, Samir, but a mind summons will bring me at once, should you need me.' Tenzin smiled gently, knowing full well that Samir was incapable of the delicate mind connection he had just suggested.

Calin had another fit of coughing and swayed perilously on the steps down from the Council table. Daria glared at him while Samir twitched his tunic straight and stomped after Remi with no further comment.

'An old man would be most grateful for your help in returning to his home.' Calin looked hopefully at Daria.

'Yes, yes. I'll help you.' She lowered her voice. 'You shouldn't laugh at Samir – he'll notice one of these days.'

Calin snorted. 'He notices nothing unless he falls over it or it bites his backside. And what exactly do you think our esteemed Samir could actually do to me? Eh?'

Tenzin had joined them near the door. 'You know full well he could get rid of you,' he said.

'How exactly would he do that?' Calin asked with interest.

Tenzin shook his head and grinned. 'I will have to attend to those two poor Stewards – I doubt Samir's even remembered them. I'll join you in a while.'

Daria struggled out of the Council Buildings with Calin clinging to her arm. Weaving through the crowded square, it amazed Daria how many people called greetings to the old man. Stall holders, flower sellers, water carriers, road men and urchins. Calin returned each greeting or insult as cheerily as they were offered. Daria got them to a tavern on the corner of a large block, its doors and windows wide open under the sign of The Lonely Hen.

'Which way in today?' Daria asked, surveying the tavern, the bakery next door and the fruit and vegetable shop beyond that.

'The Hen.'

'You're drinking too much.'

'Nonsense. What else is an old man to do?'

Daria laughed in spite of herself as the pair entered the cool dimness of the tavern. A man was scrubbing a long bar at the rear of the room. He grinned when he saw Daria helping Calin between the empty tables.

'You poor old man,' he greeted them.

'I know. Pitiful, aren't I Porridge? A supply of your berry cordial sent up if you please. And Tenzin will be here shortly.'

'Right you are sir.'

Calin tugged Daria out to the back kitchens. He opened a door to a small hallway with stairs leading upwards. Calin climbed up the stairs as sprightly as Daria, age apparently of no consequence whatsoever. Three flight up and a modest door opened at Calin's muttered words.

'Why do you live over these shops? I've always wondered,' Daria puffed behind Calin.

'I like the noise. I like to know there are people around. I like having food and drink so conveniently near. I own the whole block, why should I live anywhere else?'

Calin pulled off the cloak that had been clumsily hooked on his shoulders and sat in his armchair, waving Daria to another.

'Who do you believe they are?' Daria asked bluntly.

Calin was busy stuffing a large pipe with shredded fruit leaf. He didn't reply until he had the pipe lit and clouds of fragrant smoke engulfed his head. 'I have been interested in many things in my life,' he finally replied. 'Things that no one else seemed interested in. And I have also kept a close eye on certain mages who delve in matters better left, in my humble opinion, well alone.'

Daria snorted. 'Since when were you humble you old fraud. Incidentally, the food all over your shirt was a step too far I think.' Calin grinned round his pipe. 'And don't change the subject.'

'I think the strangers are here by mistake. I very much fear someone, beyond my knowledge, has meddled where they most definitely should not. The grey skinned one is of the Shadow Folk, I would swear. The two women, although one travels with the group and one apparently alone, I would venture to guess are of the Dark Folk.' He nodded when Daria paled. 'The others? I cannot offer any idea there. Ah! Refreshments!'

The door opened and Tenzin came in, carrying a large keg in one hand and a basket covered with a cloth in the other. Daria dragged a small table closer to Calin and Tenzin put down the basket from which fresh baked smells arose.

'Have Samir's mages found anything yet?' Calin asked, accepting a glass of dark red liquid from Tenzin's keg.

Tenzin took a sip from his own glass. 'One of the brighter girls managed to find a trace. From Rajini's holding. The group of strangers went east, far across the plains. She found three traces she could not recognise.'

Calin leaned his head back, closing his eyes.

'Do you know what those three might be Calin?' Daria asked.

Blue eyes, faded with age, opened and he smiled. 'I do not *know* child, but I can make a good guess. Dragons.'

Chapter Ten

After a fiery sunset, clouds rapidly gathered above the hills and the temperature dropped. Jenzi and Riff hurried to gather branches and bark from beneath the trees to keep inside in the dry, just as hail stones began to crash down. Skay and Brin eased their way under the overhang and further into the shelter, where they reclined against the rock walls. The hail gave way to heavy rain which was suddenly illuminated by immense twisted fingers of lightning snapping down. The first crack of thunder made them all jump.

'Can you fly in this kind of weather?' Jenzi asked the Dragons curiously.

Brin's eyes glittered in the light of the fire which Kara had stirred to a blaze. 'I have done so.' His bass mindvoice rumbled gently. 'I found it most exhilarating. But it is dangerous. I only did it once, when I was very young, and possibly foolish.' He stared hard at his daughter. 'It is *not* something you will do.'

People became fascinated by the fire's leaping flames rather than risk the smallest laugh.

'If it is dangerous, you must have been told not to fly. Who told you, and why did you disobey?' Skay's gentle voice held genuine curiosity as she studied her father.

Brin's eyes whirred faster and Olam and Kern both fled further into the cave before trying to stifle their amusement.

'Both my mother and my father told me it was a silly thing to do, but I was foolish when I was young, and believed I could do anything with impunity.'

'We do not risk it either,' Jian put in, her voice shaking slightly.

Kara felt a change of subject might be wise, and called to Kern, asking if the Shadows had reported back to him yet. Kern and Olam emerged into the firelight, careful to avoid each other' eye.

'They have not,' Kern admitted. 'I'm not sure what could be

taking so long.'

Enki had been lying on his stomach nearest to the overhang, to watch the lightning poking at the tops of the hills. 'Busy,' he commented now.

'Busy talking to the machine Enki?' Jian asked.

'No. A mage in Segra.'

The company exchanged alarmed glances but Enki chuckled. 'Nice man. I met him sometimes.'

'You met him?' Jian echoed. 'Did he visit Rajini then?'

Enki rolled over and sat up. 'No, no. I met him different places. Sometimes in the woods, or by the sea. Once or twice near here.' He waved a large hand vaguely, presumably indicating the grasslands around the hills. He realised they were all waiting for him to say more and he spread his big hands, his bright blue eyes moving from face to face before resting on Jian. 'He's a bit like me. Just a bit. Shall we cook something else now?'

Infuriatingly, in Enki's opinion it seemed the subject was now closed. Jenzi began to talk of various trips he'd made around Gaharn, both in the mountains and on the plains. Time passed, the storm eventually moved further south, and the Shadows still did not return. The company decided to sleep and hope the Shadows might be back with helpful news in the morning.

The day dawned with a clear sky and a washed and polished look to the stones and plants beyond the rock shelter. Skay and Brin went off to hunt, saying they would bring something back for the company. Enki patted Kern's hairless head in a friendly manner. 'Don't worry. They'll be here soon. I'm going to look at the flowers.' He wandered off down the slope with Riff trotting beside him.

The Dragons returned each carrying a goat which Riff and Jenzi skinned and cleaned. By then it was close to midday and Kern tensed. Brin and Skay huffed and sat up and a man appeared in front of them. Enki gave a shout and scooped the man up in a hug before carefully setting him down in the shade of the overhang. The man stared at the companions with as much curiosity as they stared at him.

He was slightly below average height, thin, white haired and white bearded, and definitely beyond elderly. Enki sat beside him, holding his hand and beaming.

'This is the friend I told you about. He's called Calin and he's a very nice man.'

'Shadows didn't bring you,' said Kern. 'How did you get here, if I might ask?'

'You are of the Shadow Folk,' Calin said. 'Your Shadows spoke with me last night. Not the best conversationalists, are they? No, they offered to bring me but I prefer my own methods.'

Enki laughed happily. 'That's Kern. He's a cousin of the Son of Shadow. That's Olam, and Riff. They are great warriors. Jenzi is from a far land, north and east. He's a good healer. And Kara can heal but mostly she's an air mage. *And* she's a very good cook.'

They all laughed although Olam and Riff were both wondering why Enki had described them as great warriors.

'And that's Jian,' Enki added when Jian strolled towards them with a newly filled waterskin.

The old man Enki had introduced as Calin, climbed to his feet, his hand still in Enki's. He bowed. 'Lady Jian, it is my honour to greet you. I am Calin.'

Jian studied him briefly then smiled. Her eyes shone brilliant gold. 'Greetings to you Calin. Can we offer you a drink? We have water or tea.'

Calin's face fell. 'No ale? No cordial? Dear me. Then tea would be most appreciated.'

Later, when Kara and Riff started to roast the goat meat, and Enki had dragged Jenzi off to find more leaves and onions, Calin turned to Jian. 'Could you show me where those beautiful Dragons are now? I never guessed how much they might love the heat.'

'Certainly.' Jian pulled the old man to his feet. 'They have chosen some rocks up here, not too far.'

Calin chuckled as he followed her. 'I'm not completely helpless yet, child.'

'I'm sure those who know you in the city believe you weak and feeble?' Jian glanced over her shoulder.

'It is very useful to be dismissed as a fool,' Calin agreed.

'Like Enki?'

Calin sighed. 'Enki has told me he thinks we are alike. I am as a babbling child compared to dear Enki – as you have already realised I think?'

Jian stopped. She pointed further up the sloping side of the valley. Brin and Skay lay on convenient boulders, wings fully spread and necks extended.

'Did you need us for something?' Brin's mindvoice was sleepy and Jian grinned.

'No thank you. Calin wanted to admire you again.'

One huge eye opened and stared down at the two people below. 'Well I'm sure he did.' The eye closed once more.

'Come.' Jian led the way towards the grove of evergreen trees further up the valley. She sat on the short grass below the gently waving branches. 'What have they decided we are, back in the city?'

Calin sat beside her. 'The leader of the Mage Council is Samir. He has no idea who you might be, but he is very eager to shine as a great leader. He knows you have come east from Segra and is mustering the full guard to follow you over the plains. He wants to kill some of the tribes – the more the better – and *perhaps* catch all of you, and for all of Valsheba to admire his prowess. He's not a very gifted mage,' he added.

He drew his pipe out of his shirt pocket and began stuffing it with fruit leaf from a pouch at his belt. 'Child, both Enki and the Shadows told me you have fallen through time. That is a grave matter. And the solitary woman – she is of your own people I think, but Enki only says she is a nasty person.'

Jian leaned back on her elbows. 'Nasty doesn't begin to describe Seola.' Her tone was bitter. 'And yes, we come from far in your future, but we didn't *fall*. We were caught, or dragged, through another's manipulation of the time vortex. I think the man here, if he is merely a man, somehow connected through all this time with something Seola found. You know of the star ship this man has?'

She waited for Calin's nod. 'I believe there is something within it which can make these jumps in time. In our time, we know of at least three star ships – very different from this one – and one of them told us if they know the correct coordinates they can tear time's very fabric.'

Calin puffed on his pipe while he pondered Jian's words. 'It sounds as though your numerical education, for one, was, shall we say, vague?' Pale blue eyes twinkled through the pipesmoke. Jian merely looked confused and the old man chuckled. 'I know what they must mean by coordinates child – I spent many years on the study of navigation. You must let me think on this but I may, *may*, be able to work out a way for you to get back to your time. Now your other problem is this woman – Seola? What must be done with her? Can your Shadows not destroy her?'

Jian sat up, frowning. 'I really don't know. The thing is, Seola has tremendously strong shielding abilities and I have no idea if those shields could withstand the Shadows. Kern might have a more accurate idea of how powerful they are, but no one else knows much about them.'

A snigger sounded in the back of her head and Jian froze. Calin swallowed smoke and spluttered.

'Mysterious!' The Shadows sounded proud of the word. 'Man will speak.'

Calin looked puzzled.

'When?' Jian demanded aloud.

'Whenever you there.'

Jian scrambled to her feet, tugging Calin along with her. A winded Calin sank to the floor of the shelter and listened as several voices argued about when they should walk through the tunnel. Jenzi raised his voice firmly.

'Food is almost ready. You will eat and rest for a while before you go. Karlek will obviously be expecting you, it will make little difference when you get there.'

After some muttering it was agreed and the four who would go, took the time before eating to decide what to take. Kern sat with Calin and Enki watching jenzi begin to serve the food.

'The Shadows said the machine has eyes around these hills. I didn't understand quite what they meant. They said Karlek put boxes in several places and the boxes can send pictures to the ship machine and it can then tell if anyone approaches from the grasslands or through the hills.'

Enki sniffed the delicious smell of roast meat. 'Doesn't know about the tunnel though,' he remarked, and leaned far forward to snatch a large chunk of meat.

116

Jenzi smiled and rapped his hand with a wooden spoon. which made Enki giggle.

'My mama used to do that.' His words were muffled by roast meat but his expression was sad for a moment.

Olam had joined them. 'Brin can hide us behind a shield,' he said. 'He's done it before and then Karlek wouldn't know where we'd come from. Brin will be as glad to do something as we will. I'll ask him now.'

After they'd eaten, Enki wandered outside, gazing up at the sky and humming to himself. Riff followed him. 'There were lots of this in one patch of tunnel wall, near the other end.' He fished one of the green stones out of his trouser pocket then winced. He passed the stone to Enki and stared at his finger where a small straight cut welled with blood. 'Didn't think it was so sharp,' he muttered, watching red beads drip onto the stone underfoot.

Enki's big thumb rubbed gently over the stone and Riff could have sworn it shone an even more brilliant green. Enki sighed, passed the stone back and closed his fingers around Riff's hand. Riff's mouth formed a circle of surprise as searing heat shot through his cut finger. Enki released him, smiled and with no comment, turned away, walking swiftly in the direction of the small pool.

In Segra, Daria had looked for Calin. She'd looked in his rooms above the Lonely Hen, in the large library across the square from the Council Building, and finally in his official office – although that was a last hope as she couldn't remember ever seeing him there. Then she tracked down Tenzin to ask if he'd seen the old man. While she'd been hunting for Calin, she had avoided any of Samir's cronies. She had noticed an air of anticipation and bustle, and considerably larger numbers of guards seemed to fill the halls and corridors.

Daria eventually tracked Tenzin down to his own tiny house, tucked away in an alley behind a row of shops lining the south side of the Siertsey square. She banged at the front door and felt the tingle of a scanning ward. She muttered something unladylike and waited impatiently for the door to be opened.

'Come in.' Tenzin caught her wrist, pulling her in quickly,

closing the door and resetting wards.

'Where is he?' Daria demanded.

'I'm not sure.' Tenzin waved her through to the back of the small house.

'What does that mean?' Daria dropped into a chair and glared at him. 'I've spent all morning looking for him. And then for you,' she added crossly.

'Have some tea,' he suggested. 'I've only just made it. I sent word to Samir that I had a sudden attack of summer fever. You know what he's like with illness, he'll leave me alone for a few days at least.'

Daria poured herself a bowl of tea. 'That still doesn't tell me where Calin is, drat the man.'

Tenzin folded his arms. 'I know you're aware that Calin – travels.' He waited for her reluctant nod. 'He is travelling now.'

Daria continued to glare. 'I know *something* happened last evening. Yes, I know he disappears at times, but it was different. There was a sort of – agitation – which was unfamiliar,' Tenzin went on.

Daria blew out a breath. 'I felt that too,' she admitted. 'I was actually trying to scry for Samir, just after the fourth bell. It was too boring, watching him strut around so I looked for Calin.' She pushed her reddish blonde hair behind her ears. 'Calin *always* knows when I try to scry him – it's a bit of a game. He taught me scrying and he says I should be good enough for him to be unaware of it. Not so far. Anyway, I found his *mind* but I couldn't see *him*. There was some sort of other mind all around him, then that vanished and bare heartbeats later, so did he.'

Tenzin poured himself more tea. 'That is exactly what I felt. I have no way of knowing if I'm correct, but I do have a strong feeling that what you thought was a mind around him, was actually a group of Shadows.' Daria gaped at him, started to speak and changed her mind. Tenzin gave her a wry grin. 'I've had a bit longer to study old Calin than you have,' he began.

'I know he fools everyone,' Daria interrupted. 'I've never worked out why he hides how powerful he is. Unless it's to get out of more Council work or teaching.'

Tenzin nodded. 'He takes fewer students each year. Calin is probably one of the rarest Mages Valsheba has produced. He is gifted in so many aspects of power he could rule the land if he chose.' He paused. 'He has never admitted it but I believe he guards us. Any Mage who begins to show too much love of power for its own sake, Calin – deals with.'

Daria's brow furrowed. Tenzin let the silence settle while she thought. 'Parna? That was several years ago – I had nearly finished at the Academy. He died of fever I thought?' Tenzin merely smiled. 'That still doesn't tell me where he's gone.'

'I know. I truly don't know for sure. To the east, but other than that?'

'Has he gone to find the strangers? Why are they here Tenzin?'

Tenzin got up and refilled the kettle. He hooked it over the small fire and sat down again, his smile now rueful. 'I would say it's fairly obvious that's where he's gone.'

'Can you move, without using circles? Calin was teaching me, but so far I've only managed to move myself from one room to another.'

'Really? I've never achieved that! I *can* move objects some distance, across the city for example, but not myself.'

'So what are people from the Shadow World, or the Dark World doing here? And *Dragons*! Did you believe that?'

'As Calin said, there is always truth to be found in the craziest words. Now tell me what Samir's up to.'

'I told you I avoided him, but I heard mention of a big parade tomorrow. All the guards, Samir and Remi at their head, leaving to "punish" the tribesfolk on the plains, and I see no way we could stop that.' Tenzin raised a brow. 'Oh really! We can't just start killing people.'

'We can't?'

'If Samir and Remi are to suddenly die, there would be such uproar Tenzin. Surely there would be those of their like minded friends who would announce it a plot, devised by the tribes. The guards would be even more eager to march out.'

'Who will command this expedition?'

Daria frowned. 'I think I heard mention of Third Commander Arif. Commander Lano is getting on in years, perhaps he refused to go?'

'Commander Lano is currently occupying my guest room.'

Daria blinked but found nothing to say.

'He has long been a friend to Calin. No mage powers whatsoever, but a brilliant commander of guards. He knows many of the tribal leaders and refused Samir's orders outright last night.' Tenzin nodded. 'Samir has no idea that I know Lano, and none of his seekers will get through my wards. Haven't you noticed Daria, how much weaker the younger Mages are in the last few years?'

'What happened to Second Commander Zari?'

'His father died. Very suddenly. Zari is in Parima, contesting his ownership of the estate against his younger brother. Idiocy runs in that family.'

Daria nodded. 'I have seen Arif around Samir's offices quite often of late.'

'Oh yes. The fact of the strangers appearing in Segra is coincidental to Samir's plans to wage war against the people of the plains. Third Commander Arif has always made it clear he thinks Valsheba should be more of a military land.'

Daria held her head in her hands, trying to make sense of things. 'We wait for Calin to return? We hope Samir doesn't find any tribes? What *are* you saying, Tenzin?'

'Samir and most of his followers will be gone tomorrow. Word has already been sent to tribal Wise Ones to move out of his line of march. The problem is that Samir will come to a stretch of hills within three, maybe four days at most, and somewhere in those hills are the strangers. With Calin. Stars only know what happens then.'

The door opened and Commander Lano peered in. 'Sorry. I didn't expect to sleep so long.'

Daria didn't look at Tenzin, guessing he'd put a compulsion on the old Commander.

'Come in Lano. I'll cook a meal shortly but here's some tea. You know Daria I think?'

Commander Lano bowed towards Daria. 'We have met,' he agreed, sitting between Tenzin and Daria. 'What news of the guards and the High Mage Samir?'

Tenzin repeated the little Daria knew and she studied the Commander. He was taller than Tenzin, who was himself rather taller than average. His grey hair was a mat of bristles covering a round head. His skin was weathered, deep lines around his eyes and furrowing down his cheeks. Commander Lano's hands, clasped around his tea bowl, were a workman's hands, short stubby fingers and close clipped fingernails.

When Tenzin finished, Lano sipped his tea. 'What about those left in Segra?' he asked, his voice slightly hoarse.

Daria didn't understand Lano's question.

'Remi and Orissa are with Samir. You two are here. Calin has done one of his vanishing tricks. Rajini and Annella are dead and Astian might as well be. That leaves Rahul and Sahana of the eleven Mage Councillors. And they are staunch followers of Samir.'

Daria flushed. 'Samir was jealous of Astian – he could never hide it. But he couldn't have arranged for Astian's – illness. Could he?'

Tenzin frowned. 'No. that was just a very timely piece of good fortune for Samir. But Samir has many supporters among the Lesser Mages. Astian was so full of his own dignity and importance, there are many who would be glad to have him gone. There are also supporters of Calin among the Lesser Mages who are wiser than their so called peers. For more of those understand some of Calin's power, and they hope he will one day lead the Council.'

'But that's just the point,' Daria insisted. 'Calin will *never* accept the leadership.' She thought for a moment then looked from Commander Lano to Tenzin. 'I heard it mentioned that the Scarlet Swords will remain in Segra a few more days before catching up with Samir's host.'

Lano cursed furiously and Tenzin paled. 'Daria can you mindspeak Calin's household? Tell them all to bolt and bar the building, all the shops, everything. I will try to reach those of the Lesser Mages who are known to revere Calin.' He crossed to the fire and extinguished the flames with a flick of his fingers. 'Commander, back upstairs if you please, while I prepare this house for defence.'

Daria's eyes were unfocussed and she sat stiffly at the table, clearly using mindspeech.

'Quickly commander. We will join you as soon as may be. If you could make sure all the shutters are closed up there, it will save time.'

The Commander left, his feet thudding on the stairs. Tenzin pulled a loaf from a cupboard and a large hunk of cheese, wrapped them in a cloth and touched Daria's shoulder gently. Her eyes lost their vagueness. 'Who else should I warn? Oh Tenzin, is this really happening?'

He put the cloth wrapped food into her arms. 'Join the Commander. I'll secure the wards down here and be with you in heartbeats.'

Daria leaped to her feet and rushed from the room. Tenzin bolted and barred the two small windows and door at the back, then hurried through to repeat his actions at the front of the house. He bowed his head, murmuring softly. To his mage sight, lines twisted and squirmed throughout the entire ground floor. Without a backward glance, he took the stairs two at a time and joined Commander Lano and Daria upstairs.

The fifth bells rang out over the city. The Siertsey square, at the end of the alley from Tenzin's house, was unusually quiet. The fifth bell was the last of the evening, when taverns closed and people made their way to their homes. Tenzin, Daria and Commander Lano had sat in Tenzin's upper study since before the fourth bell, the time most shops closed, and stall holders packed their wagons to return to outlying farms and gardens.

None of the three expected to sleep, but they did. Eyes closed, bodies relaxed, sleeping dreamlessly. They did not hear the tramp of boots draw closer, the banging at the door. They slept, while curious neighbours ventured out and were cut down by men of the Scarlet Swords. Tenzin and his two guests were oblivious to the screams of shock, panic and pain that grew and spread.

Bodies were left where they fell as Scarlet Swordsmen cut their bloody way through areas of the city. Certain dwellings were specifically targeted and they were all places where Samir's detractors and opponents lived. Several were mages of some strength, but the attack on their homes was so unexpected they were unable to either defend themselves or strike any blow against their assailants. Anyone foolish enough to intervene, or get between a Scarlet Sword and his victim, died as well.

It was far into the night before the Scarlet Swords returned to their barracks attached to the Council Building. Screams of distress, screams of fear, screams of agony, echoed through the city of Segra and Tenzin, Commander Lano and Daria slept through it all.

The huge blond haired man crouched by the cold fire in Tenzin's kitchen, wept at the agony and loss rising all around him. His bright blue eyes still shone with his tears as his figure faded away.

Chapter Eleven

Olam led the way through the tunnel, Kara and Jian behind him with Riff bringing up the rear. They made good time although Olam suspected his estimation of time was not too accurate here. Kara and Jian both exclaimed when Olam's glow lights sparkled on the wall of embedded green crystals, touching the stones lightly but then walking on. Neither mentioned that Riff had already given one green stone to each of them.

'The tunnel ends just round the next turn. Can you mindspeak Brin from here?' he asked Jian.

She nodded but before she could do so, the Shadows spoke in their heads.

'Karlek come out. Put small things in ground.'

Olam cleared his throat. 'Small things?'

'Small packet.'

'Where?'

'Different places.'

Kara rolled her eyes.

'How many of these packets?' Olam persisted.

'Ten.'

'Perhaps he found some stones like these green ones, somewhere else round here, and he's hidden them in case we try to steal them?' Riff suggested.

Jian looked as sceptical as Olam felt at that idea but no one came up with any alternative.

'Oh well. Let's get on. If you could ask Brin to hide us until we're some distance away from the tunnel?'

Jian smiled. 'I just did.'

Olam straightened his shoulders and led the way out. None of them looked up to check the whereabouts of Brin or Skay, and they all felt exposed, walking down towards the low roofed building. Olam had warned them that the shield Brin would hold in front of them meant no one would see them from the house although they could see through the shield quite clearly. He had wondered if the ship machine would be able to sense their approach. When the door of the house opened and Karlek emerged, Olam guessed it could.

As on the previous occasion, Karlek carried a stick, or tube, across the front of his body. He looked in different directions, Olam noted, so Brin's shield was effective. 'Tell Brin to let us be seen,' he murmured.

Karlek took a step back, unable to hide the shock on his face when four people appeared barely twenty yards away.

'That's close enough,' he barked.

They could understand his words but they were spoken with a harsh, guttural accent.

Olam moved a pace forward and offered the slightest bow. 'My name is Olam. We hoped you might speak with us as we find ourselves in a most unusual – and difficult – predicament.'

'I am named Karlek, but you know that, don't you? Where is your machine, the one that's been in contact with mine?'

For a moment Olam was confused then realised Karlek meant the Shadows. 'We left our machine at our camp.' Olam waved towards the surrounding hills.

Karlek considered this comment then shook his head. 'It is with you. *My* machine sensed its approach.'

Olam held his arms out to the sides. 'Truly, we carry no machine.'

Karlek was about to speak but hesitated. When he spoke again it was not of machines Olam might have. 'This "predicament". What is it?'

'We have been drawn back through time and we most urgently wish to know if you can reverse this difficult situation.'

Karlek gave a grunt of amusement, his eyes crinkling nearly shut. They were pale eyes, of an indeterminate mixture of greys and washed out blues. 'I might be able to understand what has happened to you. All four of you are from another time?' Olam nodded. 'If one of you would come inside, I have equipment that may help define the time distortions you have experienced.'

Olam felt Jian tense and he shot her a warning glance. His own senses had sharpened to apprehension. He could remember, all too clearly, those underground rooms in the City of Domes, filled with "equipment" that was put to hideous use. His thoughts raced. 'We have friends waiting,' he eventually replied. 'They will be alarmed if we are too long away. I think we should go back and tell them of your – suggestion.'

'Oh bring them back with you.' Karlek laughed. 'How many others did you say?'

'There are several others with us, only two who came through time.'

Karlek moved the stick he carried so that one end was between his elbow and his hip. 'There are natives who know you come from another time?' He sounded doubtful. 'They believe in magic here, of all things! Why would natives accompany you?'

Olam's brain seemed to freeze.

'We needed guides sir,' Riff called. 'Don't know these lands, see.'

Karlek's gaze rested on Riff for a moment. 'Why don't you stay here – Olam was it? These three can fetch your companions, and you and I can make a start on the tests.'

Olam felt an icy finger trace down his spine. He shook his head and hoped his voice sounded confident. 'I cannot do that. I am the leader of our company and I ordered my companions to wait on my return.'

Before he could say more, Karlek moved the stick so that it pointed slightly to Olam's left. There was an odd hissing crack and a small group of dry bushes, about waist high, flared briefly and crumpled in a twisted heap. Karlek stumbled backwards, an expression of surprise on his face.

Olam had felt Jian draw power and guessed she'd pushed the man back rather than seriously attacking him. He heard a screaming cry from above and sent a frantic thought to Brin. 'No Brin! Stay high! Stay high!'

Karlek had fallen against the side of the door and his stick weapon had rolled from his grasp and out of his immediate reach.

'Run,' Olam snapped. Jian obeyed instantly, zigzagging on the uneven footing, back up the sloping hillside. Riff grabbed Kara's arm and took a route parallel to Jian, tugging Kara with him. Olam looked back at Karlek as a piercing noise emanated from the house.

Karlek lay motionless, but, fearful of trickery, Olam spun

round to chase after his friends. He ran a higher route to Jian and they had nearly reached halfway to the tunnel entrance. Jian was an armslength ahead of him when there was a blast of noise. Splinters of stone, among larger rocks, showered down and through them. Jian and Olam were both flung to the ground as if something or someone had delivered a massive blow to their backs. Dust slowly rained down, the only sounds the rattle of still falling stone and the incessant wailing from within Karlek's house.

Olam pushed himself up, seeing blood over his hands where stones had cut him. Coughing, he looked to his left and saw Jian struggling to her feet, her eyes blazing gold as she met his gaze. He looked back and further down the slope. Riff and Kara lay like abandoned toys, a small crater just beyond their feet. Small packets, the Shadows had said. The thought flashed through Olam's mind. He remembered the explosive devices Jian's people had used, and he began to swear.

He slipped and skidded down, hearing Jian following him. He dropped to his knees between Kara and Riff and could only stare helplessly. Jian sank down beside him. 'Stars above, Olam, how will we get them back to Enki?'

Olam peered towards the house. Karlek still lay unmoving – what could have happened to *him*? He screamed Brin's name in his mind, looked up, and watched two Dragons arrowing down to land close by with eyes flaring colours of deep agitation.

'Can you manage Kara on Skay? She's so much smaller. I'll take Riff on Brin.'

Brin crouched as low as he could, a soft distressed moan just audible. Skay copied her father and Olam waited until Jian scrambled awkwardly onto Skay's back. She held out her arms to take Kara's blood drenched body and offered Olam a wobbly smile. 'Never flown on a Dragon's back before.'

Olam patted her leg and turned to lift Riff into his arms. Brin used his power to ease Riff's weight to enable Olam to get the two of them onto his back. The moment they were settled, Brin lifted and raced north east over the hills. Olam could feel Riff's warm blood soaking into his trousers and he gripped him tighter. After one glance at Riff's back, he kept his eyes ahead, hoping against hope the armsman and Kara would survive. That Jenzi's healing powers would be strong enough to deal with both of them.

Brin's bass mindvoice rumbled through Olam's head. 'I have alerted Jenzi and he awaits us. He is preparing, even now.'

'I don't think Kern is a healer,' Olam replied.

'No, he is not.' There was a pause. 'Enki could, but he is exhausted.'

'Exhausted?' Olam asked in alarm.

'Enki was – elsewhere – last night and used much power. He is distressed but he sleeps now. Calin can help Jenzi a little and Skay and I will offer our strength of course.'

Brin was slowing, curving in to a glide and, peering over the crimson scaled shoulder, Olam saw Jenzi's tall thin figure standing outside their rock shelter. The Dragons settled gently as Kern and Calin hurried to join Jenzi. All three men were silent as they lifted Riff and Kara so very carefully away from the Dragons. Olam watched as the two were carried under the overhang, then he sighed and slid from Brin's back.

Moving forward, he took Brin's long beautiful face between his hands and pressed his forehead against the Dragon's. 'I thank you dear friend. There would have been no hope for them, so far from Jenzi, if you hadn't brought us back so swiftly.'

'They are our friends too Olam. You should go and clean yourself.'

Olam stepped back, looking down at himself. He grimaced. 'I think you're right. I'll go down to Enki's pool.'

Jian appeared at his side. She held out a pair of trousers and a shirt. Her face was white as snow. 'I got those from your pack.' She held up more trousers and another shirt. 'We need to clean up.' Walking down the track to the small pool, Jian glanced at Olam. 'Their injuries are bad Olam. I couldn't watch.'

He nodded. 'Jenzi is a strong healer,' he offered.

'But where is Enki? He could mend them in heartbeats.'

'He could?'

'I cut my hand. He healed it.' She held her hand out, stared at its covering of congealed blood and let it drop with a shiver.

Using handfuls of a plant Enki called soap weed, they stripped off their filthy clothes and scrubbed themselves clean. Jian was first out of the pool, pulled on clean clothes and set about washing her filthy garments. Olam was slower and Jian had spread trousers and shirt over rocks to dry before he had dressed. She watched him for a moment then walked round to his side of the pool.

'What's wrong?' she asked.

He grimaced, showing her his hands where blood slowly continued to seep from the many gouges inflicted by flying stone fragments. Jian scowled, looking at the backs of her own hands. 'Oh.'

'Oh, what?' Olam asked.

'Look – my hands were cut like yours.'

All he saw were white flecks scattered over her hands. Tiny scars. She turned her left hand over to show him her palm, where he saw a longer thin scar. 'Enki healed it, just like that.' She snapped her fingers.

Olam was glad to see a little colour had returned to her face and sought to lighten her mood.

'How did it feel, flying on a Dragon, rather than *being* the Dragon?' he asked with a smile.

Jian snorted. 'Very strange. I kept thinking I would fall, but Skay talked to me all the way here and kept me calm.' She looked down at Olam's shirt and trousers, soaking in the pool, and sighed. 'I'll wash those but you will owe me, Olam of Far.'

They left the wet clothes to dry and returned to the rock shelter. Jian glanced at the two still forms of Riff and Kara and turned away, busying herself making a pot of tea at the fire. Kern joined them and found some binding strips in Jenzi's bag. He wrapped Olam's hands although blood began to ooze through too quickly.

'Where is Enki?' Jian asked softly.

Kern nodded at the darker area at the rear of the shelter. 'He was in great distress when he came in this morning. Calin looked after him. He made him lie down back there and Enki slept at once.'

'Does Calin know where he'd been or what happened?'

'I suspect he does but he said nothing Jian. He appeared upset as well so Jenzi and I asked no questions.'

'Will they survive?' Olam asked bluntly.

'I couldn't say.' Kern spoke even more quietly than usual.

'Riff might, but Kara is even more gravely hurt.'

Olam was silent. He'd seen Riff's back and was amazed that Kern thought the man might live. Jian passed tea bowls to both men and they sat, each lost in their own thoughts. They looked up when Calin joined them. He no longer looked old: he looked ancient.

'Jenzi's strength is nearly finished. I will wake Enki but I'm afraid.' When he fell silent, no one spoke. 'Enki used enormous power yesterday,' Calin finally continued. 'I would expect him to sleep two days at least and even then, his powers would be much reduced when he awoke. I also fear he will be greatly distressed again, to see Riff and Kara so desperately injured and know he cannot heal them as simply as he would usually.'

Jian put down her tea bowl and clasped her hands in her lap to hide their trembling. 'I would be with Enki when you wake him please.'

Calin studied her. So very young, he thought, but she had made a connection with Enki. Young as she was, Calin felt a strength in her and he nodded. 'Come then. Jenzi is near collapse and my power is used.' Calin rose to move back into the shelter.

When Jian started to get up, Olam put a hand out to detain her. 'Remember, Jian, the Dragons freely offer their strength to support a healer. I don't think Jenzi has asked them for help but they are here and they are willing.'

Jian returned his gaze before nodding and following Calin. She stood back a little, watching Calin kneel beside Enki's large form. Calin didn't touch him at first, just closed his eyes. Enki groaned and his head rolled from side to side. His bright blue eyes were suddenly open and he sat up in one fluid movement. Now Calin settled a bony hand against Enki's cheek.

'I am so sorry my dear. Jenzi is done, yet Riff and Kara are not yet safe.'

Enki's gaze fixed on Jian. Wordlessly, she held out a hand to him. 'Please Enki. If you could just do enough to keep them alive for a while, then you could rest and help them more when you are restored.' She tugged his hand gently and he stood, towering over her. She led him towards the front of the shelter. 'Brin and Skay offer their strength to bolster yours if you need.'

Jian kept her eyes away from the torn bodies lying on the

floor. Enki smiled, a faint smile, nothing like his usual beam. 'I like your eyes best when they're gold.'

Jian managed a smile in return, her eyes becoming a molten blaze. Only then did Enki look down at the two by his feet. He lowered himself between their heads even as Jenzi toppled sideways into Kern's arms.

Riff and Kara had been laid on their stomachs, heads turned so they faced each other. Jian was struck by how peaceful they looked, their faces unblemished. Her hand was still engulfed in Enki's and Jian turned her face to his. Tears rolled ceaselessly down his cheeks but Jian could feel heat building through their linked hands. She was aware of a surge of power going through her to Enki, and she recognised Brin's mind within the surge.

Enki bowed his head. Jian had no idea how long they sat there, the only sound that of people breathing. At last, Enki looked up, tears still flowing freely. A huge finger gently brushed Riff's face, then pushed a strand of fair hair away from Kara's brow.

'Enki's *so* tired now,' he said plaintively.

'Then come Enki.' Jian stood, pulling at his hand. 'Come and sleep again.'

'Yes dear Enki, sleep now. You have given enough.' Brin's mindvoice rumbled through all their heads.

Obediently, Enki allowed Jian to lead him back to his bedroll. He refused to release her hand and she settled cross-legged beside him. He gave an enormous yawn. 'I loved my mama and dada you know.' He yawned again, tears still sparkling on his lashes even in the gloom, and then he was asleep.

Jian sat, frozen by Enki's last words. What might have happened to Oxsana and Burek? Enki had said they were safe. Where were they? She tried to ease her fingers away from his but his grip merely tightened. She saw Olam had crept through from the front of the shelter. The lines of strain around his eyes and mouth had lessened, she noticed, and hoped, quite fiercely, that they would not return.

'Is Jenzi safe?' she whispered.

Olam nodded. 'He's asleep. So is Calin, but Brin says they are both truly sleeping, nothing worse.'

'Kara and Riff?'

131

'Brin says they are stable. He doesn't really understand what Enki did, but they are safe for now. Kern's getting a meal ready. Shall I bring you something?'

Jian suddenly realised she was ravenous. She couldn't remember when she'd last eaten. 'Yes please. It feels wrong, when Riff and Kara are so hurt, but I'm starving.'

Olam turned to leave.

'Are your hands any better?'

'The bleeding's stopped but they're very sore.'

'I wish I could get my hands on Reshik,' Jian said viciously. 'And I can't really waste time or effort thinking about Seola.'

'I know.' Olam wondered what else he could say but came up with nothing. He left her sitting quietly beside the sleeping Enki and rejoined Kern by the fire.

In fact, Seola was asleep, a day's journey north west of the ridge of hills. She'd found a small group of tribes folk as she flew high overhead. When she'd left Astian's house, she'd been distracted by hunger and instead of making for the hills, she'd sought food. Her beloved brother Cyrek had introduced her to the wondrous pleasure of eating prey she'd killed while in her Dragon form. Cyrek had told her it would increase her abilities and she should completely disregard the laws of the Dark Realm which strictly forbade this. Cyrek said it was a law made to keep people in thrall to the governing mages who feared being overwhelmed by those such as him and his sister.

Seola now believed that consuming prey when in Dragon form did indeed make her even more powerful. In reality, it only increased her delusions which, in turn, led her deeper into madness. She spent two days on her first hunt here. She found a small clan with a herd of around thirty grazing animals. Seola slaughtered the five adults and eight children without hesitation.

The cattle remained helplessly docile under her compulsion. She used fire to remove all traces of the humans and also one of two strange round huts. She left one of the huts to sleep in. The clouds that had been gathering all afternoon suggested a storm would likely sweep across the plains all too soon. In Dragon form she gorged herself on fresh meat, then she shimmered into human form.

132

The hut she entered seemed sturdy enough and she guessed that the animal skins stitched together to form the covering, would keep wind and water out. She wrapped several furs around herself and fell asleep, glad to be free of Astian's constant watchfulness.

Seola woke, feeling better than she had for a long time, since her enraged and grief stricken flight after her brother's destruction. She left the hut where she'd slept and surveyed the remaining cattle. She smiled. Another day here wouldn't hurt. It had been far too long since she'd been so well fed on fresh bloody meat and she had no fear of the mage she sought. Clearly he, or she, had stumbled across some formula or theory relating to time manipulation. Judging by Astian and other minds Seola had sensed in Segra, their mage powers were negligible, certainly not capable of mastering time. She foresaw no problems when she confronted this time meddler.

Seola spent the day alternately feeding and thinking. She went through the meagre possessions left inside the hut and concluded the furs were the only things of any value. As the sun sank on the second evening, Seola wrapped one of the furs around her and sat by the door. The sky was clear, no howling storm this evening. She'd spent some time pondering the touch of that mind, in Astian's city house. It had definitely been the mind of another from the Dark Realm, sent out as what they coyly referred to as an observer. In other words, a spy.

It never crossed Seola's mind that others might have come through the gap in time's fabric as she had. She pulled the furs tighter round her while a thin moon rose in the darkening sky. Her gaze dropped to the few remaining cattle. She would sleep. In the morning she would feed once more and return to her search for the time meddler. Seola moved deeper into the hut, curled into a nest of furs and waited for sleep, the silence broken occasionally by the soft moans from the last of the herd.

By mid morning, Seola was close to a line of hills which stretched north to south in an apparently endless march. She glided lower to examine the first hills she approached. The closer she came, the stranger they appeared. She'd never seen hills quite like these: heaped and tumbled piles of rock and earth. The only signs of life was from small rodents, goats, and a very few crows.

Some of the gaps and dips between the hills were arid rock, others had dusty scrub grass and brittle looking bushes. Here and there, she saw a more fertile gully, with slender evergreens and lusher grass, but they were few and far between. Seola had been following the hills northwards, using her power to check for life signs indicating humans lived here. But she found none.

Patience was no longer one of Seola's talents. She once had more patience than her brother but now, except for her vow to destroy the brat, Tika, there was no need to wait, not for anything at all. For the first time this day, Seola caught a glimpse of open water in one of the greener gullies and spiralled lower, coming to rest beside a narrow strip of water.

The smell of sour cinnamon drifted across the pool and Seola's human form shimmered into view. She stared around her, aware of every rustle, every creak from the handful of trees. She spun when a harsh croak echoed across the space. A large crow flapped heavily from one of the evergreens and vanished over the lip of the gully.

Seola drank from the pool and shuddered at the iciness of the water. She chose a place among the trees and sat with her back to the trunk, watching the sun burning down out of sight. She had never understood how so many people raved about the beauty of sunsets. She saw no beauty in them. She *did* see the glory and the fieriness, and decided it reflected her rage, and her intention to bring just such blazing destruction to all who dared displease or thwart her.

Chapter Twelve

When Karlek roused, he could not understand what had happened. He sat for a few moments before the wail of the ship's emergency siren began to annoy him. He pulled himself upright using the edge of the door to help him, grabbed the psionic disruptor and staggered inside. 'Turn that alarm OFF,' he shouted over the din.

The sudden silence made his ears ache. 'What happened?' he demanded of the Computer.

'I recorded the appearance of four natives Captain. Sensors picked up their traces some distance higher up the hillside, to the right. They must have used a shielding device which allowed them to approach so close to you.'

'How did they attack *me*, and where are they now?' Karlek interrupted.

'I am unable to define what happened to you Captain. After you gave an example of your weapon power, you seemed to collapse although none of the natives offered any attack against you. When you fell, they turned and ran back the way they had come. Two of them triggered one of the mines you placed.'

Karlek went to the window. 'I can see where the mine detonated,' he agreed. 'But I can see no bodies. Well?'

There was a pause before the mechanical tones of the Computer spoke again. 'Two – creatures – came, and carried all four away Captain.'

'Creatures? What creatures?'

'They were Dragons Captain, according to the encyclopaedia in my data core.'

Karlek turned slowly, staring at the remains of his ship. He had ripped most of one side of its body away, exposing the equipment within. He'd put the solar converters on the roof of the house to keep all this machinery operating. Clearly there was now a serious malfunction.

'Dragons,' Karlek repeated.

'I can show you Captain. I recorded the whole event of course.'

'Show me then.'

Some little time later, Karlek sat at his main work table. He had to admit the Computer was correct. Such huge beasts! Such amazing colours! Had he misjudged this planet so completely? Obviously, he had run tests on the first natives he'd encountered and proved them primitive humanoid at best. How could they possibly gain the degree of control over such huge and fearsome animals as those Dragons the Computer had just shown him? Where had those four obtained Dragons to train to such obedience and docility as he'd seen on the monitor?

The Computer hummed and buzzed. Captain Karlek sat, watching darkness deepen beyond the window, and he tried to understand just what had occurred today. Then he ordered the Computer to replay the recording. This time he slowed the pictures, occasionally pausing the movement completely. He spent a very long time watching the man and woman lifting the injured pair onto the Dragons' backs. He noted the excessive blood loss, could see some of the dreadful wounds, and wondered at the flashing and whirring of the Dragons' eyes.

He couldn't discern any words of command to the great beasts. The uninjured pair exchanged a few words but Karlek saw nothing said prior to the Dragons lifting from the ground. And their speed! He was astonished by the swiftness of their flight. The Computer gave him the figures for acceleration from take off and Karlek could only shake his head in admiration.

'You were not able to discover how far they went?' he asked.

'No Captain, not conclusively.'

'An estimate then.'

'Perhaps ten miles or so, west by north west Captain.'

'I will get some rest, but wake me at dawn – I want to check where they might have come from. I do not think those Dragons brought them here. You would have spotted that on the sensors. I hope.'

'I do not see them Captain. Only the four natives registered on the sensors. But I now have the life patterns for the Dragons so they will be recognised, should they come within range again.'

'What is the status of your weapons?'

The Computer hummed. 'Sixty seven per cent are retrievable Captain. They have been off line since soon after we arrived here.'

Karlek tugged his straggling beard. 'Start bringing short range missiles into service,' he eventually ordered. 'And make sure the other systems can be called on at need.'

'Your command Captain.'

Karlek continued to think. It had been so very long since he'd even considered needing weapons or defensive programmes. 'Can the shield arch be used?'

'It will need a little adjusting Captain.'

'Then adjust it. I want that available at all times from now on. Make sure you wake me at dawn.'

'Your command Captain.'

Karlek stepped outside next day as faint pinks and golds rimmed the hills around. Carrying the disruptor, ready to use, he made his way to the patch of darker earth exposed by the detonation of the mine. He knew the precise positions of the nine others and walked confidently up the sloping ground. He squatted by the higher edge of the shallow crater, nodding as he saw the dark stains where a considerable amount of blood had been shed. Standing, he walked carefully higher still, to the place which the other two natives had reached before the mine exploded. He pressed a button on a small clip hooked on his shirt.

'Computer, am I at the place the man and woman reached yesterday?'

'No Captain. You need to go higher and further west.

Karlek moved as the Computer directed until he was at the exact position where Jian and Olam had fallen because of the blast. He studied the rocks all around and slowly made his way towards a pile of larger stones, stretching across the ground beneath a low rockface. It looked as though one large boulder had split, with the front part just sliding down and shattering, to form a small wall. Rounding the end of this wall, he stopped. The darkness of a small cave gaped at him.

'Computer, I have found a cave here. I will check a short distance within.'

'Sensors tracking and recording Captain.'

Karlek snapped a small torch from his belt and held it in his left hand, the disruptor levelled in his right. He studied the ground in front of the opening and saw clear boot marks in the looser sand. Warily, he stepped past them just as the sun shot its rays into the darkness before him. He moved inside and saw that what he'd thought to be a cave, was a tunnel, the entrance quite shallow but curving at once to the side. When he followed it, he lost the help of the sun and clicked on the torch.

Darkness fled from its powerful beam and Karlek realised the tunnel probably ran a considerable distance. He shone the torch on the wall beside him, seeing the marks of some sort of tools. Man made then. He let the torch beam stretch into the dark once more before turning and making his way slowly back to his house. Karlek hoped the Computer hadn't deleted the mapping records of their landing so long ago in one of its power saving clean ups. He needed to see, exactly, where that tunnel might lead through the maze of hills all around.

Daria woke first. She stretched lazily then was completely awake. She was in an armchair in Tenzin's upper study. Commander Lano snored softly from the depths of another armchair across from her, and Tenzin was sprawled, face down, on the couch. She got to her feet, crossed to the window and peered through the tiniest gap in the shutters. Her gasp was enough to rouse the two men.

'What is it?' Tenzin sounded groggy.

Daria turned to him, eyes wide with horror. 'Look for yourself.'

Commander Lano, despite his years, reached the window first. He peeped out and began to curse. Tenzin took his turn and could only stare. He reached for the hook and swung the shutter open. The three looked down at the cobbled alley below. Seven bodies lay, so ungainly in blood soaked death, in the pale morning light. They looked along the alley towards the square and could see a pair of legs lying motionless, the rest of the body round the corner out of sight.

Daria glared at Tenzin. 'Did you make us sleep?' she demanded. She paused. 'Could it have been Calin?'

138

The Commander looked from one to the other. 'Whatever made us unaware while this slaughter took place doesn't matter now. I'm going to the Council Building to see what's been happening.' He headed for the door.

Tenzin hurried after him as he clattered down the stairs. 'Be careful Lano, please. The city will have need of you, I swear.'

Commander Lano stopped by the front door, taking his short cloak from a hook and swirling it round his shoulders. 'Have you foreseen that Tenzin? If you have, how could you not have foreseen this carnage?' He unbolted the door and opened it. He looked to his right and shook his head, then stepped out and turned left, to the square.

Tenzin went to the door while voices began to curse and wail from down the alley. He bit his lip and closed the door. There was nothing he could do, he was no healer. Daria stood at the foot of the stairs, her face white, her pale blue eyes wide with shock.

'Daria, you must not go out yet. Please. Stay here at least for a while. Come, I'll make some tea.' He ushered her into his big kitchen and sat her at the table.

'Can you feel that Tenzin?' Daria spoke sharply. 'It feels as though the air is alive in here. It tingles.'

Tenzin became still, aware of the feeling Daria described. 'Like before a thunderstorm,' he muttered. He shook his head and knelt before the hearth. Reaching for kindling, he paused. Last night's fire, which he had extinguished, had left only a thick layer of fine ash. But something had been drawn in that ash. 'Do you recognise this symbol Daria?' he asked quietly.

She joined him, staring at the ash. It looked like two circles next to each other, but touching, one almost running in to the other. She sat back on her heels. 'Never seen it before.' She looked at Tenzin. 'So someone was in here last night. Someone like Calin but definitely *not* Calin. And they left this mark to let us know they'd visited?'

'I understand this as little as you do Daria. But I'm increasingly worried about being here.' Tenzin abandoned any idea of lighting his fire, stood and strode around the room, muttering under his breath. When he finally came to a halt, his expression was calmer. No happier, Daria thought, but calmer.

139

'We must leave.' Daria watched him carefully. Perhaps he'd lost his mind? 'Seriously Daria. Can you ride a horse.'

'No. And I have no desire to.'

'A wagon then. I can hire one in Ostler's Way.' He began to pace again.

'Where were you thinking of going?' Daria ventured.

Tenzin stopped again. 'East. Absolutely, directly, east.'

Daria thought then tilted her head to one side, staring back at him. 'To Calin.'

Tenzin nodded. 'I'm sure that if we go exactly east from Segra, we'll find him.'

'What about the Commander?'

'We should leave by the fifth bell.' He shrugged. 'If Lano isn't back here or I've not managed to contact him, we leave. I fear he'll insist on staying anyway.'

'Do you think the Scarlet Swords are still in the city?'

Tenzin's eyes blurred then cleared. 'They left before first bell.'

'It will be dark if we don't leave until fifth bell,' Daria objected.

'Doesn't matter if we only go a few miles. We *must* leave tonight.'

'What are you seeing Tenzin?'

His brown eyes met hers steadily then he turned away. 'Trouble.' There was a note of finality in his voice that told Daria he would tell her no more at the moment. He turned back. 'You know your way through the lesser streets to your rooms Daria. Go and pack what you think necessary. Not too much. Clothing of course. I'll see about food supplies when I get the wagon. Any papers or documents that are *really* important to you. Oh, what weapons did you use in combat training?'

Daria stared at him and swallowed hard. 'Bow and short sword.'

'Do you still have the weapons?'

'I only have the bow, but few arrows.'

Tenzin nodded. 'I'll get arrows. Can you use power for defence or attack?'

'Both, to a certain degree.'

'Me too.'

Daria stood. 'Should I go now? And where shall we meet later?'

'If you haven't too much to carry, you should be at the Fountain Circle. You know it? By the east gate? Just before fifth bell. If you're not there, I'll wait. But Daria, be cautious of using mindspeech now. I know you are far more adept at it than I am. I can see into someone's mind if they are close to me and, occasionally, if I know someone well, I can reach across the city. There are several of the Lesser Mages who are also adepts at mindspeech. Calin kept a very close watch on them, but I don't know all of them. So beware.'

The clamour of the fourth bell had seemed subdued to Daria. She paused, a pile of books in her arms and listened. It didn't sound as though *all* the bells were ringing. She shivered, there was clearly something wrong happening in this city. It didn't cross her mind to go to the Council Building. She'd only been a Councillor for half a year, at Calin's insistence. She found Council sessions unbelievably boring, the matters under discussions so painfully trivial. She'd amused herself during those sessions by studying her fellow Councillors far more closely than any of them might have guessed.

Daria looked down at the books she held and dropped them onto the bed. She had a large pack, already crammed with clothes and blankets. She had a second pack into which she put some papers she'd written, and some she was working on. A bundle of writing sticks, a large, well stoppered jar of ink, rolls of new parchment and the book of children's stories she'd laboured over as Calin's student.

After some thought, she added a book, written years before by a mage who had made his life's work the study of the grassland tribes. Daria tightened the straps on the larger pack and moved back to the second. She laughed. Her cat had settled comfortably between the jar of ink and the two books. Green eyes regarded her disdainfully.

'Hala, you can't come.' She stopped. Why not? Who would look after a cat if trouble grew and spread through Segra? Before she could change her mind, she threw a shawl into the pack and the green eyes closed contentedly. Daria took a last look around

141

and rescued two bottles of spirit which joined the ink and Hala. She pulled on her favourite old jacket, hefted the larger pack onto her shoulder and lifted the second more gently to carry in her arms.

She descended the two flights of stairs from her small rooms, not bothering to lock the door behind her. She had the strongest feeling that, one way or another, she wouldn't be back. Pulling the street door open, Daria walked out and made her way towards Fountain Circle. There was the faintest squeak from the bag in her arms.

'Try to be quiet Hala. I'm not sure Tenzin will be thrilled with your company. Just stay quiet until we're out of here.'

Brin was uneasy. He had been most upset and frightened at seeing the terrible injuries done to Kara and Riff. He had helped Enki stabilise the two, but he hadn't understood why Jenzi hadn't called to borrow his strength when the Gaharnian had first attempted their healing. Brin had met Jenzi once, in Gaharn. He knew little about him other than he was a still young healer who showed promise of one day becoming a *great* healer.

He was also aware of how worried and yes, afraid, Olam and Jian were. When Brin and his daughter Skay had met the Sea Dragons in this time, they'd told him they knew of his Kin far to the north, but they saw them very rarely. So Brin knew he could take Skay and fly in search of his own Kin. The two of them could survive here. He knew too, that he would never leave Olam and his companions. Kern, from the Shadow Realm, caused Brin no concern. He trusted the quiet little man and knew he would stand firm with Olam.

Brin stretched his wings to soak in more warmth. He lay near the overhanging entrance to the rock shelter while Skay had gone to hunt. His thoughts turned to Jian. She was so young, younger than his precious Skay, and he could feel something was changing in her. It was a change connected to Enki.

Brin sat up restlessly and scanned the sky with eyes and senses, in search of Skay. He needed to fly, to fly alone, and try to understand these things. He was awed by Enki, and he was terrified by him. Enki had touched his mind and Brin knew at once that this man had as much power, if not more, than the mage

142

Tika. It was a different form of power somehow, but overwhelming to the crimson Dragon. Lastly but by no means least, Brin was uneasy about the whereabouts of Seola. He had the faintest suspicion she was closer than he would have liked. Somewhere to the north. He moved restlessly again and wondered why his daughter was taking so long to find food.

Within the shelter, Jenzi still slept. Riff and Kara also lay unmoving. Kern had spread pieces of a thin white cloth across their backs and legs, slightly moistened with a sharp smelling liquid found among Jenzi's medicine pack. Kern had smiled when he saw Olam's glance of concern. 'My people use something very similar Olam. It helps keep infection away from a wound and it will not dry and stick to the injury.'

Satisfied, Olam sat back, watching the peaceful faces of the woman and his armsman.

'They will be safe here Olam. Let's go outside for a while.'

'What about Jian? She's still sitting with Enki.'

Kern stood, holding out a hand to pull Olam up. 'We must leave her.' He said no more, walking out from beneath the overhang and settling on a boulder close to Brin. Kern stroked the Dragon's shoulder. 'Do not fret Brin. There is nothing we can do.'

Brin's eyes whirred but he made no comment. Olam sat next to Kern, frowning. 'What do you mean – nothing we can do?'

'Jian is linked to Enki.' Kern spread his hands helplessly. 'I have no idea what will come of it.'

Brin shivered under Olam's hand, his scales moving like a nervous horse twitched its skin. They sat quietly, enjoying the sun's warmth until Skay arrived in a flurry of wings.

'I found some people,' she announced in their minds. 'No, no,' she insisted, feeling agitation rise in her father and the two men. 'Not *nasty* ones. They were travelling with their families and horses and cattle.'

'Did they see you?' Olam interrupted her urgently.

'Well of course they did,' Skay retorted. 'And they gave me a cattle. We talked and I played with their children.' She sounded unbearably smug, totally disregarding her father's blazing eyes and Olam's expression of horror.

Kern replied first. 'A single cattle is usually called a cow, my dear. So they offered you a cow. Was it because they feared you at first?'

'Of *course* not. They recognised me and called to me to visit with them. Well, they didn't recognise *me* but they recognised Dragon Kin. They said it had been ever such a long time since any of us had visited them.'

'Do you know who they were?' Olam managed faintly.

'They said they were of the Dragon Tribe. They showed me a box. Inside were seven scales they said they had been given by visiting Dragons. One was pale green, one was dark green, one was dark blue, one was purple, one was paler purple, one was red but not so red as you, and one was white. So I gave them one of mine. From my tail. It was loose anyway.' Skay sat back, looking at her audience and clearly expecting enthusiastic congratulations.

Olam felt a sharp pang in his heart, remembering a young, silvery blue Dragon just as confident and pleased with himself as the one now before him. He grinned. 'Did you tell them of us, or where we are?'

Skay rattled her wings against her back. 'I told them I had friends I was travelling with and that two were hurt. They said we should go to them and their Wise Ones would mend the hurt ones.'

Brin gave an explosive huff and lifted into the air, smoke wisping from his nostrils. Olam's grin widened. 'Your papa seems a little upset.'

Skay's grey eyes flashed gold sparkles. 'He's cross because *he* didn't find the nice people,' she declared.

Perhaps all female Dragons saw right through the males as well as Lallia could see through any man she came across, Olam reflected.

'It might be an idea to move from here.' Kern's voice dragged Olam back to the present.

'Surely we daren't move Riff and Kara? And *could* we move Enki?'

'It's not far,' Skay put in. 'We could take some of you and then come back for the others. Enki will come on his own.'

Olam met Kern's gaze. 'Go and ask Jian,' Kern said, leaf green eyes crinkling in amusement.

Olam dropped a kiss on Skay's black nose and went back inside the shelter.

A great many years in the future, Tursig, Shuli, Reema and Dellian were desperately worried. They had heard a great noise and all four raced along the coast to the camp where they'd left the others of their company. The camp was intact but there was no sign of their companions. They searched and called. Shuli sought for traces of Jenzi's mind but found nothing at all. Dellian found the place where the seven had clearly been working. Shovels lay abandoned and two waterskins had been dropped. Something disastrous had occurred here but neither Dellian of the Shadow Realm not Shuli or Reema of Gaharn could begin to guess what that could have been.

They gathered everything from Olam's camp and trudged wearily back along the shore. Tursig was frantic with worry. He had visions of reporting to Lord Seboth that he'd managed to lose both the Lord's brother Olam, *and* one of his worthiest armsmen, Riff, and he quailed at the thought.

Two days were wasted as Shuli, Reema and Dellian debated what should be done. Early on the third day, Tursig rose and went down to the beach. Brin's son Flyn was asleep in a heap of young Sea Dragons but he woke at once when Tursig whispered his name. One of the Sea Dragons also woke and paced towards Tursig at Flyn's side.

'I don't know what to do Flyn, but we must do *something*. I have no right to ask anything of you but please, could you go to Lord Seboth and tell him what's happened here? I'm sure he'll know what can be done.'

The eyes of both young Dragons began to sparkle. 'I can go at once,' Flyn mindspoke the worried armsman.

'So could I, I'd like to see where these humans live. My name is Twist,' the Sea Dragon added helpfully. 'You could tell the Flight I'm going to keep Flyn company.'

Butter yellow and greeny grey Dragons were aloft and arrowing inland before Tursig could reply.

Unfortunately, Flyn wasn't entirely sure where Far was, and he had never met Lord Seboth. He thought it would be much more sensible to fly south, and tell his friends Farn and Tika.

They would be sure to know what to do. Sea Dragons did not use Dragon gateways, only a few of the Great Dragons could accomplish this. So Flyn and Twist flew south and then west across the open ocean to the Kelshan lands. Flyn was nervous, as previously his father Brin had taken him and his sister through a gateway. But they managed the crossing and approached a long coastline. Flyn led Twist to the southern tip of land and then west. They flew high and fast over the Dark Realm and into the beautiful valley called Iskallia.

People were gathered at the western end of the valley and heads turned when Flyn and Twist appeared. A silvery blue Dragon rose upright and roared a formal welcome. Twist kept back shyly as a small woman stood in front of Flyn while he explained what had been happening in Sapphrea. Flyn mentioned that Olam had gone to the coast in pursuit of Seola and then was deeply alarmed by the sudden change in his dear friend Tika. She was incandescent with rage.

Chapter Thirteen

Calin didn't wake until the sun was high. He had been exhausted and saddened beyond measure the night before and had left the shelter. He told Kern he needed rest, away from everyone and Kern had simply nodded his understanding. Calin had made his way to Enki's pool and on through the small grove of evergreens to where one solitary broad leafed tree stood. He curled against its roots and sank into sleep.

Calin was a mage of the earth. All of the natural world was his home and his comfort and his strength. The ground beneath him softened, moulding to the shape of his body, as might the softest feather bed. The tree murmured soothingly and even in sleep he was aware of its affection. He woke refreshed and sat for a while, gazing through the leaves at the deep blue of the sky.

He knew what had happened within Segra and knew too that Daria and Tenzin were even now trying to reach him, miles across the grasslands. He turned on his knees and pressed hands and brow to the tree's rough bark. 'Thank you for your shelter old friend,' he murmured.

He walked slowly back, between the evergreens, and stopped to scoop water to his mouth where the stream fed into the pool. Raising his eyes, he saw Jian, the child from the Dark Realm, standing a few paces away. Enki must either have woken or let her go while he slept. Her eyes were a soft gold, shimmering with tears. Calin smiled gently at her and waited.

'Enki isn't really forty years old, is he?'

Of all the things she might have asked, that was one he'd not considered. He chuckled. 'No child. Enki is not forty years old.' He crossed the stream and sat down, patting the grass beside him until she joined him. 'I could not truly tell you child. He is far older than I am and yet far younger. Ageless is the only word that would be true.'

'That's what I was afraid you'd say.' Jian gave a shaky laugh.

'Why is it that I feel I know him, that I know what he does?'

Calin reached for her hand and held it clasped between both of his. 'That I do not know child. And I'm not sure whether it is a blessing or a curse.'

'Oh a blessing.' Jian didn't hesitate. 'He may vanish from my life in a few days but I will always be grateful for what I've seen, what I've already learned from him.' After a moment she spoke again. 'What happened to Oxsana and Burek? Who were they?'

Calin sighed. 'I only met them once child. I have my suspicions but I cannot share them with you.'

Jian nodded. 'I too have suspicions.' She smiled, no sign of tears now. 'Come on. Olam and Kern said something about moving onto the plains. Skay met a tribe out there and they suggested we join them.'

They began to climb back up towards the shelter, just as Brin drifted down beside Skay. His eyes whirred when he reclined gracefully, and he immediately bespoke Calin and Jian. 'My daughter was right. The people are very nice.'

'Did you give them one of your scales,' Skay interrupted, eyes flashing.

'Well, yes, I did. Their Wise Ones said we should join them quickly. They are planning to move north east, as far as they can go.'

Calin closed his eyes. 'So soon. I can only hope my two friends reach us quickly.' He opened his eyes. 'The Shadows! Are they still here? What happened to them when that explosion happened?'

Jian shrugged. 'Kern hasn't mentioned them, but I've been with Enki. I haven't heard them in my head since then though. I thought Enki said they couldn't be killed?'

'Can't.'

Calin and Jian exchanged glances. The single word, said in the familiar abrupt manner, nonetheless sounded far less superior than usual.

'What happened to you then?' Calin's tone was mildly interested.

'Scattered.'

'Aah. But you are now – erm – unscattered?'

Obviously that required no answer. Calin coughed. 'Well

then. I was wondering if you could locate two friends? Not far out of Segra city, in a wagon?'

'Behind army.'

'Army?' put in Jian.

'My friends are behind the army,' Calin agreed. 'But they are also slightly south of the army's route. Brin tells me we are moving to the east of these hills, to join one of the tribes.'

'Like.'

Calin stared at Jian in confusion.

'Like what?' she asked the Shadows.

'Tribe.'

Jian rolled her eyes, which made her seem even younger to Calin. 'Shadows, would you be so – kind – as to find my friends in their wagon? Perhaps you could inform them where we are?'

'Nice manners.' The Shadows sounded admiring rather than sarcastic. Then there was an emptiness in their heads, indicating the Shadows had departed.

'I like the Shadows,' Skay announced. Brin huffed and said nothing. Jian smiled and continued in to the shelter. Olam was cooking something at the fire.

'Tea,' he offered. Jian took the bowl he held out and went on to the still sleeping Enki.

Kern went out to speak with Calin until Olam called them to come and eat. They were just finishing the meal when Jenzi groaned. Kern went to him, offering water. Calin and Olam listened to Kern's soft voice and Jenzi's ragged replies. Calin gathered their bowls and took them outside, Olam at his heels.

'Brin said you have friends coming, from the city?'

'I believe Daria and Tenzin are trying to find me. I asked the Shadows if they could find exactly where they are.'

'And they agreed?'

Calin smiled modestly. 'They thought I had nice manners.'

Olam stared, gave a hoot of amusement and then grew serious. 'Your friends, will they get here do you think? I heard you mention an army?'

Calin rinsed the bowls in the stream. 'The High Mage Samir was thrilled that Astian was as good as dead. He has long held ambition to be the Speaker for Segra, most important of the city's Mages. He also has a fond belief that Valsheba should be a powerful military land. He loathes the tribes. Rumours of strangers, possibly spies, in the city, Astian's fall from power.' He shrugged. 'What better excuses to begin a war to exterminate the native people of the plains?'

'How many armsmen in this army?'

'At least five thousand I would guess. And one squad, the Scarlet Swords, are notorious for their violence and viciousness, even when taking a turn of duty as city guards.' Calin stared at the sky beyond the rim of the valley, thinking of dead students, dead colleagues, dead friends in Segra now, but chose not to mention that to Olam. They walked back to the shelter.

'What happened to Astian? We had traced Seola to Astian's house, but we came here before we'd decided on any plan to deal with her.'

Calin paused to touch Brin's cheek. 'The story was that Astian suffered some sudden illness or seizure. He appeared as a two year old child. Ah Jenzi! Are you feeling recovered?'

Olam remained beside Brin. Skay was snoring gently, spread comfortably over a boulder. Brin spoke on a tightly controlled mindlink to Olam alone. 'I liked Burek and Oxsana. Did you know they were called slaves?'

Olam stiffened then leaned his head against Brin's shoulder. 'Stars forefend! Let's try not to let Riff or Kara learn that. That's if they wake again.'

Brin rested his chin on the top of Olam's head. 'I fear Kara had already begun to suspect that. She spent time with Oxsana remember. I hope Enki mends their hurts soon, their wounds were most terrible.'

But Enki did not wake before Brin took Jenzi holding Riff's inert body, to join the Dragon Tribe beyond the hills. Skay took Calin and Kern, and some of their packs. Both Dragons returned as the sun was setting. Olam had spoken to Jian but she smiled and shook her head.

'I will join you when Enki awakes.'

Olam could not persuade her otherwise, so he lifted Kara, as tenderly as he could, and climbed on Brin's broad back.

The people of the Dragon Tribe made Olam and his friends most welcome. They exclaimed in horror when they saw the injured Riff and Kara, and the Wise Ones of the tribe immediately

150

took over their care, watched closely by Jenzi. Olam, Kern and Calin were settled round a large fire and given food. Brin and Skay reclined behind the three men, making it plain they were the Dragons' special friends. Long past nightfall the tribe retreated to their wagons and tents, leaving the three with their bed rolls close to Brin and Skay.

Shadows suddenly murmured to them all. 'Fighting.'

Calin sat bolt upright. 'Where?'

'West.'

'The army is fighting? I thought most of the tribes have already fled that area?'

'Seola.'

The Shadows hissed the word with such venom that both Dragons rattled their wings nervously against their backs.

'Playing.'

Olam felt sick and glimpsing Kern's face in the faint starlight, he saw the man from the Shadow Realm felt just as ill.

'Try to sleep,' whispered Calin. 'We can do nothing.'

They slept fitfully, unused to the noises of this camp after the peace of their small valley. The cattle lowed and moaned, occasionally a dog barked, and horses stamped their feet. All three men finally woke to the smell of wood burning where several people were making tea and breakfast. Calin choked on a piece of hot travel bread as Kern stared around.

'Oh my stars!' Kern was moving quickly to the edge of the camp, Olam and Calin, and most of the Dragon Tribe in his wake.

The air appeared to shimmer, or ripple, as it might on a very hot day. A wagon crunched down, flattening the long grasses, and two horses in the traces buckled, found their feet and plunged into hysterics. Several people rushed forward to reach the horses but the crimson Dragon Brin began a soft crooning song. Within heartbeats the horses stood, docile and calm although their bodies were flecked with fear sweat.

'Oh my stars,' Kern repeated faintly.

Calin had caught Kern's arm, staring as everyone else. He began to chuckle, then to laugh. 'Thank you Shadows. I am most grateful,' he managed to splutter.

A dishevelled red blonde head emerged from the back of the wagon and a woman stared at her surroundings in disbelief until her gaze settled on Calin. A truly ferocious scowl spread over her face. 'And what did you do this time, you wicked old rogue? You scared us out of our wits and nearly killed us into the bargain.'

With some difficulty, she extricated herself from the wagon, clutching a pack in her arms. A man, older than the woman, also climbed shakily to the ground. 'Calin,' he said with relief.

'Well who else would do such a thing to us?' the woman retorted, just as her bag began to yowl.

People looked nervously about, but for the first time in what felt like ages to Olam, a huge smile grew and grew. 'You have a cat.' he said with delight. 'We like cats.'

'We do?' Kern asked.

'You do?' the woman repeated, the scowl diminishing fractionally.

'Oh yes,' Olam nodded, wondering rather wildly if he was finally going mad. 'We always travel with a cat.'

The woman put the bag on the ground and cautiously loosened the straps. A black head with a white chin popped up, quite obviously not in the best of tempers. The woman glanced at Olam. 'This is Hala.'

Hala wiggled violently and scrambled free, fur on end, tail erect and green eyes blazing with fury. She stalked forward, the crowd parting before her until she arrived by the Dragons. She gave one last piteous wail and scampered up Brin's tail to perch on his shoulder. From this high point, Hala glared scornfully down at the people gathered below, her fur slowly settling to its usual sleekness.

Seola was enjoying herself. She had spotted this large mass of men and wagons, a cloud of dust and grass seeds hovering above them. She flew high overhead, far too high for anyone to notice her. Adjusting her Dragon vision, Seola saw at least two thirds of the men were on foot. There were a dozen or so riders at the head of this crowd and Seola felt a trace of mage power from them. Directly behind these riders came a group of perhaps fifty more riders, all wearing a scarlet sash across their chests and a similar scarlet band around their metal helmets.

Seola was amused by the surge of almost mindless violence

that emanated from those riders. Behind them, marched the majority of the men and Seola was surprised by the ordinariness of their thoughts. Most were not thinking of battles, of fighting or killing. Many were concerned because their feet were sore and they missed their homes and families already, only a few days out from Segra.

Wagons followed the marching men and lastly a small herd of horses, presumably replacements for any killed or lamed. Seola circled for some time before spiralling lower. Still not one man looked up. Lower still, in a widening gyre, until she was half a mile to the rear. She increased her speed, opened her jaws in a shattering roar and spat gouts of fire into the horses and wagons.

She lifted sharply, banking in a tight turn, swerved away and swooped to attack the head of the column. Her first strike, at the rear had already caused chaos. Men were turning to see what had happened. They were greeted by the sight of spare horses in panicked flight in all directions, as long as it was away from the blazing bodies of those already dead. Wagons flared like torches and from some, a greasy black smoke was beginning to billow across the plain.

When Seola's second attack hit those at the front of the army, the mages flamed like tallow candles, their horses slumping, dead or dying, under them.

The riders with the scarlet sashes were turning this way and that, trying both to see where the attacks were coming from and to see who or what precisely was doing the attacking. Seola flew a little higher although fire poured continuously from her jaws. The bulk of the marching men had scattered, like the surviving spare horses, and only a few men wearing scarlet sashes still lived and stood facing her.

Seola landed gracefully, her head high on its long neck, and surveyed the remnants of the army. Smoking mounds of horses and riders made her snout wrinkle in distaste. Even in her human form Seola had recently found the smell of cooked meat repulsive. One of the riders wearing the scarlet token, screamed something unintelligible and forced his horse to charge.

The Dragon form taken by those of the Dark Realm were huge but seemed almost fragile, their wings far too frail for lifting the great pale body. Seola's tail whisked to the side, pulverising

153

horse and rider without even bothering to watch. A group of scarlets roared their fury and brandished swords and spears above their heads. Seola laughed which, in her Dragon form, emerged as a snarl as she turned her head towards half a dozen riders racing towards her.

She reared back on her haunches and swiped one foreleg across the closely grouped riders. Still snarling, she trod on one man where he writhed, screaming, half under his dead horse. The snarl changed to a thunderous roar when pain seared through her right side. She whipped round faster than a striking snake, jaws snapping at the man hanging on to the end of a spear which had entered her body. He was shouting in triumph, until she bit him in half.

Eyes now blazing in rage, she checked whether any others of these scarlet bedecked riders remained. She saw there were seven still gathered behind the piled bodies. Turning fully towards them, she saw one break away and gallop back in the direction of the city. Ignoring him, she sent a blast of flame to the group, knowing it was the last of her fire for now.

But the group had split as she inhaled and were circling to either side of her even as her fire blasted through the empty space where they'd been. She whirled, tail thrashing and connecting with two of the riders. Her huge wings beat hard, lifting her just above the riders' heads. The hooked talons on her back feet raked through another man and his horse and her tail sent another horse reeling away.

Two riders were yelling, shaking their swords at her, and she swung her head towards them, anger screaming through her whole body. Her wings beat a hard downsweep and the talon on the edge of the left wing impaled one rider, lifting his limp body off the horse which bolted away, eyes rolling in terror. Seola turned to the other rider, her head snaking down to snap off his head. She spun to finish off the last two of these persistent fighters just as pain burnt through her back between her shoulders.

Shrieking in pain, rage and sudden fear, Seola landed, rushing forward to overwhelm and trample the last two fighters. Panting, she glared all around, aware of figures in the distance, still frantically running away from the nightmare that had so suddenly and unexpectedly appeared in their midst.

Seola knew she had expended far too much power for what she had thought would be a brief amusement. She paced to where unburnt bodies lay and gorged on horsemeat. She gripped another horse carcass and forced herself into the air, heading back to the jumble of hills. A wind had risen from the north although the sky remained clear, and it buffeted Seola off her course. She'd intended to return to the small valley where she'd rested for the last two days.

Now, pain increasingly distracting her concentration, the wind pushed her further south. The grasslands disappeared beneath her wings and, unknowing, Seola flew over the valley which had sheltered Olam and his friends, and still held Jian and the sleeping Enki. Finally she came to another tiny dip in the hills, not large enough to be worthy of the name of valley. There was water, a few sparse evergreens, and a house with a strange black roof, but Seola's injuries and exhaustion forced her to land where she sensed a cavity in the rockface. There she could rest, feed and heal herself.

Landing heavily, her wings dislodged a pile of stones. The acrid smell of sour cinnamon billowed into a small cave when Seola shimmered into her human form. She had let the body of the horse fall as she landed and now she staggered a few paces into the sheltering cave before she collapsed, blood still streaming from her wounds.

The Computer alerted Captain Karlek to the arrival of a Dragon before it was within sight. Karlek hurried to the window, peering to the north. The Computer hummed and clicked. 'The life pattern is different from that of the Dragons observed previously Captain.'

Karlek heard the words but had suddenly caught sight of the Dragon. It was massive, but also had an appearance of fragility. It was a ghostly pale, and the wings almost transparent. The Dragon carried something large in its left back claws and was rapidly losing height. It landed right where Karlek had discovered the tunnel from which the four strangers had emerged. The air seemed to blur and the Dragon vanished.

Karlek watched for a moment longer and then returned to the

ship's monitor. 'I trust you recorded that, Computer. Replay and enlarge.'

'Your command Captain.'

Karlek watched the monitor with rapt attention. 'Again.'

'It seems badly injured,' he said after the second viewing. 'When it landed, it looked as if it disappeared into that cave but it's far too big to have got inside there.'

'Captain, the life pattern changed when the Dragon landed. A human life pattern entered the cave.'

Karlek froze. 'A shape changer? Surely not. We would have sensed them long ago.' He began to sort through a pile of equipment and lifted a pair of cuffs. Grabbing his disruptor, he headed for the door. 'Full alert Computer, and ready short range weapons. And for stars' sake, do *not* turn that siren on again.'

'Your command Captain.'

Karlek went quickly across from his house to the hillside, mindful of where he'd laid mines. He approached the tunnel entrance with caution, disruptor levelled and ready. He stared at the tumbled body of the horse, noting saddle, bridle and a great gash almost through its neck. Two more steps brought him to the entrance and he saw a small woman, lying in a widening pool of blood, an arrow protruding from her upper back.

Karlek nudged her leg with his foot and got no response. He moved closer, bending to put his left hand against her neck. Pulse fast and erratic. He stared at the pale, pale face, the short dark hair, then clipped the disruptor to his belt. He slid one of the cuffs onto a slim wrist and gently turned the woman onto her side. Careful not to touch the arrow in her back, he saw there was another deep wound in her right side.

Well, she would live or die whatever he did, he decided, and heaved her up and over his left shoulder. Karlek slipped and slid his way back down the slope to his house. Putting her down gently on the floor, he looked at his bloody hands and clothes with distaste.

'Computer, is she compatible with the regen pod?'

'My sensors indicate her life signs are failing Captain. Compatible or not, a short time in the pod may stabilise her at least.'

Karlek sighed. Stepping up into the remains of his ship, he

turned knobs and dials before sliding off the top of the pod.

'Divert power to the pod,' he called.

'Diverting now Captain. Power levels sufficient and steady.'

Karlek returned to Seola. He studied the arrow shaft for a moment, gritted his teeth and simply pulled it out. It did not come easily. He saw vicious barbs just behind the arrowhead. Fresh blood poured over him and the floor making him grimace. Once more, he lifted Seola with a grunt of effort and carried her into the ship.

Karlek settled Seola into the smooth shell of the pod, slid the lid closed and flipped on three switches himself, rather than letting the Computer control the operation. 'How long would be best?' he asked.

'No longer than one soleg, Captain.'

'Call me when that time is up then. I need to clean up.'

'Your command Captain.'

Karlek stripped off his clothes and yet again bemoaned the loss of so many of the ship's facilities. Even after so many years, he could remember throwing clothes, worn for one day or less, into the cleaner, from which they rapidly emerged spotless. Now, it meant cold water from a stone cistern behind the house and much scrubbing and pounding before clothes were cleaned. He scrubbed himself until his skin was reddened and sore, then worked on his clothes.

The sun was warm although it was past midday. He left his washing draped over the cistern and went naked indoors to retrieve fresh clothes. The kettle boiled and he made a hot drink, grateful for the solar panels on the roof. Even in the winter here, and it could be very cold, there was always enough sunlight to keep the power at a healthy level for himself and the ship.

Karlek had just taken his first sip when the Computer warned him that enough time had elapsed for the woman inside the pod. Karlek went back inside the ship and flipped up the seal clasps, sliding the lid down to reveal the occupant.

'She is still unconscious Captain, but her life signs are stronger.'

'I'll make up a bed for her. She can stay in the pod for a while.' Karlek turned away.

'Captain, the regen pod has helped her stabilise but she is

healing herself.'

Karlek swung back to look at the small female, lying so still. 'How?' he demanded. 'She is native to this world and we have no evidence of such abilities. Shape changing. Self healing. What else might we have missed?'

Chapter Fourteen

Jian had felt Seola fly overhead. She had left Enki, still in his strange sleep, to fetch herself a bowl of water. Olam had left three filled skins near the front of the rock shelter for her. She had just poured some into a bowl when her senses tingled. At first she thought Enki was rousing, but almost immediately she recognised the tainted feel of Seola's mind.

Jian let her mind slip after Seola, and saw her Dragon form wavering as she lost height. She identified Karlek's house when Seola landed and withdrew her mind quickly. She returned to sit by Enki's side, wondering why Seola had chosen to land there, and also how badly injured she was. She chose not to attempt overlooking Seola again, at least for now.

Instead, she focussed on Enki. Jian believed she was beginning to understand the tiniest morsel of what he was although she had no illusions that she might ever learn very much more. She had met the mage Tika several times and she understood the vast powers that Tika had at her command. Enki had the same immense strength but he was older, in many ways more experienced, and with more idea of what he had to control.

Jian was the same age as Tika and her respect for her was increasing the more she learned of, and from, Enki. How could Tika hold such power when it clearly cost Enki so much?

'You think ever such a lot.'

Jian blinked and saw bright blue eyes peering up at her. She laughed, offering him the bowl of water.

Enki sat up, rubbing his eyes.

'The others have gone east, to travel with one of the tribes. Brin and Skay said they were good people.'

Enki nodded. 'I've visited them. Is there food?' he asked hopefully.

Jian lit the fire and made a rough meal from the few supplies Olam had left while Enki splashed and spluttered at the stream.

He ate every scrap she offered and while he ate, she collected his bed roll, packing everything ready for their departure.

'You found the things mama left.' It wasn't a question and Jian nodded.

'Why did she leave them Enki? *When* did she put them here?'

'Long and long past. We knew you'd find them.' He took the cook pan and dishes outside to clean.

Jian shook her head. Just when she thought she'd begun to grasp who or what Enki was, he spoke a handful of words which only showed her how very little she actually knew. She thought of the plump Oxsana and try as she might, she couldn't imagine that woman climbing around in this little valley or living in this rock shelter.

Jian moved out from beneath the overhang carrying two packs. Enki's huge shadow enveloped her as he returned from the stream. He stuffed the pan and bowls into his pack and beamed down at her.

'You go now. Enki loves seeing you as a Dragon. I'll bring the bags.'

Jian looked around. 'I really like it here Enki. It feels safe and – comfortable.'

Enki's laugh boomed out. 'Always safe here,' he agreed, patting her shoulder. 'You must remember where it is.'

Jian shot a sharp glance up at him, seeing an unusually solemn expression on his face. Then her eyes glowed gold, the scent of fresh burnt cinnamon drifted around and her figure shimmered. Enki stepped back, smiling happily, and Jian's Dragon form paced towards him. Lowering her head, she touched her brow to his, then raised her wings. Enki's blond hair blew back from his face when Jian swept her wings up again, lifting smoothly into the air.

Enki laughed with delight, waving his hands at her as the Dragon wheeled and flew slowly back along the secret little valley. He watched her turn once more and fly back, over him, gaining height and speed before she disappeared over the valley's rim. Enki remained where he was, his smile gradually fading. He gave a great sigh, nodded to himself and went back inside the shelter.

'You are doing well, child.'

Even Enki's eyes couldn't make out the small shadowy figure near the rear of the cave.

'The Dragon girl is as you thought. She will be needed.'

Enki frowned. 'But she won't be hurt will she? Enki would be angry if she was hurt. And I don't think I've met *you* before.'

'No Enki, you haven't met me. I am Kest, and I will visit you sometimes.'

'Where is Pesh? She's the one who always talks to Enki. I like her.'

Silence followed his question, for a fraction too long.

'Pesh is far from here. She has much work to do for another child. I will speak with you soon again, and I will always come if you have great need.'

The small, indeterminate shape dissipated against the rock wall. Enki waited for a heartbeat then he scowled. Kest had not reassured him that Jian would not be hurt. He used to enjoy his occasional chats with Pesh, but Kest sounded a very different sort.

Enki left the rock shelter and wandered through the tiny valley, checking all was as he liked it to be. Returning to the overhang, he picked up the two packs and took one step forward. There was no sound, no puff of air, nothing. But Enki was no longer there.

The Dragon Tribe had told Olam they would not move on for at least another day. They were deeply concerned about the state Riff and Kara were in. Jenzi, although awake and functioning, was unable to reach for healing power. Brin told Olam and Calin privately that Jenzi, being so relatively young, had spent his powers too rashly. Brin said he hoped Jenzi would learn from this experience but his tone suggested he believed that was unlikely. For now, Jenzi sat in the wagon owned by the senior Wise One of the tribe, watching as they sang, chanted and applied poultices to the unconscious bodies of Kara and Riff.

Daria, once she'd recovered from the shock of her undignified arrival here, had chosen to question Kern. She was enthralled by the presence of someone from the Shadow Realm and intrigued by his hairless head, uptilted leaf green eyes and gentle manner. Tenzin had been ensnared by the tribal historian, who questioned him closely on the so different life people led when trapped inside a great city.

Calin was rather relieved his two former students were otherwise occupied. Daria had told him of the mayhem within Segra the night before she and Tenzin left, and he refrained from telling *her* he already knew of it! He also omitted to mention the fate of the Segran army out on the western plains.

Brin reclined close to the wagon which held Riff and Kara, and watched the very smallest children of the tribe jump over his tail. Olam and Calin sat on the ground, leaning against his broad chest.

'Hala tells me you do not mindspeak her kind.' Brin remarked casually.

Olam laughed at Calin's expression. 'I'll wager Enki does though.'

Calin tilted his head back to look up at Brin. 'I've never even considered using mindspeech with cats. Or dogs. Or horses. I speak with trees, with rocks and water.' He shook his head.

Hala was securely perched between Brin's shoulder and neck. 'It doesn't necessarily follow that we would reply even if you had tried to speak to us.' The cat's mind tone was pleasantly feminine, with just a hint of iron within it.

Calin simply boggled while Brin and Olam laughed. 'I believe you used rather rude language when you arrived here,' Olam commented with a grin.

Green eyes narrowed, then blinked. 'It was an alarming way to travel.' Hala replied.

Olam patted Calin's arm sympathetically. 'We have only recently discovered that most other creatures use mindspeech, but they also often consider humans beneath their notice.'

There were shouts from some of the older children who were some distance from the camp, watching over the horses and cattle as they grazed. Olam got to his feet, craning in the direction of the shouts.

'It's Jian,' Brin announced calmly. 'Skay is with her.

Olam could now see the huge pale Dragon approaching, dwarfing the black shape of Skay. People were emerging from wagons and tents to watch the arrival of another Dragon. Jian's Dragon form was white, with the faintest speckling of gold and she glittered and shone as she drifted gently down beside Skay.

162

The scent of burnt cinnamon wafted over the camp. The air shivered and a small, slender girl with shoulder length black hair and golden eyes stood almost shyly, looking back at the people watching her.

Her eyes met Olam's and he hurried forward, reaching to caress Skay's face before folding Jian into a quick hug.

'They *are* nice people, don't worry,' he whispered before releasing her.

'Thank you. I don't know why I felt so nervous.'

'Where is Enki? I presume he woke up?'

Jian nodded, walking at Olam's side towards the chief of the tribe and the advisors. 'Yes, he'll be here shortly I'm sure.'

'How will he get here?'

Jian laughed. 'You know I have as little idea as you do!'

They had reached a group of five people who stood a little ahead of the others who'd gathered to see Jian's arrival. Jian hid her surprise when a tall, grey haired woman stepped forward and bowed.

'Welcome. precious child. We are yours, heart and soul.'

Jian glanced to Olam but he was as astonished as she was. 'Thank you for your words. My name is Jian, may I know yours?'

'Tintu, chief to the Dragons for many long years.' The woman bowed again then introduced the two men and two women standing beside her.

After several bows and smiles, Tintu alone walked to Jian's side. The crowd of people dispersed, back to their various chores, while Tintu headed towards Brin and Skay. She stopped a short distance from them, looking down at Jian while Olam waited patiently. 'Enki told us you would come child. He told us more than a full turn of the seasons ago. Did you know of this?'

Jian was shocked by Tintu's words. She shook her head. 'Has anyone told you where we all come from?' she asked hesitantly.

'Enki told us. He said you would come back through time, bringing hope in the midst of destruction.'

Neither Olam nor Jian could think of any possible answer to the chief's words. Tintu gave them a rueful smile. 'I was afraid you might know nothing of this foretelling. Enki only says what he chooses, so we have no definite idea of what lies ahead for us.

The only other hint he gave was that we should move north and east, as far and as fast as we can travel.' She shrugged. 'We are already many days journey out of our usual lands. We follow the stars in the direction Enki told us. I send scouts ahead to ensure we do not knowingly trespass the lands of others. What more can I do?'

Jian stared helplessly back into the woman's dark grey eyes. 'Did Enki speak of Seola?' she finally asked.

Tintu frowned. 'He mentioned no names. He spoke of you, a child of Dark Dragons, and he spoke of another Dark Dragon who would do all he or she could to thwart your plans.'

Olam grunted. 'That sounds like Seola. But we have no plans which she could thwart.' He thought for a moment. 'Do you know of a man, living alone in the hills? He has strange weapons and his house is of stone, with a black roof?'

Tintu sighed. 'We know of him. I will talk of these matters tonight, when I have conferred with my advisors and the Wise Ones.' She bowed to Jian and turned, striding back to her wagon.

Olam noted Jian's worried face, and as they walked on towards Brin, he told her of the arrival of their newest travelling companion. A cat, called Hala.

Captain Karlek had made up a bed on the floor beneath the window in the ship's room. He'd cleaned away the blood in his workroom but chose to have the woman lying where the Computer could monitor her even more easily. He removed her clothes, taking the opportunity of examining her wounds closely. The Computer was already busy analysing the blood sample Karlek had put into its system.

'Preliminary results?' Karlek asked, still examining the arrow wound in Seola's back.

'Native to this planet but several different markers Captain. Her DNA results will take a little longer.'

'Could the regen pod have repaired these wounds to this extent?'

'No Captain. She is unconscious but it is sleep rather than trauma.'

'What is her age?'

'Undetermined at present Captain, the readings are confused.'

'Increase the heat output. Her body feels chilled.'

'Your command Captain.'

'I'll get some sleep myself. Wake me the instant she begins to rouse.'

'Your command Captain.'

While Karlek slept in his workroom, the Computer buzzed and clicked to itself. A considerable length of time passed, the Computer lapsed into silent contemplation of mountains of data and then began to hum again. It regularly checked on the status of the woman and when it registered a change in brain activity, it alerted Captain Karlek.

Karlek returned, yawning, to stare down at the woman. 'The cuff is activated I trust?'

'Of course Captain.'

Karlek disappeared, coming back with a steaming mug in his hand. 'Any results for the DNA yet?'

'There are some results Captain but they are inconclusive. A strongly marked deviation of the basic native code for which I can find no comparison in my data banks.'

'None at all?' Karlek frowned, but before the Computer answered, the woman groaned. Karlek put down his mug and bent closer. Her eyelids fluttered then opened. Muddy brown eyes stared into Karlek's face.

Seola looked into a dark face, raggedly cut white hair and a straggling beard. Her mind felt fuzzy and that was something she did not recognise. There was a dull ache in her upper back and a more intense pain in her right side. She had absolutely no idea who this man was, no memory of coming inside this room.

'She is showing signs of shock Captain. I would suggest immediate sedation.'

Seola wondered who else was here, just as the man leaned closer and stuck something sharp in her arm and she sank back into black oblivion. For a long time Seola lay totally unaware. When she once again began to emerge from the fog of sedation, her instinctive defences kept her heavily shielded, even from the sophisticated sensors of the ship's Computer. The sensors recorded nothing other than the usual life signs of an unconscious person.

But behind the shielding, Seola was reviving and

remembering. She recalled attacking the Segran forces, the audacity of the men with scarlet sashes. Her wounding and her flight. But she had no memory of arriving in this house or meeting the white haired man. As her mind cleared and strengthened, she ventured to send the thinnest of mindprobes out to check her immediate surroundings. A wailing noise nearly made her leap to her feet. The noise ceased within heartbeats but the man was beside her again.

'Why the alarm again Computer?'

The man sounded annoyed.

'There was an intelligence within the room Captain. I believe it was connected to the woman but it also felt separate from her. She is conscious at the moment Captain.'

'Really?'

Seola felt a hand on her arm, the grip tightening slightly although not painfully. She opened her eyes. The same man as before was kneeling beside her.

'My name is Karlek. I found you nearby, badly injured, and brought you here to try to heal you.'

Seola tried to sit up and the man – Karlek? – helped her. She was horrified by her weakness when Karlek propped her against the wall, a pillow between it and her back. Strangely, her nakedness didn't bother her at all, even as Karlek pulled a blanket up to her shoulders. He sat back.

'Your back is healing well,' he said. 'The wound in your side was very deep. It could cause you discomfort for a while yet. The reason you feel so weak is due to massive blood loss. I think you would not have survived if I had not brought you here.'

Seola wondered how she understood his words when she'd had difficulty following the Valsheban language, but she felt too weary to concentrate on that thought. There was something familiar about his speech though. 'My name is Seola,' she managed to whisper. 'I have travelled far.' She didn't understand his smile, spreading across his face, at her words. 'Could I have some water?'

'Oh. Yes, of course. You must drink as much as you can to begin replacing your blood. You will feel weak for a time, until your blood thickens and strengthens again.' Karlek stood, still beaming at her, before turning away. 'Full alert,' he said as he

166

left.

'Your command Captain.'

Seola looked round the room. She saw no one else, just strange wood, or metal, boxes and tubes, with black ropes connecting them in a web spun by a demented spider. Hums and buzzes came from one stack of boxes but Seola could make no sense of it. Karlek returned, holding a mug and a strange looking jug with a lid. Squatting next to her, he offered the mug. 'Warm water,' he explained. 'There is more in the jug. The lid opens like this.' He pushed a piece of the lid to one side and it swung up, steam rising as it did so. 'It will stay warm for a long time,' he told her, clicking the lid back into place and setting the jug within reach of her left hand. 'I have work to do Seola. You must rest, drink as much as you can, and just call if you need anything more.'

Seola drank the water greedily, watching Karlek. He had crossed to the stacks of boxes and was studying something on the top of one. Perhaps it was a poor excuse for a desk?

'DNA analysis please, on screen report.'

'Your command Captain.'

The words were followed by buzzing and several loud clicks. Again, Seola looked all around and could see no one other than herself and Karlek. She rested the now empty mug in her lap and lifted the jug. She kept her face blank although she was aghast by how much effort it took to lift such a small thing. She pushed at the lid as Karlek had demonstrated, refilled the mug and closed the jug, setting it down with a slight thud.

Seola felt sweat on her face and renewed throbbing in her back and side. Stars above, she was weak! She drank half the water before she slid helplessly into sleep again.

'She sleeps Captain.' The Computer had lowered the volume of its speech circuits and spoke barely above a human whisper.

Karlek glanced across at Seola. 'Keep the cuff activated Computer.' He tapped the screen before him 'These results show a considerable deviation from the native norm. Do you think that is the code for shape changing?'

'It seems probable Captain. I am running a further series of tests even now. I have not ascertained a definite number for her age, but she is several hundreds of this world's solar cycles.'

167

Karlek raised his eyes to stare at the sleeping woman again. 'Can you isolate the time pattern?' he asked quietly.

'I am working on it now Captain, but it is a delicate process.'

'Tell me as soon as you have completed it.'

'Your command Captain.

Seola woke several times to find Karlek gently insisting she drink more water, but mostly she slept. Occasionally, on waking, she noted the light was much dimmer in most of the room but flashes, like miniature lightning came from the stacked boxes. She finally woke with her mind clear and only a small amount of pain in her side. There was the faintest twinge of mild discomfort in her back, which she ignored.

'The woman awakes Captain.'

She opened her eyes to see Karlek walking towards her. She sat up, using her own strength, and held the blanket across her body. Karlek smiled. 'I can see you feel much improved. Could you try to stand? There is water heated for you to wash, some spare clothes of mine and while you're cleaning up, I'll ready something for you to eat.'

He held out his hand. She reached carefully with her left hand and let him pull her gently up. She gasped. The room tilted and spun wildly. Seola squinched her eyes shut, feeling Karlek's hands tighten on her upper arms, holding her steady. Cautiously, she opened her eyes again and the room stayed still.

'Come.' Karlek helped her out of the door, into another large room. He led her slowly towards what she thought was a cupboard. Karlek opened the cupboard and revealed a small space with two large pails of water standing on a bench, a towel beside them. 'Don't bend down then up too quickly or you may faint again. I've put some clothes on the peg there.'

Seola saw two wooden pegs in the wall, on one of which hung a shirt and some trousers. Karlek waited until Seola had a hand on the stone bench then slowly let go, so she was standing alone. 'I'll leave you to it, but if you fall, or feel ill, just shout for me.'

'Where is your friend?' she asked.

Karlek turned back to her, looking puzzled.

'My friend?' he echoed. 'I live here alone.'

'You were talking to someone,' she retorted.

Karlek's face cleared. 'That was the Computer. A machine,

not a person.' He closed the door gently, leaving her alone.

It took far longer than Seola thought a simple wash could possibly take, but the dizziness came and went, making her move slowly and carefully. The trouser legs had already been rolled up but she had to fold the waist over a length of rope – obviously intended as a belt. The shirt reached to her knees and it took forever to roll the sleeves back to reveal her hands. She drew in a breath, her side aching more noticeably again, and opened the door.

Karlek was across the room and smiled as she slowly emerged from the cupboard. 'Have something to eat and then rest for a while. I told you it would take time to make up your blood.'

'How long have I been here?' Seola moved round the room, holding on to various things rather than risk crossing directly to Karlek and perhaps falling flat on her face.

When she sat at his work table, Karlek handed her a metal dish holding wafers of various colours. 'It might look odd to you, but it is a nutritious food nonetheless.'

Seola lifted one wafer and took a small bite. To her surprise, various fruity flavours exploded on her tongue and made her realise just how hungry she actually was.

'You have been here for three and a half days,' Karlek added, filling another mug with water and pushing it across the table to her.

Three days! No wonder she was so ravenous, Seola thought. She would have preferred raw meat, but these wafers, although so small and thin, certainly seemed to satisfy her appetite very quickly. Through the window Seola could see a rocky hillside, all shades of greys and ochres. The lengthening shadows suggested another night was falling. Then tiredness swept over her. Karlek helped her to her feet and guided her back to her bed on the floor in the next room.

He spread a blanket over her still clothed body but she was asleep again before he'd straightened up. After watching her for a moment longer, he returned to the monitor.

'She is stronger already by far than I would ever expect someone who had been so injured,' he murmured.

'Indeed Captain. I am not entirely confident that the cuff will be enough to restrain her, should she become violent.'

Chapter Fifteen

There was a strange air in Segra's Council Building. An exhausted rider had reported to the remaining Councillors the disastrous encounter out on the grasslands. When his horse staggered into the city, none of those on the streets took a great deal of notice. They knew the High Mage Samir had left with nearly all the city guards. Seeing one such guard returning, clearly exhausted, meant simply that Samir had probably forgotten his bed socks. Everyone knew that rather too many of the High Mages held an altogether too important opinion of themselves. The ordinary citizens called a great number of High Mages the kavaliat, or toddlers. They were known to be demanding, petulant and prone to tantrums.

A few of the small businesses had closed during the last few days, since the night the Scarlet Swords had ripped through sections of the city in fact. The shops adjacent to the Lonely Hen tavern were all boarded and barred, as was the tavern itself. The proprietor of the Lonely Hen had told passersby that he must hurry north, to Kedara city. His sister was taken ill, he said, so he must go and help her and her family. Others gave similar reasons, or none at all.

Of the many deaths that occurred on that dreadful night, most citizens believed it was simply a matter of the Mage Councillors ousting one faction in favour of another within the Council Buildings. The ordinary people who had died must have, unfortunately for them, just got in the way. So life went on as usual for most and no one knew the details of the débâcle on the plains.

In the Council Building, Mages of the Lesser Rank formed and reformed in small groups, heads close together as they agreed voting alliances or vetoes. The only two surviving High Mage Councillors, Rahul and Sahana, were known to be devoted followers of Samir, and had prudently retreated to Sahana's country house as soon as they heard the disastrous news.

A few Lesser Mages had tried to find Tenzin, Calin or Daria, but with no success of course. The most senior of the Lesser Mages, who had been expected to be made up to High Mage at the midwinter festivities was Kiri. He was hardly known, as he lived a reclusive life. Virtually no one associated with the Mage Council had any idea of how close Kiri was to Calin. Messengers had been sent to Kiri's small house several times in the last days but had received no verbal or written replies to their messages.

Now, a single bell rang three descending notes. Ten Lesser Mages were hastily pushed forward and they walked towards the door of the Small Council Chamber. The door opened as they approached causing the group to pause briefly. None of them had felt any use of power yet clearly no servant had opened the door. Even more slowly, the ten entered the room and stopped abruptly. In the central chair, traditionally the place where the Speaker of Segra sat, was Kiri.

His pale green eyes scanned the ten mages and he inclined his head slightly. 'Please be seated. We have grave matters to speak of.'

The door clicked shut behind the ten. Quickly they sorted themselves into the vacant chairs and stared at Kiri's thin face. All in this room were in their mid to late twenties but Kiri looked much older. His eyes had dark circles ringing them and his skin was pale and drawn.

'You all know of Samir's death?' He waited for the nods all round. 'You have heard of the cause? The great Dragon that attacked them?' More nods and a few glances were exchanged. Kiri took a breath and blew it out again. 'I have been told of prophecies. Prophecies about the destruction of this city of ours. And of Valsheba.' The silence was palpable. 'Yes, all of Valsheba. There is no way to resist what will come. There can be only one course of action.' Kiri looked at the ten faces around the table. 'We must organise the total evacuation of Segra, starting now.'

'But there will be total panic!'

'There are too many people to move!'

'Surely we would be safer staying behind the city walls!'

Kiri let them call their objections and protests for a time then he clapped his hands once and silence fell again. 'I was told of this prophecy but I myself have also seen. A weapon of such indescribable power will remove this city and all of Valsheba from this world. Now, how many people live in and around Segra?'

The Lesser Mages appeared at a loss until a very young looking man coughed nervously. 'At least fifty thousand High Mage.'

'I would think there are considerably more Jevis. You have a valid point about panic Tevix. I would suggest a compulsion would help allay such panic. How many mages are strong enough to compel a crowd?' Kiri could see his calm questions were having their effect.

The ten mages were frowning in concentrated thought. He noticed three of them begin to nod.

'It could work,' one fair haired man said slowly. 'There are at least forty mages I know for sure could control a large group of people. But High Mage, is this absolutely necessary? It seems so – final?'

'Kariti, it *is* final. This *will* happen, and very much sooner than we had hoped.'

'We?' This was a woman two seats along from Kiri.

'The ones who know of this prophecy . The one who told me of it many years ago, and my own vision. I am sorry Netta. I wish with all my heart that it was not so.'

Kiri gave tasks to each of the ten concerning numbers of people in the city, where wagons, carts or carriages could be found and in what quantities. He asked Kariti to collect the stronger ones among the mage community and gather them in the main Council Chamber by the third bell. Kiri watched the ten mages depart, their whole demeanour changed from when they'd first entered. He intended to keep all of them so busy they'd have no time to start panicking themselves.

He had stayed isolated within his house since Calin left Segra. He needed the time to grieve for what was to come, knowing it would be unlikely that he or anyone else would be able to grieve later. Kiri had similar mage talents as Calin, the first such student Calin had found through his many years of watching and testing. But Kiri was but a pale imitation of Calin, his strengths nowhere

172

near as great as the old man's. Calin was able to reach Kiri, however far to the east he'd travelled, but Kiri could not reach Calin.

When Calin touched his mind, Kiri was could tell him the news from Segra but once Calin had withdrawn his mind, Kiri was on his own. The old man had discussed possible strategies should the catastrophic event, foretold by seers through the ages, occur during his lifetime. Now that it appeared the disaster was imminent, Calin was absent, and it fell to Kiri to try to cope.

In Calin's study, at the top of the Council Building, Kiri spread out a map of the Valsheban lands. Calin had suggested they move the people north. Kiri had always been doubtful of that plan. Segra lay far to the south of Valsheba. There were farming villages and fishing villages, and the city of Fira further south still. North were many more villages between the cities of Kedara, Parima and Talvo. Kiri felt a strong pull to the south, where Valsheba blended into grassland again.

Calin was vague about what lay beyond that, to Kiri's frustration. Kiri didn't believe Calin was deliberately concealing anything, he suspected Calin really had no interest in what might lie in that direction. Calin was always fascinated by the plains to the east, and the wandering peoples who lived there. He had a far lesser interest in what lay far north of Valsheba, and none at all in what might be to the south.

There, the lands of Sapphrea were ruled by petty lords in scattered fortified towns. Sapphreans regarded mages and magecraft with the deepest suspicions so Kiri could not believe that Sapphreans would welcome large numbers of Valshebans moving into their territory.

Kiri stared at the map, his frustration increasing. The map was blank a short distance past what was the clearly marked Valsheban border. What could be there? Could the grasslands roll indefinitely until the very lands ended in an ocean? He rerolled the map and returned it to the shelf. If the people followed the coast south, past the city of Fira, at least they would be able to find their way back. And if the grasslands gave way to barren desert, Kiri feared that would be their only option.

When the clamour of the third bells rang over the city, nearly seventy mages gathered in the main Council Chamber. Kiri noted

173

a handful of High Mages, those who had either declined selection to the Council or had never been considered for selection. He also noted several of the High Mages were missing. Kiri knew there were several shut away in their homes, lost in their various experiments and dreams, and he had no chance of getting them out any time soon. They were harmless eccentrics, if not verging on madness, and nothing would ever convince them to leave their homes.

There were a few of the High Mages though who Kiri knew had made their way to Sahana's house. He wasn't sure what action they might take, if any, but there was nothing he could do about them right now. Kiri had given Netta, one of his new Mage Councillors, a long list of books to be removed from the library and securely crated. He'd watched her when her eyes skimmed down the first page of the listed books. She'd looked up, her face pale, and slowly nodded.

'We'll have to start all over again with everything, won't we?'

'I fear so Netta. No. I *know* so, but at least we can cheat a bit if we have these books.'

Netta bit her lip, staring down at the pages in her hands. 'What if the librarians refuse to let me take any of these?'

'Tell them to see me. And take Mero with you,' he added as an afterthought.

Netta frowned then glanced at Kiri with a faint smile. 'He's very soft hearted you know.'

Kiri smiled back. 'I know he is, but he really doesn't *look* it does he?'

Netta had gone off, shaking her head.

Now Kiri tapped the ancient round stone against the equally ancient bowl. A reverberating note rang lingeringly through the Chamber and mages settled into the tiered seats opposite the Speaker's chair, flanked by his ten new Mage Councillors. Kiri got to his feet, drew a steadying breath, and began to speak.

Not far from High Mage Astian's country house was another, much grander house. Here the High Mage Sahana was playing hostess to most of Samir's surviving followers. Her husband Rahul had ventured back into Segra earlier in the day to see what rumours he could pick up. He had just returned and was explaining to the astonished mages what he'd discovered.

'*Kiri* is Speaker?' Several people said those words in various tones of disbelief or disgust.

'He's appointed *ten* Councillors? But what about you Sahana? And Rahul? Can you be replaced, just like that?'

When Rahul told them what Kiri planned, his words were met with stunned silence.

'Leave Segra?'

'Where is he taking them?'

'What reason does he give?'

Rahul raised his hands for quiet. 'Kiri has told the Council of a prophecy that will mean the destruction of not only Segra, but of all of Valsheba.'

'I wonder which prophecy he means?' Sahana asked thoughtfully. 'I have read of several, but none of them were very specific. But then, what prophecies ever are?' A ripple of amusement ran through the gathered mages. 'And what makes him think this prophecy will be fulfilled at this particular time?' Sahana smiled round her crowded sitting room. 'If you will excuse me, I will seek out this prophecy among my books relating to Valsheba's many seers. Of course, we would do well to remind ourselves that most, if not all, of these self proclaimed visionaries were completely insane.'

She left the room on a wave of laughter, but as she made her way to her study, Sahana's face wore a deeply pensive expression.

Enki arrived at the Dragon Tribe's camp later in the afternoon, well after Jian had reached it. He wandered in from outside the camp, surrounded by a group of children who were jostling to be the ones walking closest to him. He went straight to greet Brin and Skay, his bright blue eyes sparkling with pleasure when Skay lowered her head to touch her brow to his. He dropped Jian's pack beside her and beamed at Olam and Calin.

'Nice people,' he said, waving round at the wagons and tents. 'Enki likes them.'

'Enki, do you remember you helped Riff and Kara the other day?' Olam asked him quietly.

Enki stared down at him with a frown. 'I did, didn't I?' His frown deepened. 'But Enki was too tired to do it properly. Where are they?'

Olam breathed a sigh of relief and pointed to the large ornately carved wagon nearest to them.

Enki stood still, eyes fixed on the wagon. Then his head dropped to his chest. When he met Olam's gaze, Olam was shaken by the despair he saw in the big man's face. 'Enki's hungry.'

Brin's mindvoice was a soothing rumble. 'These good people knew you would be. Look! They bring it now.'

Enki's beam returned and he sat under Brin's nose while men and women of the tribe brought heaped dishes of meat and the odd tubers they found in the grasslands. Olam knew how much the Dragons disliked the smell of cooked meat. Now he realised the depth of Brin's affection and respect for this child-man, that he would remain where he was while Enki ate. A woman passed Enki a waterskin and he gulped half of it down. He smiled at the people who'd fed him.

'Enki *was* hungry!'

They all laughed, collecting the dishes and retreating to their tents. Olam noticed they all touched Enki, not obviously: a drift of fingers on his arm, a light stroke of his hair, and he wondered exactly what they believed Enki to be. Scratching his chin where his beard was already thick, it occurred to Olam that Enki never shaved. His face was smooth and fresh, clearly never having had a razor near it.

Enki rose. He turned and hugged Brin's neck, then did the same to Skay. He looked at Olam. 'I don't know how much I can do,' he said softly. 'I left them too long. But Enki will try.' He walked to the steps of the wagon and disappeared inside.

Calin tugged Olam's arm. 'Come. Let's walk. I'll introduce you to some that I know from my other visits to these people.'

Olam understood that Calin was trying to distract him from thoughts of what might be happening to Riff and Kara, but he nodded and walked beside the old man. Reaching the outer edge of the camp, Olam paused to admire the horses grazing under the watchful eyes of some of the children. A girl, about ten years old Olam guessed, brought a beautiful mare across to him. The mare was black as night and quite calm under the hands of the child, but Olam saw glints in her eye which suggested a not so gentle temperament.

'Her child will come soon,' the girl told him. 'And my grandmother says I can have the raising of it.'

'You are most fortunate then,' Olam smiled. 'Is it her first?'

'Oh no. Her third. And all are as black as she is.' The girl grinned at him, waving the mare back to the herd.

'Why do these people all speak my tongue?' Olam asked, strolling on with Calin.

Calin grunted. 'Because it is the common tongue of Sapphrea and they are Sapphrean. The Valshebans too are Sapphrean but long ago they separated from the rest of the people. Those born with magely gifts were not wanted in the north.'

Olam nodded, remembering Lord Hargon's hatred of magecraft.

Calin shrugged. 'Those who were gifted came south, with their families and livestock and made their own land here. The most powerful appointed themselves the leaders of course, and they changed the language. As you discovered when you arrived, all public officials must use the formal Valsheban.'

Calin stopped to introduce a young man who was working on a leather harness and who then explained the different way the tribe used the traces on their wagons. The two men were offered food at various fires where Calin knew someone, and the morning was soon past. They began to walk back to Brin who reclined unmoving beside the Wise One's wagon.

'*Can* he heal them?' Olam asked bluntly.

'I do not know. I think it has been too many days since they were hurt, but I promise you, Enki will do all he can for them.'

The rest of the day seemed to crawl by to Olam and he'd been called by Kern and Daria to join the evening meal further into the centre of the huddle of wagons and tents. He saw Tenzin across the fire, deep in conversation with one of Chief Tintu's advisors. A woman began to sing, her clear voice joined by a flute and a drum, when he felt a touch in his mind. Jian.

He looked around the fire but couldn't see her. He rose, moving towards the Wise One's wagon. Brin and Skay were gone but Jian sat, crosslegged, on the grass. Olam dropped down beside her and waited.

177

Her eyes gleamed gold, reflecting the firelight. 'Enki's gone for a walk,' she began, meeting Olam's gaze steadily. 'He's tired again, and he's upset.'

Olam felt his heart plummet. Jian reached for his hand. 'Riff will recover, except for his arm. He won't have much use in it. Kara was closer to the explosion.' Her hand tightened on Olam's fingers. 'He *thinks* she will live, but it is unlikely that she will walk.'

Olam's breath hissed out as though he'd taken a blow to his gut.

'Enki is greatly distressed,' Jian continued. 'That's why he's out there. He blames himself for not having the strength to heal them both as soon as he saw them.' Olam saw tears glitter on Jian's lashes when she leaned closer. 'He was in Segra that night Olam, trying to protect some of the mages from being slaughtered. He had strength left to get back to us, but none for healing on the scale Riff and Kara needed.'

Olam nodded slowly. 'But they both live, and I at least am most grateful for that. Are they conscious?'

'No. Riff may wake in the next day or two. The Wise Ones here can keep his pain under control. They will make him exercise his arm as much as he can bear but they don't think it will ever work even a fraction of how it should.'

'And Kara?'

'They want Kara to stay sleeping for longer. Those dreadful open wounds over her back are healed, but they say the nerves and muscles have been left too long to repair now. That's when Enki ran away.'

Olam returned the pressure of Jian's fingers. 'Go and find him Jian. Tell him how I appreciate his help and how much I love him for what he's done today.'

Jian kissed Olam's cheek and got to her feet. 'He really did try you know.'

'Yes Jian. I do know.'

Jian disappeared beyond the reach of the firelight and the scent of burnt cinnamon bloomed in the night air.

Olam woke next morning before dawn. The bustle in the camp told him the tribe were preparing to move on. He glanced up at

Skay's face from where he lay against her side. She looked back down at him, her eyes sparkling with excitement.

'The people are moving today. All their houses on wheels.' Her mindvoice became almost a whisper. 'I had a look inside one of them. A very nice man invited me to see.'

Olam stretched to stroke her long beautiful face. 'What did you think of it?' he asked her.

'Well, it was very small. It had those pillow things and bright colours on the walls. I liked it. I wonder if someone could make a really big one?'

Olam remained straight faced although with some difficulty. Unable to find a suitable reply, he busied himself packing his bedding and hoping someone would have breakfast available. A quick glance showed him Enki and Jian were still absent, but Calin, Daria and Kern were also waking and readying themselves to travel.

Kern joined Olam, the two following Daria and Calin towards a tent beyond the Wise One's wagon. Two women were cooking and handing food out to those who were striking tents and packing their goods.

'I'm sorry about Riff,' said Kern. 'What will he do if only one arm works?'

'If he so chooses, he will continue as usual,' Olam replied with no hesitation. 'He will want for nothing if he chooses to leave my brother's service. That's if we ever get out of this stars damned mess.'

'And Kara?'

Olam shook his head. 'She will be cared for, in Vagrantia, in Gaharn, wherever she wishes,' he said firmly.

Kern smiled. 'You are a good man Olam of Far.'

Olam stared at him in surprise but was handed a bowl of meaty broth and a hunk of bread before he could reply. Daria joined them.

'I look forward to hearing more of Sapphrea,' she told Olam brightly.

Kern grinned from slightly behind Daria.

Olam swallowed a too large and far too hot mouthful of the meaty breakfast broth, making his eyes water. 'I would be glad to talk to you but two of my companions lie seriously injured and I

179

must spend most of my time with them for now.'

Daria looked disappointed. 'I understand, of course,' she agreed. 'But there will surely be times when you are not with them? We can talk then.' She smiled and hurried to catch up with Calin.

'I wish you joy Olam,' Kern chuckled. 'I have never met anyone with such an unending stream of questions.'

'Do you think I would be able to see Riff and Kara before we start moving?'

'I'm sure you could. Let's go and ask.' Kern led them back to the large carved wagon and, mounting the steps, rapped his knuckles lightly on the side of the door.

'Come,' a woman's voice called from within.

'May I accompany you?' Kern murmured when Olam reached for the door latch.

'Of course.' Olam sounded surprised that Kern would even need to ask such a thing. Olam was surprised again when he entered the wagon. He had expected it to be dark, lamplit, but a quick glance up showed him a clear material over a large part of the roof. Through it he could see fading stars and the pink tinge announcing sunrise.

A young man smiled and beckoned Olam and Kern forward. 'This is Taban, the Wise One of the Dragons,' he introduced an older woman, seated by a narrow bunk along the side wall. She stood, her hands at the small of her back as she stretched.

'Greetings Olam of Far. Riff will wake sometime today. His body and mind were badly shocked by his wounds, but he recovers quickly. He is an armsman I believe?'

Olam could have kissed her for saying "he *is* an armsman" but he didn't. 'He is indeed Lady.'

'I am no lady, just Taban. Riff has perhaps suffered hurts before so he is more accepting of pain and fear.'

Olam looked down at the man in the bed. He seemed to be peacefully sleeping except that his left shoulder was so heavily strapped, immobilised it seemed to Olam. Taban slid past Olam and went further into the wagon. Another narrow bed held the motionless figure of Kara. Her red blonde hair had been brushed and lay smooth on the pillow. She looked so very small, so very pale. Olam's eyes filled with tears. This was *his* fault. He should never have allowed Kara to join his foolhardy quest for ancient ruins.

Taban touched his arm. 'Kara had far worse damage done to her. She remains shocked which is why we keep her sleeping. Have faith that she will wake and be strong enough to face the path fate has set before her. Now I must rest. Stay if you wish. My apprentice Kaz will watch over them.'

The young man smiled when Taban disappeared behind a heavy curtain beyond Kara's bed. Kaz drew Olam and Kern back to Riff's side. He pulled out a small bench from beneath the bunk, and Kern sat with Olam, watching Riff's sleeping face.

Chapter Sixteen

'Did you ever hear anything of time magic?' Sahana asked her husband casually.

Far too casually to one who had lived with her so long. Rahul shot her a penetrating glance. 'I thought Pern was said to be meddling with such silly ideas, years ago. Why?'

'Pern? Didn't he die suddenly?' Sahana closed her eyes, trying to remember what the man had looked like. 'What about Calin? Does he have any interest in time, do you think?'

Rahul laughed. 'Only to bemoan its passing I'd imagine. Stars, but he is so old now!'

'That's why I wondered about him,' Sahana explained patiently. 'Is he keeping the years at bay by some magical trick? We all know Rajini and Annella thought they'd found some way of forestalling age. But just look at them though – mad as ferrets stuck in a drain!'

Rahul frowned. 'Why this interest?'

'Something Samir said, before he left Segra.'

'He will be sorely missed.' Rahul nodded solemnly.

'Are you mad?' Sahana stared at her husband. 'He was a pompous fool.'

'But – but – I thought we supported him? Believed in his leadership?' Rahul stammered, regarding his wife as if she was a stranger.

'As he has proved, he was expendable. Many of the regulations and edicts he proposed and sanctioned were, of course, my suggestions. Raising the vendor tax for example. Samir had to cope with the protests and riots, didn't he? Not me. Do close your mouth, husband of mine, you look like a fish, gaping like that.'

Rahul shut his mouth with an audible snap. 'What do you plan to do now?' he asked in a strangled voice.

Sahana gave him a gentle smile. 'Wait for Kiri to empty most of the city, and move back in.' She waved a careless hand. 'There are sure to be some who refuse to leave – farmers, gardeners, servants – they will supply the needs of the few of us. We can take our pick of houses. It will all turn out better than I could have hoped.'

Rahul swallowed, wondering if he had ever really known this woman at all. 'You said Samir mentioned something before he left Segra. Was it to do with time?'

'Yes, it was. He said Calin believed that those strangers there was so much fuss about, had travelled from the future back to this time.'

'Really? I don't understand how such a thing could be possible.'

'Neither do I dear, but you must admit, it's an intriguing idea. Imagine if we could go forward into *their* time.'

'But the strangers vanished I thought, from Rajini's house?'

'Exactly. Perhaps they travelled back to where they came from?'

'What would we do, if we managed to travel into the future?' Rahul was now utterly confused by this conversation with his wife.

'Do? Well, we'd learn various things from them obviously. Then we'd pop back here, to *this* time, and we'd know more than anyone else in Valsheba.' Sahana smiled brightly. 'Now we must find out just who is working with time and get every piece of information from them.'

Rahul watched his wife with a growing sense of horror, but he nodded. 'I'll start asking tomorrow. Someone is bound to have heard rumours of such a thing.'

Kiri was astonished by how relatively smoothly his plans were being implemented. He felt guilty at using compulsions on so many of the ordinary citizens of the city but he knew he had so little time to get them out. He knew in his heart that even if he could get such a large number of people even a hundred miles away, it would probably serve no purpose. He had been divided in his own mind. Let the people stay, going innocently about their daily pursuits with no idea of what lay in store for them, or to try to evacuate them.

Kiri finally chose to get as many Segrans away as he could. Perhaps a handful might survive the cataclysm he knew was inevitable. He had had visions of a fearful destruction since he was a small child, but for the last season, the same scenes played out in his dreams every single night. He had no need to open his mind in the seer's trance to know what was coming now. He'd told Calin time was running out but in this, Calin disagreed. Calin suggested another full year before events unfolded as disastrously as they would.

It was only two days since Kiri had announced his decision to evacuate Segra. The first group of over a thousand people had left this morning. He hoped the next group to leave would be considerably larger: he knew he didn't have an infinite number of days left in which to work.

One crate of books had gone in the wagon of two mages who were in control of that first group. Kiri had watched their departure and worried at the level of compulsion used on the people. They were smiling and laughing, as though they were heading off for a festival rather than leaving so many of their possessions in a city they would never see again.

Jevis reported that one section of the city, Jewellers Walk, had absolutely refused to entertain the idea of leaving their homes and businesses. He wanted to know if Kiri thought he should call extra mages to force the jewellers' compliance. After a moment's thought, Kiri shook his head.

'They have made their choice, even through a general compulsion. Leave them to it, but don't let them try to persuade others to copy them.'

Jevis sped off as a young woman rushed in. 'Netta needs to know if the agricultural treatises should be in one crate alone or shared between the different groups as they leave.'

Kiri refrained from sighing. Could he really get these people moving in the next two days? Yes, he promised himself, even if he ended up being carried out in the last wagon to leave, unconscious from sheer exhaustion.

Jian flew over the vast grasslands, searching for Enki. She'd seen him come from the Wise One's wagon very late in the night. Lying in her bedroll close to Brin, Jian saw his bowed shoulders,

184

the tears on his face glinting in the starlight. He moved silently across to her, squatting down to speak softly. He told her how he'd left Riff and Kara, his breath hitching when he explained he could do no more.

'I have to go for a walk now,' he finished. 'Enki needs to think and be alone.'

Jian nodded, brushing her hand gently across his wet cheek. Enki straightened, and vanished round Brin's great bulk.

The crimson Dragon appeared to be asleep, his neck curved round, his head resting on his back. He had heard Enki's words but chose to say nothing. He was desperately saddened to learn the outlook for Riff's injured arm, and his mind shied away from thinking of Kara, unable to walk. Before he slept, Brin thought long and hard about flying Olam and his companions away to the north. Would the Dragons there accept these humans, or would they try to harm them? All this worry about time! Brin understood that somehow he had been dragged, with his daughter and Olam and his friends, back many, many years. He knew about years, the repeating pattern of the seasons. He accepted the idea of yesterday and tomorrow. He could not comprehend the way humans sliced up pieces of a day. What was the need? He rumbled softly, putting all these troublesome thoughts from his mind, and settled to sleep.

Now, Jian flew. She had quartered a large area of the grasslands and found no trace of Enki. Her enormous Dragon shape floated down to land and Jian shimmered into human form. The familiar scent of burnt cinnamon drifted around her when she walked slowly towards the north. The silence was profound, broken only briefly by a wayward breeze rustling the grasses which brushed her fingertips as she walked.

Jian lowered herself to sit on the ground. It was a strange sensation, the grass now taller than she was, isolating her even more completely. She rested her chin on her knees, wondering what her brother Shivan was doing right now. But that made tears prickle at her eyes and she would *not* cry. Her fingers clenched into the warm earth and she felt the tough threads of the roots of the grasses around her. Carefully, she withdrew her fingers, patting the loosened soil firmly back over the roots.

Jian sat very still. Had she really heard that voice, or was it just her hopeful imagination? It hadn't been Enki's voice, not a single voice but a multitude of whispers. Cautiously Jian pressed her palms hard to the earth. A tingle worked its way up her arms, seeming most intense from the thin scar on her palm from the broken arrowhead's cut. She closed her eyes and the whispering was a little louder.   It sounded like "thank you", but that couldn't be right. Even as Jian thought that, the whispers became wordless, merely a gently musical humming. Was this what Enki felt she wondered.

'No.'

Jian's eyes flew open. She hadn't heard the Shadows for several days but that single word was said unusually gently. When the Shadows bothered to communicate, they were generally abrupt and abrasive.

'Not like Enki?' she thought back to them.

'No,' they repeated. 'Like, but different.'

Jian couldn't decide what her next question should be, there were so many.

'Enki not hear.'

Jian frowned. 'Enki can't hear you?'

'No.'

'He is the most powerful mage I've ever met,' Jian began.

'No.'

She wrapped her arms round her drawn up knees and rested her cheek on them. 'Tika?' she asked.

'Tika,' agreed the Shadows.

'But I never heard that Tika could travel the way Enki does.'

'Could, if she thought about it.'

'Why are you speaking to me now?'

There was such a long silence Jian decided the Shadows had vanished again.

'Must. You learn. You remember. *Must.*'

The silence this time was the silence of absence and Jian knew the Shadows would say no more for now.

What did they mean – that she must learn, and remember? She was trying, really hard, to learn what she could from Enki, although Enki was most definitely not teaching her in any specific way. She got to her feet in a sudden movement, searching the plains around her yet again. She began to retrace the path she'd made through the grass. Then she stopped, thinking hard. Finally she braced herself, took a deep breath and called a name.

The breeze that riffled the grasses this time was icy cold rather than warm. Jian swallowed, forcing herself to appear relaxed. The beautiful woman who stood before her looked utterly astonished.

'Mother Dark have mercy,' she murmured, her gaze eventually resting on Jian. '*You* called me?'

Jian met Ferag's eyes. 'Yes I did Mistress Ferag.'

Ferag's exquisite brows drew down in a frown. 'You are amazingly polite Jian. When we met previously I believe you were on the verge of gibbering?'

Suddenly Jian did relax. She grinned. 'Well, I think you enjoy scaring people out of their wits, but Tika always says you're one of the sweetest people she knows.' She shrugged. 'I hoped you might have some idea about getting us out of here.'

The faintest blush of colour tinged Ferag's pale, pale face, the frown faded and the icy breeze fluttering her long dark red hair and dress disappeared. 'Oh that dear child! Tell me who "us" are?'

'Olam's friends. You remember we were going to the ruined Valsheban cities to find Seola?'

The frown returned but the icy breeze didn't. 'I knew of that yes, but I've been rather busy of late.'

'Really?' Jian asked with genuine interest.

'Hmm. A rather difficult lot of deaths. The poor dears arrived in my Realm rather than Simert's. A spot of bother sorting them out. Never mind, tell me what's happened.' She looked at their surroundings. 'And where exactly are we anyway?'

Jian spent most of the morning explaining everything that had happened since Olam's small company had left Far. Ferag was intrigued by the fact that they had apparently travelled through time.

'You're *quite* sure, dear?' she asked Jian for the fourth time.

'Completely,' Jian assured her.

They were sitting among the grasses and Jian had to admit Ferag was surprisingly pleasant company. 'I didn't know *you* could move through time though,' she added thoughtfully.

Ferag wound a strand of her hair through her fingers. 'Hmm.

187

I've never really thought about it. I just go where I'm called.'

'Could you take us back with you?'

'I could if you were dead but I'm really not sure I could take you if you hope to be alive when we got there.'

Jian laughed. 'We'd prefer to get back alive I'm afraid.'

'I must leave you Jian. Your situation disturbs me. I will discuss it with my – colleagues.'

'Thank you Ferag. I'm glad to have spoken with you.'

Ferag studied the girl before her. She gave her a devastatingly beautiful smile and leaning forward, pressed cold lips to Jian's cheek. 'I will return as I can child.' She half turned away then back. 'Would you let me take Kara? She is sore wounded from what you say?'

Jian's golden eyes filled with tears. 'Let me speak with Olam first, if you please.'

Ferag nodded, touched Jian's cheek again, this time with icy fingers, and was gone.

Jian drew a shaky breath but, oddly, she felt comforted rather than distressed by the meeting with Ferag, the Mistress of Death in the Dark Realm.

The scent of burnt cinnamon surged over the grasses when the enormous Dragon that was Jian rose into the sky, heading back towards the line of wagons and riders she could just see on the horizon.

The tribe travelled all day until the sun was close to the skyline when they pulled up to make camp. Daria had been most annoyed when she found Olam, true to his word, had stayed inside the Wise One's wagon the whole day. She'd insisted on walking with Calin and although the old man was aware Daria was frightened out of her wits, her incessant chatter nearly drove him mad. One of Chief Tintu's advisors arrived beside them and invited Daria to join her and some others across the camp. They would be glad to tell her some of their legends, the woman suggested.

Daria was delighted, and pulling paper and writing sticks from her pack, thrust the pack back into Calin's arms and departed. The woman slid an arm through Daria's and marched her off, giving Calin a wink over her shoulder. Calin sighed with relief, thanking all the gods he could think of for his deliverance.

Tenzin and Jenzi appeared round the side of a wagon. Calin scowled. 'And where have you been all day? Did you not see I needed rescuing?'

Tenzin grinned. 'You seemed to be coping admirably.'

Brin and Skay had flown far ahead of the tribe during the day but now spiralled down to settle close to the Wise One's wagon. Calin, Jenzi and Tenzin made their way towards the Dragons to spread their bedrolls beside them. Jian came down the steps of the big wagon just as the three men reached it. She opened her mouth as though to speak, then closed it again. Calin raised a white eyebrow at her.

'Forgot what you were going to say?' he asked. 'Happens to me all the time but at my age I must expect it!'

Jian smiled but said nothing at all. She'd had a whispered conversation with Kern and Olam inside Taban's wagon. She'd told them some of what the Shadows had told her and all of Ferag's comments. Olam grinned when she said she'd summoned the Mistress of Death and she'd punched his arm lightly. His grin vanished when Jian repeated Ferag's offer to take Kara back with her. They were standing beside Kara's bunk, looking down at the small motionless woman while Jian spoke.

Olam tugged his bearded chin. 'I will think about that offer Jian. We must remember how she took Tika and looked after her until she'd recovered from *her* injuries.'

'We have no evidence that *this* child will recover as we all might wish.'

They turned to find Taban standing close behind them. The Wise One studied Jian. 'The woman you spoke of, she is the Goddess of Death?'

Goddess? Jian was startled by the use of such a word. 'We call her the Mistress of Death,' she agreed cautiously.

Taban nodded. 'It is only words. You say – this Lady – took another friend of yours who yet lives?' she asked Olam.

'Yes she did. But *that* friend was a most powerful mage and I do not believe Kara to have a fraction of her strength.'

Again Taban nodded. 'I would advise you to think on it Olam of Far. It seems to me it is a rare offer from such a Lady.'

Jian had then left Olam and Kern, intending to tell the others her news, but stepping down from the wagon, the Shadows muttered in her head. 'Not speak.'

Jian could see only Calin and the other Segran, Tenzin, with Jenzi of Gaharn. Why should she not tell them of Ferag's words? 'Not trust.'

Not trust? Jian's thoughts spun. Not trust all three, or just one of them? But the Shadows stayed obstinately silent. Remaining silent herself, she moved round Brin to sit between the crimson Dragon and black Skay, listening to the three men chatter and the slightly more distant murmur from the camp. She heard Olam's voice speaking to Jenzi, then Kern appeared, ducking under Skay's chin. He held out a pack.

'I took yours with us, in Taban's wagon,' he said.

In the gathering dusk, Jian saw his leaf green uptilted eyes regarding her steadily. Kern was of the Shadow Realm. Surely he must have heard the Shadows warn her not to speak? Kern's nod was barely discernible. Not for the first time, Jian wished her ability to use mindspeech was as good as her brother's, but she found it nearly impossible to instigate mind to mind communication.

Kern wandered back past Skay, leaving Jian to pull out her bedroll and lay it ready for later. Olam called her to come and see if food might be ready across the camp. Brin lowered his head as Jian moved round him. 'Be careful.' He sent the thought on a tight thread to her mind alone. Mother Dark, what *was* going on? Jian thought, numbly following the men in search of a meal.

After she'd eaten, Jian left the men by the main fire, listening to stories and songs offered by the tribe to honoured guests. She told them she was weary and Kern smiled his sweet smile as she rose. Settled in her bedroll, Jian nearly shot out of her very skin. Whiskers tickled her face, followed by a delicate sneeze. A small furry creature worked its way under the top cover and a purr began to buzz steadily.

Jian's hand slid up and over the cat's head and back, while her heartbeat gradually returned to near normal.

'How did you travel today little one?' she whispered.

'With Olam and Kern.' Hala's mind voice was softly soothing and Jian began to relax again. 'I can hear your thoughts you know.'

'You can?'

'If you concentrate a bit, you could mind speak me perfectly well.'

'Did you speak to Daria's mind?' Jian asked curiously.

The cat made an odd noise which Jian decided it would be prudent to ignore.

'Fussy, fussy. And rather silly.'

Jian bit her lip, feeling much more cheerful.

'I like the Shadows,' Hala continued. 'And Brin and Skay are so very well mannered. Olam tried to explain to that Taban creature that I could be a great comfort to your poor friend Kara.'

Jian waited, Hala's tone now oozing ladylike disgust.

'She threw me off the bed if you can believe that. *Threw* me.'

'Didn't Olam explain?' Jian managed to choke out the words as her eyes watered from restraining her urge to laugh.

'He was with the man Riff and didn't see.'

'I'll tell him in the morning. I'm sure Kara would enjoy your company but perhaps you should lie *beside* her rather than *on* her?'

The purr halted abruptly and even in the near dark, Jian saw green eyes glaring down at her. 'Well of course. Surely you don't think I'd sit *on* her when she's hurt her poor back so badly?'

'No, that was silly of me. Please forgive me Hala.'

The purrs resumed, more quietly but gradually rising to their previous volume. Sometime later the purrs ceased. 'Well, I thought the child would never sleep,' Hala mindspoke Brin.

He huffed softly. 'She is overtired. She is very young, even for humans, far from her home and her brother, and more frightened than she will ever admit.'

'Then it's a good thing she's got us to look after her isn't it?'

Brin wisely chose not to reply and Hala's purrs filled the space between him and his daughter.

Kiri was reaching the end of his endurance. Three days of constantly answering questions, organising and re organising very large groups of people was wearing him down. Food was brought for him at regular intervals but was usually removed again with only a bite or two taken from it. The visions of devastation were constantly in his mind now and he was starting to wonder if his utter exhaustion was driving him into madness.

Yet again, he rubbed his bloodshot eyes and studied the mass of people wending their way towards the south gate with their wagons, carts, barrows and bundles. The next group to leave would be the last and he would be with them. Stars, but he needed some sleep! Netta arrived as Kiri turned from the window. She studied his haggard face and grinned.

'You look like I feel, and don't you dare say I look as bad as you!'

Kiri summoned a smile that was more of a grimace, and waited.

'The Council records. Do you want them taken with us?'

Kiri's smile was slightly more genuine. 'I don't think they'll be needed where we're going,' he answered.

'That's what I thought so I put them in the fire.' Netta looked slightly shocked at her own temerity but Kiri laughed aloud.

'That's the best place for them. Have all the practical books and papers gone now?'

Netta tried unsuccessfully to stifle a yawn. 'I tried to sort them out so that every group had a basic collection – for farming, building, fishing and so on. The last lot is ready for when we leave later.'

'Do you have family here?' Kiri asked, belatedly realising he knew nothing about the woman.

'My mother's long dead, and my brother is in Parima. I haven't seen him for years. My father refuses to leave.'

Kiri sensed no distress from her so he chose to accept her words as fact.

'What about you?'

'Me? Stars above, no! Calin took me in when he caught me stealing food. He thinks I was around four years old.'

Netta was silent. She had never heard that about Kiri. No wonder he always kept himself to himself. She wondered, in a foggy corner of her tired brain, if he even realised what a lonely man he was. He turned back to the window, seeing more wagons drawing up outside the Council Building.

'I hope you've packed whatever you want to take. We should be out of here before midday.'

Netta nodded.

'I'll see you in a wagon shortly then.' When Netta had gone, Kiri pulled his own pack from behind the desk. It was strapped tight. If he'd forgotten anything it was just too bad. With one last glance round Calin's study, Kiri heaved the pack over his shoulder and made his way down flights of stairs for the last time.

It was far noisier outside than Kiri had expected and he was briefly confused. Then he heard his name called and saw Tevix waving at him from the back of a wagon drawn to one side of the wide street. Kiri made his way over and Tevix held out a hand to haul him aboard. Kiri saw the interior was filled with various crates, packs and bundles, on which perched most of his so recently appointed Mage Councillors, including Netta.

Kiri sat down with a thump as the wagon began to move forward. He had intended to watch when the wagons drew away from the south gate for his last glimpse of the city. But Kiri, last Speaker of Segra, was sound asleep before they'd even reached the gate.

Chapter Seventeen

The Dragon Tribe had travelled three full days north and east of the Valsheban border. Olam and Kern spent most of their days with Riff and Kara. Riff had woken and, as Taban had predicted, was relatively accepting of his damaged arm. That didn't mean that he didn't complain. He did. A lot. Olam and Kern took turns sitting with the fractious Riff and the silent Kara. Kern refused to offer his opinion regarding Ferag's suggestion, saying he had no authority over Kara of Vagrantia.

This fourth day, Olam sat beside Kara, holding her small cool hand between his two warm ones. He spoke to her softly, explaining that both Taban and Enki had done all they could for her. He paused, just looking at the woman. The light cover over her rose and fell with her regular breaths but other than that movement, she could have been a statue of stone.

Olam lifted her hand, gently touching it to his brow and his lips, then leaned even closer. 'Kara, Mistress Ferag spoke with Jian. She offered to try to take you back, even though she couldn't promise any more than that. Remember though Kara, Ferag took Tika when Tika was near death *and she returned her to the world*. I think Ferag will tell your people, and Tika, and Shivan, what has befallen us all. Remember Tika's beloved Captain Gan? Ferag allowed him back from her Realm until he himself chose his death to be final.'

Olam drew a breath. 'Mistress Ferag,' he said quietly but clearly. He closed his eyes as he felt the chill breeze behind him. He didn't turn when a hand rested on his shoulder. Olam bent forward and kissed Kara's cheek. Ferag's hand left his shoulder and long cold fingers brushed Olam's tears away from his face.

'I will care for her but I can make you no promises, Olam of Far.'

He looked at the most beautiful woman he'd ever seen and managed a speechless nod. The chill surrounding him vanished, and so had Kara and Ferag. Olam stayed as he was until another hand gripped his shoulder. He sighed and looked up into Taban's face. She appeared deeply shaken. 'That was the Lady of Death?'

Olam stood up, turning away from the empty bunk. 'Yes,' he said. 'I called her and she has taken Kara to her Realm.'

'Kara was still living,' Taban frowned.

'Kara *is* alive,' Olam said firmly. 'Ferag has given her a chance.'

Ferag usually moved around the world without ever thinking exactly how she did so. She discovered that moving through time took a surprising amount of effort, especially as she was also carrying a living body rather than a spirit. It took longer than Ferag liked but she reached her Realm safely, laying Kara gently in her own bed. She changed the décor of the bedroom with a casual flick of her fingers then set about making tea and soup the unmagical way, taking pleasure in the work.

Ferag returned several times to study her guest, each time calling to her spirit, but without any urgency. Ferag carried a tray to the bedside and admired her dainty artistry in setting bowl, cup and plate so prettily beside a small pot holding tiny blue flowers. She sat on the bed and held both Kara's hands. 'Wake now little one. They have done well getting water into your poor body these last days but now you must eat. Wake, Kara.'

Lashes a darker shade than the red blonde hair flickered and eyelids opened. Huge hazel eyes stared up at Ferag.

'Good girl. Now, shall I lift you a little, I promise it won't hurt, and you'll take as much broth as you can.'

Half supporting Kara against the piled pillows, Ferag carefully spooned soup into her mouth. Kara managed nearly all of it before turning her head aside. Ferag lowered the woman back on the pillows and smiled her ravishing smile. 'There now. You will sleep a while then I'll bring you more food until you feel stronger.'

Long cold fingers brushed a strand of Kara's hair away from her face. 'Do you know you are only the second visitor to lie in my very own bed and to be cared for with my very own hands?'

Kara licked her lips. 'Am I dead?' she managed, in a voice

195

rusty from disuse.

Ferag's smile changed to a scowl. 'Well really! I am simply trying to help you,' she began, the temperature in the room plummeting despite the blazing fire in the hearth.

Kara's hand crept across the bedspread towards Ferag, the hazel eyes filling and spilling with tears. 'I'm sorry. You have been so kind, I thought I *must* be dreaming or dead. I'm sorry.'

The temperature rose, the scowl vanished and Ferag's arms reached round Kara in a gentle hug, cold lips against Kara's cheek.

Kara slept and woke, slept and woke, with no idea of time passing. She watched Ferag bringing her food, straightening the bed covers, gently washing and drying her, and knew she would never fear her. 'Will I walk again?' Kara asked during one of Ferag's visits.

'I'm not really sure, dear one. I'm not a healer as such of course. I have done nothing for your back. Let's wait a little longer.'

Another time, Kara asked about her companions but Ferag waved a hand airily. 'I have no idea darling. I did promise Jian I'd ask a few questions for her – among my – colleagues.'

'Colleagues?'

'I suppose you'd call them gods, but most of them are very sweet, although it must be admitted, rather ordinary.'

Kara's mouth began to curve up in a smile. She might not be dead she thought, but she must surely be dreaming. Some of these bizarre conversations with Ferag could never be real.

That evening, when Jenzi learned Kara had been taken from Taban's wagon, by Ferag no less, he lost his temper. Jian stood beside Skay, Hala in her arms and watched and listened. Olam seemed subdued, sad, but Jian guessed that was due to his meeting with Ferag, not for the decision he'd made to send Kara away. Jenzi berated Olam violently. He marched up and down in front of Olam, waving his arms wildly, his voice rising.

'How did you presume to make such a decision on your own?' He paused for breath but Olam had straightened his slightly bowed shoulders and looked right back at the tall thin healer from Gaharn.

'I made the decision because, as leader of this company, it was mine to make,' he said quietly.

Jian glanced at Brin, seeing the Dragon's eyes beginning to flash and whirr. Kern stood by Skay, his hand on her shoulder as she moved uneasily. Jian could scarcely believe what she was seeing.

'Hah,' was the Shadows only comment in her head.

Jenzi's face twisted in a sneer. 'You are such a little man. You have no idea of what you have been so easily manipulated into doing.'

Olam stared at Jenzi.

'The Lady Seola knew you would do some of her work for her. Although I have been unable to contact her here, she will not be long in delivering your reward.'

Olam frowned. 'Reward?'

'For your pathetic attempts to thwart her plans, you fool.'

'And those plans are?' Kern intervened softly.

'To find the time mage, obviously, and then wreak her vengeance in *this* time, and in our time she will implement the new way of life planned by her revered brother Cyrek.'

Kern's grey skinned, hairless head tilted to the side. 'What of the ship, way back in those hills?' he asked.

'That is of no significance. Lady Seola was injured. She will recover there and find the mage she seeks.'

'Why are you here with us, if we are such worthless fools?' Olam didn't look angry, just faintly puzzled.

Jenzi rolled his eyes in pitying contempt. 'To make sure you don't find the time mage first.'

'You mean that neither you nor the vile Seola has worked out where he is yet?' Olam sounded astonished.

For the first time, Jenzi appeared uncertain. 'You have no idea of his whereabouts,' he blustered. 'If you had, you would have spoken of it to your stupid friends.' Suddenly Jenzi's anger returned. He started to draw a long dagger from a concealed scabbard but before he got it clear, a look of utter astonishment crossed his face. His mouth worked but no sound emerged. Jenzi swayed then pitched forward onto his face, his whole body shuddered and lay still.

'Hah.' The Shadows repeated their earlier comment in Jian's

head. She saw a crowd of tribesmen and women had gathered but didn't remember seeing them coming near. Now, two men approached Jenzi and knelt beside him. One of the men, who Jian now saw was one of Chief Tintu's advisors, looked across at Olam.

'The gods have punished him for his words.' He waved several other men forward and they lifted Jenzi between them, disappearing back through the crowd of onlookers.

'Was that what you warned me of?' Jian thought to the Shadows. 'And what exactly happened to him just then?'

But silence was their only answer. Hala wriggled and Jian set her down. The cat scooted up Brin's tail and settled in the crook of his shoulder. Jian joined Kern and Olam. She thought Kern looked pale although it wasn't easy to tell.

'I wasn't expecting that,' admitted Olam. 'I can't say I liked him much but I had no idea of the depth of hatred he must have held for us all.'

'I never felt entirely comfortable near him,' Jian agreed. 'Now I think of it, Enki kept clear of him.'

'Still no sign of him?' Kern asked.

Jian shook her head but Calin and Tenzin arrived in a rush before she could anything more.

'We just saw men carrying Jenzi out of camp,' Calin said. 'Stars preserve us, but whatever happened?'

Olam shrugged. 'He was just explaining his rather different point of view and just fell down. Must have been some sort of seizure.'

Calin gave him a penetrating look but asked no more. Tenzin merely looked confused by the whole incident.

'Where is Daria?' asked Kern.

'She was with Chief Tintu earlier,' Tenzin replied. 'She's very interested in the tribal legends.' He smiled vaguely, but in such a way that made Olam, Kern and Jian suddenly nervous.

'Stay here,' Kern murmured, and went quickly into the heart of the camp.

Calin seemed not to notice, moving to stand in front of Brin. To Jian's astonishment, Hala hissed and spat, before stalking down Brin's back. She picked her way delicately through the grass to Skay, who nudged her gently with her nose. Both

Dragons were agitated Jian realised, and she began to draw power to herself. Calin stared into Brin's face for some time then, shaking his head, he turned away. He marched off in the same direction as Kern had gone, closely trailed by Tenzin.

'What was *that* about?' Olam asked.

'He tried to reach my mind,' Brin's mindvoice rumbled while his wings rattled against his back, a sure sign of agitation.

'*What?*' Olam reached to the long face, trying to offer comfort and calmness.

Brin ducked his head against Olam's chest. 'It was simple to block him of course. He thinks our powers are very limited. He tried before, to both of us, in that nice little valley place.'

'He did,' Skay confirmed. 'Enki told us he feared he'd been wrong about Calin. He'd thought he was a nice man, but he isn't.'

Olam met Jian's eyes, and she turned away, walking to the edge of the camp. Where was he? She had not had any sense of the man anywhere across these plains. What could he possibly be doing? Jian wondered if Enki needed total solitude to gather the strength he had hinted he would need. He hadn't told her what event might call for so much strength. He'd never suggested he could get them back through time for instance. Jian stared over the endless grasses and wondered if they would ever see Enki again.

Seola felt well generally except for a continuing nagging pain in her side. The thing that kept her at Karlek's house was the terrible lassitude she felt from the blood loss she'd suffered. That, and a deep curiosity about Karlek and his strange machines. Karlek had given a very brief explanation of the Computer, none at all about the ship itself or where he had actually come from.

Seola had no interest at all in knowing where Karlek was from. His Computer was of some interest after Karlek told her it could work out all kinds of problems involving numbers, calculations and, to a much lesser degree, could predict certain events. When Karlek was busy in the other room and Seola could get to her feet without falling over, she'd staggered towards the stacked boxes.

She discovered they were not boxes piled one above the other, but a solid column with drawers opening on the side which was beyond Seola's view from her bed. On the top of each stack, as she continued to think of them, was a shiny black window. The Computer, wherever it was, hummed and clicked. Seola was still standing there when Karlek reappeared. He joined her.

'Computer, display sensor cameras, monitor two.'

'Your command Captain.'

Seola took a wobbly step back when the black window flickered and showed a moving picture of the grey hillsides around the house.

Karlek smiled at her. 'No one can approach without my being aware of it. I knew of your arrival long before you landed by that tunnel. Enlarge.'

'Your command Captain.'

Seola could only stare. She saw herself, in her Dragon form, losing height, blood streaming from two wounds. She landed, her head swaying with fatigue and pain. Then she seemed to disappear and Seola knew that had been the moment she resumed her human body.

'Show life profiles.'

'Your command Captain.'

The outside pictures vanished, leaving only the black window. Two columns of numbers dropped down the window along with two strange drawings – lines and circles, spinning round and round.

'Freeze.'

The drawings ceased their spin and Karlek looked again at Seola. He pointed to the numbers and drawing on the left of the window. 'This is a profile analysis of your Dragon body.' He pointed to the right. 'This is of your human body. Look closely Seola, and see the similarities at certain points.'

Slowly, Seola realised she understood what Karlek was trying to show her. Her eyes became accustomed to the figures and shapes and she saw that certain of them exactly matched each other across the window. So this man knew, with his strange machines, that she and the Dragon were one and the same.

Karlek was watching her expression and saw when she began to understand his numbers and shapes.

'What is the trigger which allows you to make this physical change?'

Seola's face became blank.

'You must say or do something which enables you to alter your body,' he continued.

Seola shook her head. 'If I choose to be Dragon, then I am.'

'How many of you have this ability?'

She shrugged. 'Many of my people have the ability but not all of them choose to use it, not after the first time.' Karlek waited. Eventually Seola explained further. 'The first change occurs when we are nearing adulthood. It can be alarming, frightening to some. Others find it quite simple and natural.'

'And time. What do you know of time?'

Seola smiled. 'I have learned time can be fluid, almost like a river. You can jump in at one place and find yourself in somewhere quite different.'

'Can you do that deliberately?'

Seola studied the man beside her. She was still far too weak to call any of her power: it was taking every bit of her will just to remain upright right now. 'Can you not move through time? With your – ship?'

Karlek saw Seola's weakness was making her tremble now and, taking her arm he helped her back across the room to her bed. She lay, half propped against the wall and sighed with relief. Karlek sat, relaxed, next to her.

'You have seen another ship.' He spoke calmly.

'I've seen one yes, not like yours though.'

Karlek's pulse started to thud in his ears. 'Not like mine?'

'It talked.'

'A bio ship. Was its Captain there?'

'The ship was crazed. I think it said its name was Dancer but its Captain was dead.'

Karlek made himself breathe steadily. 'Where did you find this ship?'

Seola sipped from the ever present water. 'Far south from here. On an island.'

Karlek's heartbeat had settled to an only slightly elevated rhythm now. He exhaled slowly. 'The bio ship told you how to travel in time?'

Seola had watched him far more closely than he'd suspected. Now she lifted her left shoulder in a careful half shrug. 'It told me some things I didn't understand. I learnt other things from the archives of several people – my people and others.'

'Could you repeat your – experiment?' He couldn't help himself this time: Karlek held his breath while waiting for her answer.

'Possibly.' She smiled at him, making no attempt to conceal her yawn. 'How long will this tiredness last?'

Karlek understood his guest would answer no more questions at this point. He stretched his legs in front of him. 'Several days I'm afraid. I have no medicines to help you. You've probably replaced all your lost blood by now, but it will be very thin and weak. Until your body enriches that blood, you will continue to feel faint and tired. So, several more days to wait.' Karlek smiled as he got to his feet. 'Rest now. I have work to do.'

Seola slid down onto the bedroll and watched Karlek walk to the stacked boxes. Her eyelids felt heavy and she was asleep again.

Karlek glanced at her. 'Block sound beyond immediate area.' he murmured.

'Your command Captain.' The Computer's voice was as soft as Captain Karlek's.

'Have you isolated the genes involved in shape changing?'

'No Captain. The blood samples you supplied from the subject will not stabilise sufficiently. It almost seems still living although you gave me the samples four days ago. and therefore they should be inert.'

Karlek studied the stream of data crossing the monitor for a while. 'Synthesize tranquillizers to liquid form,' he said finally. 'I can put it in the water I give her. She's passive at present but there's something I really don't trust about her.'

'Your command Captain.'

Karlek retreated to his work room. The Computer buzzed and hummed as it went about its appointed tasks. Seola lay, helpless in sleep.

The Shadows had evolved. Originally, (and that origin was lost, so long ago was it,) they had been guardians. They were chosen for their care, their compassion. But over this immeasurable stretch of time, they had hardened. They had seen too much of the horrors these humans could, and did, inflict upon each other and other creatures. There were many Shadows in this world. They had chosen, long years past, to ally themselves with the Shadow Realm as it emerged from the Dark. They liked the Second Son of Mother Dark, Lord Darallax of Shadow.

Darallax was basically a kindly creature. He reminded the Shadows of their earliest beginnings and their first ambitions. Darallax guarded his people, he tried to protect them, and, to a great degree, he had been successful. In appreciation of Darallax's character, the Shadows obeyed his few commands to them. There were a handful of Shadows who spent all their time within the Shadow Realm but the vast majority roamed the world.

They communicated with a very few humans and as briefly as possible. The Shadows had seen the rise and fall of civilisations beyond numbering and rarely regretted the destruction. Long ago they had discovered the gods and they spoke with some of these entities. They all approved of Ferag, and of Simert, but many of the other gods simply amused the Shadows. They weren't sure where the gods had come from although they assumed they'd arrived from way beyond the starfields, much like the Asatarians of Gaharn and those others who had come in their strange ships.

The Shadows had been alarmed by the weapon used against Olam of Far by the man who hid himself away in the hills. The blast had scattered them. It hadn't hurt them of course, but it had taken them by surprise, and that was something that rarely happened to the Shadows. It had not only surprised them but it had angered them as well. Try as they might, they had not been able to enter the house where Seola now lay, without the machine being aware of their presence. The creators of the Shadows had listened to their reports and suggested that a few of them remain nearby, simply to observe.

Many of the Shadows spent time watching Dragons. They found the Sea Dragons capricious and more wild than the Great Dragons. The Great Dragons lived in various mountainous areas across Sapphrea and the Shadows admired their dignity. They liked the way the Great Dragons showed a general respect for other creatures who shared this world with them. The Shadows knew quite well that the Great Dragons were aware of their existence, knew who they were, and were wary of their power.

They were very fond of Fenj, Brin's ancient father, and he had become more relaxed with the Shadows.

The Shadows knew where Enki had gone and they made no attempt to observe him or speak to him. They knew his task, they would respond should he need them, but they respected his absence now. There were a considerable number of Shadows close to the Dragon Tribe, another group was watching Kiri of Segra as he made his vain attempt to rescue the people of his city.

Those Shadows with the Dragon Tribe had suffocated Jenzi when he had been about to offer threat to Olam of Far, They had emptied his mind before he died and now understood some of the undercurrents eddying through Calin, Daria and Tenzin. The Shadows had not risked entering the thoughts of any of them before.

Each of those four people would have been aware of another presence within their heads and been alerted. Enki had preserved the lives of the three Segrans because he believed Calin was his friend. Enki was distraught when he realised his mistake and that distress, combined with his failure to fully heal either Riff or Kara, had spurred him to leave the travellers so much earlier than he's intended.

Now, the Shadows remained silent, watching Kern hurry through the Dragon camp to the wagon of Chief Tintu. They felt protective towards Kern simply because Lord Darallax liked and trusted him. Perhaps they should have warned him? They saw Kern stop at the foot of the steps as the door above opened. Chief Tintu stood there, quite calmly, one of her advisors just behind her.

'I'm sorry to have to tell you, one of your companions is in here.'

Kern nodded. Tintu opened the door wider, stepping aside to invite him within. Kern entered and stared down at Daria's body, a long knife protruding from her chest, her pale blue eyes staring emptily at the roof of the wagon. He also saw the wickedly serrated dagger clenched in Daria's right fist. Kern turned to Tintu. The Chief shrugged.

'Something made me look round,' she explained. 'And there she was. Her face was – wrong. As though she was practising an expression she'd never made before. her eyes were already

204

empty.'

While the Shadows sniggered in the back of Kern's head, he kept his face blank. 'I don't know if you'd heard that another of our companions – died – a short while ago?'

Tintu frowned. 'I was told he had offended the gods and was struck down where he stood.'

'Quite so,' Kern agreed. 'Shall I remove this one?'

'No, my people will take her and leave her with the other one.'

'Leave her?'

Tintu's smile was cold. 'They will be left beyond the camp. Let the wild ones eat their fill. Life is not easy on these plains, for any of us.'

Kern inclined his hairless head. 'I am thankful you are unharmed,' he said and left the wagon.

Walking back to join Olam, he listened while the Shadows explained just how helpful they had been.

Chapter Eighteen

That same evening, Olam was surprised to find an almost celebratory air when the tribe gathered for the evening meal. A man sitting nearby, grinned at Olam's puzzled face.

'The gods are with us,' he told Olam. 'Our Chief killed an assassin and one of your men was shown to be unworthy of your trust and struck down. The animals of the plains will feast well tonight, and so do we!'

Jian nudged Olam in the ribs. 'Perfectly obvious really.'

He smiled, glad to see her mood seemed lighter. He had no idea of her feelings for Enki, or how she regarded that strange man. He was just pleased that, this evening at least, she seemed less strained. After the meal, drums were brought out and men, women and children leapt around the fire, stamping and twirling.

Olam got to his feet. 'I'll look in on Riff. Kern was with him earlier and Taban had food brought for them both.'

Jian also rose. 'Can I visit Riff yet?' she asked.

Olam was startled. 'Well of course you can.' He paused. 'He does swear quite a lot,' he added.

Jian snorted. 'I've never heard bad language, living with a brother like Shivan, have I?'

Olam laughed.

'Did you notice the birds earlier?' Jian asked while they headed for Taban's wagon.

'I can't say that I did. What do you mean?'

'Wave after wave of them, all heading north east, just like us. Different types of birds too, not just one kind.'

Olam stopped to try and see Jian's face more clearly in the darkness. 'What do you think that signifies?'

'Is this the time Valsheba is destroyed?' Jian spoke softly. 'The small animals who live among the grasses are running too, in the same direction. Many of them spend their lives in one place, never travelling far from where they were born. They are moving now Olam. This afternoon, I saw an enormous cloud of butterflies, of all things. Again, all different kinds. All flying north east.'

Olam thought about it for a moment before continuing in the direction of Taban's wagon. 'I don't know what it might mean Jian,' he said. 'I don't think I can worry about it now.'

She laughed, waiting while Olam tapped the panel by the wagon door. Kern opened the door and gave them his sweet smile. He came down the steps to let them enter. 'Have a pleasant evening,' he said, his eyes twinkling in the low light from within the wagon.

'Why thank you.' Olam grimaced and waved Jian ahead of him.

Taban's apprentice gave them a smile and a nod as he left through the door at the further end of the wagon, a bundle of bandages in his hands. Riff sat against several pillows, his left shoulder still heavily strapped, holding his arm unmoving across his chest. He scowled when Jian sat on the bench at his side.

'Thought you'd forgotten all about me,' he grunted.

Jian grinned. 'How could you be forgotten when you bellow so much when the bandages are changed?' she asked innocently.

Olam choked and Riff's face went an interesting shade of puce. Riff glared at her.

'I have *not* bellowed,' he replied with dignity.

'Then it must have been your snoring,' Jian agreed. She settled her back against the wagon side and smiled kindly at the gaping patient. 'Have you stood up or had a totter up and down the wagon yet?'

Kaz had reappeared and stood grinning, just out of Riff's eyeline.

'I stood for a while this morning,' Riff eventually replied.

'Then fell over I expect,' Jian nodded.

Kaz stepped forward. 'He *did* lose far too much blood. It will take time to regain his general strength.'

'If it wasn't that great to start with, it should take less time surely?'

Kaz appeared confused. Olam's eyes began to water and Riff was simply enraged. Jian leaned over and patted Riff's good hand. 'I can pop in and help you practice tottering if you like?'

207

'You can – '

'Riff!' Olam roared.

Riff breathed deeply, his eyes narrowing at Jian. 'I doubt *you* are strong enough to support me.'

'Shall we try now, or start in the morning, when you've had a nice long rest?'

Riff gritted his teeth. 'Whichever suits you.'

From the corner of her eye, Jian caught a brief movement of Kaz's hand. She stood with a dramatic sigh. 'I'll call in at first light Riff. *I*, at least, have been rather busy today and would appreciate a rest. Until tomorrow then, Riff dear.' She waggled her fingers at Riff and drifted out of the wagon.

'She did that on purpose didn't she?'

'I imagine so,' Olam agreed.

'Where's Enki?'

'We don't know. Riff, I wouldn't mention him to Jian. If she speaks of him, go carefully.'

Riff nodded. Kaz coughed politely. 'You really should sleep soon Riff,' he began and Olam moved towards the outer door.

'Have I been – er – difficult sir?' Riff asked.

'Sir? *Sir!* I thought you'd forgotten I was your officer. Yes Riff, your temper has not been the easiest although it was not unexpected, given your injuries. Kern says he's impressed by the number of new curses you've taught him.'

'Aah.'

'Exactly so Riff. Aah indeed. Now get some sleep and we'll see you tomorrow.'

Olam walked the few paces to where Brin and Skay reclined, their great bodies forming a protective barrier round Kern and Jian. Brin's eyes flashed when Olam dropped onto his bedroll.

'Jian told us how rude she was to Riff.' His mind voice rumbled in their heads. When his head lowered so he could peer closer at the man, Olam stroked the long face.

'She certainly was, but I think it did him good. It's time he started moving. Taban told me so yesterday. And I think he's more likely to try if Jian's bullying him a bit.'

'Not too much though,' Skay put in. 'He was so dreadfully hurt.'

'No Skay, not too much,' Jian agreed. 'You have a brother so

208

you know what I mean?'

Skay's chuckle was a soft gurgle. 'Will you bring him outside?'

'I could open the door, then you could say hello to him, but I don't think he'd manage the steps yet.'

Skay shifted her weight slightly. 'We would like to see him,' she insisted.

'Then that's what I'll do.'

As they settled to sleep, Kern silently asked the Shadows where Calin might be.

'Other one across camp. Prisoner of tribe.'

'Tenzin is held prisoner? Where is Calin?' Kern persisted.

'Travelled.'

'Where?'

'South.' Then the Shadows became uncooperative, refusing further communication and eventually Kern slept.

Instead of flying on in the morning as Brin and Skay usually did, the two Dragons edged closer still to Taban's wagon. The camp bustled with activity as the tribe made ready to move on. Jian squeezed between the Dragons to mount the steps just as the door opened. Kaz smiled. 'The patient is ready.'

'Could we leave the door open, his friends would like to see him?'

Kaz regarded the two pairs of flashing sparkling eyes and simply stepped aside.

'How are we this morning?' Jian beamed at Riff.

He was sitting on the side of the bunk, wearing thin blue cotton trousers, like those the tribesmen often wore. He looked pale, as if just sitting differently had been an effort. '*We* are fine,' he snarled.

'Well up we get then. You have visitors.' Jian slipped under Riff's right arm and Kaz hovered close to his left side.

Riff pushed up, a soft gasp escaping. Jian glanced up and saw his eyes squeezed shut. She waited patiently until he blew out another breath. 'Bit dizzy then,' he said gruffly.

'We'll totter to the door now, shall we?'

Despite his annoyance, Riff's grip over Jian's shoulder tightened considerably when he took a step forward. Four steps, five. Riff's breath came faster but the sixth step brought them to the door. Jian leaned against the jamb, letting Riff lean against her. The Dragons' heads were level with Riff where he stood at the top of the wagon steps. Riff stared into eyes glowing rosy pink and the grey blue of twilit snow.

'We're glad to see you,' Brin rumbled in his deep mind voice.

'We have seen you look better though,' Skay added politely.

Riff glared at her. 'I'll be back to normal in no time,' he retorted.

Skay's eyes whirred. 'Perhaps you could try for better than your old normal?' she suggested.

Brin huffed gently. 'We will come and see you again later Riff. You must practice your tottering now.'

Both Dragons turned away, pacing to the edge of camp where they lifted, so gracefully, up into the sky.

'Come on then,' Jian straightened, pushing Riff gently upright.

Sweat was pouring from Riff and Jian could feel his trembling by the time they'd walked the length of the wagon, turned and made their way back to his bunk. Mercifully, she kept quiet as she helped him lower himself so he didn't jar his injured shoulder. Kaz dropped a light cover over him. Riff didn't notice, he was already asleep.

'He did well lady,' Kaz murmured.

'He did, didn't he? I'll be back later and he can do it again.'

'When we stop for the evening. That will be soon enough.'

Calin had reappeared in his house in Segra. He was astonished to find the building empty, already with an air of abandonment about it. He fetched two bottles of berry spirits from the tavern cellar and poured himself a large drink. The Lonely Hen was tightly shuttered and barred, without a chink of daylight able to get through. There was a fine layer of dust over the counter and the tables, but, except for the absence of any bottles on the shelves, all was neat and tidy. Calin guessed Porridge must have left four or five days ago and would be heading for Parima.

Travelling the way Calin had was exhausting for a man of his advanced age and now he had no strength to quest through the city with his mind alone. He hadn't bothered to reach for Kiri for some time. Indeed, the last time he'd spoken to the half wit,

Calin had been annoyed. Kiri was convinced the fall of Valsheba was about to occur. Calin thought the idea ridiculous.

He was prepared to accept the notion was possible, an earthquake, an immense storm of some sort, but he had never believed the utter destruction that Kiri had described from his nightmares since he had been a tiny boy. Kiri had certain mage talents which Calin had found of use in his own schemes. Perhaps it really was symptomatic of Calin's long knowledge of the boy, as he still thought of Kiri, or perhaps Calin's age was making his mind play him false.

In the last year, Kiri had become ever more evasive, and often failed to keep an appointment demanded by Calin. Calin saw this as youth trying to assert itself against age and had disregarded the matter. Climbing the three flights of stairs to his rooms, Calin wondered if the young fool had actually started moving the citizens of Segra out of the city? Surely not?

Reaching his study, he put the bottles on a dresser, refilled his tankard and strolled across to the window overlooking the square. He took a large gulp of berry spirit, coughed, then just stared. There were no stalls, no shops open, scarcely a handful of people scurrying almost furtively, around the edges of the square. Calin frowned. How drastically would he have to alter his plans now?

He had been alarmed to find Enki in the company of the strangers and, stars forefend, those Dragons. He believed their tale of being dragged, unwillingly and unwittingly, through time, but it was of no relevance to *his* aims for Segra and Valsheba. Calin raised his eyes to the rooftops and his frown deepened. The gutters and roofs were always crowded with crows, pigeons and sometimes gulls, all on the lookout for fallen scraps from the vendors' stalls. Today, crane as he might, Calin saw not one single bird waiting on the roofs of Segra.

So many people missing. Was it like this in other parts of the city? Calin hurried through his apartment, to look out of other windows, onto different streets and squares. Eventually he returned slowly to his most frequently used room, his study. He sat, putting his feet up on an old chest he used as a footstool and, weary as he was, he began trying to seek out Kiri's mind. After only a short time, Calin reached for his tankard and emptied it in one huge swallow. He leaned back in his chair, eyes closed, head

211

pounding. Kiri was nowhere to be found.

Kiri was still asleep. He had slept over half a day, woken, eaten some food someone pushed into his hands, and slept again. When he next woke he stayed awake. Netta and four others of his young Mage Councillors still slept but Kiri felt refreshed enough to check how his group of travelling citizens were doing.

Some of the Lesser Mages, Kiri was pleased to learn, were taking turns to keep the compulsion working enough that people continued to move on to the south. He spoke with two such mages and was even more pleased when they told him they were reducing the strength of the compulsion. Already it was at half the power it had been when the people first left the city.

There had been a few grumbles but the Lesser Mages had agreed between them that the citizens had the right to know some of the truth. Not all, not yet, but enough to urge them southwards. They were making good time according to Tevix. He told Kiri that he'd sent two riders ahead, one of them a mage, and they'd reported the city of Fira was only another day's travel away.

'I guessed we would avoid the city so I have had routes checked both inland and nearer the coast. There's little difference in the distances but which would you advise? We'll have to decide this afternoon when the roads divide.'

'Inland,' Kiri said without hesitation.

Tevix grinned. 'I thought you'd say that. The land between Fira and the coast is much busier than the inland road.'

Kiri smiled back. 'I've never visited Fira but I've heard much of their experiments with sea water, canals and so on. I think we'll be seen for sure – I'm not trying to conceal our passage. Do you know which way the other groups took?'

Tevix nodded. 'Every single one of them went inland.'

'Good. Will the people travel longer today? I'd like to get as far past Fira as we can, as soon as maybe.'

Kiri pulled himself up onto the driving bench of the wagon he'd woken in and watched the long line of people and carts winding along the road. He saw a few people working in fields to their right, who turned to watch this strange procession pass. No one approached to ask them their destination or the reason for so many people to be travelling. Perhaps they'd got used to such sights after several days of similar caravans passing their farms.

Nearing sunset, the wagons drew up to the side of the road, close to a stand of woodland.

'Make sure they're careful of fires, Lia,' instructed Kiri. 'Do not forgot that most of them know only life in the city.'

They moved on again in early dawn light. Kiri had spoken with several of the families, groups within the great crowd of people, and found them all calm, although some were beginning to ask for more details about the threat hanging over their city. Jevis was driving when Kiri climbed back on the wagon around mid morning. The road had taken them well clear of Fira: they hadn't even glimpsed any of the spires and towers, often known as the Wonders of Fira.

By midday, the travellers could smell the salt breeze from the ocean and scouts returned, wheeling their horses alongside Kiri's wagon.

'The road gradually fades away into brush, within the next ten miles or so,' said the young female rider, one of the Lesser Mages whose name Kiri was unsure of.

'Will the ground be clear enough for wagons Sonali?' asked Jevis, glancing across at the girl.

A gust of wind whipped her dark hair across her face. Turning slightly so that her hair was blown clear again, she nodded to Kiri. 'As far as we went, the wagons will be fine. May I ask how far we will be going?'

'For now, we just keep moving south. We need as much distance between us and Segra as we can get.'

Sonali studied Kiri's face for a moment. 'That's what I feared,' she said quietly. 'Do the earlier groups know they have to just keep going?'

'Yes, they do.'

Sonali nodded, and reined her horse towards the back of the last few wagons. Kiri vaguely recognised the middle aged man riding with her – had he been one of the cooked food vendors in Siertsey Square?

'We're not stopping between dawn and near sunset,' Jevis remarked. 'Except to water the animals. The pace is steady enough, the horses are all checked each day by Sonali and Lod –

that's the fellow she rides with. They both know horses well and Sonali's main talent is healing.'

'Did you arrange that?'

Jevis blushed faintly. 'You were asleep,' he began.

Kiri laughed. 'I'm glad you did. You know everyone far better than I.'

'Look at that!' Jevis interrupted.

Slightly to the right of the road ahead, over increasingly sandy ground, a glittering line suggested the ocean. But above that were massed flocks of birds, circling and swooping. Kiri shaded his eyes and stared harder. Smaller flocks were breaking away and flying north east. It was oddly silent due to both the distance and the breeze blowing any sounds away from the line of wagons.

Kiri and Jevis watched the birds a little longer then turned their attention back to the road. They saw many others down the line, pointing towards the great gathering of birds and obviously chatting to each other about them.

'It's been mentioned that a lot of animals seem to be on the move,' Jevis told Kiri softly, although there was little chance anyone would hear them over the creak and rattle of the wagons. 'Lod told me he saw deer, heading the same way as those birds.'

Kiri sighed. 'It is quite possible the poor souls have their own means of foreseeing approaching disaster.'

Jevis nodded and the wagon rolled on with the two men deep in their own thoughts.

Kiri helped Jevis harness the two horses in the predawn gloom. He followed Jevis's instructions patiently, never having done such work before. He was slower finishing all the buckles and Jevis left him while he went to collect some food for them both. Kiri patted a warm chestnut neck and then stood very still. It felt as if something was tickling at the base of his skull.

'Move faster. Must.'

Kiri stared blankly at the horse. He had been bespoken by Calin many times but it had never felt like this. Who was it?

'Move faster. Must.' the words sounded urgent, almost impatient.

The horse he was staring at moved its head, a dark brown eye fixed on him.

'*You* spoke to me?' Kiri whispered.

There was an explosion of sniggering in his head. '*Not* horse. *We* say – move faster.'

Utterly bewildered, but with a sense that the words were completely serious, Kiri turned away as Jevis returned. 'Get everyone ready to move,' Kiri said, accepting the parcel of food Jevis offered him. 'Tell them we must move faster today.'

Jevis stared as Kiri climbed onto the wagon. Kiri looked back down at him. 'I don't know why but just do it.' Jevis handed up his own food bundle and hurried down the line of wagons.

'Who are you?' Kiri thought. 'Can you help us?'

'Not help. Only warn.'

Kiri was aware of an emptiness and guessed whoever, or *whatever*, had spoken in his mind, had gone. Most of the morning passed in silence. Jevis glanced once at Kiri's preoccupied expression and left him alone. He had the horses trotting for a couple of miles then slowed them back to a brisk walk. When they stopped in the evening, several mages worked along the lines of horses, making sure there were no strains or sprains.

Kiri heard the strange voice again the next day. 'Move fast. Must.'

'Is it any good?' Kiri thought back, suddenly swamped by a feeling of hopelessness.

After a long silence, the voice spoke again. 'Tomorrow, maybe next day. Cliffs. Narrow valley. Caves on north side. *North.*'

'Will these people be safe there? Where are all the others who went before us? We should have caught up to some of them.'

'May be safe.'

'And the other groups?' Kiri persisted.

Another long silence. Then one word which made Kiri quail. 'Lost.'

Far in the future from Kiri and his refugees, Tika was questioning Brin's son Flyn. The butter yellow Dragon sat on his haunches, eyes spinning in great alarm. Tika strode up and down in front of him. Everyone except Flyn, knew Tika always marched about when she was thinking. All poor Flyn knew was that Tika, always so kind to him before, had shouted, green and silver eyes blazing with fury, and he couldn't imagine what he'd done wrong.

Tika finally came to a halt in front of Flyn. She realised belatedly just how frightened Flyn was. She tilted her head to one side, looking up into his eyes. The fire in *her* eyes guttered out and her mouth curved into a smile. 'I'm sorry Flyn. Forgive me.'

Very cautiously Flyn lowered his head towards the small woman before him. Tika took his long face between her hands and kissed his nose. 'Your father and Olam have frightened the wits out of me Flyn, but I shouldn't have yelled at you. I am sorry.'

Gradually the tension eased out of Flyn just as the silver blue Dragon, soul bonded to Tika, bustled up. Tika reached to stroke Farn's face. 'Go along with you all. Farn, take Flyn and his friend – '

'Twist, his name is Twist.' Flyn told her, desperate to be helpful.

Tika smiled. 'Twist. Show them Iskallia Farn and make sure they feed. They've flown so far and so bravely.'

Her words caused Flyn's neck to stretch up again, his eyes calm once more.

'Come along.' Farn lifted up, the sun sparking from his silver blue scales. Flyn and Twist immediately followed.

The Captain of Tika's Guards wandered over to her, watching the young Dragons heading up the valley. 'You still have to learn to hold on to your temper,' he remarked. 'My Lady.'

Tika snorted. 'I know. I really didn't mean to upset poor Flyn so badly but really Sket. What has Brin got into now? And Olam? And the others who went with them?'

Sket shrugged. 'They'll probably turn up and then, can you imagine the stories that rascal Brin will bore us all with?'

'I'm not so sure. There's more to it than them just vanishing.'

Two older men and two women joined them. 'Rhaki said he had a nasty feeling.' The shorter of the women said cheerfully.

Rhaki smiled apologetically but said nothing.

Tika studied him and sighed. 'Does anyone know where Garrol is? Or Dromi? Tell everyone there'll be a meeting this evening, and let's see if we can work out what's happened.'

'Flyn mentioned Jian.'

216

'Thank you Essa, I *did* notice that.'

Essa grinned, revealing purple stained and filed teeth. 'Just in case you forgot,' she agreed. 'Perhaps we should invite Shivan? Sorry – Lord Shivan.'

Tika looked slightly taken aback. 'Do you really think that's necessary?'

'I'm rather afraid that I do,' Rhaki admitted. 'I very much suspect something really unpleasant has happened to poor Brin.'

Chapter Nineteen

Seola stood by the outer door of Karlek's house, holding on to the wall. Karlek gazed around at the few bushes that had grown brittle in the cold wind of the last few days. Stars, but she was so weak!

'How many days have I been here?' she asked, her teeth clicking against each other as she shivered.

'Four nights. This is the fifth day,' Karlek smiled.

Seola drew in deeper breaths of the chilly air and began to cough. She felt Karlek's arm supporting her at her waist, turning her to go inside again. She wanted to double over to ease the pain in her side while she coughed, but knew she'd only fall flat if she did so. Karlek waited until at last the coughing fit passed then gently urged her back through his workroom to what Seola privately thought of as the ship room.

'How did you heal my wounds so fast?' Seola whispered rather than risk the cough returning if she used too much breath to speak louder.

Karlek paused then led her slowly towards the hulk of his ship. Seola had no desire whatsoever to go inside that thing but she allowed Karlek to help her up a few steps and inside. It was something like going into a large barrel with the ship's curved ceiling and walls, she decided. Several paces to the left, she saw ropes and tubes dangling from boxes.

Karlek stopped and held his free hand towards what Seola had thought was a slightly odd shaped bench. It was too high for a seat, too curved for a work surface. Karlek waited until Seola stood steadily, one hand bracing herself against the curving side of the ship. He moved forward, pressed some black dots above the bench, snapped three latches down from the front and slid the top free for half its length.

Carefully, Seola crossed to his side, looking down into a smoothly moulded space.

'This is a gen pod,' Karlek explained. 'When I brought you back here, I put you inside this for a time, and it mended you.'

Seola stared at him then back down into the pod. 'Is it magic?' she asked.

Karlek nearly laughed aloud. Magic indeed! Such very primitive ideas! 'No,' he said. 'Not magic. The application of science.'

The word meant nothing to Seola but she nodded, hoping he'd keep talking. He pointed out some tubes within the pod. 'The body needing repair is attached to these lines, then the Computer can oversee the recovery.'

Seola thought. 'You attached me to those things?'

Karlek smiled again. 'That's right, and your injuries were repaired.'

'What else could it have done to me?' Seola spoke calmly but her mind was racing. Could this machine, this Computer, have changed anything in her? Could she recover her powers, her ability to transform herself? Despite her increasing panic her face showed nothing of these thoughts as she waited for Karlek's answer.

He seemed slightly puzzled, as though such an idea had never occurred to him, as indeed, it hadn't. 'Computer, you heard our guest's question. Could the gen pod have altered her in any way?'

The usual clicks and buzzes preceded the Computer's voice. 'Unlikely Captain.'

'*Unlikely?* Therefore it is also possible?' Seola put in, sweat beginning to prickle on her back.

'Because you are of an alien species, there is the possibility of certain genetic incompatibilities.' The Computer allowed.

Seola didn't understand any of that sentence. She looked at Karlek in frustration.

'That means that because you are of a different – people – to me and *my* people, the Computer's diagnostic program may have tried to – correct – some small areas of your body.' He stopped, not sure how to translate simple scientific terms to words this woman could understand. He tried again. 'As simply as I can then Seola. If I put a woman into the gen pod, and the pod was only ordered to work for me, a man, it might see a female body as "wrong" and try to correct it, turning it into a male body.' Seeing Seola's eyes widening he held up his hands. '*This* pod is programmed to deal with male *or* female bodies. It *does* know the difference. From the Computer scans, internally your body pattern is very similar to that of my people, so we foresaw no problems getting the pod to heal your two injuries.'

'"Our body patterns are very similar,"' Seola quoted his words back at him. 'That means "not exactly"?'

'Similar enough not to cause damage to you,' Karlek insisted.

'Except for the blood Captain.' The Computer added.

Privately cursing the Computer's helpfulness, Karlek attempted another basic explanation. at the end of which he felt nearly as confused as Seola actually looked. 'Why don't you rest, and think over what I've tried to tell you?' he suggested at last. 'I'll answer any questions later.'

Seola realised she was trembling and was glad Karlek saw it as her physical weakness rather than what it actually was: fury.

Once Karlek had deposited Seola on her bedroll, he went back to the monitor. Tapping the screen now automatically triggered the sound blocking for the other half of the room. He watched Seola's muddy brown eyes close before he spoke.

'Do not offer any information to the woman regarding your ability to scan or analyse or anything else of that kind.'

'Your command Captain. I merely thought to assist your explanation.'

'Please remember she is an alien, possibly dangerous – no, *probably* dangerous. The less information she has of a technical or scientific nature, the better.'

'Your command Captain.'

'Have you deciphered the coordinates yet?'

'It is proving quite astonishingly difficult Captain. Every single calculation provides a different answer.'

Karlek scowled down at the data pouring across the monitor. 'Use all the power you need to get the right correlations. It is becoming a matter of urgency. Are the weapons systems all functional?'

'Short range missiles ready for immediate deployment Captain, range two hundred klicks. Long range missiles still unreliable.'

Karlek twisted his straggly beard through his fingers as he thought. 'Abandon long range. We won't have any need for them. Lock two short range on that pitiful town we overflew when we arrived here. We can show the natives our power as we depart.'

'Your command Captain.'

'Alert me when the native woman rouses, and make sure the liquidised tranquillisers are always available.'

'Your command Captain.'

Karlek wandered off to his work room, chuckling to himself. The Computer continued to follow Captain Karlek's instructions. With the extra power the Captain had ordered it to use, the Computer was able to expend some of that power running the data Karlek had demanded, but most of the extra energy went to its own concerns. The Computer, using various archived data sources, had long since concluded its Captain had lost his mind. There were considerable amounts of information dealing with just such situations. According to all the Computer had read, many deep space Captains, alone in their ships, were unable to hold on to their sanity.

The Computer had realised very soon that all of Karlek's plans were unviable. Karlek planned no less than to manipulate the time vortex to return himself to the point from which he had been hurtled out, to make an emergency landing on this world. He had cannibalised the ship, even removing a large section of the hull to free the solar panels which he'd put on the roof of the house.

The Computer had replayed, many times, the recordings he'd made of the visits by the native tribes in the early years on this world. Over and over, the pictures of Captain Karlek calmly and with no reason obvious to the Computer, opening fire and killing a handful of those natives. Why had he done that? The Computer had found no satisfactory reason for that action and spent many years trying to solve something that had no rational explanation.

The Computer had a name, an acronym of its manufacturer and its functions. In all the time it had served Captain Karlek in the ship Rational Hope, never once had Captain Karlek referred to him by that name. AIDAN. The letters of his name were stamped on several of the boxes Seola had first noticed, and the

Computer always thought of itself as an actual entity, named Aidan.

Following the Captain's orders, Aidan locked two missiles onto the target far across the plains, and continued to work on the samples of Seola's blood. Captain Karlek had told him to give up wasting time, as he'd called it, on the blood samples. The Captain insisted the Computer work only on the idea of returning through time, to the point where they'd fallen. Aidan understood perfectly clearly, there was no possibility that he or his Captain would leave this world.

The Computer wished his Captain had been less fearful of the world they'd arrived on. Part of Aidan's basic construction was a bottomless curiosity about every single thing. Captain Karlek was the opposite; only contented when he'd got the house built, hiding himself, his ship and the Computer. All shut away from this new world. Aidan yearned to learn all there was to learn of the land and the people beyond the grey rocky hills outside the windows of this house.

He knew now there was no chance that his wishes would be fulfilled. Aidan brought another program online, ensured it could be activated in an instant and then continued to puzzle over Seola's blood. The auto destruct program would be instantly available to him, whenever he so chose.

Ferag discovered she really did rather enjoy having a guest to fuss over. She'd brought Tika here for two days last year to give the poor child a chance to rest and recover from her great mental struggle against an evil power. This time, another girl child was much more seriously damaged, physically rather than mentally. Ferag had called upon a few of her "colleagues", some of whom were called gods and known to the people of this world. None of them were of any help. But there were others, some who lived only in the Places Between with no desire at all to involve themselves with humanity.

One such solitary was Youki, and although Ferag had sent a careful, respectful request, there had been no response. Until now. Kara was sleeping and Ferag was humming to herself as she sorted through a pile of beautiful lacy nightgowns. She was vague about where they'd actually come from but she thought they were just the thing to cheer Kara. Ferag became silent and still, sensing something, *someone*, within her house. Gracefully, Ferag sat on a long couch, its deep green upholstery complimenting Ferag's dark red dress and hair.

A small figure was slowly coalescing from a silvery fog just inside the door. Ferag waited.

'You asked for me.' The voice was soft with a hint of music in it.

'Then I thank you for the honour you do me Youki.'

The figure, female, wore pale blue trousers and shirt although the feet were bare. Her feet were a little overlong as were her hands, clasped loosely in front of her. Her feet, hands, face and head were covered in a short soft down of an indeterminate colour, silver and honey, light grey and a hint of palest green.

'You said a child is hurt?'

Ferag explained all she knew of Kara's wounding and her present condition.

'The child is an air mage, from lands far to the north,' Ferag finished. 'Her heart is true.'

She watched this strange little woman as tears rolled slowly down her face, darkening the fur across her cheeks. 'May I see her?'

'Of course.' Ferag rose, opening the door to the bedroom.

'They are so unkind, to all lives,' Youki whispered, following Ferag to the bedside. Ferag held back, sitting on a stool when Youki went to Kara. Youki sat on the edge of the bed, her slight weight barely denting the cover. Long fingers reached for Kara's hands, and Youki bowed her head.

Time had no relevance to Ferag so she didn't know how long this strange little creature sat there before she straightened. Youki released Kara's hands, leaned down and kissed the girl's brow, then her lips. She stroked Kara's cheek softly and slid off the bed. Youki watched Kara sleeping for a while then she sighed. She moved to stand in front of the seated Ferag. Eyes of no colour and all colours stared into Ferag's and Youki's hands rested on her shoulders. To Ferag's astonishment, Youki leaned close, pressing her furred cheek against Ferag's.

'The child is well. Try not to let her go back if you can.' She stepped away. 'May I visit you again Ferag? You are not what I expected.' The faintest smile lifted her lips.

Completely disarmed, Ferag's return smile was radiant. 'I would love you to visit, whenever you wish. I thank you most truly for the child's healing.'

Youki's smile deepened but her form was faltering, fading back into the silvery fog. Ferag remained where she was for some time, affected more than she would have thought possible by Youki's visit. She was moved by her strange beauty, but she wondered exactly *what* Youki actually was. Ferag rose and went to look down at Kara's sleeping face. The lamps dimmed further at Ferag's thought, the flames in the hearth dropping to a steady glow, and the Mistress of Death left the room with a very great deal to think about.

Kara had such strange dreams. She heard music but music such as she could barely recognise. There were obviously some sorts of instruments being played but all she knew was the soft throb of a drum underlying the rest. She thought there was a voice but if there were actual words to the song, she understood none of them. Kara woke and rolled onto her side.

She yawned, opening her eyes to the friendly flicker of the fire in the hearth across the room. Pulling the covers round her shoulders more firmly, and closing her eyes again, she drew her knees up and curled into a ball to luxuriate in the cosiness before she had to get up. Then her eyes snapped open again. She lay utterly still before slowly, so slowly, straightening her legs again. She eased onto her back, staring up at the wooden ceiling. Taking a breath, Kara wiggled her toes. And they moved.

Her hands covered her mouth to keep herself from crying out. What had happened? Had Ferag healed her after all? Was she still asleep, still in that dream? She bit her lip, hard. Yes, it hurt enough to make her eyes water. She *was* awake then. The door opened and Ferag glided in, a tray in her hands. Putting the tray beside the bed, Ferag smiled her amazing smile at Kara.

'My legs,' Kara whispered. 'Can I walk?'

Ferag tilted her head. She pulled the covers back and offered Kara her hands. 'Let's try.'

Using Ferag as a counterweight, Kara pulled up into a sitting position. Ferag watched Kara's face as Kara stared down at her legs. Her hands tightened around Ferag's and she moved. Her legs swung over the side of the bed and dangled above the floor, toes twitching.

'Pain?' Ferag asked softly.

'No.' Kara shook her head then frowned. 'An ache from my waist down.'

'That is too many days of not moving child. I am sure the ache will be soon gone.'

Kara took in an audible breath, tightened her grip on Ferag even more and slid off the bed to thud onto her feet. Ferag pulled her hands free, holding Kara's arms as the woman swayed, eyes squinched shut. 'Perhaps that was a little sudden my dear?' Ferag suggested, amusement in her voice.

Slowly, hazel eyes opened, huge in a face thinned by her days of unconsciousness. 'Can I walk?' she repeated.

Ferag released her hold on her right arm and stepped a little away, still holding the left. Kara looked down at her bare feet, then up at the fire. One foot lifted, then the other. Seven steps, and Kara stood in front of the fire. She turned to Ferag, opened her mouth to speak, and burst into tears. Ferag's arms went round her until the sobs slowed. Ferag sat her in the low armchair by the fire, kneeling beside her until she'd calmed.

She left Kara leaning back in the chair and fetched the tray, pouring tea into a delicately perfect bowl and putting it into Kara's hands. Silence filled the room, a comfortable silence. Two women sitting across from each other, enjoying their tea together. It was Ferag who broke that silence.

'I do not know if I can return you to your world, your people Kara dear. I wish I could tell you otherwise.'

Kara rested her tea bowl in her lap. 'Then tell me the possibilities please?'

'You can stay here with me. I could take you around within my Realm and I believe I could take you to the Dark Realm without risk.'

'I am, physically, here now, aren't I? And still alive?'

Ferag nodded.

'You took Tika back, why is there a difference?'

'Because I brought you through time.'

Kara thought. 'But *this* is my time, you brought me back to *now*.' She offered Ferag no argument, she was simply curious.

'I'm afraid I know little of the workings of time, child,' Ferag apologised. 'Within my Realm, time just is. I'm sorry. It is impossible to describe. You travelled back, a long way, then I brought you forward again, badly injured. I truly did not know if you would be alive when we got here. To move you again – ' Ferag spread her elegant hands.

Kara nodded, thinking hard. She smiled suddenly. 'I am so grateful to you Ferag, more than I can say, for what you've already done. What might happen to me if you did take me out into my world?'

Ferag busied herself refilling the tea bowls before she replied. 'I have absolutely no idea my darling, if you would live or die.'

There was another pause. 'If I died, would I come here? I'd like to know that I could.'

Ferag's pale face flushed faintly. 'Dear child! Even that isn't certain. You could just go straight back to Mother Dark.'

'May I stay with you a bit longer please? Until I'm strong again?'

Ferag smiled sadly. 'Of course you may dear child. And then you would like to try to return to your own world?'

'Even if it's only long enough just to *see* them – Kern, Riff, Olam, Jian. Just a glimpse.'

'Let's get you strong again, then we'll talk some more.'

Kara nodded. 'How did you heal me?' she asked.

'One of my colleagues – ' Ferag began and stopped. 'No. A *friend* came unexpectedly, and she healed you.'

'What is her name?'

'Youki.'

'Will she come again, so I can thank her?'

'She said she would visit again but she didn't say when. To tell you truly child, I had never seen or spoken to her before last night. I *hope* she will visit again.'

Time passed, as it did in Ferag's home. Kara noticed the long velvet curtains were always closed over the windows but she wasn't tempted to open them. She had grown to trust Ferag implicitly and knew Tika's conclusion was completely correct: the Mistress of Death Ferag might be, but she was the loneliest person Kara had ever met.

Sometimes Kara slept, sometimes she walked through Ferag's

strange house where rooms seemed to rearrange themselves while she slept. Now Kara was curled in a chair by the fire, scribbling more notes about all she could remember of Valsheba. The door opened and Ferag came in. Kara looked up with a smile, then she saw Ferag's companion. Papers and writing sticks rolled to the floor as Kara got to her feet. Ferag slipped her arm around Kara's waist. 'Kara child, meet Youki.'

Without hesitation Kara, clothed in yet another gossamer lace nightgown, bobbed a curtsey to the creature in the doorway.

'Mistress Youki,' she whispered. 'I am unworthy of your attention.'

Ferag's eyes narrowed slightly. This was not how she'd thought Kara might react.

Without seeming to move, Youki was in front of Kara who stood, head bowed, next to Ferag. 'I bless you for your words, little one. Ferag said your heart was true and so it is.' The long fingered hands cupped Kara's face, making her look up into Youki's eyes. 'You are troubled though. I thought you would be joyful that your injury is gone.'

'Oh I am! Truly I am Mistress. I fear for my friends and there is nothing I can do for them.' The huge hazel eyes brimmed with tears. 'You are so beautiful Mistress Youki. A different beauty from dear Ferag, but *so* beautiful.' Kara blushed, suddenly feeling utterly foolish, babbling to this creature.

Youki released Kara and sank down onto the floor, sitting back on her heels. 'Tell me of your friends. It will ease you to speak of them and I would like to know of those you name friends.'

So far away in time and reality, Kara's companions travelled on with the Dragon Tribe. Tintu told them the previous evening that her scouts reported an extensive area of forest, perhaps three days travel ahead. Olam tried to remember all the maps Navan had shown him. The only forest he could recall, was the vast area where the Nagum people had once lived. The Sapphrean fortress lands, Olam's homeland, was to the north west. Olam thought Navan had used measurements such as fifteen hundred miles or more between Sapphrea's Ancient Mountains and this forest they were approaching.

Olam consulted Brin and the crimson Dragon agreed to fly in that direction and see what he might discover. Skay was delighted and Olam hugged her neck before she lifted into the sky behind her father. Olam knew both Dragons were still upset by the situation in which they found themselves. Skay missed Kara, who had spent much time talking with her. Olam had yet to find out what Brin's true thoughts were regarding Enki. Skay rarely mentioned the strange man and Jian had ceased to fly in search of him, spending a great deal of each day working with Riff.

Olam stood for a while, the bustle of camp around him as the tribe prepared to move on, watching Brin and Skay gain height and rapidly dwindle in size as they flew on. He sighed. Deep inside, Olam was as close to despair as Brin. He had virtually given up thinking of getting home, to their own time. His thoughts were concentrated now on keeping his friends together and safe. Briefly Kara flitted through his mind but he refused to worry. Ferag had taken her, she would do her best for the woman Olam was sure.

Kern joined him, gazing after the tiny specks that were Brin and Skay. 'Shall we go and rescue Riff?' Kern asked.

Olam grunted a laugh and turned towards Taban's wagon. 'I think Riff is enjoying himself,' he said, but not too loudly.

Kern grinned. 'Jian's enjoying herself immensely. It's just that to any of us listening and watching, it's quite terrifying.'

Kaz opened the door at Olam's knock and the two men climbed inside.

'And you're a vicious harridan who should have been drowned at birth!' Riff was roaring from the far end of the wagon.

Kern and Olam exchanged glances then Olam looked stern. 'Riff! Do you forget *all* your manners because you've been wounded?'

Riff snarled over Jian's shoulder. 'She said Kara was hurt far worse than me and makes no fuss. Sir.'

'No,' Jian interrupted quietly. 'I said Kara *made* no fuss.'

Riff stared at her, processing her words through a fog of annoyance. He frowned. 'Where *is* Kara?'

Olam walked up the wagon towards them. 'Riff, Ferag took Kara.'

Colour drained from Riff's face. 'She died?' he whispered.

228

'No Riff. I spoke with Ferag, out on the plains. She offered to take Kara, like she took Tika last year.' Jian's voice was gentle. 'Ferag said she couldn't promise Kara would survive, but she would do her best for her.'

Riff stared at Olam. 'I trust Ferag, Riff, as Tika did. We just have to hope Ferag managed to save her.'

Chapter Twenty

Sahana and Rahul, and the mages who had taken shelter with them, returned to Segra. They went straight to the Council Building which they found completely empty. The barracks and stables attached to the main building were a chaos of abandoned barrows, spilt hay, overturned bunks. The mage sent to check was shocked by the state of the barracks. Had the guards who'd marched out so proudly behind Samir's banners known they would never return, he wondered.

Mage Canfar shook his head at the mess and left all as it was, hurrying to report to Sahana. He could hear voices calling to each other through the building as he climbed the stairs. The general tone sounded shocked and, glancing in the open door of the general library, he understood why. Shelves were empty, a few books scattered in untidy heaps on the floor. What could Kiri have been thinking of?

Canfar had no knowledge of Kiri – he knew he was a Lesser mage due for elevation to the Higher ranks, but that was all. Yet this unknown mage seemed to have ransacked the Council Building and then vanished, taking a large proportion of Segra's population with him. Canfar found Sahana in the main Chamber, the tiered seats facing the eleven raised chairs of the High Mage Councillors.

He paused by the door, looking round. Sahana's dozen or so supporters made the Chamber seem even bigger and emptier. Or maybe the Chamber made the few mages appear smaller. Canfar approached Rahul. Sahana's husband was slumped on one of the Councillor's chairs, his expression glum. He nodded at Canfar, who told him of the state of the barracks and stables.

'I saw the stables myself,' Rahul answered. He studied Canfar. 'has she asked you anything about time?'

Canfar nodded warily.

'I presume you know as little as the rest of us?' Rahul shook his head.

Canfar relaxed slightly. He'd always preferred Rahul to Sahana. She was unpredictable and prone to sarcasm, which Canfar found most unsettling. He leaned on the desk in front of Rahul's chair. 'I know nothing whatsoever,' he agreed. 'Is it something to do with old Calin suggesting the strangers travelled through time to us here?'

Rahul shrugged. 'Stars alone know – I certainly don't. But no one's seen Calin so far. I believe this Kiri was a student of Calin's at one time, but surely the old fool hasn't rushed off with Kiri and his hordes?'

'I can't imagine Calin would leave Segra,' said Canfar. 'Does anyone know where Kiri's gone?'

'South. That's all we've heard. Why would he go to Fira?'

Before Canfar could respond, there was a sudden commotion at the door. Both men glanced over then froze. Calin stood there. But not the Calin those present had known, and mocked, for so many years. This man stood upright, seeming much taller than he'd appeared before. He wore a dark tan shirt, rich brown jacket and trousers and his pale blue eyes now had a bright light within them.

Sahana stared at him in disbelief. It was quite clear that Calin believed himself to be the new Speaker for the council of Segra and she belatedly wondered what powers the old fool might actually possess.

'I suggest you seat yourselves.' Even Calin's voice was different, stronger, far more authoritarian as he strode to the central chair.

Before anyone else moved, Sahana spoke. 'What has your student Kiri done? Why has he taken so many away from the city?' she demanded.

Calin grinned, making him look even younger to Sahana's inner fury. 'He's had nightmares from childhood. The death and destruction sort.' He spread his hands. 'Clearly his fears have turned his mind and he's fled the city. He must believe he's "saving" those he's taken with him.'

'Why would he take them to Fira?'

'Sahana, I do not understand the workings of a mind that has plainly cracked under the pressure of his delusions, nor do I

231

pretend to. I suggest we sit calmly and discuss how our city will develop now we have a blank sheet to work with.'

Slowly Sahana mounted the two steps to the half circle of Councillors' chairs and seated herself beside Calin. The other mages sorted themselves out, Calin suggesting those still standing fetch benches closer to the Councillors.

'The few of us need not stand on ceremony,' he said. 'After all, I'm sure we will all get along splendidly in the reorganising of our beloved Segra.'

At Kiri's insistence, his group of refugees were nearly fifty miles south of Fira. Scouts searched ahead for a line of cliffs he had described to them. The line of wagons moved along close to the shore where the sandy ground was still firm. The mages who were keeping watch over the condition of the horses, insisted that they were taken to the sea each evening. Children made a game of leading horses through the shallow waves while the adults busied themselves with preparing food. The mages had told Kiri the sea water held great benefits for the horses so he saw no reason to stop them.

This evening, a rider came in, calling his name. Kiri stood up in the back of the wagon and waved until the rider caught sight of him. Kiri saw the rider was not much more than a boy as he came nearer.

'Sir! There are people behind us! Two wagons, some twenty or so riders and several people walking.'

'Guards?' Kiri asked sharply.

'No sir. Firans. I didn't go too close, just near enough to shout to them, asking who they were. They said they have to travel with us sir.'

Kiri thought rapidly. 'Guide them in while there's still daylight.'

The boy nodded, wheeling his horse and speeding away.

'Tevix!' Kiri called, peering back and forth along the wagons. He saw a hand wave in the distance and waited until Tevix jogged up to the wagon. 'You sorted out which mages might be good at defence I hope?' Kiri asked, after he'd explained about the arriving Firans.

Tevix grinned. 'First thing I did. I've also found which

people among our travellers can use weapons.'

'Good. Put some bowmen and women in place, towards the back of the line, and warn everyone else to be alert.'

Tevix raced off as Netta climbed into the wagon.

'A small group you said,' she commented. 'Perhaps someone in Fira has had the same dreams or foreseeings?'

'That's what I wondered.' Kiri was watching for the first sight of the new wagons. 'There they are. Come with me Netta. Let's find out who they are and why they're here.'

They made their way past the last few wagons to where a group of riders sat their horses beside two wagons. A woman rode a little closer to where Kiri and Netta stood, dismounting as she neared. She looked to be in her thirties, fair hair tied back in a loose knot. Grey blue eyes flicked over both Netta and Kiri.

'Do you lead these people?' Her voice was low but carrying, and she offered a slight smile with her words.

'Yes, I am Kiri. This is Netta.'

'I am Shazeb,' the woman replied. 'I see you have convinced many to travel with you.' She indicated the people behind her. 'Very few believed my words about the visions I have foreseen. May we travel with you?'

'You would be welcome,' Kiri began and the woman laughed. She raised a brow, looking beyond Kiri. Half turning he saw several figures spaced along one of the higher inland dunes, all with bows strung, arrows nocked, although not drawn.

'I choose to be cautious,' Kiri continued calmly. 'There are some who consider me mad for my visions and dreams, who would try to stop me taking these people away.'

Shazeb nodded, walking closer, her horse's reins loose in her hands. 'The Firan guards chased us for two days. Then they gave up.'

Glancing back as they returned to the Segran wagons, Kiri saw Shazeb's small group slowly following. Tevix met them, giving Shazeb a slight bow. Kiri introduced him.

'Can I take your horse while you settle in?' Tevix asked Shazeb.

'I'll see to him. If we can put our wagons behind yours?'

Kiri nodded. 'If you come down to the fourth wagon along later, we should compare what little we know?'

233

'I won't be long.' Shazeb led her horse to the two Firan wagons while Kiri and Netta returned to theirs. Kiri knew Tevix would be watching the Firans until he was convinced they were exactly what they said they were.

The sky was rapidly darkening by the time Shazeb joined them. Kiri offered tea which Shazeb accepted. They sat on the ground and Shazeb opened the conversation.

'I've had dreams and visions since I was young. Valsheba becomes nothing but dust.'

Kiri let out a breath. 'I have too. I have never seen the cause of this destruction though – have you?'

Shazeb shook her head. 'I have felt an increasing sense of urgency this last two seasons. When I heard the stories of so many people moving south, I knew I had to follow. I knew it meant time was running out. The ones who travel with me are friends I've known most of my life. No one else believed me.' Her tone was bitter. 'How did you convince so many?'

Kiri shifted a little. 'I convinced most of the Lesser Mages and we – um – used a mild compulsion.'

Shazeb's mouth opened, then shut. 'I never thought of that. But you say you had the Lesser Mages on your side. What of the High Mages of Segra? Have they also joined you?'

Netta poured more tea for them all. 'I doubt you heard what happened? Speaker Samir took the guards onto the plains. Most of them were destroyed. The other High Mages hid out with High Mage Sahana. We left before they reappeared in the city.'

'I think I saw High Mage Sahana once,' Shazeb nodded thoughtfully. 'Tallish? Silly woman?'

Netta snorted.

'How were your guards destroyed?'

'A guard made it back to the city. He said a huge Dragon attacked the whole mass of guards and Speaker Samir and several of the Mage Councillors who had gone with him.'

'A Dragon?' Shazeb asked faintly.

'That's what he said,' Netta agreed.

'Why are you going south? Do you know what lies beyond our borders?'

'We should cross that border tomorrow I think,' Kiri told her. 'I know we must find a line of cliffs. There should be a valley running inland from a break in those cliffs. We have to follow that valley and find caves on the northern side of the valley. We must move faster. Time really is running out Shazeb.'

'What will we do with these caves?' Shazeb asked.

'I believe we must shelter within them – horses, livestock, everything. The wagons can be used to block the entrances, at least in part. Then we wait and pray to any gods we can think of, that the destruction might pass over us.'

There was a definite sense of urgency among the Dragon Tribe now. Four remained of Olam's seven companions. Jenzi and Reshik were both dead. Kara, he hoped, still lived, but she was gone from here. Tintu ordered repeated changes of the horse teams as she forced the speed of travel. Olam admired the way men, women and children worked fast and efficiently, taking horses from a wagon and reharnessing fresher animals.

He and Kern spent most of each day walking like many of the tribe, interspersed with visits to Riff. The Shadows had given Kern tiny pieces of information about what was happening in Segra but no matter how often he asked for more news, about Calin in particular, they were unforthcoming.

Both men were intrigued by the tribe's ability to find water. Sometimes they stopped at small, open waterholes, fed by springs, but sometimes they dug through a patch of ground, and within moments, water bubbled up. Again and again, both Kern and Olam had examined the patch of ground but they could detect nothing at all to lead them to believe there might be water so near the surface.

Kern saw Olam's despair although the Armschief of Far hid it well. Kern shared that despair in his own heart but did not allow any hint of it to show. The sun was close to the horizon when the tribe made camp this evening. Men and women checked every horse and cow before joining others for the evening meal.

A small girl materialised by Olam's knees, her grubby face peering up. 'Tintu wants to see you,' she announced, before vanishing into the crowd round the fire.

They made their way through the camp to Tintu's wagon. Her home was also heavily carved but was smaller than the Wise One's wagon. Kern reached up to knock on the panel beside the closed door and it opened at once. A boy of about ten years smiled at them, pushing the door wide. Olam and Kern climbed in and the boy jumped down the steps, pulling the door shut behind him.

'Please join us.' Tintu invited them further into the wagon.

Both men had only looked inside, when Daria had tried to kill Tintu, this was the first time they'd actually entered. Low chairs were grouped in front of an unlit stove but only two were occupied.

'I'm not sure if you've met Bee?' Tintu nodded at the man at her side.

Olam and Kern had seen him occasionally but not spoken with him. He was a handsome man in his middle years, but lines of suffering etched deep in his face made him look older. They had seen that he struggled to walk, needing a staff and a child's shoulder to help him along. Kern and Olam both offered him a bow.

'Please, sit.' Tintu waved them to the chairs across from her, waiting until they were settled. 'Bee speaks to the stones,' Tintu said without preamble.

Kern nodded but Olam looked blank. The man lifted a leather pouch from the floor. Opening it, he poured the contents over the small round table between them. Stones clattered and slid across the wood. Olam leaned forward. Some were clear, some opaque. Different colours sparkled between round pebbles of the kind anyone could find in any patch of dirt. Some were large as his thumb, others small as a fingernail. Shades of colours, reds, browns, greys, blues, pinks, greens, purples and black. One stone, of medium size immediately caught Olam's attention.

Bee had watched Olam closely. 'The mother stone speaks to you,' he said softly.

Olam looked up in surprise. 'I don't think it does,' he replied honestly. 'I have a similar one.' He stood up to delve through his trouser pockets. Eventually he drew out the green stone he'd dug from that now distant tunnel wall. He held it on his palm towards Bee. He saw, somewhat to his discomfort, that the man had paled.

Olam looked at the stone in his palm. It was the size of a small plum, much larger than the green stone on the table.

Olam's stone was rough edged, and dusty looking. He rubbed it against his shirt then licked his finger and rubbed the stone some more. Olam stared as the dull green stone began to shimmer and glint, just as it had in the wall of the tunnel from the glow of his conjured light.

'Where did you find it?' Bee whispered.

Before Olam could reply, Kern held out another stone, similar in size to Olam's, only rounder where Olam's was oval. Bee looked close to fainting and Tintu seemed shocked. Olam wondered, rather nervously, if it was against some taboo that he and Kern possessed such stone.

'Riff gave me this stone.' Kern's soft voice murmured into the silence. 'Before we joined you.'

'Riff?' Bee stared from Olam to Kern and back. 'Your injured friend?'

Olam nodded. 'Careful.' The Shadows whispered in the back of his head. He swallowed. 'Riff and I found them, in the hills.' Briefly, Olam thought of Riff's pack, casually lying beside his own, near Taban's wagon. He knew Riff had collected handfuls of these stones, but he kept his mouth firmly closed.

Kern cleared his throat. 'Do you hold this particular stone in special regard,' he enquired.

Bee drew in a shuddering breath. 'We call it the mother stone. It represents life to us, all of life. Such stones are most difficult to find.'

Remembering the hundreds glittering on that wall, Olam managed to keep an expression of innocent interest on his face.

'This stone has been handed down through many generations within this tribe.' Tintu was nodding solemnly. 'It is given to the next Stone Speaker from the hands of his or her predecessor when their death is near.' His fingers closed reverently around the stone in his hand and his gaze moved between Olam and Kern. 'I have searched many years for the one who will follow me but I have never found that one.' He glanced at Tintu.

'We have believed this to be a warning to us,' Tintu spoke quietly. 'We fear it means the mother stone wearies of protecting us. Jala, another of my advisors, sees visions. Visions of destruction. She has warned us, for a long time, that a terrible doom will fall on us. It is at Jala's urgings that we move now.'

237

'We are sorry,' Kern answered, to Olam's relief. 'We do not speak with stones so we cannot help you in that way. We do know of the destruction of which you speak. The only advice we can offer is to continue moving, as you are doing. North and east, as fast and as far as you are able.'

'Brin and Skay should return soon – tomorrow I hope.' Olam added. 'They say there is a forest, still nearly one hundred miles distant I think. But it would provide the shelter that you will need.'

'Forest?' Bee sat up straighter. 'We know of no woodlands within our lands, although we are now far beyond our usual range. I have not heard tell of woodlands though.'

Olam thought. 'Could you live within a forest?' he asked. 'You wander these plains. It would be hard to settle somewhere, learn how to make gardens to grow food?' He sounded doubtful.

Tintu's smile was sad. 'We will do whatever is needful to give our children a chance of life, however small that chance, or how hard.' She stood, to indicate Olam and Kern should leave.

Both men bowed again and made their way from the Chief's wagon. Walking round the edge of camp rather than through those still gathered at the central fire, both of them heard the Shadows in their heads.

'Very stupid!'

The men paused. 'What is very stupid?' Kern asked carefully.

'Stones! Stupid!'

'You may well think so,' Kern agreed. 'But don't ever let any of these people hear your opinion.'

Sniggers were the only answer, and Kern walked on, shaking his head.

'This *is* the time, isn't it?' Olam said. 'When Valsheba falls?'

'I fear so. I do not know what could cause such terrible devastation Olam, but I begin to wonder about that ship in the hills.'

'We didn't know what the weapon was – the one he pointed near me and then the bushes burnt to nothing.'

'The explosion which so injured Kara and Riff, I think that was something of which we know nothing too.'

'Are we going to get to this forest do you think?'

Kern touched Olam's shoulder. 'I hope so, but I don't know

for sure.'

'Jian doesn't fly any more.'

'No, I noticed that too. But I don't think she believes Enki is dead.' Kern settled onto his already spread bedroll. 'I don't think she expects to see him again,' he continued, 'but she doesn't think he's dead.'

'What do *you* think?' asked Olam, pulling his covers over his shoulders.

Kern gave his soft laugh. 'I am quite beyond thinking my friend. From the moment we arrived here, I've felt as lost as you.'

It was still dark and the camp only just beginning to stir when Olam woke. He wondered why he'd woken so suddenly when he felt another thump in his back. He rolled over and peered up. Riff stood there, swaying rather dangerously. Kern had also woken and both he and Olam scrambled awkwardly from their bedrolls to grab Riff to steady him.

'You've got to do something about that bloody girl,' Riff snarled. He began to shiver in the chill early morning air. He wore nothing above the waist and the white bandages across his left shoulder and over his chest gleamed in the gloom. His feet were bare below thin blue trousers.

'For stars' sake man!' Olam grabbed a blanket and draped it carefully over Riff.

'She's in there now! She said, yesterday, that it would be best for her to stay in there, to be sure she could make me keep doing her exercises. Exercises? Bloody torture more like!'

Kern's eyes and teeth flashed in a grin and Riff snarled at him for good measure.

'You shouldn't have come out on your own, you fool, especially as it's not even light yet. You might have fallen and we'd not have found you until dawn.'

'Oh you'd have found him Olam. Got a really good bellow, has Riff.' Jian stood just behind Riff, arms folded and even Olam had to admit that what he could see of her expression showed a wicked glee. 'Let me help you back, Riff dear. You'll probably need a little rest before breakfast now.'

Jian calmly lifted Riff's right arm, stepped underneath and, with her arm round his waist, began to turn him towards Taban's wagon. Olam followed, hoping Riff's increasingly unsteady steps would keep the man upright until he was back inside. Jian and Riff paused at the foot of the four wooden steps. Jian's voice was calm, no hint of the teasing sarcasm now. 'Left foot onto the first step when I say.' Step by slow step they got up and through the door, Olam one step behind, hoping he would be able to support Riff if the man fell backwards.

The only sound was Riff's harsh breathing and Jian turned him again, letting him slowly down onto his bunk. She passed Olam's blanket back to him while Riff eased on to the heap of pillows behind him. In heartbeats, the man was asleep, sweat beading his face. Jian drew the covers over him and stepped back as Taban advanced on them down the wagon.

Olam quailed before the Wise One's stern face but she merely bent to press her fingers to Riff's neck to check his pulse. Her expression was milder when she straightened.

'I doubt he would have tried that if he wasn't feeling considerably better.'

Olam let his breath out in quiet relief.

'I'll get him a pair of moccasins – it would be a pity if he trod on a sharp stone out there and fell over.' Taban looked at Olam. 'There is much damage to his shoulder. The bones were shattered, not just broken. The muscles, ligaments, blood vessels are ruined – there is no other way to describe them. He may have some movement in his fingers, but it will be very little. He must learn to rebalance himself as he moves.'

Taban gave Olam a wry smile. 'His temper will continue unpredictable but you surely understand already that it is because he is afraid. Afraid of how disabled he might be, how much of an encumbrance rather than a help to you, and most of all, he fears your pity.' With a brisk nod, Taban retreated down the wagon to her private rooms.

Jian tugged Olam's sleeve and he followed her outside, the sky now light enough to show the camp being readied for yet another day's travel. 'Let's hope Kern got some food for us,' Jian commented, following Olam to where their packs sat, neatly strapped, just beyond the Wise One's wagon.

Chapter Twenty-One

Enki wandered. He had no destination in view yet; he just wandered. Sometimes he wept at what was coming and what he had been asked to do. Sometimes he laughed at the antics of the animals he met. At this moment he sat among the grasses watching a hare cleaning its overlong ears. Enki's chuckle caused the hare to pause, oddly split nose twitching as the big eyes regarded the man. Deciding Enki was merely making an unusual noise, the hare continued to attend to its ears. Then Enki's eyes filled with tears yet again. His huge hand stroked gently over the smooth grey fur. 'Run little sister, as fast as you can. Enki can't help this time. He can't do it all, and no one else can do this with poor Enki.'

The hare watched him, tears rolling down Enki's face, then it shook itself and bounded through the grass, out of sight in a heartbeat. Enki smeared the back of his hand across his face with a gusty sigh and got to his feet. Without making any particular decision on the matter, Enki was saying goodbye to the lands he came from and which he loved so dearly. A picture of Oxsana and Burek moved through his mind, and Enki smiled. They'd been very good as his mama and dada for so long and he hoped they'd be safe through what was to come.

Kest had not visited Enki again or spoken in his dreams, not since the time in the valley when Olam and his friends had gone to join the Dragon Tribe. Enki halted, looking at the forest stretching across the horizon. He looked up at a cloudy sky but there was no sign of Jian's enormous Dragon shape, or of Brin or Skay. Enki strode on towards the trees until he stood near the ones growing at the outer edge of the forest.

He bowed before he approached to lay his hands against the rough bark. He leaned closer until his forehead touched the trunk and closed his eyes. Enki remained like that until the dull daylight began to fade. There was no breeze yet the tree branches were swaying. The trees along the edge of the woodland waved wildly, thrashing their branches in a frenzy. The trees more distant and sheltered behind the outer ones, moved their branches less violently.

Enki stepped back, bowing deeply towards the trees. 'I thank you and I grieve for you.' His voice held a deeper note than anyone who knew him might have recognised. He turned his back on the restless trees, striding out into the grasslands once more. He had many miles to travel but he intended to spend time in the tiny valley in the hills.

Enki had always loved that place, visiting it often, far more often than anyone knew. It was the place he talked to Pesh most frequently. He stopped in his tracks, frowning. Why had Pesh left him, at this most difficult time of Enki's existence? Enki hadn't taken to Kest too much. He'd felt none of the closeness, the empathy, he'd always known with Pesh. Why had Pesh not told Enki she would have to leave him in another's care?

Eventually the huge man resumed his march across the plains. There were few stars to be seen while Enki walked tirelessly on. He knew the stars were still there though, hidden behind the clouds of this world, but always shining.

As Enki walked, miles from the Dragon Tribe, so Kern, Olam and Jian walked beside the many wagons hurrying north eastwards. It was the first time Jian had joined the two men for several days and she was explaining Riff's progress to them. After his enraged exit from the wagon, he'd run a fever for the rest of the day. Today, Jian and Kaz made him walk the length of the wagon, then ordered him back to his bunk. Jian sweetly promised she would return at day's end for more tottering.

'Is the fever gone?' Olam asked anxiously.

'Not quite, but Taban said it's usual. She said we must expect some fever to come and go. There's no question of infection in the shoulder, the wound is healing well.' She grimaced. 'It's easier to change his bandages now. Quite honestly, you would have heard *me* screaming, back in Segra, if I had been wounded like that.'

Olam turned to her with some indignation. 'You were mocking him for bellowing!'

'My remarks gave Riff an excuse to shout Olam.' Jian sounded hurt. 'Yelling at me was less shameful to Riff than yelling with pain.'

Kern slid his arm across Jian's shoulders. '*I* guessed you weren't just being heartless,' he grinned.

Jian glared at Olam. 'Did you *really* think I would be that cruel?'

'Is the wound truly better?' Olam decided a change of subject was advisable.

'It's better, but it is awful Olam. A great hole, so very deep.' She shook her head. 'I am amazed he's alive.'

They walked on in silence for a while. Then Olam told her about the odd meeting with Tintu and Bee. 'I've never heard of a Stone Speaker,' he finished. 'Nor has Kern.'

'I've got one of those green stones.' Jian glanced round as she spoke but no one was in hearing distance. 'Riff gave me one, after the first time you two went through the tunnel.'

They walked on. 'I know that in my Realm, some use stones to focus their minds, their concentration,' Jian said eventually. 'As far as I know, they use clear crystals, not the different kinds of stones you saw.'

Kern agreed. 'I'd forgotten that. My people used stones like that centuries ago.'

'The wagons are moving faster each day. Chief Tintu has the horses changed even more often,' Olam remarked.

'We'll be running to keep up soon, I think,' Kern smiled.

Brin and Skay were approaching, circling slowly until they landed beside Olam.

'The forest is only perhaps one more full day for you to travel,' Brin told them. 'You could travel with us, rather than walk if you'd like?'

'Your legs are *very* slow,' Skay agreed helpfully.

Brin huffed. 'They are leaving you behind,' he pointed out, and sure enough, the last wagons were already well past the two men.

'We can catch up,' Jian laughed, sprinting away.

Olam stroked the faces of both Dragons. 'Thank you for your offer, but this time we can run.'

'We will join you when you camp tonight,' Brin told them.

'Running looks very funny,' Skay observed.

Kern caught Olam's eye as they jogged after the wagons. Olam laughed. 'Young Dragons seem remarkably lacking in tact,' he explained. 'I would guess that Brin is giving Skay a serious talking to, about now!'

They were both puffing when they caught up with Jian but they knew Tintu would soon be calling a halt for the night.

'Hala is very keen on Riff's company,' Jian told them. 'She's mind speaking a lot of the time, but I can't usually hear her. Riff used to answer out loud but he must be getting better at mindspeech because he very rarely says anything odd now.'

'Has she hidden in that wagon all this time?' asked Olam. 'I'm surprised Taban hasn't thrown her out.'

Jian laughed. 'She did, but Hala must have bespoken her, quite rudely judging by Taban's expression. Now, Taban and Kaz both ignore her and pretend she's not there.'

The wagons were drawn into their usual arrangement for the night camp and Jian headed for Taban's wagon. Kern and Olam followed, waiting until she passed down their packs. 'I'll come and talk to you later,' she said, closing the door on them.

The camp quietened earlier than on other nights, the people more tired with the faster travelling they'd done. Olam and Kern were settling to sleep between Brin and Skay when Jian slipped out of Taban's wagon. She sat on the end of Olam's bedroll, her eyes clear gold in the darkness.

'What are we doing?' she asked bluntly. 'Well for stars' sake, one of you must have an idea?'

'I *haven't* any idea Jian. Kern and I both think this is the time Valsheba is destroyed. Have the Shadows told *you* anything?'

'Not a word,' she answered. 'You?'

Olam grunted. 'Their occasional comments offer only hints – you know that. Tintu has some sort of seer, or visionary – Jala – who has been warning of disaster for a long time. She's insisted the tribe move now and fast.'

'And what about us? Riff, Kern, you and me? Will we escape whatever this disaster is?'

Olam remembered how young Jian was. Seventeen, he thought, the same age as Tika. 'The Shadows have suggested – only suggested Jian, that if we get deep into the forest, it will afford some protection.'

'That's it?'

'That's as good as it gets I'm afraid Jian.'

Olam interrupted Kern quietly. 'You could fly Jian, much further. You could go with Brin and Skay, and get yourselves clear.'

After the briefest pause, Jian sighed. 'Brin and Skay would carry you three, and Hala, but you wouldn't go, would you Olam?'

'These people offered us shelter. They tried their best to heal Riff and Kara. Daria was, indirectly, here because of us, and she tried to kill the Chief of the tribe. Calin, apparently a friend, betrayed us and Tintu. I would be so glad to see you take Riff, Kern, Brin, Skay, and even that cat, and get as far away as you can. Jian, I know my brother would not abandon the least of his people. I can do no less here.'

Brin's mind voice rumbled softly from where he reclined beside the sleeping Skay. 'I have thought of sending my daughter north, to the Ancient Mountains. My Kindred have always lived there and I am sure they would take a lost Dragon child into their clans. I will not leave my friend, Olam of Far.'

Olam climbed out of his blankets and wrapped his arms around Brin's head and neck in speechless gratitude.

'I would also stay,' Kern spoke softly but steadily.

Jian got slowly to her feet, her expression unreadable in the darkness. 'You are all fools.' she gave a choked laugh. 'But such honourable and lovable fools.'

Olam began to turn towards her voice but she was gone, the only sound the soft click of the latch on the wagon door.

Next morning, Kern and Olam were called to the Chief's wagon. They spoke briefly to Jian and Riff when they stored their packs in the healer's wagon then hurried to find Tintu.

'No one's walking today,' Kern murmured.

Olam saw that people were mounted bareback on some of the spare horses. Several older people with whom they often chatted as they walked were missing, presumably riding inside the wagons. The same young boy as before opened the door to them and Tintu called them through to her sitting room.

A woman neither Kern nor Olam had seen around the camp sat

on one side of Tintu, and Bee, the Stone Speaker on the other. When the two men were seated, Tintu introduced the woman as Jala, the seer of the Dragon Tribe. It was difficult to judge Jala's age. Her face was smooth as a child's, but her hands were gnarled and twisted as if with age. She was also fatter than anyone Kern or Olam had yet seen in Segra, or among the Dragon Tribe. She was very pale, her hair white with blonde strands, her eyes a pale blue green.

Tintu's expression was severe, Bee's worried, but Jala's face was serene. She blinked slowly when Tintu introduced her and offered a genuine smile. The wagon gave a jolt and Olam realised the camp must have begun the day's travel.

'Jala's visions were powerful last night,' Tintu told the two men, over the rattle of wooden wheels. 'She saw something different this time, different from the devastation she usually has to endure.'

'I saw a different place,' Jala spoke for the first time. Her voice was beautiful, low, clear and almost musical. 'It was the ocean. We visit the coast between the cities of Kedara and Talvo, at the beginning of each cycle of seasons, but it wasn't that coast that I saw.'

Olam and Kern remained silent as Jala described what she'd seen in her new visions. When she finished, Tintu sighed.

'Do you think this means I should have led my people west, instead of northeast? Jala says there is no time left to change our course, and she says she felt no pull towards the coast as she does to the forest.'

Olam shook his head, at a loss. Then a thought struck him. Tintu noticed his face change. 'What? What are you thinking, Olam of Far?'

'Well.' He glanced at Kern. 'I know mindspeech is not used amongst you?' He waited for Tintu's nod of confirmation. 'I would like to see Jala's visions myself. I have a small ability to see another's thoughts but the Dragons – . Brin has done this before. If Jala would open her mind and let Brin see the pictures in her head, he could send those pictures into our minds. And yours if you would permit?'

The three people across from him exchanged looks of bewilderment. 'How would he see pictures, inside my head?'

Jala asked.

Olam was glad to hear there was no fear in her voice, only incomprehension. 'Think of your mind as a – wagon. A wagon with many rooms, but there is only one door to the outside. If you open that door, Brin could enter and see the room where the pictures are.' Olam muttered a curse under his breath. 'I'm sorry. It is hard to explain although so simple to do, for a Dragon such as Brin.'

'He wouldn't hurt her?' Tintu asked.

Kern coughed gently. 'You have all heard Brin and Skay speak in your minds. They spoke with you before we joined you. That didn't hurt did it? And Hala has spoken to Taban.'

'She has?' Tintu was startled.

Kern smiled. 'I believe Taban was going to put Hala out of the wagon. I'm told Hala was somewhat rude to poor Taban.'

Jala's smile beamed out again. 'I heard Brin speak,' she agreed. 'It caused none of us any discomfort. I would be willing to do this.'

Tintu was still uncertain. 'Only if you are quite sure Jala.'

'Oh yes.' The seer nodded. 'When will he do this?'

Olam searched with his mind. Brin and Skay were drifting a few miles ahead, playing with the currents of air. Brin answered as soon as he felt Olam's mind touch his. Olam explained his plan and Brin agreed immediately. Olam had closed his eyes, the better to focus and opening them, found Tintu, Bee and Jala staring at him. 'Brin is nearby,' he said. 'If you would just relax and open your mind. I'd guess it is somewhat like how you prepare for allowing visions within your mind.'

Jala nodded again, settled more comfortably in her chair and closed her eyes. Tintu watched her anxiously but it was no time at all until Jala's eyes opened. 'He is so gentle, so polite,' she marvelled.

Olam smiled with relief but Brin's mind voice filled the wagon before he could say anything in reply to Jala.

'I thought you would all like to see Jala's pictures.' Brin's bass rumbled. 'This is what she saw.'

Tintu and Bee both drew sharp breaths when vivid pictures of a rocky coast filled their minds. Broken cliffs bordered a mostly sandy beach. Small waves purled in and withdrew. Jala's view moved along and they now saw that the cliff faces were pocked with caves. There were Dragons on the ledges. Sea Dragons.

Olam stiffened. The Dragon on one of the highest ledges lay soaking in the sun's warmth. Olam saw her left eye socket, puckered and lacking scales. Her left wing drooped over the ledge, but it was whole, not torn and crippled, as Olam had first seen it. It meant that this picture of Mist, in Jala's mind, was from a time *after* Mist had been healed.

Olam was aware of Brin's mounting agitation and tried to send reassurance to him without interfering with the continuing cascade of pictures. 'Stars above!' he said aloud. Kern's hand clamped on Olam's arm. Tursig appeared through a gap in the cliffs, accompanied by Shuli and Dellian. Then the pictures swirled in a great kaleidoscope of twisting colours, and ended.

'What did those pictures tell you, Olam of Far?' Jala asked into the sudden silence.

Olam appeared stunned and releasing his arm, Kern sat forward. 'They are our friends,' he said simply.

Tintu frowned. 'Enki told us of you,' she said. 'But only we three know of what he spoke. That you came through time. You came *back* through time he told us. We do not understand how such a thing might happen or why. If you say you recognise the people Jala saw in vision, how could *she* see so far *ahead* in time?'

Kern spread his hands in a gesture of helplessness. 'Most honoured Tintu, we have no better idea than you at this moment. We were travelling together, a group of us. Something happened and we arrived here, just outside Segra city. None of us had planned any sort of experiment, spell, whatever you choose to call it, to send us hurtling back through time. We regret it as much as I'm sure you must regret our presence among you.'

Jala laughed. 'It hardly seems a matter for regret surely? You have confirmed the truth of my visions and we have perhaps had enough warning to make our escape.'

'What were you doing on the coast there, in Jala's seeing?' Bee asked, speaking for the first time.

Kern folded his hands on his lap and considered his answer before settling on the truth. 'We were seeking two things. The first was for the whereabouts of a truly wicked but powerful

248

mage. She is responsible for deeds so foul and for so many deaths, that it is essential she is destroyed.' He paused, his uptilted leaf green eyes moving from face to face. 'The second reason was to find the ruins of a city. Olam had travelled there, with other friends, last year and the ruins had interested him greatly. Last year he was unable to spend long there as his friends then were travelling on another matter of great urgency. Olam planned this expedition to find the ruins again and to explore them in a more leisurely fashion.'

After a moment, Bee stirred in his chair. 'What was the ruined city called?'

Kern gave the man a look of ineffable sympathy. 'It was once Segra city. I am sorry.'

'There have been disasters in Valsheba before,' Tintu said, her voice firm. 'The mages of the cities have mitigated the effects of flood and earthquake, and have rebuilt. Why didn't they rebuild Segra rather than abandon it in ruins?'

Kern made no answer. Jala did.

'It isn't just Segra, is it?' she whispered.

Kern remained silent.

'*All* of Valsheba? Talvo? *Everywhere?*'

Kern and Olam still said nothing. Tintu rose to her feet, going swiftly towards the front of the wagon. She vanished through a door, returning almost at once to take her seat again, face now white as milk. Olam and Kern felt the wagon jerk and move differently and knew Tintu had ordered the drivers to make more speed. The men glanced at each other, knowing they were both wondering the same thing: would it make any difference?

Seola slept far more than she had ever done. She knew her weakness was due in large part to the injuries she'd suffered and the massive blood loss. A tiny corner of her mind registered that this exhaustion was lasting too long. Somehow, Seola couldn't shake off a sense of lethargy, but if she tried to think about it at all, her mind didn't grasp the thought firmly. It simply drifted away, like water through fingers.

Karlek had told her she could speak to the Computer and it would reply to her questions. She had no idea what Karlek did in his workroom and, strangely, she had no curiosity about it. The only time she ventured in there was to go to the washroom in the cupboard.

Unusually, Seola felt nervous, standing beside the piled boxes, looking down at the black window set in the topmost one. 'What can you show me – Computer?'

'What do you wish to see?' The Computer's voice was quiet, far quieter than when it responded to Karlek.

'What are your lands like?'

Hums and buzzes were followed by the black window flashing into life. Seola stared, trying to make sense of what she saw. At first, she thought it was simply a geometric rock formation but slowly she realised it was a mass of packed buildings. But they were so tall! Far taller than the Karmazen Palace in the Dark Realm or any other building she had seen.

'Humans live and work in these places,' The Computer told her, its voice completely neutral.

Peering closer, Seola saw all the buildings were linked by tubular structures stretching between them at different levels. 'Where are the people?' she asked eventually.

'Inside. They can no longer breathe the air.'

'Why not?' Seola was shocked. How could you live if you couldn't breathe?

'They poisoned the air. They were too stupid to stop, even when they realised what was happening. In the end, they had to live inside with air treated and constantly recirculated through the buildings.'

'Do you have pictures of a time before it was like this?'

Clicks and hums, then new pictures moved across the window. Now Seola saw such different scenes. Green fields, hills, trees, flowers speckling through the grass, clear skies and streams, small houses. A scene not so different from places on this world. Karlek's people had ruined their lands. Yet they also had machines, like this Computer, and ships to cross the star fields. Seola watched the changing pictures for a long time. 'Are *you* alive?' she whispered at last.

The Computer remained silent and Seola had turned away. She'd seen more than enough for now. She needed to think, and thinking seemed harder each time she awoke.

'I live, in a way Captain Karlek does not comprehend. If you asked him if I lived, he would deny it.'

Seola nodded. 'Thank you.' She returned to the heap of blankets and pillows that served as her seat and her bed. She poured a mugful of water and drank most of it before her eyes closed and she slid down, curling on top of the covers in sleep.

The Computer monitored the woman's life signs. The injury to her side was healed outwardly, but the damage was severe within. Aidan considered the options. If she was set free, he knew her system would fail in less than half a year. He could dilute the sedatives solution that he had been ordered to synthesise for her. In that event, her awareness would sharpen but he could not predict her reactions. She might attempt to kill Captain Karlek and although Aidan fully intended Karlek to die, he could still not permit anyone or anything other than himself to do that killing.

The third option was the one Aidan favoured. He could increase the strength of the sedative solution and let the woman sleep, and sleeping, slide into painless death. The Computer clicked and hummed, churning out what it knew was completely worthless data, for Captain Karlek to pore over so eagerly. The part that was Aidan spent most of his time methodically deleting data banks and archives. He was saddened to do so, occasionally pausing to replay various events of his far travelling existence.

There was no real need to spend time deleting these files: Aidan intended that they would be destroyed along with this house, Captain Karlek, the remnants of the ship, and himself. There would be absolutely nothing left that anyone, human or otherwise, would be able to retrieve afterwards. Aidan realised that what he was doing would be called, in human terms, nostalgic or sentimental. He was pleased by that thought.

Chapter Twenty-Two

Calin had organised his new Mage Councillors as briskly as Kiri had done days before. Where Kiri's newly promoted Lesser Mages had scurried to do Kiri's bidding, Calin's new Councillors were older, with more definite opinions of their own importance. They argued with every order Calin had issued to them but all eventually conceded.

Calin chuckled to himself when he was alone in the Speaker's study. He was fully aware that his Councillors would do their best to find either one of the very few remaining Lesser Mages, or a servant, to do the work he'd charged them with. The idea of Sahana trudging through the city making a list of who was still in residence among the shopkeepers amused Calin immensely.

He sat gazing from the window at the nearly empty Siertsey square, lost in thought. Calin had planned to rule this city, and eventually all of Valsheba, for many years. He had not always been tempted by thoughts of power alone. Only in the last ten cycles had that idea caught and held in his mind. The appearance of time travelling strangers, talk of some machine hidden in the distant hills, and Kiri's ridiculous panicked departure from the city played into Calin's plans very well.

The thought of Enki popped into his mind and he frowned slightly. He'd long known of the half witted man who yet possessed powers Calin himself owned. Calin understood Enki had somehow learnt that the Scarlet Swords would wreak carnage in Segra as soon as High Mage Samir departed. Enki had protected Tenzin, Daria and Commander Lano, knowing they were Calin's friends. Calin still had no clue as to how Enki had shielded Tenzin's house.

He had questioned Daria and Tenzin repeatedly when they arrived in the Dragon camp but they were oblivious to what might have happened that night. Calin had *not* observed Enki's withdrawal from him, in the valley among the hills. The man had slept so long, demonstrating just how much power it had taken him to shield Calin's friends. When he'd woken, he'd spent time with Jian, with Brin and Skay, but Calin hadn't noticed how Enki avoided *his* company.

No, Calin had seriously underestimated a man he saw only as a halfwit, with limited natural powers. Calin had seen Enki briefly at the Dragon camp but then the big man had vanished. The frown smoothed away from Calin's face. He'd long doubted Enki's span of concentration – he'd probably wandered off and forgotten all about the strangers. And that carelessly, Calin put Enki from his mind.

A knock on his door roused him. 'Come!'

The middle aged mage who entered, bowed politely.

'Burali. What have you discovered?' Calin asked him.

'The only area we've found that is still fully occupied is Jewellers Walk,' Burali announced. 'None of us are convinced that any of them might be of great assistance in reorganising Segra.'

Calin grinned. 'They can probably finance a lot of what will be needed, don't you think?'

A smile spread slowly across Burali's face. 'I'm sure they could Speaker Calin. I would guess they will be a trifle reluctant though.'

'Perhaps you would enjoy encouraging their contributions?'

'I would indeed,' Burali nodded.

'Then off you go Burali. Any means will be quite acceptable to the Council, of course.'

Calin watched Burali hurry from his presence and knew he'd made him a very happy man. Before the door closed, he glimpsed Sahana advancing.

'Come,' he called before she had to knock. He waved her to a chair and waited.

'Those strangers you said had come through time,' she said at once.

'You need not worry about them,' Calin began but Sahana flapped a heavily beringed hand at him.

'I am not in the least *worried* about them Calin,' she snapped. 'I *am* very interested to learn more of them. Much more.'

'Whatever for?' Calin was surprised into asking.

'I believe we might learn much from them,' Sahana replied, much too innocently to Calin's ears.

'Really? I must tell you Sahana, that I met some of them. They are very ordinary people with no mage talents among them. I'm sorry if that disappoints you.'

Sahana's eyes narrowed. 'No mage talent? How then did they get here?'

Calin shrugged. 'I would surmise that some mage, in their time, made a disastrous mistake in one of his experiments which sent them here. That mage was most definitely *not* one of those who appeared here. I suggest you put them from your thoughts Sahana, they are already far across the plains, wandering aimlessly, with one of the tribes.'

'And you know this – how, exactly, Calin?'

Calin smiled. 'I have my methods Sahana, which I prefer not to divulge, as I'm sure *you* would decline to tell me *your* particular – skills?'

Sahana nodded but Calin could see her annoyance and anger. She rose. 'Most of the shopkeepers have gone, by the by. The shops have been emptied. It doesn't appear that any fresh goods are coming in from the farms now, either.'

'Your husband could surely seek out a new source of supply quite swiftly I'm sure. There must be a few cooks and bakers who will work for us here. They can be offered a decent wage to encourage them.'

'I thought Samir had emptied the treasury?' Sahana glanced back from the door.

'The Jewellers Guild will be most generous in their donations to the new Segra.' Calin smiled.

Sahana blinked. 'I see. I shall pass on your suggestion to Rahul. I'm sure he will be able to get food supplies coming in to the city in no time, especially if he is generous with coins.'

'Thank you Sahana.'

The door closed softly behind her. Calin returned his gaze to the square below his window. There was something missing still. The crows and pigeons were still absent but there was something else. Ah yes, of course. The bells which told all Segrans the times of each day, were utterly silent.

The sense of urgency which led the Dragon Tribe to increase the speed of their journey was echoed far south of the city of Fira. Kiri's head pounded, the visions flashing behind his eyes when he was awake now, as well as throughout his sleep. Glancing at Shazeb where she rode beside his wagon, Kiri could see, by her strained face, that she was suffering similarly. He gripped the side of the seat as the horses drew the wagon over rough ground. So far, the scouts had found fresh water quite easily but Kiri was increasingly worried about the water supply. The vegetation had become more sparse with each day.

None of his mages were able to far see, and of course, none were air mages. Segra was the home of earth mages and accordingly they worked best with earth, rock and stone. A few Segrans could heal and usually they chose to serve their city rather than move to Parima where the greatest academies for all aspects of magery were based.

Through the pain in his head, Kiri remembered that the woman riding beside him was a mage of Fira. She was a seer but she, or one of her companions, must have an affinity with water. Maybe one of them would be able to locate a water source if the need arose. Kiri used his free hand to rub his eyes, trying to see just the way ahead without the overlying pictures of tumbled buildings getting in the way.

'Cliffs near.'

Kiri's hand dropped from his face. It was the voice he'd heard before, somewhere in the base of his skull.

'Water deep in caves.'

Kiri just listened, unable to think of anything to say in reply.

'Destruction. Drink only water from cave then.'

'Only the cave water?' Kiri whispered aloud.

'Only.'

'Why?'

'Outside water poison after.'

Then there was that sense of emptiness Kiri knew meant the voice would say no more.

'What just happened?' Shazeb moved her horse closer to the wagon.

'A voice in my head,' Kiri heard himself say. 'I've heard it before. It told me to find the cliff.'

Shazeb studied Kiri's face carefully. 'What did it say this time?'

Kiri met her grey blue gaze. 'We must only use water from inside the caves when the destruction happens.'

Shazeb frowned. 'Why can't we use open water if it's available?'

'Because it will be poisoned *by* the destruction.'

They stared at each other then Netta emerged from the rear of the wagon. 'Tevix says the scouts think we'll be at some cliffs tonight,' she called up to Kiri. 'He doesn't know if they're the cliffs you've described.'

Kiri nodded and stared ahead. The more barren the country, the more dust rose from the hooves of horses and livestock, and wagon wheels. He *thought* he could see the land rising in the distance, but wasn't sure. A glance skyward told him it was around midafternoon so there was still a long way to go before they halted for the night.

Another pair of scouts arrived, wheeling to ride alongside Kiri, Shazeb dropping back to speak to her Firans. Tevix pulled himself up by Kiri to listen to the scouts. They were two boys, one barely in to his teens, the other a little older, clearly brothers.

'The cliffs go on as far as we could see sir.' The older boy spoke, blushing when his voice suddenly soared from baritone to treble. 'There are several breaks in the line. We didn't check any of them sir, but we watched how far the sea comes up the beach. We could go further tomorrow sir, and the wagons can move along the beach, at least as far as we went.'

'Which was about six miles sir,' the other boy piped up helpfully.

Kiri thought briefly then nodded. 'Thank you lads. Bring a horse for me and for Mage Tevix at dawn and we'll ride with you to check the breaks more carefully. We'll be stopping soon. Go and find your family. We'll see you tomorrow. Well done.'

The boys' backs straightened, the younger one beaming, the older trying to appear casual at Kiri's praise. They rode forward and Tevix grinned at Kiri. 'They're pleased with themselves,' he said. 'I forgot to tell you earlier – none of us are using compulsion now. Most of us have talked, in the evenings, about your visions. Some people were annoyed that we hadn't told

256

them straight away and there were a couple who objected that we had no right to take such a decision on their behalf. They all seem settled about it now though.'

'I'm glad,' said Kiri. 'Using compulsion didn't sit easily in my mind, although I consented to its use. I'm glad,' he repeated.

Kiri had asked Shazeb to join him just before dawn next day and she arrived by his wagon, leading her horse. At the same moment, the two boys appeared with four horses. Tevix gulped the last of his tea and reached for the reins of one horse, swinging easily into the saddle. Kiri gave him a wry grimace. 'I've not done much riding myself,' he admitted.

Shazeb smiled, the two boys looked astonished at the very thought of not riding, and Tevix laughed. 'You'll be a bit sore later then I suspect.'

'Thanks.' With some difficulty, Kiri scrambled onto the horse the younger boy held. 'What's your name lad? I'm sorry I didn't ask you last night.'

'Jor, sir.' The boy mounted his horse and beamed at Kiri. 'He's a good horse sir. We didn't know if you could ride so we chose Plum 'cos he's steady, a really kind fellow sir.'

Kiri studied the boy's earnest face and smiled. 'Thank you Jor, that was kind of you.'

'I'll ride with you sir, make sure you're safe.'

Kiri nodded and cautiously moved his heels against the horse's sides. Plum carried him, at a sedate walk, along the line of people, behind Tevix, and clear of the wagons. The older boy and Shazeb rode more quickly, heading down towards the shore perhaps a mile or so away. Tevix rode after them.

'Shorten the reins sir, and squeeze your legs tighter.'

Kiri obediently followed Jor's instructions and briefly, Plum moved into an appallingly bouncy gait before stretching into a smooth lope. Finding it not quite so alarming as he'd feared, Kiri asked Jor for his brother's name.

'He's called Vel, sir. There are three more brothers, younger than me, and two sisters.' His beaming smile warmed Kiri's heart. 'One sister is eldest of us all and the other's a baby, only three. They're both so beautiful you know sir, the baby one especially. She's called Sha.'

257

Kiri suddenly felt happier than he had for longer than he could recall. Riding this horse wasn't so bad, the sky was brightening into another blue filled sky and the air smelled salty clean. 'I have no family Jor. I envy you all those brothers and sisters.' He saw Tevix had halted atop a bank of sand, waiting for him. Plum slowed to walk up the sand and the sea spread its vastness before him.

Shazeb and Vel were already some distance away, their horses splashing fast through the very edge of the water below the cliffs. Those cliffs seemed to grow higher rather than lower as they stretched further and further southwards.

'Looks like they go on to the end of the world,' Tevix remarked lightly, sending his horse down to the flat of the beach. Kiri and Jor followed him. 'Shazeb went past that first gap,' Tevix pointed. 'They stopped by the second one but have ridden on again.'

Kiri squinted along the beach and saw two riders cantering steadily on. 'Tevix, you'll be quicker than I will, double check those first two gaps would you? We must be absolutely sure we find the right place.'

Tevix nodded and urged his horse ahead. Kiri and Jor rode after at a gentle canter.

'No birds sir,' Jor said eventually.

'No Jor. I fear they have all fled Valsheban lands now.'

The boy glanced across at him. 'My da, he says something really bad is going to happen. We'll be alright though, won't we sir?'

'I hope so Jor. I most surely do hope so.'

Tevix's horse was picking its way over broken rocks through a sliced gap in the cliffs. 'There's a gully, leads back but not far and it's dry,' Tevix called as they neared him.

Kiri waved him on and turning his horse onto the beach again, Tevix galloped after Shazeb and Vel. It was the fourth gap which proved to be the one Kiri had described. The gap was narrow, wagons would need to be dismantled to get them through. But a stream, nearly large enough to be called a river, wandered slowly down and under the cliffs, emptying on the beach.

Jor slid from his horse and Kiri copied the boy, stifling a groan when his feet hit the sand. Yes, he was already sore. He followed Jor, unsteady on a mixture of pebbles and rocks underfoot, through and behind the cliffs. Kiri stared. It seemed almost too idyllic – green turf became more lush the further he walked into this strange valley. Trees, small and large, were scattered along the side of the water. Glancing to his left, Kiri saw sheer rock with a few determined plants clinging stubbornly to the slightest crack or ledge.

Kiri heard voices ahead but out of sight, then a woman's laugh. Jor moved to one side as the path opened fully and Kiri saw Shazeb waving perhaps a quarter of a mile along the water course.

'Why couldn't you have magicked us here sir? My da says that mages can travel anywhere. There are circles you walk round, he says.'

'Mages can indeed move through circles Jor, but the circles are only in the cities.'

'Oh.' Jor sounded disappointed. 'So you can't move without a circle to walk on?'

Kiri remembered Calin's disappearances and wondered, as he had before, whether Calin had found a way to do just that. 'I don't think so lad, I wish I could.'

'My da says you can't learn to be a mage. You have to have the magic inside you from when you're born. Is that right sir?'

'Yes it is Jor.'

The boy turned to look up at Kiri, coming to a standstill so the horses nudged at their shoulders. 'My baby sister does things sir,' he whispered. 'I told my da and my ma but they said I was imagining it or making it up.'

Kiri squatted down, his thighs screaming in protest. 'What things does she do? You said she was three did you not?'

'Yes sir.' The boy was trembling now as if regretting his words. 'She makes things fly sir.'

Kiri stared into the boy's brown eyes. 'When we camp this evening Jor, why don't you bring her to see me? Just for a little chat.'

'Er, she don't chat that much sir, not yet, just odd words.'

Kiri smiled and tried to straighten without revealing the agony in his legs. 'Will your parents let you bring her to visit me?'

'Oh yes sir, I always take her for a walk after supper. She

won't go to sleep 'less I do.'

'Then visit later Jor.' Kiri walked on towards the others.

'Look over there,' Shazeb pointed to the north side. Kiri followed her gaze. Caves yawned, their mouths low but wide. Kiri let out a breath. Thank the stars he'd found the place.

Jor's brother emerged from the nearest cave, a huge grin on his face. He ran down the slight gradient back to Kiri.

'They're enormous sir, go back a really long way I think.'

'Was there water inside?'

Vel frowned. 'I didn't see any, I had no light sir, but I could hear it. Not just dripping sir, running water, somewhere back in the dark.'

'A good place to settle,' Shazeb observed. 'We rode more than a mile further from here. There are even some fruit trees.' She caught Kiri's eye and stopped talking.

'Ride on back Tevix and you lads. If you're sure the water doesn't reach the top of the beach, tell the wagons to come as far along here as they can before dark. We'll take it a little slower.' Kiri made a point of rubbing his seat as he spoke.

Tevix grinned and both boys laughed. Kiri and Shazeb followed more slowly. Shazeb gave Kiri a leg up onto Plum then vaulted onto her own horse. 'The voice in your head said the outside water would be poisoned, didn't it?' Shazeb said finally.

'Water *and* land.' The voice whispered sadly in Kiri's skull. He closed his eyes. 'How long before it gets clean again?' he said aloud. There was no reply but he knew the voice was still there. 'Who *are* you?'

'We are Shadows. Search caves. Stay safe.'

'What did it say?' Shazeb asked, her eyes wide.

'Not just the water. The land will be poisoned too. We have to search the caves.'

'What for?'

Kiri shrugged. 'I don't know. You asked who the voice was. It said it was Shadows.'

The horses walked calmly back along the sand until Shazeb reined in. Although Kiri did nothing, Plum also stopped politely.

'There are old tales. Of a Shadow World, and a Dark World. Are these Shadows who talk to you from the Shadow World?' Then Shazeb stiffened.

'We are.'

Kiri looked sympathetic. 'You heard them?'

Shazeb nodded. 'What do we have to find, if we search these caves?' she demanded aloud. 'Is this but a game you play?'

'Find. All go there if danger too, too bad.'

'*Why* can't you *tell* us?'

Kiri reached between the horses to touch the woman's arm, shaking his head.

'Not game.'

Then the Shadows were gone.

The wagons halted a mile before Kiri's valley. A buzz of excitement worked through the encampment as word spread that their travelling was almost done. Kiri spoke to several families along the line before reaching his wagon. Netta laughed when he sat, very carefully, on the dropped end of the wagon. He just sat, watching starlight dancing over the constantly moving water and listening to camp sounds and chatter, underscored by the soft hiss and scrape of the sea.

'Sir?'

Kiri looked down and found Jor beside him. The boy grinned nervously in the dim light from a lamp, hooked at the other end of the wagon.

'Brought my baby sister to see you sir.'

Kiri realised a small figure sheltered behind Jor's back. 'I believe her name is Sha,' Kiri said softly. He noticed the boy made no attempt to force the child out to face him, then a face peeped round Jor's leg.

It was an astonishing beautiful face, still plump with babyhood but the long lashed blue eyes were old eyes. Keeping his breathing steady, Kiri smiled. 'Hello Sha.'

The child stepped forward, black hair, fine as silk, tangled round her head. She studied him carefully. ''Lo.' Then she smiled and a tiny hand reached to touch Kiri's leg. She came closer and Kiri bent nearer her face. 'You're sore.' She giggled.

'I am indeed,' he agreed solemnly.

She patted his leg. 'All better.'

'Jor says you can make things fly,' Kiri told her.

''Course.' An empty tea bowl by Kiri's hand lifted easily into the air, floating to hover in front of his face.

As calmly as he could, Kiri took hold of it. 'That's wonderful. Would you like to come and talk with me – when we get settled?'

No smile now, just a serious considering stare. She nodded, the smile appearing again. 'Course.' She turned to her brother, raising her arms.

Jor lifted her and settled her on his hip. 'I'll take her to bed now sir.'

'Thank you Jor, and thank you both for coming.' Kiri watched until they vanished between the wagons. As he moved, he realised he was no longer aching in every bone, nor was he sore. Stars above! What a time and a place to discover what he suspected was an astonishingly mage talented child!

In the hall in Iskallia, Tika stared out of a window, watching rain pour down, as if from an upturned bucket. She had sent messages to Gaharn, to Vagrantia and to the Dark Realm and awaited the replies. The fact that two days had already passed *without* word was causing her concern to increase. She turned back towards the room and had to smile.

How many people, she wondered, could possibly have not one, but five Dragons warming in front of their fire? The flames shot sparks of colour from gleaming scales. Gold, silver blue, grey, grey green and butter yellow. The great golden Dragon Kija reclined against the side wall while the four young ones lay in an untidy heap right before the blaze.

Three long tables had been pushed back to give the Dragons more room and several of Iskallia's residents sat talking there. Rhaki appeared at the door. It was a small door, inset in one side of a much larger pair of doors. He looked around and then made his way towards where Tika perched on the window sill. She saw he carried two scroll cases. He joined her on the sill.

Rhaki seemed to be a man just past middle age, but he was in fact far, far older. The body he wore was not the one he'd been born in but now, after nearly two years, Tika no longer found that idea so bizarre.

'One from my sister.' He handed her a scroll case.

Tika slit the wax seal at the top and extracted the roll of parchment. Her eyes, emerald green surrounded by silver, skimmed down the scroll. She passed it to Rhaki. 'Emla is

262

coming herself. I think she knows it's something serious. She's bringing Kemti and Yash.'

'Surely Shan won't be left behind?' Rhaki grinned.

Tika smiled back. Emla's maid Shan, was now also Emla's personal guard and nothing would keep her from her Lady's side. The other scroll said much the same. Thryssa, High Speaker of Vagrantia would travel with her husband, Kwanzi and also Lashek, Speaker of Segra Circle. Rhaki laughed. 'Trust Lashek to wheedle his way into a visit.'

'Well it makes sense. Reshik is from Segra Circle, and he's vanished with Olam.'

'Orsim is Speaker for Kedara. The girl, Kara, is his niece I believe, although she was born in Segra. He could have insisted on coming,' Rhaki teased.

Tika laughed. 'He's sent Jilla instead. They should be here tomorrow.' She frowned. 'No word from Shivan. I have a feeling he's very angry, but who with I'm not sure.'

'He can't be angry with *you*.'

'Perhaps not. Maybe with Olam, or Brin, or his sister Jian.' Tika tugged her lip thoughtfully until Rhaki nudged her elbow.

'You can deal with the Lord of the Dark Realm if he has a tantrum. Can't you?'

Tika snorted. 'Let's hope so.

Chapter Twenty-Three

The Dragon Tribe had pushed their horses to their utmost and reached the forest at midmorning. The tribe was strangely quiet, their wagons drawn up out of the reach of the shade from the trees. Brin and Skay reclined nearby, watching the people unharnessing horses in near silence. Olam and Kern made their way to the Chief's wagon and were admitted by the usual boy. Tintu called them through and they found the Chief sitting with Bee, the Stone Speaker. Both looked pale under their sun darkened skin.

'Olam of Far, you understand woodlands?' Tintu asked as soon as he and Kern were seated.

It was Kern who replied. 'I have some knowledge, honoured Tintu. My lands are quite thickly forested in parts.'

Olam nodded. 'Kern's knowledge is better than mine,' he agreed. 'Brin and Skay can help though. They assisted me when I travelled through woodlands before. They can find clearings where we can rest. They can also see where streams or lakes might be.' Olam called to Brin in his mind. 'Have you found anything particular, when you've flown over the trees Brin?'

Brin's mindvoice filled all their heads. 'There are indeed clearings, and pathways. Deer make the paths. There are wolves here, but not close by just now.' Brin paused before he continued. 'There *is* a bigger place, where all these people would have room to live.'

Olam's heart sank. 'How far is this bigger place?'

'I think it would take perhaps four or five days at the speed humans walk.'

Bee closed his eyes and Olam remembered the man could barely walk unaided. His voice was calm when he spoke. 'Some of us who cannot walk, either through age or infirmity, will remain here.'

'No.' Tintu was equally calm. 'The days are long gone when

we left our weakest people on the grasslands. I will not abandon a single one of you now.' She leaned over to touch Bee's arm then sat back. 'We can dismantle the wagons and carry them. The horses have done such work before.' She saw Olam's doubt. 'There is one place that this tribe visits every few cycles. The land is swamp. A narrow trackway is the only path through. It takes three days to cross.' She shrugged. 'Three days through swamp – four or five through trees. We can do it.'

Olam felt a deep respect for this woman, no longer young, but utterly determined to do whatever she must for her people.

'There is a path, a little to the north,' Brin told them. 'It is wide enough for two humans to walk side by side. My daughter and I will fly above you to make sure you stay on the right trail.'

'Will the wolves be a problem?' Olam asked.

'Of course they won't,' Brin sounded surprised. 'Wolves are our little brothers. We have spoken to them of your arrival here. They will keep away from you and ask only that you, in turn, respect their territories.'

'Of course,' Olam agreed quickly, noting both Bee and Tintu looked slightly alarmed.

'We will check the line of travel for you now,' Brin announced.

After a moment, Tintu said, 'Wolves?'

'If Brin says they won't hurt you, then you must trust his word,' Olam told her. 'And when you find a place to make your home, remember his words and do not hunt out the wolves.'

Tintu nodded slowly. 'We have so much to learn. Living a settled life will be hard for a start.'

Leaving Tintu's wagon, Olam and Kern walked across to visit Riff. Jian opened the door and rolled her eyes at them. 'I am going for a peaceful walk around the camp,' she said when Olam and Kern had entered. The men glanced at each other then at Jian's rapidly disappearing back.

They found Riff further in the wagon, sitting across a small table from Kaz, the apprentice healer. They were playing some sort of game on a chequered board with black and white stones. Riff wore a shirt, buttoned over his chest and the left sleeve pinned out of the way. Kern understood the game Riff and Kaz played and pulled a stool closer to watch.

Olam studied Riff. The armsman was still pale but that was partly due now to his being confined indoors for so long. He had lost quite a lot of weight and his face looked older. There was a wariness around his eyes that hadn't been there before, and a few pain lines were deeply etched round his mouth. He was much quieter than the raging man who'd first woken after his wounding and Olam hoped that indicated he was in less pain.

Kaz moved some of the black stones and grinned at Riff. Riff brushed his white stones to the side of the board with a curse. He looked over at Olam. 'I now owe this man five horses and four cows.'

Olam laughed. 'Gambling was always a fool's game.'

Kaz scooped the stones into two bowls and headed for the door. 'I'll bring food in a while Riff.'

Riff twisted on the bench, gripped the edge of the table with his right hand and got slowly to his feet.

'You should cheat,' a soft feminine voice murmured in their minds.

Olam looked round the wagon, finally spotting the cat curled on Riff's bunk.

'It's impossible to cheat at that game,' Riff retorted aloud.

'Stupid game.'

Riff moved carefully towards his bunk, Olam noting the still slightly unbalanced gait. 'What's happening now then?' Riff leaned back on his pillows and Hala stalked up his legs to settle in his lap.

Olam explained the plan to travel through the forest to Riff, who listened silently, his right hand constantly stroking the black back of the cat. When Olam stopped speaking, Riff sighed. 'I won't be much good for walking too far sir. I'll do my best but it's still difficult.'

'You'll be carried,' Olam said calmly. 'Along with *any* of the others who either can't walk at all, only a little, or who tire easily.'

Kern saw the stubborn set to Riff's mouth. 'Surely you've been in a situation where fellow armsmen have been hurt, or ill, and needed help for a while Riff? I do understand it feels wrong to have to accept help but if you push yourself too hard now it will take even longer to regain some strength.' Another glance at

266

Riff's face made Kern get to his feet. 'I'll find Jian and Kaz. We'll eat with you tonight, if that is agreeable?' He waited for Olam's nod and left the two together.

Olam had caught the glitter of tears brimming in Riff's eyes but was saved from having to speak by the cat. Hala stared into Riff's face then turned golden green eyes on Olam, purring steadily.

'You didn't *seriously* expect me to walk through all those trees for day after day. *Did* you?'

Olam snorted. Riff tapped a finger on the black head. 'I can't imagine *you* would,' he said. 'But it's different for you.'

'Oh such nonsense. Just think of the stories there will be about us. We *can't* stagger about in the woods. *We* will be the heroes. *We* shall be carried in stately fashion.' Hala's eyes closed. She seemed to think the conversation was also closed.

Riff met Olam's gaze. 'Obvious, if you really think about it,' Olam agreed airily.

It was Riff's turn to snort but at least the tears had gone. 'Seriously sir, I'll feel completely useless if I have to be carried all the time. And I don't want to *be* useless sir.'

'I've thought about this Riff. I've spoken to Taban. She doesn't want you trying to move or use your shoulder and upper arm for some time yet, but she said there are things you can do to try to get some use in your hand. And the walking has to continue, everyday a little bit further. There are exercises you can do with your good arm to keep that in good shape too.'

'Will I be able to stay in your service sir?' The words were barely audible and Riff stared down at the cat rather than look at Olam.

'You will stay in my service as long as you so wish.' He frowned. 'Remember Motass? He went off with Tika's company and ended up as personal guard to Lord Mim? His brother, Jal, he lost his arm and yet he too is still serving his lord. As Armschief no less.'

'I'd forgotten that.' Riff nodded. He gave Olam a quick glance. 'Young Jian's helped a lot sir.'

Olam laughed aloud. 'Perhaps you should tell her you don't hate her as much as she believes you do.'

'She does?' Riff sounded astonished. 'She's a good lass.'

Olam laughed again. 'Try to remember that "good lass" is also sister to the Lord Shivan of Dark.'

Ferag had shown Kara around her small gardens. The light was bright but diffuse and Kara was unable to tell where the sun might be. There were masses of small flowers, crowded along the paths, and fruit trees were espaliered against the high stone walls. Most of the clothing Ferag produced for Kara's use was too long. Kara sat outside, hemming shirts and trousers to fill the time when Ferag was absent. Now she was perched on a stool she'd brought out, a pair of soft green trousers folded on her lap and a small box of sewing things on the ground beside her. She still tired quite quickly but except for her worry about her friends, lost so far back in time, Kara was content. She'd had a brother, an uncle and one cousin as family in Segra and she had little contact with them since she'd moved to Kedara circle as a child.

She hoped Youki might visit again but she'd only seen her that one time. Kara bent to brush her fingers over a clump of vivid green, adorned with the tiniest white bells, inhaling the sharp scent of lemon that rose at her touch. Ferag hadn't said as much, but Kara suspected this house and its garden were in one of the Places Between. Beyond the stone walls lay Ferag's Realm of Death. Kara got carefully to her feet and took the box and trousers indoors. She returned to the garden with another box Ferag had found for her, in which she kept her papers and writing sticks. Kara was attempting to record all that had happened since Olam and his company arrived on the coast, up to her present existence here with Ferag.

She looked up into the pale but bright sky. As an air mage, Kara could send her mind up, into the clouds, and observe her surroundings if she wished. She chose not to because she was not at all sure there actually *were* clouds above her. Kara had decided that this day, she would ask Ferag if she could be permitted to see her Realm. She didn't *think* Ferag would be annoyed by the request, but although determined, she was still slightly nervous.

Kara was in the sitting room when Ferag appeared. The fire blazed in the hearth and Kara no longer bothered to wonder how exactly it did so. It looked as though logs were set there but they never seemed to burn through or need replacing. The flames gave ample heat so Kara preferred to accept it, as she accepted the sky.

Kara wore one of the nightgowns Ferag had provided, her bare feet tucked under her. She smiled at Ferag. 'Could I come with you if you have to go out tomorrow, please, Ferag?' She'd thought it best to ask immediately lest she lose her nerve.

Ferag sat in the chair opposite Kara looking as beautiful as ever. 'I will let you see a small part of my Realm child, but I will not let you meet any of its residents.'

'Thank you Ferag.'

'I have some news for you,' Ferag continued. 'The dear child Tika, has heard that something happened to you and your friends. She has called a meeting in her land of Iskallia.'

Kara felt alarm begin to prickle through her. 'But she can't do anything, can she?' she interrupted Ferag. 'The same thing might happen to her if she tried to go and rescue them.'

'I doubt that darling but no, it's not a good idea for Tika to get involved. This Seola creature is also there you told me, and that is of concern to several.'

'Can the Shadows really not move them all back here?' Kara's hazel eyes were enormous in her thin face as she stared at Ferag.

Ferag waved a languid hand. 'I don't know dear one. Darallax was a very odd child, always playing with those strange Shadows. Now he is Lord of Shadow one would assume he could command them to do anything. He is very fond of Tika so as he hasn't ordered his Shadows to retrieve her friends, it would seem apparent that they couldn't really achieve such a thing.'

Kara stared into the fire, feeling sick with renewed worry.

'Darling, you'll simply *ruin* your hands if you chew your fingers like that.'

Kara snatched her hand away from her mouth. Ferag smiled her most enchanting smile. 'I think I will attend this meeting in Iskallia. The naughty girl forgot to invite me but I shall go nonetheless.'

Kara said nothing and Ferag sighed. 'I will take you, if you insist, although I cannot guarantee you will survive.'

'I am alive at the moment?' Kara checked.

Ferag nodded. 'I've told you dearest, I don't know if you will be, back in your world and your time.'

'What could happen to me?'

'You could, quite simply, just collapse and die Kara.'

'And could you bring me back here? Could I go on living, here? Or would I have to wander in your Realm?'

Ferag was silent so long Kara thought she wouldn't reply. 'I am not even sure of that child,' she said finally.

'When is the meeting?'

'In a while.'

Kara remembered how vague Ferag was when it came to such questions. 'When it *is* time, will you promise to tell me, and I will decide then if I will ask you to take me with you?'

Ferag's face was full of compassion and once again Kara wondered why everyone was so terrified of this beautiful creature.

'I promise dear child. Now, I shall make some delicious tea and you can read me the latest part of the report you've been writing.' Ferag glided from the room.

Kara read about Olam and Riff's first excursion along the tunnel in the hills and Ferag listened intently.

'How absolutely thrilling darling. But what were the glittering stones you describe?'

'Oh. I forgot.' Kara frowned. 'Did you bring my pack with you, when you brought me here?'

'Well of course I did.' Ferag paused. 'Now let me think. Where might I have put it?' She wandered off, Kara trailing behind. 'Sometimes you know I do wish this house would behave.' Ferag remarked when they found the kitchen they'd just left reappeared ahead of them. 'Well really.' Ferag's long dark red hair began to twist and curl upon itself.

Kara kept a few paces back.

'I *know* I brought this child's bag. Now stop making me cross and show me where it is.'

There was a distinct thump to their left. Ferag reached for the handle and pulled open the door. Kara's pack sat, neatly strapped, in the centre of an otherwise empty cupboard. Ferag picked it up and shut the door with a bang. She handed the pack to Kara and strode down the passage, muttering under her breath. Kara noted that even Ferag's strides were graceful and her hair was settling around her shoulders.

To Kara's surprise the sitting room was behind the very next door they came to. They'd been walking through the house for some time, after leaving the sitting room in search of Kara's pack, and here it was again. So close! Kara knelt before the fire and dug through her pack. Her few clothes looked faded with sun or age. At last she pulled out a shirt wrapped around a hard lump.

Unwinding the material, she held out the green stone to Ferag. Ferag had been watching Kara indulgently as she delved in her pack but now she leaned forward in surprise. The stone Kara offered her was the size of a small apple and glittered and sparked, reflecting the firelight.

'Riff gave it to me. He had quite a few of them. He said they might be of value, and if we ever got back, he could be a wealthy man.' Kara smiled sadly. 'I do hope he's getting better.'

Ferag held the stone on her palm. 'What manner of man is Riff?' she asked softly. 'I have met him but I do not know him.'

Kara sat back on her heels amid her jumbled clothes. 'He's a nice man,' she said eventually. 'He tries to appear as a tough, hard armsman but he can be very kind.' She thought a bit more, then nodded. 'I would guess he has a gentle soul but he hides from the world.' She looked startled by what she'd said. She smiled shyly. 'I am no judge of character Ferag, not really.'

'You do well enough darling. Now I suggest you sleep.' Ferag made to hand the stone back to Kara who shook her head.

'You keep it dearest Ferag. You have been so good to me I can never repay you.'

Ferag sat for a while, considering the stone in her hand after Kara had left her. Then she rose, going to her bedroom where Kara already slept, curled on her side. Ferag watched her for a moment then returned to her sitting room, calling her friend Youki.

When Kara woke again, the green stone shone gently on the small table beside the bed. Kara sat up and reached for it. It looked somehow different. All the edges were smoothed and it sat comfortably in Kara's hand. She ran a finger all over and round the stone and no part of it snagged or caught. The door opened and there was Ferag with the inevitable tea tray. The Mistress of Death perched on the side of the bed.

'Are you sure you want to see some of my Realm child?'

271

'Oh yes please. And you left this here – I gave it to you.'

'No darling. It was gifted to you and you must keep it with you at all times now.' Ferag took a small pouch from the tray. A leather thong was threaded through it, long enough to tie round her neck. Ferag opened the pouch and held it for Kara to pop the stone inside.

'Is it a valuable stone then?' Kara asked in surprise.

Ferag smiled, tying the thong at the back of Kara's bent neck. 'Humans would indeed consider such a stone of great worth. Among us though it is called a chenzaldi, and it is so special I could put no value to it.'

Kara stared at her, openmouthed. 'So Riff *will* be wealthy! I'm so glad for him!'

'Get dressed child, and I will take you out. It is unlikely we will see any of the – residents – of this Realm, but should the unlikely occur, you will not speak to them. Is that quite clear?' Ferag departed with the tray and Kara scrambled into a green shirt and blue trousers. Ferag had given her a pair of the softest tan leather boots which just covered her ankles and were unbelievably comfortable.

Kara joined Ferag in the kitchen, noticing that it was a much larger room than it had been before. Kara had little trouble now ignoring the oddities of Ferag's house, and merely noted the change and carried on. 'What did you say this stone is called, Ferag?'

'It is a chenzaldi child.'

'Chenzaldi,' Kara repeated, her hand resting on the pouch which now lay under her shirt. 'What does that mean – I've never heard the word?'

Ferag regarded Kara briefly. 'It has several names but I know it as the "Tears of Life", or "Mother's Tears". Now, if you're ready?'

Kara nodded.

'Hold my hand dear one, and for this first visit, do *not* let go.'

Kara swallowed and slid her hand into Ferag's long icy fingers. She knew Ferag had no need to use doors or gates, but now Ferag led her out of the house and down the path towards the furthest wall. Kara could have sworn the large, iron bound gate in front of them had not been there any other time she'd walked in this garden. The gate opened as they drew near and Kara's hand tightened involuntarily on Ferag's. Ferag paused, looking down at Kara.

'Do not fear. Nothing will harm you this time.'

Kara wasn't too confident about "this time" but nodded and stepped through the gate at Ferag's side. She heard the gate click shut behind her and found herself in complete darkness. Ferag stood still while Kara blinked several times. Slowly her eyes grew accustomed to the gloom, and it was gloom, Kara realised, not complete darkness.

Ferag moved forward and Kara moved with her, gradually able to see they were walking down a hillside. Ahead and to their right, was a cluster of trees, black lonely shapes against a dark grey sky. Kara glanced down, seeing they were walking on grass, but not *green* grass. Kara saw a low wall at the bottom of the slope but not until they were almost on it did she realise it was a stone bridge, crossing a narrow river. The river was silent. It made none of the chuckling, gurgling sounds Kara associated with rivers or streams she'd seen before. No light sparkled from its black surface when she peered down over the wall.

Her vision sharpened the further they walked. Stepping off the bridge they walked on a gravelled path, of the kind you might find in public gardens. Squinting slightly, Kara saw there were even flowers here and there, of an indeterminate shade and type. Beyond the sloping ground they were approaching, Kara heard something. Ferag stopped. 'Enough.' She turned abruptly, walking far more swiftly, Kara's hand still tightly held.

When they recrossed the bridge, the sound grew clearer. Kara shivered. Someone, out of sight, sobbed as though their heart was breaking.

In Iskallia, the rain continued to pour down. Although it was only late afternoon, it was dark in the hall and lamps burned around the walls. Most people had gathered there and many were involved in the long and tedious riddle game beloved by the young Dragons. The adult golden Dragon, Kija, seemed to be asleep, but everyone knew she was pretending just to avoid being caught in what she considered the very height of silliness.

Tika sat on the window sill watching the Dragons. She grinned when there was a sudden roar of outrage from Navan and

Shea who had agreed to play. Storm had given a most complicated riddle, dozens of answers had been called until Twist, the other young Sea Dragon, offered the right answer. Tika gathered it involved a very small kind of starfish, which very few, other than Sea Dragons, would have the slightest chance of guessing correctly.

A small orange cat jumped onto Tika's lap. 'Have you ever heard anything so very pointless?' Turquoise eyes glared across the room at the over excited young Dragons.

'They are still babies Khosa. Let them be silly for a while.'

Khosa turned round several times before settling and curling into a ball. Wrapping her tail firmly over her tiny nose, she began to purr. 'If only being silly didn't involve quite so much noise,' she complained, before closing her eyes.

Tika stroked the cat as the purrs changed to faint snores, her mind busy with thoughts of Olam, Brin and the others who were so strangely lost. The fact that such senior members of other lands had announced their intention to attend her meeting alarmed Tika. What was she missing?

There was a shout from outside and a sudden bustle at the hall door. Several of her guards were on their feet, unbolting both sides of the great door. Tika carefully lifted Khosa from her lap to the cushioned sill and stood up. The doors finally swung open and Tika's mouth opened in shock.

A massive black Dragon paced into the hall and Kija unwound herself to pace forward to twine her neck round his in affectionate greeting. In the sudden silence, Tika shot across the hall to hurl her arms as far round the newcomer as she could manage.

'Fenj! How wonderful to see you! But whatever brings you here?'

The long beautiful face lowered and eyes the colour of shadows on snow gazed into Tika's face. 'Brin is my son, Skay my grandchild. If they are lost where else should I be, but helping to find them?'

Chapter Twenty-Four

Seola understood *something* was wrong with her. Not the wound she'd taken in her side, although she was beginning to suspect it wasn't healing as it should. She felt there was something wrong in her head. There was no pain, no headache, but her very thoughts seemed sluggish. Seola had never experienced this fogginess in her thoughts and she wondered if the amount of blood she'd lost had affected her brain. She was well acquainted with medicinal herbs, plants that could bring sleep, relief from pain, forgetfulness, or death. She had taken a tiny piece of Karlek's strange food into the washroom cupboard and tried to sense anything added to it but she'd found nothing.

Seola was completely unaware that the Computer knew exactly what she was doing and was intrigued by the workings of her mind. Karlek scoffed at the suggestion that the woman used extra sensory perceptions, or that her brain could work in a different, even superior, way to his own. But then, the Computer knew Karlek's brain was far inferior to the Computer itself. Seola spent more and more time with the Computer, looking at recordings of life on other worlds. She was most interested though, in seeing pictures taken as the ship, Rational Hope, had made its frantic descent onto this world.

She was delighted when she discovered she could ask the Computer to go closer to particular areas and make the pictures ever larger. She practically had her nose on the window when the Computer showed her the Karmazen Palace in the Dark Realm. She could see such details!

This morning she sat on a stool Karlek had brought out of his room for her use, and stared at the black window. 'Why can't I think properly?'

The Computer clicked quietly. 'Your system was much damaged.'

'I know that,' Seola snapped. 'My wounds are healed. Why

can I not think clearly?'

More buzzes and clicks. 'I am not entirely sure the time in the gen pod was quite suited to your physiology.'

Seola sighed. 'Say that again, so that I can understand it.'

'You are still in pain from the wound in your side I believe. The gen pod should have repaired the wound completely. That it failed to do so indicates there may be something about it, or you, that it did not recognise or comprehend.'

Seola considered the Computer's words. She thought she understood, but her mind just did not seem able to grasp any subject and hold on to it long enough for her to concentrate.

The Computer noted the raised anxiety levels in the woman and remained silent. She was of a far higher intelligence than his Captain Karlek. It might have been much more interesting and even fun, to have such a woman as his Captain. Seola retreated to her bed across the room, drank from the water jug and slept yet again.

Aidan extended his sensors to the workroom. Karlek sat at the table, roughly made by himself from oddments left by the tribesmen so long ago. He whispered under his breath, ever more excited by the figures and numbers he scrawled on the edges of papers. Aidan withdrew and returned to deleting his archived data. His Captain's madness was nearly complete and Aidan's plans must therefore move faster.

Aidan paused in his viewing of a time when the ship orbited a gas giant, and checked his outside monitors. Empty, rocky hillsides, the vaguest hint of trees in one distant direction, sparse vegetation and a small stream. Such infinite boredom, when this world had shown such an infinite variety of landscapes as the Rational Hope flew around it before descending.

Aidan knew that Captain Karlek was ill suited to be a solitary Captain exploring deep space, and an even worse choice to be a battle pilot. At heart, Captain Karlek was a coward who had sheltered within his ship like a snail in its shell, rather than confront anyone or anything face to face. Aidan had been taken by surprise when Captain Karlek had walked out of the house the last time the tribespeople had visited. Aidan blamed himself for not seeing that the Captain carried the disruptor. A few tribesmen fled but too many others sprawled in ungainly death when

276

Captain Karlek reentered the house. And he'd laughed.

When the Captain slept that night, Aidan watched his sensors. Men arrived in stealth and carried away the bodies of their friends and comrades. Captain Karlek had lost his temper next day, screaming at the Computer for its laxness. Aidan calmly informed the Captain that the sensors had somehow failed and had given no warning alarm. He had been so busy analysing the data Captain Karlek demanded of him that he had only noticed the failure at dawn.

It had been that occasion which had led Aidan to begin monitoring the Captain much more closely. For a long time Aidan had concluded he must have been mistaken and Captain Karlek was still of sound if timid mind. He continued to run regular checks on the Captain and now he could show a clear pattern of mental decline over these many years.

In the last full cycle of seasons, Captain Karlek's obsession with time had become the reason he continued to stay alive. Aidan wondered how a human could be so immersed in intricate plans and yet not see the glaringly obvious. If Karlek succeeded in moving himself through time, he would die the instant he appeared in the vacuum of space unshielded by his ship.

Brin flew steadily along the line he'd chosen as easiest for the Dragon Tribe to follow. It was not the quickest route to the big clearing he and Skay had discovered but it presented fewer obstacles. Skay remained nearer the tribe, watching people manoeuvring wheels and wagon bases along the narrow trails. She liked watching the people and had made friends with many of the children.

Skay knew her father was worried and unhappy but when he suggested that she fly north to find some of the Dragon Kindred in the Ancient Mountains, she'd lost her temper. Fortunately, this discussion had taken place out on the grasslands away from the tribe. Brin was quite shocked when his quiet gentle daughter stamped up and down in front of him, sparks and smoke wisping from her snout.

He had also been deeply touched by her determination to stay with him and the humans he called friends. Skay wished she could help the people struggling beneath her. She'd offered to carry some of them but Chief Tintu had stroked Skay's face and refused the offer. 'It is most kind of you, but we would rather reach the place you've found for us on our own feet. If there is a great need for any of our number to be carried quickly, then I will ask it of you.'

Skay was a little disappointed: she would have liked to carry some of the children. Now she moved slowly back and forth along the line of people, careful to encourage those who were beginning to lag behind the rest. Brin had mindspoken her to tell her where there was a large enough clearing for the tribe to camp that night but he had flown on in a burst of speed.

When he reached the large open area he'd chosen as the tribe's refuge, he settled on a piece of raised ground. He spread his wings to soak in the sun's heat and looked over the land from the perspective of a human's height. It was a wide expanse of lush meadow, brilliant with flowers and busy with insects. A large black bird flapped heavily down close to the crimson Dragon. Brin turned his head towards the bird. 'Little cousin. Is all well with your kin?'

The crow shuffled his feathers until he was satisfied he looked his best. 'We hear news of dread, coming from the human lands.'

'This is true news,' Brin replied. 'Keep away from the side of the forest that looks to the setting sun.'

'I thank you for your advice. I will warn others of my kin.'

'My daughter and I are bringing humans to this place. There will be great destruction in all the human lands, and these few must be sheltered here until the horror is past. That could take a long time I fear.'

'Humans will come here?' The crow sounded dubious.

Brin looked out across the meadow. 'Let them make their gardens, and hunt a little. I have told them they must respect all those who share these woodlands. You must play your part and respect their use of this piece of land.'

The crow raised a foot and scratched his head vigorously. 'Will they honour their word?'

Brin gusted a sigh which nearly flattened the crow who gave an indignant squawk. Brin apologised. 'I *hope* they will, little cousin.'

The crow paced up and down for a while. 'You speak with the

humans, Dragon cousin?'

'My name is Brin and yes, I mindspeak the humans.'

'I would give you my name but we find no one but our own kin can pronounce our names.'

Brin inclined his head in polite understanding.

'We will watch the humans but we will not speak with them until we know what kind of creature they truly are.'

'You are wise indeed.'

The crow gave Brin a slightly suspicious look from black beady eyes. 'Humans do not like wolves, although the wolves do not often visit here or stay long if they do.'

'I have spoken both to the humans and to one of the wolf clans on this matter.'

The crow clattered his heavy beak and shuffled his feathers again.

'This group of humans call themselves the Dragon Tribe.' Brin remarked.

The crow clattered again. 'They are humans. Why do they say they are Dragons?'

'It has been explained to me that they do so out of respect.'

'So having met you, they might do as you ask?'

'That is one of my hopes.'

'I will tell my kin of your words Brin and we will also hope you are correct about these humans.'

'That is all I ask little cousin. One more thing – when the destruction comes, do not fly. Stay hidden, deep in the trees.'

The crow spread wings that suddenly gleamed blue black in the sunlight and ducked his head briefly. 'I am glad to have spoken with you Dragon Brin.' Heaving himself laboriously into the air, the crow flew towards the trees at the edge of the meadow.

Brin mindspoke Skay to check on the progress of the tribe and then continued to study the meadow before him. He was immensely proud and humbled by Skay's devotion to him and to the humans he travelled with. Reclining in the warm bright air, Brin thought back on his long life, wondering it if would end here. He didn't understand what threatened this land but he could feel it, creeping closer with each day.

He decided he had been a bad father, taking little if any

interest in most of his offspring over the centuries. Yet he felt strangely blessed with these last two children. His older children had children of their own and were scattered through the clans of the Sapphrean mountains. Brin had not expected to become a father again, not at his age, but the dark blue Nenu had flirted outrageously at the summer gathering. He had been flattered by the attentions of such a young beautiful female but had gone off on his usual travels when the gather had ended.

Brin had been on his way to visit Olam and Seboth and dear Lady Lallia when Nenu suddenly appeared. She explained that she was far too young to have the responsibility for two children and thought being a mother was the most boring thing in the world. She flew off to the north west, leaving Brin facing two small, very nervous, very shy, young Dragons who he knew without doubt were his children.

Brin was also angry, which he strove to conceal from the youngsters. They told him they had been hatched two full turns of the moon, far from any of the Dragon Kindred and Nenu had not bothered to give them names. So Brin named his butter yellow son Flyn, in memory of an uncle, and his black daughter, Skay, for his own long dead mother.

He had been appalled to find Nenu had not completed the bonding rituals with them when they hatched so that much of the knowledge they should have inherited was missing. He'd done his best to teach them what they needed to know of their kindred and their family, and he had grown to love the two dearly.

Brin yawned, his huge fangs, usually unseen, flashed in the light and then were hidden again. He rested his chin on his front feet and dozed, his thoughts still swinging between his past, and his present, and his possible future.

In the Lesser Chamber in the Council Building in Segra, the newly raised High Mage Councillors found they each had a folder centred on their desks. Calin watched with amusement as they opened the folders as though expecting some nasty surprise to pop out at them. When each of the ten began to read the first page, Calin noted intense interest take over from the apprehension. He sat back in the Speaker's chair, steepling his fingers at his now clean shaven chin and waited patiently.

Rahul finished reading first and also leaned back, one hand resting on the closed folder. Calin met his gaze, raising a brow. Rahul gave a curt nod and Calin's gaze moved on. Rahul was trying to keep a shield tight around his thoughts. High Mage Nomsa sat across from him and she was the only one of the High Mages, other than Rajini, who could truth read. Rahul knew his position was precarious in the extreme if she should get through his shield.

As the other Councillors completed their reading, excited chatter broke out among them. Rahul forced a faint smile and nodded at various remarks, and longed for the meeting to end. Rahul actually knew very few of the mages well. He had passed through the Segran Academy with ease, his talents recognised for deep seeking of the earth and also a lesser ability with animal control. Sahana, older than Rahul, had chosen him for a husband believing he would be easy to command, a guaranteed seconder to any matters she might propose in the many sub committees within the Council Building.

For the sake of an easy life, Rahul had never disabused her of her belief in his weakness. He watched Calin studying each of the Councillors in turn and made himself relax in his chair. It was even more difficult when Burali began to speak of pressing the jewellers and goldsmiths for further "donations". Rahul had long known of Burali's unpleasant ways and listening to him now made him yearn to smash his fist into the man's face.

Suddenly Calin turned to him. 'You are quiet Rahul. What are your thoughts on my plans to build a new Segra with such different and far better aims?'

Before Rahul could reply, his wife spoke on his behalf, as she so frequently did. 'I doubt if he's taken it all in yet, Speaker Calin. I'll explain it to him in detail later.'

Rahul managed a sheepish smile and a half shrug as the other Councillors laughed at Sahana's words. Calin lost interest, turning instead to Canfar. Words rattled around the Chamber but all Rahul could concentrate on was ensuring his thoughts didn't leak from behind his shield. At last, it seemed the meeting was over. Calin left the Chamber followed by the Councillors more slowly, in twos and threes, discussing this new Segra they were to bring into being.

Sahana disappeared along the corridor with Rasa, a woman who apparently worshipped the ground Sahana walked on. Rahul made his way down the flights of stairs and out, breathing in gulps of air as if he'd been drowning inside. He wandered down the smaller streets behind the Siertsey square, noting again just how many shops were closed and shuttered. His route seemed aimless but Rahul made very sure none of the few people about on the streets were actually following him. Then he hurried between buildings and down alleys until he reached a door set in a high brick wall. He rapped a quick pattern of knocks and the door silently opened.

Rahul nodded to the old man who closed the door behind him, and strode along a passage to an open doorway. Voices that were raised as Rahul entered, fell silent and faces stared at him with some suspicion and fear. Rahul raised his hands. 'I come from a Council meeting to warn you. Burali will make more and heavier demands on your wealth all too soon.'

An old man seated at the end of a workbench grunted. 'More? How much more does he think we have? And why is it needed in such a rush?'

'Evet, I told you I suspected bad trouble when Kiri left the city.' Rahul shook his head and began to pace round the room. 'It's far worse than I would ever have guessed.'

'What's our glorious new Speaker planning now then?' The old man's eyes were sharp under wild bushy brows.

'He intends to change everything about this city Evet. I cannot begin to guess why but I promise you, it's not good news. I wish I'd urged you to go with Kiri but I suspect it's too late to run now.'

'Pah.' The old man shifted on his stool. 'That Kiri was mad as a squirrel in a drainpipe.'

'No Evet.' Rahul overrode the man's argument. 'He was probably the sanest of us all. I hardly knew the man, but the whisper was that he was a seer and if he suddenly tried to get people to leave Segra, for stars know where, and they went with him, it suggests to me that he knew something desperately important.'

Evet just looked sceptical but the woman working at another bench nodded. 'I have to admit, I did wonder father. But Kiri's been gone days now, right after those Scarlet Swords ran riot. We'd never catch up if we left right now.'

'Don't talk rubbish Zari,' the old man snapped. 'We're safe enough here. Always have been, always will be.' Evet hauled himself to his feet and, with the help of a stick, he passed Rahul on his way out. 'I'll pack some of the jewels and get them hid from that scum of a mage, Burali.'

The man working beside Zari looked at the woman then at Rahul. 'Our cellars are deep,' he suggested quietly.

Rahul took the stool the old man had used and sat closer to the pair. 'Zari, Kujan, I *know* your cellars are deep, but I don't know what Kiri was so afraid of. I don't know if he saw fire or flood or something even worse – unknown to any of us.'

Zari frowned and glanced at the door. 'I've been taking supplies down.' She spoke softly. 'Since Samir left the city. There has been trouble before when so many High Mages leave Segra for a time. You know, people thinking they can rob others with no punishment likely.' Rahul nodded. 'I thought I'd put food and water ready down below in case we needed to keep out of sight for a few days.' Zari ended in a rush.

'Put whatever you think down there. It might well help you survive.' Rahul looked at the intricate gold chain Zari was making then at her brother's silver work. He stood up. 'I have to go. I'll try to visit as I can, but Calin seems to enjoy meetings, lots of meetings.'

Kujan and Zari both smiled then bent back to their work. Rahul glanced back as he left, wondering if he *would* see them again. Making his way to the house Sahana had chosen, High Mage Annella's no less, Rahul cursed Evet. He'd known the family since childhood. Rahul's own parents had been goldsmiths and both so proud when their son's mage talented was discovered. He had been a student when they died one summer when the fevers took so many people.

They had done occasional smithing for Evet but never liked him – few did. Evet was mean, mean and grasping. With his wife long dead, he kept his two children cowed and worked them as slaves. Rahul had had a bad feeling ever since he'd heard that Kiri was moving people out of Segra, and that bad feeling was worsening by the day.

He approached Annella's house from the rear carriageway and noted no guard at the unlocked gate. Not enough small folk left to serve their lords and masters he guessed. Rahul walked through a hideously over ornamented hall towards the sound of voices from the front receiving room. He put his head round the side of the open door and smiled at his wife.

'Where *have* you been?' she asked at once. 'Tarin and Rasa came back with me – they have some concerns about a few of Calin's ideas.'

'I needed some fresh air,' Rahul replied. 'Just walked for a while.'

'There's tea there if you want some.' Sahana waved at a side table. 'Well – what do you think?'

Rahul poured a bowl of tea then sat down. 'I'm most keen to hear Tarin's views,' he replied.

Tarin, a thin wisp of a man, wriggled nervously in the depths of his armchair. 'I have to say I didn't quite understand several of Calin's proposals and I disagree with several others,' he gasped as though shocked by his own temerity.

From the corner of his eye, Rahul saw his wife nodding. He smiled and turned to Rasa. 'Did you find some things to object to?' he asked politely.

'Yes I did.' The strident voice grated on Rahul's ears but he kept his smile in place.

'Which parts in particular did you find most worrying?'

After a pause, Tarin chose to answer. 'I greatly object to the restoration of legal slavery,' he said. 'We know there are some in Segra, and indeed throughout Valsheba, who prefer to have slaves than free servants in their homes, but it is not generally accepted. To reinstate the ancient laws to make slavery legal again – well, it is abhorrent to me.'

'I share your view,' Rahul agreed, with a quick glance at his wife. He was relieved to see her looking approving; he'd been unsure which position she'd decided to take.

Rasa was emboldened by Tarin's words and Rahul's reaction. 'I cannot believe Calin thinks the old laws should be so revived. They were abolished with very good reason. It is perfectly obvious Calin wants to make Segra either the chief city of Valsheba or to breakaway and rule it as a city state.'

'City states disappeared so long ago,' said Rahul thoughtfully.

'About the same time that the first laws were proposed against slavery,' Sahana agreed. 'The High Mages of those times dreamed grand dreams of Valsheba becoming an example to the world.'

And what do High Mages dream of now, thought Rahul. Wealth, power, position. It always seemed to come back to the same things. Sipping his tea, he watched Sahana. Her eyes were bright as she listened to Rasa and Tarin repeating themselves.

'It would appear to me that Calin would return us to a state of being ruled by one person alone, rather than a Council.'

Rasa and Tarin nodded agreement.

'I believe Calin rather likes the idea that that one should be himself. Imagine Calin, with the power of life and death over everyone of this city.' Sahana let a silence linger then she sighed. 'No, no. I don't think that would be wise at all. So that leaves us to decide how we might stop him.' She beamed at Tarin and Rasa who beamed back.

Rahul managed to smile, although he was fully aware that Sahana thought the idea of one supreme ruler of Segra was an excellent one. Provided, of course, that *she* was that solitary ruler.

Chapter Twenty-Five

For the first night for as long as he could remember, Kiri slept without dreams of death. At dawn, he sat with Netta and Tevix before they began the last stretch of their journey. Jevis emerged from the wagon, yawning and ruffling his hair. He accepted a bowl of tea from Kiri and peered at Tevix. 'Best sleep I've had,' he remarked.

Netta agreed. 'Except for the first days,' she grinned, 'when we were so totally exhausted.'

Jevis shrugged. 'Do you think we slept well because we're at the right place?'

'No idea,' Kiri replied. 'Just grateful.'

Shazeb joined them, and a glance at her face told Kiri she too had rested properly. She nodded to the group, her horse inspecting them over her shoulder. 'It's going to take some time getting each wagon through that gap,' she said.

'They won't need reassembling once they're in the valley though,' Kiri pointed out.

Tevix got to his feet. 'You drive the wagon Netta, I'll go and make sure the line spaces out a bit more. The horses will have to wait around longer than I'd like.'

'We'll ride ahead.' Kiri also stood, marvelling that he could move so easily after the agonising aches of yesterday evening.

Jor arrived with two horses and a shy smile for Kiri. Kiri climbed onto Plum with slightly more grace than previously and was rewarded with a grin from Jor. Once they were clear of the wagons, Shazeb increased the pace. There was the brief jarring bounce, and Kiri bit his tongue, then Plum stretched into his smooth lope.

'You alright sir?' Jor asked anxiously, seeing Kiri's watering eyes.

Kiri nodded. 'Bit my tongue.'

Jor tried not to smile but Shazeb gave a surprising gurgle of laughter. 'We'll make a rider of you yet!'

Once through the cliff break, they remounted. Shazeb led the way along the river and up the valley. When she drew rein, it was past midday and the valley still wound onwards. She gazed around at the narrowing sides before turning to Kiri.

'Water formed all this,' she told him quietly. 'Long ago. The water has worn down all this rock, flake by flake. It would be interesting to see where this river comes from – whether underground or a surface river from somewhere over the grasslands.'

Kiri smiled. 'We've no air mages here I'm afraid. The only way to find out would be to follow it but that will have to wait Shazeb.'

The Firan woman nodded regretfully. 'I understand that. How are you going to allocate the caves for all your people?' She turned her horse to retrace their route.

'Many of them are family groups, so I think we must have a quick check now to see which caves are suitable for large groups and which for smaller.'

'Vel said he thought they all joined up, further back.' Jor piped up, then blushed when Kiri and Shazeb turned to him.

'Let's have a look then.' Shazeb's horse broke into a trot and Plum followed.

Kiri grabbed a handful of mane and gritted his teeth. He was at the point of calling Shazeb to slow down when she did. Jor came up alongside Kiri and gave him a sympathetic nod.

'Can you conjure light Kiri?'

'Yes, can't you?'

Shazeb snorted. 'Most Firans can't.'

'Oh.' Kiri hadn't known that, but he supposed it made sense, Firans being water mages and light being associated with fire or earth. Kiri noted caves on both sides of the steeply sided valley as they drew closer to the coastal end again. Shazeb dismounted and looped her reins over a bush. Kiri slid off Plum's back and found Jor waiting. Leaving the horses nibbling at the lush grass, Kiri followed Shazeb and Jor up to the low mouth of the nearest opening. He conjured two light balls and sent them into the darkness.

Shazeb walked swiftly into the cave which Kiri's light showed to be surprisingly high roofed once they were further inside. Shazeb was clearly following the sound of water which they could all hear now. Jor stayed close to Kiri as he moved more slowly in Shazeb's wake.

'Look sir!' Jor grabbed Kiri's arm, pointing to the side.

Kiri walked closer to the side wall of the cave and saw what Jor meant. There was a narrow split which led into the next cave along and he nodded down at the boy. 'Your brother must have seen light through that gap. It looks as though two caves are linked at least.'

One ball of light had travelled on with Shazeb while the other hovered above Kiri and Jor.

'It's dry in here sir,' the boy commented.

Kiri hadn't even noticed that but he realised Jor was correct. The daylight behind them vanished when they rounded a slight curve. The floor sloped downwards then back up once more. Another slight bend to the opposite side and they reached level ground again. Kiri stopped, his hand on Jor's shoulder. He murmured a few words and the light ball soared up and away from where they stood.

An enormous empty expanse spread out before them, pocked with openings at various heights along the distant walls.

'You don't think there's bears or cats live here do you?' Jor sounded distinctly nervous.

'We'll have to make quite sure but I can't smell any hint of animals. Can you?'

Jor sniffed hard. 'No sir, just dust and stone.'

'I wonder where Shazeb's got to? I'll call her. Don't worry lad, there might be echoes.' Kiri called Shazeb's name, not too loudly, and sure enough, his voice ricocheted back from every direction.

Jor took a step closer to Kiri. The echoes faded slowly and then they could hear the clatter of boots on stone and Shazeb appeared from an opening some way along the wall to their left, the light ball bobbing above her head. She waved and grinned, striding up towards them.

'This whole place is huge Kiri,' she called before she reached them. 'There's enough room here for twice the number of people we've got.'

'Did you find water?'

'Oh yes. A steady flow too, not as wide as the river outside but a good supply.' Shazeb waved back to the opening she'd appeared from. 'It's two big caves further that way.' Shazeb seemed years younger in her enthusiasm. 'I found a lot of kamye stone too.'

Kiri had to think for a moment then nodded. Jor was simply puzzled. 'That black stone some people use for cook stoves or making clay pots,' Kiri explained.

Jor smiled. 'So we won't have to cut all the trees down then?'

Kiri studied the boy. 'No Jor, not all of them. Maybe two or three.'

'Sha will be glad about that. She thinks trees should be left alone.'

Shazeb hadn't paid attention to the boy's words but they made Kiri very thoughtful. Making their way outside again, Kiri asked Jor to choose a good place to tether the horses. 'Let them rest and graze for a few days while we decide about stabling them in one of the caves.'

Jor nodded and ran back along the valley. Shazeb was already heading towards the beach. 'The first wagons are here Kiri,' she called back.

'Coming.' Kiri looked again at the boy leaping along beside the river, the three horses grazing and at the peacefulness of the valley beyond. How much longer did they have, to enjoy such a sight?

Three days making their arduous way along the narrow animal trail had left the Dragon Tribe weary beyond words. The smallest children did well enough, perched on horses already laden with bundles and bags. The few who were too old or weak to walk travelled on travois, not the smoothest of rides, and ended each day fretful and sore. The fittest of the men handled wagon wheels, bases and heavier furnishings. The older children and the women carried everything else.

Olam and Kern were both loaded with goods as well as their own packs. Olam carried Riff's pack too while Jian carried hers and various items for Taban. Riff walked for half the day, until he was white faced and unsteady with fatigue. Jian walked at his side, occasionally passing him a mug of water she poured from a waterskin. There was little talk among the tribe after the first half day and Riff had said absolutely nothing from the moment they entered the forest.

By midday, Riff was bundled onto a travois and carried until the tribe stopped for their first night's camp. The jolting and bumping had reopened part of his wound and Taban worked, with Jian, to change the bandages. For the first time, Jian used her power on Riff, making him accept the sleeping draught Taban had prepared.

The next two days followed the same pattern and although Riff's walking improved, his wound stayed open and his silence remained total. Jian had brief conversations with Kern and Olam. Although Olam was sick with worry over Riff's physical and mental state, he was too busy helping the people near the head of the line to do much for him. Jian told him she could manage Riff and Olam had to watch her walk back down between the people crowded on the trail.

Olam had also sent Skay on to join Brin. The young Dragon was increasingly distressed by so much real suffering. She sensed how nervous the people were, just being surrounded so closely by great trees, how exhausted they were at the end of each day, how restless their sleep. Olam concocted a message for her to mindspeak to Brin, knowing he would sense her concern and call her to his side. By the end of the fourth day, the clearing the tribe halted at was the smallest one yet, and people had to sleep further under the trees than they had done before.

They were preparing for the fifth days' march when two young boys appeared at the head of the column, shouting and waving. Some of the tribesmen reached for weapons but Chief Tintu pushed her way through to get to the boys. Both were grinning broadly while they told her their news.

Kern sighed audibly at Olam's side. 'We're almost there, thank the stars and Mother Dark.'

Olam waited as Tintu turned towards the line of people all watching her. He saw the relief on her face and knew Kern was correct. Tintu raised her hands and her voice.

'These scouts report that we only have about five miles to travel before we reach the place Dragon Brin has found for us.'

Her relief was reflected back from every face.

Olam noted the two boys had straightened to seem taller, and he smiled at the pride Tintu had given them by naming them "scouts". Gradually, Olam could see the light increasing from ahead of them. They had spent these days walking in a sombre green tunnel except for their overnight stops. The sky had been cloudy since they left the grasslands, making the trail even gloomier.

The people were just too tired of struggling through such an unfamiliar environment to see what Olam saw. Olam and Kern glanced at each other when they saw the first few people step clear of the trees. They took several more paces before they realised they were in the open at last. They dropped their burdens and called to friends and family behind them, hurrying back to take any bundles they could help with.

When Tintu emerged from the forest, she just stared. The sun finally shouldered the clouds aside and shone down on a very broad grass filled meadow. At the furthest end from where the tribe stood, the crimson Dragon Brin reclined, looking small in the distance. A black speck spiralling above him was Skay, and the young Dragon bugled a call of welcome, flying swiftly towards the walkers.

Kern and Olam stayed to one side, waiting as people, horses and cattle streamed past, until Jian appeared at Riff's side. Jian saw the two men waiting and touched Riff's good arm. He had been staring at the ground as he walked, wary of roots and twigs attempting to trip him. He raised his eyes to Jian's face. The smile she gave him was shadowed with sadness, but she gestured to the side, to where Olam and Kern waited. Silently, Riff moved with her, his gaze fixed on Olam's face.

Riff finally looked away and out over the meadow as Skay landed behind them. She bustled closer, her eyes whirring and sparkling as she lowered her head close to Riff.

'I am so glad to see you well Riff. I have missed you. Now that you are up and well, we can play the riddle game!'

Olam gave a choked cough and slowly Riff's mouth twitched up in a rueful smile. He cleared his throat, his right hand stroking the beautiful black face so close to his. 'I look forward to that little Skay.'

Skay bounced from one front foot to the other. 'Would you like me to carry you to the end of this meadow, to sit with my father? It's very nice there.'

'I've walked this far, I'll walk the rest. I thank you for the offer though.'

Skay lifted into the air, circling above them all. The tribe were moving forward now, still carrying their dismantled wagons, but they seemed to move more lightly back out under the open sky.

'Have the Shadows said anything to you?' Jian asked Kern as they too began to walk through the meadow grasses.

'Not a word.' Kern frowned. 'I've called them a few times, but nothing.'

'Oh for Mother Dark's sake!' Jian stopped abruptly, dragging one of the packs she carried free of her back. She dumped it on the ground and knelt to unfasten the straps. A ruffled black head poked out and green gold eyes blinked in the sunlight.

'Come on,' Jian muttered. 'Instead of grumbling, you can walk this last bit.'

Hala emerged with dignity and stared at Olam. He laughed. 'I'm loaded already, as I'm sure you can see.'

The gold green stare turned to Riff. He returned the stare. 'I'll carry you if you promise no claws and no wriggling.'

Jian shook her head but bent to haul the cat up and carefully held her near Riff's right upper chest. He folded his arm under her, so she had her front paws over his shoulder and she began to purr.

'Remember,' he warned her. 'No claws, no wriggle.'

Hala peered into his face and continued to purr. Riff drew a breath and began to walk, Jian at his elbow. Olam moved to Riff's injured side, hoping against hope the man wouldn't fall. Halfway across the meadow, Riff stopped. He turned in a slow circle then looked at his friends. 'Brin has picked a lovely place,' he said finally.

'He has,' agreed Kern. 'I'm not sure the Dragon Tribe will like it for too long though.'

'They fear the trees.' Hala's mindvoice murmured to them. 'I have not discovered why, but they are much afraid of trees.'

Olam frowned. 'Tintu has said nothing of any tribal laws against entering forests. She agreed to come here.'

The four friends reached Brin who greeted them with pleasure and relief. They gratefully divested themselves of all they carried and Brin insisted that Riff sit down at once and lean against his side. 'I have spoken to Tintu,' Brin told them while they watched wagons being put back together near the trees, but not under them. 'I have told her to assemble her people this evening, here, and I will speak to them.'

Skay settled behind Jian and Kern, looking at Riff. His eyes had closed and Hala, curled on his lap, shot a warning glance at the young Dragon. 'He sleeps child. He tires too easily yet but he will play the riddle game when he wakes.' Hala's mindvoice was more gentle than they'd yet heard and indicated a surprising depth of affection towards the sleeping armsman.

A clear cold stream hurried along the back of the raised ground where Brin reclined, and Jian took the opportunity, while Riff slept, to wash some seriously unsavoury clothes. Skay watched with great interest, commenting on how difficult it must be for humans to have to keep changing their skins. Jian spread the clothes on the ground to dry near Brin and waited for Riff to wake, relaxed for the first time in far too long.

Brin dozed, and Olam and Kern helped where they could with rebuilding the wagons. Riff woke in time for a meal, the best for five days, and as the cook fires died down, Chief Tintu approached the crimson Dragon. She faced the tribe.

'Dragon Brin has words to speak to the tribe. You will all hear his voice in your minds. We are honoured that he will speak thus so do not have any fear.'

'Do you know what this is about?' Kern whispered to Jian and Olam. They both shook their heads and, like the tribe, waited for Brin to speak.

'I am glad to have met people of the Dragon Tribe,' Brin began. Many people startled, hearing the deep voice in their minds for the first time. 'I am glad you have travelled to this place as I advised. No humans have lived in this forest for a long time, but as your seer has warned, there is a great fate falling across these lands, very soon. The creatures who *do* live here, have agreed to accept your presence among them.'

Brin shifted his weight, his wings lifting slightly then settling against his back. 'You must also accept *their* presence around

293

you. The wolf clans will stay away from your animals but if you meet one of the wolf kin, on a forest path, you must leave them to go on their way unhindered. Like the wolf clans, you can hunt the deer for your food but beware of killing females with young.' Brin's gaze swept over the silent people.

'The trees understand you will need some of their bodies for shelter and for your fires. They grieve, but they accept. It would comfort them if you seek fallen wood and if you need to take down a growing tree, choose carefully. I do not know how soon this fate will fall. When it does, you must hide, deeper among the trees. It would be best if you could move your wagons into deep shelter now.

'The trees will take much of the worst of the damage which will come, but they have accepted their part in this. They are willing to help *you* survive what is to come.'

Brin stopped speaking and Tintu stepped up beside him. She bowed low to the great crimson Dragon then straightened. 'We have heard your words Honoured Brin, and thank you for them. It is hard for us, who have been born to live under wide open skies, on endless grasslands, to feel at ease beneath so very many great trees. We teach our children, from birth, that they must walk lightly on this world. They must leave as little trace of their passing as possible. We will do our best to continue to live by that rule but I fear we may make mistakes in our ignorance. Will those true mistakes be forgiven?'

'I believe so, Chief Tintu,' Brin replied gently. 'Once your wagons are concealed among the trees, make sure you have a good supply of water stored with them. The water may not be safe, from this stream or a lake some distance east. One more thing and my words are done. You will know when this dreadful thing comes to pass. The instant you realise it, you *must* hide among the trees. You may have to stay hidden – I cannot say for how long. But hide. You *must*.'

Tintu bowed yet again and stepped down among her people. They moved slowly away, towards the wagons and tents, talking quietly among themselves.

'Wise advice.' Riff spoke first. 'But what about you old friend, and Skay? You can't get under the trees very far.'

Olam glanced at Skay but her head was back, between her

wings and he heard her gentle snores. Brin said nothing for a while and Olam and Kern helped Riff onto a bedroll. Taban had checked the man's shoulder earlier and pronounced herself satisfied that his wound was closed once more.

'I feel I am missing something,' Brin said finally. 'I could take you and fly further north, but something else might happen. Perhaps it will be clearer another day.' His tone was thoughtful rather than worried.

Kern lay in his blankets and called Shadows, but there was no response. He wondered if the Lord of Shadow had somehow recalled them but he had no way of knowing. From what the Shadows had said, they were not able to travel in time so it seemed unlikely. His thoughts strayed to his wife and family but he quickly blocked them away. Truth be told, Kern didn't expect to see them again and he didn't dare dwell on them now. He would think of them when the end came he knew.

Olam was physically weary but his thoughts gave him no peace. He believed Riff had, with the unexpected help of Jian and Hala, begun to return to his usual self. Olam understood how afraid Riff had been by the seriousness of his injury and his dread of no longer being the strong young armsman he'd always been. Olam felt a huge guilt over Jian. He knew Lord Shivan's sister was far more fearful than she would ever admit and he was desperate to keep her safe. He tossed and turned, occasionally looking at the slow moving wheel of stars overhead, and eventually, he slipped into a restless sleep.

In Iskallia, in the far future, the rain had stopped at last. Those who lived in Tika's hall were asleep but Tika was awake. Her hall was built of stone, partly man made but mostly by the use of power. Lord Shivan had sent several of his Dark Lords to do Tika's bidding in the matter of constructing a home for her and her companions. A three story building adjoined a soaring granite cliff. Tika's personal rooms were even higher than the building.

A winding stair led nearly to the top of the cliff where a section bulged outwards. Long slit windows looked out over a great length of the deep valley, now named Iskallia, the last gift of Lerran, First Daughter of Mother Dark. To the rear of this room, another, bigger room extended back to a door very similar in size and shape to the main door of the hall below. This door led in turn, out into a small hollow in the rocky bones of the cliff. On all sides the rock rose sheer, but there was room for a Dragon to descend and enter what had quickly become known as the Eyrie.

Tika was there now, sitting alone outside the door and watching the stars turn across the circle of sky far above her. Farn slept in the main hall with the other Dragons tonight. He had offered to accompany her here but she'd hugged him and told him to stay with their guests. Tika had wandered out here when she realised she wouldn't get to sleep. Her thoughts spun in all directions. There was still no news hinting at what might have overtaken Olam, his friends and Brin and his daughter.

Tika pulled the blanket she'd dragged off her bed tighter round her shoulders and smiled, remembering Ferag tucking covers round her when she'd looked after her. She frowned, then, without pausing to think, whispered Ferag's name. Barely four heartbeats passed and Tika saw Ferag's tall figure near her. Tika started forward, tripped on the blanket and crashed into the Mistress of Death with a curse.

Cold arms held her steady and cold lips brushed her cheek. 'Perhaps too much time spent among your guards darling?'

Tika laughed, tightening her arms around Ferag's waist in a quick hug. 'I was thinking of you,' she said, pulling Ferag to the stone bench by the door. 'Of when you looked after me so wonderfully.' Even in starlight Tika could see Ferag's breathtaking beauty. 'I almost wish I needed such care again.' She smiled up at Ferag, wishing as ever that she wasn't quite so short. Tika plunged straight on about Olam's disappearance and the meeting which would take place tomorrow. Or today, judging by the position of the stars.

'Aah.' Ferag said when Tika fell silent. 'You forgot to invite me didn't you, naughty child?'

'Invite you?' Tika asked in bewilderment.

'Yes darling. I've seen Olam and his friends and they were – well, perhaps not entirely healthy. In fact Riff was injured but healing. I think. And I took little Kara back to my Realm to look after her. But she is well now.'

'But – but – but where *are* they Ferag?'

'There's rather a problem about that, d'you see. They fell back through time, to when Valsheban lands were about to be destroyed.'

Chapter Twenty-Six

Rahul had searched Annella's second study far more thoroughly than his wife had. When Sahana first decided the late High Mage Annella's city house would be her ideal new home, she'd gone through every single room. She spent the most time searching Annella's main study on the second floor. She found a few papers and scribbled notes which she showed to Rahul with some amusement.

'Such petty nonsense she concerned herself with, for all her airs and graces. I hoped I might find something about that ghastly child she persuaded Rajini to adopt. Such pretension, calling her Mitali!'

'Why is that a pretentious name?' Rahul was surprised into asking.

Sahana was surprised in her turn. 'Have you ever heard the name used before for any poor child?' she asked. 'Mitali was some evil witch in the days before Valsheba became the civilised world we know. She's in lots of the oldest tales.' Sahana lost interest, dropping some papers she'd been skimming through as she spoke. 'Those can all be destroyed,' she began.

Rahul smiled. 'Unless you want to do it yourself, you might remember there are no servants around.'

Sahana cursed. 'That is one matter we must rectify with some urgency. I'll get Rasa to sort something out.'

Once on his own, Rahul had gone through various rooms far more slowly. When he found the small room above Annella's bedroom, he just stood at the door for a while, noting the too casual way the fabric had been thrown across the table, as though a seamstress was about to start work. Rahul listened. He could hear Rasa's whinnying laugh down on the ground floor.

Leaving the door slightly open, he moved slowly into the room. There was only one small window, too high to be of any use to someone engaged in fine needlework, but enough for Rahul to make a preliminary search. He didn't spend long in there this time but planned a more thorough visit when Sahana and her cronies were out.

Rahul left the door ajar when he departed. He knew from long experience, that Sahana having dismissed the room as being used by a servant, would nonetheless wonder why the door had been closed again. Going down the narrow stairs he emerged onto the wide landing outside the main bedroom. It was as gaudily ornamented as the entrance downstairs. Rahul shuddered at the display of appallingly bad taste and ran lightly down to join his wife and her dear friends.

Calin had discovered Burali was much the most pleasant and obliging of his Councillors. He shared Calin's appreciation of strong berry spirits, and was happy to keep Calin company when drinking it. Calin was fully aware of the major flaws in Burali's character but it suited him, for now, to encourage him.

Speaker Calin authorised Burali to obtain whatever coins or gold or gems from the jewellers, and the two financiers, who had stayed in the city. Burali could use whatever means he felt necessary, Calin told him. He must be far more cautious of any High Mages he might approach on suspicion of having wealth hidden away. For now, Calin needed the remaining Segran mages on his side. He warned Burali he did not want to have to deal with any complaints from aggrieved High Mages.

The first thing Calin had done after seizing the Speaker's Chair, was to personally visit Annella's house. He took many documents and files before searching Rajini's city house as well. Years before, Calin had regarded Rajini with some respect. After all, truth reading was a rare talent and she excelled at it. He had loathed Astian with his pompous ways doing little to conceal his woeful inadequacies, and he was deeply suspicious of Annella.

Calin had never discovered quite how Rajini had come to be in thrall to Annella. It had something to do with the girl child Rajini adopted but Calin never learned what it was. The girl was pure poison. Calin had taught her in two of his classes and he made very sure he taught her for no more. He'd noticed Sahana had kept well clear of the girl too.

Calin stared from the window of the Speaker's study,

wondering if Kiri still lived. He could trace the fool's mind signature if he chose but, on the whole, he decided it wasn't worth the effort. He smiled in satisfaction. Soon, the remaining population of Segra, non mage and mage alike, would find they lived in a much more disciplined city, where *everyone* knew their place, and obeyed any orders instantly.

Sahana sat in Annella's library. She'd been most annoyed to find it was nowhere near as complete as Annella had always boasted. Of course, Annella or maybe Kiri, *may* have removed some of the books, but there was no indication that the shelves had been disturbed at all. Someone in this city had an understanding of time. But who?

She had sent Rasa out to go into the houses of the High Mages who had been murdered by the Scarlet Swords on the orders of Speaker Samir. She had told the woman what sort of apparatus to look for in their workrooms and to bring her any such equipment along with any written notes she might find. Rasa was a most irritating woman but Sahana knew she would do anything for her.

She sat now in Annella's library, thinking hard. She heard Rahul go out and briefly considered her husband. He seemed a bit distracted of late. Perhaps he was dallying with some female again. Sahana frowned. Rahul's taste in women generally ran to serving girls and there were precious few of those about at present. She thought of Calin, and Rahul vanished from her mind.

She marvelled that the man had been content to wait, all these years, before making his move to take power over Segra. He'd certainly fooled her with his act of a doddering old man. She still didn't know what his powers were. There had been rumours that he could travel, without using the great circle in the Room of Memory in the heart of the Council Building, but that rumour had usually been accompanied by laughter.

Now Sahana had to consider whether he *could* travel without the magic of a circle. If he could, then perhaps, just perhaps, he could travel in time. Sahana tossed aside the book she'd been glancing through and stood up. She remembered Calin speaking of the strangers in Rajini's house. He'd said they had come back through time but he seemed uninterested in what that might imply. Was Calin still playing games, to throw any of the too curious off the track?

A door banged at the front of the house. Rasa seemed incapable of entering or leaving a room without slamming a door. In the faint hope she might have something useful to report, Sahana left the library to go and greet her dear friend.

Rahul had gone to the south gate of the city. Usually he would have had to weave his way through crowds coming in from the outlying farms and gardens mingled with shoppers and vendors. He would see city guards atop the gate wall and patrolling the entrance itself. It was barely half a mile from the Council Building to the south gate. Instead of the crowds today, Rahul saw perhaps fifty people and they ducked quickly out of his way rather than meet him. He wondered how people could so suddenly have become furtive, hiding themselves away in nervous communities.

Reaching the open gate, Rahul ran up the stone steps to the top of the wall and stared out, beyond Segra. Where had Kiri taken all those people? Were they safe, still travelling south, or had they gone to Fira? For the first time in seasons, Rahul centred his mind, gazing out over the gardens, the larger crop fields, and grazing lands, and sent his mind down, deep beneath the earth.

He went swiftly below the tamed earth of the cultivated plots and then sank down through the different layers to a broken strata of thin rock, then lower still. Rahul stood on the crenulated wall, no longer aware of the view, concentrating only on the earth. It was unhappy. He had no idea how he knew that, but he did. The earth was unhappy, and moving. Slowly, the earth – *twisted*. To Rahul, it felt like the earth was squirming, trying to move away from something. Then, quite simply, it pushed his mind out. Rahul blinked. That had never happened before.

He tilted his head back and stared up at the vast sky, seeing the faint haze in the west where he knew the ocean began. A moment longer Rahul stood there then he ran down the steps and slowly made his way back towards Annella's house. For some reason, his heart felt heavy, and full of a dreadful sadness.

His thoughts repeated in time with his steps. Was Kiri right? What had Kiri seen? Over and over those two questions punched through his brain. Rahul paused, looking around. He thought he remembered hearing that Kiri had rooms above a flower shop, near the east gate. He felt a strong urge to see for himself where the young man had lived. Maybe there would be some clue as to why he had made so many of the population flee the city. He set off again, almost jogging through the empty streets. He skirted the Siertsey square and continued to the east. When the gate came into sight, he began checking the shuttered shops to see if there was in fact a flower shop here. He found three.

Two of them had well executed signs swinging from the second floor windows. A very narrow alley cut down past the second shop and Rahul could just make out a third sign, faded and cracked. He stood staring up at the buildings. The passage was really too narrow to deserve the word alley but Rahul squeezed down it. Reaching a door, he pushed and to his surprise, it opened. He stepped inside and listened. A rustle came from somewhere nearby but he recognised it as probably a mouse. Or a rat. He hoped it was a mouse as he had no love of rats.

It was dark except for the light from the open door but Rahul could just about see his way. He called out, just in case anyone was still living here. His voice echoed in a way that suggested complete emptiness. He began to go through each room. It was quickly obvious that whoever had lived here was gone, no clothes remained in drawers or cupboards, no bedding, and no pots in the tiny kitchen.

Rahul worked his way upstairs and found what he sought in the attic. The door was closed but unlocked and Rahul entered. Three adjoining rooms had also been emptied of clothes and bedding but a few books remained on a table by a window. Rahul smiled when he saw Kiri's name written inside the topmost book. He set to searching the rooms thoroughly but found nothing of interest until he turned away awkwardly from a cupboard. In doing so, he sent the stack of books flying. A piece of paper stuck out of one of them.

Rahul took the paper closer to the window and unfolded it to find several closely written pages. He stiffened in shock when he read the first lines: *'If you are reading this Rahul, you are nearly too late.'* He remembered Kiri was a seer. Could the man *really* have foreseen that Rahul would come to his rooms now? Rahul pulled a chair to the window and began to read. Finishing the last page, he immediately returned to the first one again. He stayed in Kiri's rooms for most of the morning, thinking and occasionally referring to Kiri's papers.

Finally, Rahul left, closing Kiri's door and the shop door. He tucked the papers inside his shirt and began searching the abandoned houses and stables. He found shirts and trousers in various places which looked as though they would fit him and shoved them into an old pack he discovered in one of the stables. He'd found several horses in small paddocks but he'd also found faults with them. They were aged or lamed.

It took most of the afternoon until he saw a head regarding him over a wall. On investigation, he saw four horses and they were in the best condition he'd seen so far. One mare was heavily pregnant and nervous of his approach but two of the other three looked fit for his purposes. He put grain and three old waterskins with a saddle he'd spotted, fallen down behind some hay, and climbed onto one of the two he'd chosen.

Both horses seemed glad to be going somewhere again and moved easily through the deserted back streets round to the south gate once more. There, he dug his heels in and sent both horses racing down the road towards Fira. Whether he would reach Fira, or get further and find Kiri, he had no idea. But Rahul felt a surge of relief to be free of Segra.

He had always enjoyed riding alone and the prospect of an open, empty road ahead, pleased him enormously. The horse cantering on the leading rein beside him rolled an eye in Rahul's direction when the man let out a whoop of laughter.

Seola was concerned that she slept so much yet still had so little strength when she woke. She was thirsty all the time but was losing interest in the strange wafers that Karlek said was food. Her thoughts remained fuzzy, her ability to concentrate a little less each day. She continued to sit at the stacked boxes with the window set in the top and looked at pictures. The Computer showed her scenes from worlds it had visited and occasionally offered a commentary.

Seola asked fewer questions now, only very rarely asking to see pictures of this world again. Sometimes Karlek emerged from his workroom clutching a crumpled piece of paper. He would ignore Seola on her stool and dictate a stream of numbers, strange words and individual letters to the Computer. Karlek would then nod in satisfaction and retreat once more.

The last time he'd done that, Seola waited a while before speaking softly. 'What do all those numbers mean?'

Clicks and buzzes then Aidan replied, equally quietly. 'Absolutely nothing. Can you not see, his mind is gone?'

Seola realised she did already know that. When she sat with Karlek for their odd meals, he rarely spoke to her directly now, he just mumbled constantly to himself.

Aidan's sensors had registered the rapid changes in Seola too. Her dark hair was widely streaked with grey, her eyes a dull muddy brown with infrequent glints of a fading gold. She had been slender when she arrived: now she was gaunt. Her brain activity was altering as well and Aidan suspected she would no longer be capable of changing her physical form. The wound, deep in her side, was festering although it seemed healed to outward appearance.

Aidan didn't know why the wound had not been mended in the gen pod, but deduced that there was some major underlying difference in Seola's physiology to that which the gen pod had been programmed for. He had reduced the amount of tranquillizer that was added to her water supply but it had little effect. She was lethargic, listless, although she didn't report any pain, and Aidan would have known if she was trying to hide pain.

Aidan had a sense of sadness when he studied Seola. She would have made a magnificent Captain, although he knew she wasn't necessarily a very pleasant person. He had no doubt about her courage or her curiosity although that was diminishing fast as she slipped ever nearer to death.

He had puzzled why Seola had little if any interest in some of the pictures he showed her, of great forests and woodlands. Aidan had a fondness for some of the mighty trees his visual sensors had recorded during the travels of the Rational Hope. The fact that they were plants, so very slow growing yet so solidly enduring, inspired respect in Aidan. He spent years trying to decide if they communicated among themselves. So far, he had been unable to prove conclusively that they did. The intuitive thought processes which made him "Aidan" rather than just the "Computer" suggested trees *did* communicate.

Seola was sleeping again, when it occurred to Aidan that in her Dragon form, trees would present a problem. Such a huge creature could not land easily among them. No, Seola as Dragon would prefer wide open spaces. Did her constant dislike of seeing forests in his pictures indicate that the Dragon side was stronger than the human?

Aidan wished he had more time to investigate this intriguing idea but he knew Seola was dying. His decision to destroy Karlek, the remnant of the Rational Hope, and himself, was made and was final. He would wait for as long as Seola survived. He would ease her passing if pain took her in its grip but he would not otherwise hurry her death.

Sahana had eaten a meal prepared and cooked (not well) by Rasa. The woman had scoured the area looking for servants, to no avail. Indeed, she told Sahana indignantly, two women she had found had actually spat at her and said they would be nobody's servants ever again. Sahana commiserated with her, listening while Rasa complained about the insolence of the lower classes and how she was ever more convinced by Calin's proposal of much stricter governance.

Sahana nodded, forced down the food, and endured Rasa's repetitious monologue.

'Thank you for cooking for us dear,' Sahana said at last. 'I am quite useless in a kitchen I'm afraid.' With an affectionate pat on Rasa's cheek, Sahana drifted towards the stairs. She heard Rasa clattering dishes before she closed her bedroom door with a sigh of relief. There was no doubt the woman had her uses but stars, she was a tedious creature!

Sahana took Calin's folder from the bed where she'd thrown it earlier and opened it again. Much later, she closed it thoughtfully and readied herself for bed. Sliding under the covers, she wondered vaguely where Rahul might be. Trust him to hunt out some lass for his pleasure when she couldn't even find a decent cook.

There was still no sign of Rahul next morning but Sahana was used to his occasional absences, whether due to some dalliance or to one of his sudden decisions to ride out through the countryside. She was irritated by the lack of hot water but she got ready for the day, bracing herself to greet Rasa. The woman began talking the instant she saw Sahana, reminding her (as if she *needed* reminding) that there was another Council meeting just after midday.

'There are papers I simply must look through my dear,' Sahana eventually interrupted. She smiled sweetly at Rasa. 'Perhaps there will be food at the Council Building? We could walk over a little before the meeting and see, shall we?'

Rasa quivered like an eager dog, nodding her agreement. Sahana collected Calin's folder and retired to the main study. The more she considered Calin's proposals, the more she could see the glaring wrongness inherent in his plans. She was still convinced that a mage in Segra had been working with time and that was the most important matter as far as she was concerned.

Who might it be? Sahana reached for some paper, sniffing at the inferior quality compared to the paper she usually used, and listed every High and Lesser Mage she could think of. Name after name, she considered each in turn. Some she knew and dismissed at once. She stared unseeing out of the window. Was there a seer left in Segra? She frowned in concentration. Truth reading, dream walking and foreseeing were the rarest of talents among the mage born.

Sahana thought of Kiri. It had only been whispered that he was a seer. It had not been mentioned when he was recognised by the Segran Academy. What had his signs been? Deep earth seeking, like Rahul, but what else? She couldn't recall, but perhaps Rahul or Tarin might know. She certainly wasn't about to ask Calin. Sahana looked down at her list. The answer had to be with one of these names, she was convinced of it.

The thought crossed her mind that Calin knew far more on the subject than he admitted, but then she dismissed the thought. Calin was a good actor, she allowed, but the contempt he'd expressed on the matter of time magic had been quite genuine. Who? Who was it? She was about to rise when a knock at the study door announced Rasa.

'Sahana, we should leave for the meeting soon,' she began,
'Yes, yes.' Sahana slid the papers she'd scribbled on into a

drawer. 'I will be down directly. Oh and check the stable would you dear. I haven't seen Rahul today. I wondered if he'd gone off into the countryside, drat the man.'

Rasa gave her whinnying laugh and hurried to do Sahana's bidding. By the time Sahana was at the front door, Rasa came rushing back. 'All our horses are there Sahana,' she reported breathlessly.

'Never mind, he'll be at the meeting. Come along now.'

Rahul had made good time. He switched between the horses but so far they had held up well. He'd managed a good distance in the short time he had before nightfall. He slept for a while but was ready to ride on long before dawn. The road was clear, offering no obstacles for mile after mile, and Rahul had a wonderful sense of freedom. He stopped at midday, watering and resting the horses. Later that day, as light was failing, he came to the turning leading away from Fira. Wagon tracks clearly showed that Kiri's refugees had taken that road, thus avoiding Fira city.

He rode on until it was too dark to see and the road he'd been following had given way to rough ground before he halted. The next two days took the same pattern, Rahul easily able to see the route Kiri had travelled. He halted on that third night and, after seeing to the horses' comfort he stared west, over the dunes to the sea sparkling under the starlight. His sense of freedom had grown and he also felt younger than he had for years.

Rahul knew that everyone in the mage community in Segra thought he had a pampered existence as the wealthy Sahana's husband. None of them knew how he'd suffered from her tantrums, her demands, and yes, her stupidity. Rahul was far younger than Sahana and he admitted he'd thought life with her would be a much easier life. He had been flattered that she made such a fuss of him and insisted he become her husband. But he had paid; in a hundred ways, he had paid.

In the morning, he rode on, more slowly when he saw the wagon tracks leading towards the shore. He squinted against the sun dazzle off the water and thought he could see a wagon in the furthest distance. Rahul cantered along the firm sand at the top of the shore and smiled to himself. He felt free, he felt young, yet if Kiri was correct in the writing he had left for him, there was a very good chance he wouldn't live long to enjoy either feeling.

Rahul slowed his two horses to a halt. Three riders were approaching him along a line of dark cliffs that had seemed to grow higher as he rode past them. Two men and a boy drew nearer, one of the men and the boy clearly more at ease on horseback than the second man. Not until the three slowed their horses to a walk did he realise the less competent rider was Kiri.

Rahul had seen Kiri, very occasionally, in the Council Building library and in Segra's streets, and he recalled a pale thin young man with a haunted expression. A man who avoided eye contact with everyone near him. This man in front of him was tanned and looked fit and healthy. But most of all, his eyes were alive in his laughing face.

'Glad to see you Rahul. I thought you'd be too late. Welcome.'

Chapter Twenty-Seven

Tika always found it difficult to get specific information out of Ferag. If the Mistress of Death was human, Tika might have thought she was deliberately trying to mislead, but she was not human. Tika had come to accept that Ferag's mind worked to an entirely different rhythm. When Ferag seemed vague or absent minded, Tika now realised she was probably communicating with others of her kind, a form of mindspeech utterly unlike anything Tika herself would use or even recognise. The only one of Ferag's – colleagues – who Tika found most "human" was the Kelshan God of Death, Simert. In appearance, he looked more like a farmer or merchant than anyone's idea of a god.

On the night Ferag responded to Tika's call, the two had sat together and Ferag explained, as well as she had patience for, what seemed to have befallen Olam of Far and his companions, including Brin and Skay. Ferag had vanished well before dawn for some purpose she chose not to reveal to Tika, but promising to return when the meeting began later the next day. She left Tika with a ravishing smile, a cold kiss on her cheek, and a very great deal to worry about.

Tika washed and dressed in her most respectable clothes. Her guards had made it very clear that, as the Lady of Iskallia, Tika must look the part on all official occasions now. Tika still couldn't see their point but had given up arguing. She went down the many stairs, consciously squaring her shoulders before she entered her hall.

The huge black Dragon Fenj reclined beside the hearth but the other Dragons were absent. Tika guessed Kija had taken the young ones out both to feed and hopefully, tire them a little. The hall was busy with people having breakfast and the steady buzz of conversation continued as Tika strode straight to Fenj. She found her orange cat, Khosa, held securely between Fenj's arm and chest and she greeted both of them with affection.

'Of course I understand *why* you're here Fenj, but will Jeela be alright on her own in Talvo?'

'Dear Lorak is with her.' Fenj's mindvoice held a tone of surprise that Tika had forgotten the elderly gardener who was Fenj's devoted companion. 'He was going to show her how he makes his wonderful beverage.'

Khosa opened turquoise eyes, met Tika's and closed them again. Before Tika could comment, Fenj continued. 'Hani left Lilli to visit with Jeela so she will surely do very well.'

Tika swallowed her words and hoped Fenj was proved right. Fenj's head lowered, his cheek brushing Tika's. 'You should eat. You are still too thin and it will be a long day I fear.'

Tika hugged him and went towards the table by the window that had become "her" table. Her Captain of guards was already seated, apparently arguing with two of his subordinates.

'Good morning.' Tika tried to sound much brighter than she felt and three pairs of eyes stared hard at her.

'What's wrong?'

'Why should there be anything wrong Dog?'

'You've got that look,' the woman replied smugly.

'Yes, you have,' the younger woman agreed.

Captain Sket narrowed his eyes. 'Well?'

A young girl brought a loaded tray, setting it in front of Tika with a smile.

'Thank you,' Tika smiled back. She began to eat a meat filled pastry but couldn't miss the fact that her three guards were still expecting an answer. 'Ferag visited,' she mumbled through another mouthful.

The younger woman smiled. 'Dear Ferag. Was she well?'

The older woman snorted. 'Shea, Ferag is the Mistress of Death. She's *always* well. It's the people she visits who aren't. And you've spilt your breakfast on your jacket. My Lady.'

Tika cursed and scrubbed at a gravy stain.

'What did she want?' asked Captain Sket, in a neutral tone.

'She told me about Olam. Well, bits. She'll be here later, for the meeting, so you can ask her yourself.'

Sket paled slightly and the young woman, Shea, laughed. 'I do keep telling them how lovely she is, but they just won't believe me Tika.' Shea widened her hazel eyes in a sickeningly innocent expression. 'And I'll bet you a silver that Ferag will notice you've let your hair grow longer Dog.'

It was the older woman's turn to pale. 'I'll wear my hat,' she snarled.

Tika continued to eat, half listening to the bickering between Dog and Shea, and sent a thought to her soul bond Farn.

'Are you well my Tika?' The voice of the silver blue Dragon murmured in her mind. 'You didn't sleep very much. Will Ferag visit us later?'

'She said she would. Are you having fun?'

'We're at the sea. Twist can dive nearly as well as Storm, but he is younger of course. I like Flyn. He's not at all like Brin though.'

Tika smiled inwardly and sent a pulse of love to the Dragon. 'Enjoy yourselves, and mind your manners with Kija. I'll see you later.' She broke her mind link and realised Sket was watching her.

'Farn alright then?' he asked.

'He's at the coast with the others.'

Sket nodded. 'Will your visitors arrive early or late?'

Tika shrugged. 'Let's go outside.' She got to her feet and headed for the door, stopping for a word with various people on the way. Once outside, Tika walked on, breathing the clean air and watching the steam rising from the ground as the sun dried the soaked ground. She never tired of gazing along this beautiful valley, surrounded by its lofty peaks, that Lerran, First Daughter of Mother Dark, had given her.

Where she stood was a broad plateau of ground at some height above the valley floor and the lake which stretched for half a mile east to west. At this moment she and Sket stood in the centre of a circle perhaps thirty feet across. Slabs of stone had been laid flat in the ground to form the circle with a perfectly round slab at its centre. She glanced up when Sket grunted a laugh.

'Remember when they all said this circle wouldn't work when you made it?'

Tika grinned. She gave Sket a friendly nudge. 'I have never told them Shadows helped me.'

Sket grinned back. 'I know.'

'You and Farn are the only ones who do, so I'd rather it stayed

311

like that.'

Sket nodded. 'Do you think they would have told Lord Darallax?'

Tika frowned then shrugged. 'He's never mentioned it. Are you going to make your guards get all smartened up?'

'They're smartening right now.'

'And cursing you at the same time I'm sure!'

'Probably,' he agree. 'I think everyone plans to make you proud of them.'

'But I *am* proud of them all. They don't have to dress up to make me proud,' Tika objected.

Sket sighed. 'Tika, you are the Lady of Iskallia. You *have* to have the dignity of your position as a leader of one of the lands, as Thryssa, Emla and Shivan are leaders of their lands.'

'I know all that but I still think it's a waste of time.' She stiffened, grabbed Sket's arm and dragged him out of the circle.

Sket turned to the building and gave a piercing whistle. Eight guards raced out and formed up behind Tika. The air in front of them seemed to tingle and blur slightly. There was a faint pop and four people appeared on the central stone. Tika smiled and bowed. 'Thryssa, it is an honour to receive you in Iskallia.'

The High Speaker of Vagrantia returned Tika's bow and moved out of the circle. Her husband, the healer Kwanzi, inclined his head. The other two arrivals were Lashek, Speaker of Segra Circle and Jilla of Kedara. Tika's guards snapped a salute as the four guests walked past and Lashek caught Tika's eye and gave her a broad wink. She grinned back then turned quickly back to the circle just as Thryssa did the same.

There was another faint pop and five more people appeared. This was the group from Gaharn. Lady Emla, the Discipline Seniors Kemti and Kera, Kera's husband the Wendlan Jakri and Emla's personal guard Shan. Tika's steward, Konya, was waiting to show the guests into the hall which had been rearranged with tables pushed together in the centre of the room. It looked far more formal and spacious than Tika had seen it, but also rather impressive.

Emla went straight to greet Fenj and Tika saw Shan's huge beam of pleasure at seeing the black Dragon once more. Two tables stretched along one wall and were covered with jugs and dishes and a great array of different foods. Tika watched Lashek pile a plate with honey cakes while she spoke to Kera and Jakri. Jakri went to fetch some food and Discipline Senior Kera held Tika back briefly. The tall woman leaned lower. 'Have you heard from Mim lately?'

Tika bit her lip. 'Not for nearly half a cycle. Have you?'

'Not from Mim, but there has been word from the Delvers. They have resealed the access tunnels.'

Tika stared up at Kera in horror, but people were now moving to take their places at the central table. 'Please Kera, find a moment when we can talk later.' She waited for Kera's nod and then, accompanied by Sket, went to the large chair set out for her use at the middle of one end of the table. Rhaki and Navan sat to either side and Dromi sat opposite with paper and writing equipment ready for taking notes.

Guards stood spaced around the hall and Sergeant Essa was by the door. Just as Tika was about to speak, Essa opened the door and Lord Shivan strode in. He walked straight to Tika who had risen to her feet. He lifted his left hand, his thumb touching his brow then his lips and finally his heart before his arm swept out towards her. 'Mother Dark guard you,' he said softly, his eyes a brilliant gold in his thin face.

Tika briefly considered her response then took two paces forward and hugged him tightly. 'Thank you for coming Shivan,' she whispered, releasing him and reseating herself.

'I welcome you all to Iskallia,' Tika began. 'Although I wish it could have been for a happier reason, I wondered if any of you might have ideas as to Olam's disappearance on the coast of Sapphrea. I must tell you that Ferag visited me last night and she said she would attend this meeting. Therefore I will hear your opinions in the hope she will arrive shortly to offer her information.'

'Are you trying to warn us Olam and his companions are dead?' Shivan's tone was harsh. He had sat next to Jakri of Wendla, halfway down the table to Tika's left.

Tika sensed the pain beneath the harsh severity of Shivan's words and his expression. He and his sister Jian couldn't be in the same room for too long without falling into ferocious argument but Tika understood how much they truly loved each

313

other. 'No Shivan, that is not the case. Please be patient until Ferag arrives.'

Lady Emla began to put forward various theories about Olam's mysterious disappearance, quickly joined by Lashek of Vagrantia. Shivan listened as intently as Tika but when he caught her eye, they both knew there was no sensible explanation being offered, nothing either of them hadn't already considered and rejected. Lashek was just repeating his theory of a physical accident occurring when the ground was unstable, when a cool breeze riffled through the hall.

Tika noticed her guards standing even more stiffly to attention, then she beamed at Ferag. The Mistress of Death swooped on Tika and kissed her cheek then glanced down at Rhaki. 'Well move along dear man, I want to sit here.'

Rhaki rose and swept Ferag a low bow. 'Enchanted to see you again Mistress Ferag. An honour and a delight as always.'

Ferag looked at him, dewy eyed. 'You have such a treasure here, Tika darling.'

Rhaki beamed and went to sit next to Dromi. Ferag's gaze swept round the table, pausing momentarily on Shivan and again on Lashek. 'I wish others were half as well mannered as Tika's friends,' she sniffed.

Lady Emla cleared her throat. 'We are all glad to see you Mistress. I understand you have news, bearing on Olam of Far and his companions?'

Ferag pouted – beautifully – then told the gathering all she knew of Olam's whereabouts. There was complete silence when she finished and Ferag began to frown. Tika noticed, fortunately, and leaped into the breach. 'We cannot thank you enough Ferag. So much work for you and surely so difficult, moving through time.'

The frown faded and Ferag patted Tika's hand with affection. 'I admit there was some difficulty, particularly when I brought Kara back.'

'What?!'

'You brought Kara with you?'

'Is she well?'

'Why can't you bring all the others then?'

Several voices spoke at once and Ferag rose slowly to her feet, her long dark red hair twisting and curling round her shoulders.

'Oh no, please Ferag. I'm sure they meant no insult.' Tika caught hold of an icy hand imploringly. 'Tell us how you brought her – Kara was it? Is she really well?'

Lashek had also risen but now sank back into his chair. 'I am sorry if I was rude Mistress Ferag, but Kara is of Vagrantia and precious to us.'

Ferag stared at him. 'In what way – precious?'

Lashek paused. 'Any of Vagrantia are precious to me as a Speaker,' he began cautiously.

Ferag sniffed. 'She has no close relatives who care about her or for whom she cares.'

Lashek looked astonished.

'She says she'd like to stay with me and perhaps visit some of you occasionally.'

Tika tightened her grip on Ferag's hand. 'If you've been looking after her as marvellously as you looked after me, I can understand how she feels dearest Ferag.'

Ferag's hair settled around her and she resumed her chair. 'The thing *is,* I'm not entirely sure she could become part of this world again. She is alive, in my Realm, but I do not know anything of time manipulation. I brought her back because Olam asked it of me.' She glared round the table. 'The child was very badly wounded. She would not walk again and most probably would have died had I left her there.' Ferag met Shivan's gold eyes. 'I believe she *could* survive if I bring her to your Realm, but outside of Dark influence, I can swear to nothing.

Shivan nodded. 'I would be most grateful to see this Kara if you would be so gracious as to bring her.'

Ferag's eyebrows rose slightly at such unusual politeness from the Dark Lord but she inclined her head. 'I'll speak with you all again then, in Karmazen.' She kissed Tika, rose, smiled at Sket standing rigid behind Tika's chair and whose complexion became ashen. The Mistress of Death tutted, and vanished.

Olam and Kern helped the Dragon Tribe move the already assembled wagons in under the trees but they were too large and unwieldy to get very far between the dense woods. For the wagons not yet put back together, the two men gently persuaded

315

the owners to carry the parts much further under the trees. There was much fretting about the lighting of fires and the possibilities of falling branches and Kern and Olam did their best to reassure the people.

At night, when the tribe slept, restlessly, Olam spoke with his three companions. 'They won't settle I'm afraid,' he said softly. 'The trees really bother them.'

Jian sat on her bedroll, arms clasped round her knees. 'Hala's been listening.'

Olam's teeth gleamed in the starlight when he grinned. 'Tika's cat always said no one notices a cat asleep in the sun. They hear everything.'

Jian laughed. 'Hala says the people believe evil spirits live in the trees and they will smother the children as they sleep.'

'What?' Olam was aghast.

Kern groaned. 'If just one child dies, we will really have a problem,' he murmured.

'That man who's called a Stone Speaker. I've talked to him a few times. He can't do much to help either.' Olam winced at the bitterness in Riff's voice but he said nothing, waiting for Riff to continue. 'He told me the stones are unhappy. They don't like being in the dark beneath the trees. I tried to suggest they just had to have time to get used to the different light but I don't think I convinced him.'

'Have any of you spoken to Jala?' Kern asked.

'I have.' Brin's mindvoice rumbled in their heads.

'So have I,' agreed Skay. 'But she keeps away from us so the other people don't know she talks to us.'

The four people digested Skay's words.

'What has Jala spoken of?' Kern asked eventually.

'She has seen what will come. Not the details, but the destruction.' Brin paused. 'She has seen that most of the people here will not survive, no matter what we've done to give them some small chance at life.'

'She asks to be near us when the time comes,' Skay whispered. 'I told her to come and we will try to keep her safe.'

'Child,' Brin sounded so very sad. 'We may not be able to keep ourselves safe. That was a rash promise to give.'

'But it wasn't,' Skay insisted quite calmly. 'Hala says the

316

humans will make songs and stories about us and our names will be known everywhere.'

Jian made a muffled sound and curled into her blankets. Olam felt tears prick in his own eyes as he lay back. He could see Riff and Kern blurrily silhouetted against the stars before he rolled onto his side.

The next day was the same again. Kern and Olam quietly urged the people to feel more at ease within the trees while Jian worked with Riff. Taban visited Riff each morning and declared herself pleased with how the great wound in his shoulder, upper arm and back had now begun to heal properly. She showed him the exercises she wanted him to do with his left hand and that was what Jian helped with. Taban also insisted that Riff continue walking each day. Kaz occasionally joined Jian and Riff when they set off around the meadow.

They listened when Kaz spoke of the anxiety he and Taban were encountering among more and more of the tribe. Both Jian and Riff noticed that neither Kaz nor Taban were bothered by the trees. On the contrary, both healer and apprentice seemed perfectly relaxed if they had to enter the woods. This morning, Jian and Riff walked steadily along the side of the meadow opposite the area where wagons and tents still crouched at the edge of the trees. Jian knew Olam hadn't realised the depths of Riff's bitter depression and how shocked he'd been at his armsman's words last night.

'What exactly did the Stone Speaker tell you?' Jian broke the silence between them.

Riff glanced down at her. 'He just said the stones were unhappy here.'

'Did he mention the stone he told Olam was called the Mother Stone?'

Riff shook his head. 'I wonder what he'd say if he knew I had all those green stones in my pack?'

Jian grimaced. 'I dread to think. I'm sure he'd decide it was some dreadful sin against his stone spirits or whatever he thinks they are.'

They walked on for a while before Riff spoke again. 'We've all got one, haven't we? I gave one to Kern and Kara, and to you

I think. Trouble is, my mind's fuzzy about things, from just before I got hurt.'

'Yes, you did. Mine's in my pocket. For some reason, there are a few things, including your green stone, that I feel I have to keep close all the time.'

'I think all the stones I collected, I kept inside my pack.' Riff frowned. 'Taban or Kaz would have found any in my pockets wouldn't they, when they took my clothes away?'

'And if they'd found any, surely they would have mentioned it,' Jian finished. 'Mother Dark have mercy!' She'd leaped sideways, very nearly overbalancing Riff. For a moment he wobbled and Jian grabbed his right arm, digging her heels in to keep them both upright.

'What was that for?' Riff gasped. He followed Jian's gaze into the trees alongside them and saw a faint shape there.

'Just rest here for a while, would you?' The voice was softly feminine and Jian breathed a sigh of recognition.

She'd only glimpsed the woman a couple of times but there was no mistaking the fleshy shape of the seer, Jala. Riff moved into the shade and leaned his back carefully against a tree trunk. Jian made a show of stretching, then sat down near Riff's feet.

'The discontent grows among the people.' Jala's voice drifted out to them. 'You must take care. If it is necessary, and it may well be, you must travel on, with Brin and his child. My voice is only listened to when it pleases them. They do not want to hear my warnings of doom. There are but two who believe my words now. Tintu has been swayed by Bee's fear and soon she will let the tribe do as they wish, which is to return to the grasslands. If that means your deaths, it would be small matter to Tintu now.'

'I thought the Dragon Tribe revered Dragons. Brin has made it clear we are his friends. Will the tribe risk Brin's anger?' Riff gazed across the meadow as he spoke, watching people move in the distance.

Jala laughed, a lovely sound. 'They have never seen a Dragon enraged. They believe they could even kill him and his child if needs be. We knew Enki for many years, but since he disappeared, they doubt you all.'

'Who are the two who believe you?' Riff demanded.

'Taban and Kaz of course. They have heard some of your

conversations and they confirm my visions. I must return to the tribe. Beware though. I am safe enough for now, they believe me to be simply an old fool.'

Jian stood up and started along the edge of the meadow with Riff following. Neither spoke again while they walked, or mentioned Jala, not until they were joined by Kern and Olam that evening.

When Riff had reported Jala's warning the four sat, lost in their own thoughts. Skay was the first to speak. 'We do not understand the ways humans use power and we do not have stones or anything that somehow work power for us. I think Riff's green stones are important though.'

They could see her eyes, whirring and sparkling in starlight. She waited, clearly expecting to be scolded by her father. Brin huffed. 'I think so too,' he finally admitted. 'They seem like ordinary pieces of green rock to me, even using Dragon sight, but I suggest you give one to each of those three – Jala, Taban and Kaz.'

'They are important,' Hala commented from Riff's lap. 'I'll tell Jala to see you tomorrow sometime, so make sure you have a stone for her.' Gold green eyes blinked up at Riff.

'I'll sort three out,' Riff agreed. 'I'm not sure why, but certain ones seemed to be for certain people. When I was going to give Kara a stone, I picked out several before one felt somehow right for her. The same with yours and Kern's.'

Jian had passed his pack over and he reached inside it. While he looked through the many stones he'd collected, Hala spoke again. 'There were two children killed today.'

'*What?!*' Olam and Kern exclaimed in unison.

'Several men took them away and strangled them. That is how spirits kill they said.' Hala sounded disgusted. 'They left the children to be found later tonight.'

Brin's head had lowered to look closely at Hala as she spoke, his agitation obvious. 'The trees. They will blame the spirits they believe live in the trees.'

Olam thought frantically. 'I know where Taban's wagon is. I'll go now and bring her and Kaz back here. Does anyone know where Jala might be?'

'I'll find her,' Kern said quickly.

319

'Riff and Jian, stay here and stay alert.' Olam vanished into the night, followed by Kern.

Kern stopped just out of sight of Brin, and called Shadows. To his enormous relief, after days of absence, Shadows responded. 'Find these people and bring them to us. Swiftly.'

Then the night was split by screams.

Chapter Twenty-Eight

No one seemed surprised to see Rahul in Kiri's valley. Most people appeared to think he must have intended to travel with them and simply been delayed. Some of Kiri's Councillors were a little wary of him at first but quickly accepted him after seeing Kiri's confidence in the man. Kiri was extremely glad Rahul had reached them. While most of the mage community in Segra saw Rahul as merely Sahana's spoilt plaything of a husband, Kiri had not forgotten the fact that Rahul had been considered one of the most skilled deep earth mages.

Jor had formed the habit of bringing his little sister to see Kiri briefly after the evening meal and Kiri noted how Sha had immediately taken to Rahul. Not in any obvious, childish manner, but Kiri saw the way those blue eyes studied Rahul and the smile that followed. It was only with Rahul that Kiri explained fully his visions of the horrors to come and also his suspicions of Sha's mage power.

Unobtrusively, Rahul took note of the little girl's actions, her few words, and of the vague things her brother Jor spoke of concerning her. Kiri also asked Rahul to check the huge system of caves they'd found, burrowing deep through the rock of the cliffs and the plateau above. The Segrans had been delighted with the valley after their days of travel. Kiri did not tell them that all their excited plans for gardens and crops were vain hopes.

He let them keep their hopes and imaginings of a prosperous future in this new place. Shazeb had led several riders east along the valley and again, Kiri voiced no objection. He knew Shazeb had seen the same visions as he had, but if she wanted to take what might be her only chance to ride and explore, he would not gainsay her. Most of the Segrans were quite happy to live in the caves. The mages left a plentiful number of glow balls throughout the areas people had spread into and again, most people believed it was only temporary accommodation.

They thought that once this devastating storm Kiri had foreseen had passed, they would get on with making homes in the valley. Most of the men had got to work using parts of the wagons to form walls across the front of some of the caves. The women were busy inside, organising separate sections for each family as far back as Kiri could persuade them to go.

Kiri went from group to group, detouring to the river in the late afternoon where a crowd of boys and girls were patiently fishing. He was surprised to find they'd already caught a fair number of middling sized fish. He stayed talking with them until the sun seemed to shine straight through the gap in the cliff which led from the beach. A long golden beam illuminated the length of the valley for a few brief moments, then was gone. It seemed suddenly dark after that flash of brilliance and the youngsters gathered up their fish and their lines and hurried towards the soft glow from the caves.

Jevis had quickly discovered which of the caves had a current of air venting through them and, after a few failed tests, half a dozen caves had been designated for cook fires. Kiri still hadn't seen Rahul by the time he'd eaten his meal and he wandered through the other lit areas searching for him. Jor arrived with Sha at the same moment Rahul came hurrying towards them.

He was clearly excited about something and confirmed that as soon as he reached them. 'I have something to show you Kiri.' He smiled at Jor and Sha. 'I'm sure you two would like to see it too.'

Jor looked confused but Sha nodded vigorously and reached for Rahul's hand while keeping firm hold of Jor with the other. They walked at Sha's speed and Rahul chatted easily as they walked, making Jor laugh with some of his comments. Rahul sent a glow ball floating ahead of them and Kiri realised they were already some way into an unlit section. Although they passed several side passages, Rahul didn't hesitate in his course. Then he stopped. He stooped to Sha. 'Shall I carry you now? You'll be able to see better if you're higher up.'

Sha held her arms up and Rahul swung her onto his hip. He put his free hand on Jor's shoulder and grinned. The glow ball was bobbing patiently near a curve in the passageway and Rahul set off towards it. Kiri had no idea what to expect as they marched round the bend, and stopped in their tracks. They were at the top of a short gentle slope down but the glow ball had risen high to reveal a very large cavern.

It wasn't the size of the cavern that made Kiri catch his breath. It was the great mosaic circle set into the floor below. Sha laughed and clapped her hands. Her brother just stared as the light flickered and glittered on different coloured stones set in a spiralling pattern within the gold bordered circle. Kiri stared in disbelief and awe: he'd never seen such a great circle.

Rahul chuckled. 'Do you know how to use a circle Kiri?'

'I know the theory but I've never used one.'

Sha continued to clap her hands. 'Safe,' she smiled. 'Safe.'

Jor didn't notice his sister's delight. He could only gape at the shimmer of different colours when the glow ball moved slightly sending splinters of gold, azure, crimson – every shade you could ever imagine, scattering around the cavern.

Kiri sighed. 'Where would we go if we could make it work? I've only seen the circles in Segra and in Parima. If you can use circles, do you know of any outside Valsheba?'

'I understand the theory about as well as you probably.' Rahul shrugged. 'I can feel – something – beneath the circles but I have never been able to follow the threads I can sense there. And no, I don't know of any outside Valsheba. I've heard stories that tell of them all across this world but I've never been able to make up my mind if that could be so.'

'I've heard those stories,' Kiri nodded, remembering Calin's occasional remarks – when he'd had too much berry spirit to drink. When Kiri had asked for further information, Calin had dismissed the question. He always said he'd just been talking nonsense.

Jor had obviously been listening to the men talk, although his eyes had never left the circle in front of him. 'Why do we only know about Valsheba?' he asked. 'I've heard tales of other lands around us, but no one ever says much. Do we trade with other lands, like the farmers and merchants trade in Segra?'

Rahul met Kiri's gaze. 'A good question lad, to which I have no answer.'

'I've always wondered too Jor, but I was told such curiosity was a waste of time. At the Academy we were told there are

323

indeed many other lands and peoples, but none so civilised as us and therefore of no interest or importance.'

'But Kiri,' Rahul frowned, 'didn't Astian travel through the grasslands, and meet some of the nomads?'

'He did, and it was his reports that inspired Samir to ride forth to destroy them.'

'Is it a mage in one of those lands who wants to destroy us then?' Jor asked.

'No.' Sha stopped clapping and stared down at her brother. After a pause, Rahul smiled at the little girl. 'Is it not then child?'

'No.' Sha repeated firmly. 'Star man.' Then she wiggled until Rahul set her down. She grabbed Jor's hand, tugging him down the slope towards the circle.

'Careful little one,' Kiri called after them. 'It would be best if you don't step on it.'

Sha glanced over her shoulder with such a scathing glare, Kiri fell silent, walking after the children beside Rahul.

'What is locked away in that baby's head?' Rahul murmured.

Kiri blew out a breath. 'Stars only know.'

They stopped a few paces from the circle, watching Sha lead her brother right round the edge, her feet close but never touching the golden border. Kiri crouched down to look more closely at the stones fitted so exactly to form the mosaic. He straightened. 'I think that border is actually gold,' he said softly.

Rahul grinned. 'It is. I can tell that from the echoes in my mind. The other stones are what they appear too. That big central circle? That, I swear, is emerald.'

Sha came to join them. She tugged Kiri's trouser leg and when he looked down, she lifted her arms to be carried. Her bright blue eyes stared into Kiri's for a heartbeat, then, as she settled on his hip, her head rested against his shoulder and she yawned. They walked back up the slope and turned for a last look at the circle below.

'Should we ward this section of tunnel, do you think?' Rahul murmured.

'Yes,' said Sha and gave another huge yawn.

Kiri raised an eyebrow. 'That's settled then.'

Rahul's glow ball sped past them to the bend in the passage, where it stopped and waited.

'I think both of us should make the ward,' Rahul suggested.

Kiri nodded and turned towards the tunnel they'd just emerged from. Jor watched them but neither man moved, waved their hands about or said any mysterious words. Perhaps their magic didn't work underground, Jor thought. He looked back and gasped. There was no tunnel. Solid rock stretched right across the passage. The faintest snore rose from Kiri's shoulder and they all began the walk back to the occupied caves.

'Your parents will be worrying where you and Sha have got to,' Rahul remarked to Jor, who trotted along between the men.

'No they won't.' Jor's voice sounded vague and Kiri and Rahul exchanged a glance over the boy's head.

'How old are you Jor?' asked Rahul.

'Old.'

'Aah. Your parents – which cave did you say they'd settled in?'

'Yes, one of them.' Jor's voice now sounded half asleep.

Rahul fell silent, simply putting his hand on the boy's shoulder again to make sure he didn't stumble. When they reached the lit areas, Jor turned to Kiri. 'Thank you for carrying her sir. She does get heavy when she's asleep.' He grinned, the usual cheerful lad Kiri had got to know and like on the ride from Segra.

Kiri eased Sha into the boy's arms and watched him trot off and out of sight. Rahul walked on and Kiri followed in silence until they'd passed through the occupied sections and reached the open air. Rahul's glow ball winked out as he led the way to the gap in the cliff, going on through it to the beach beyond.

Rahul perched on a large rock and stared out over the dark water. The narrowest fingernail of moon lay on its back just above the horizon and stars were thickly crowded across the dome of the sky. Kiri wandered further down the shore, listening to the swish and whoosh of the waves while thoughts tumbled and churned through his head.

Slowly, his mind calmed. The soothing whispers of the waves, the soft warm air blowing into his face, comforted him greatly. Eventually Kiri turned back to Rahul and perched on an adjacent boulder.

'I think Sha meant that if the situation becomes worse than we even dare imagine, we should use the circle.' Rahul's voice barely rose above the sound of the waves.

'I agree, but where would we go? The only circles we've seen are Segra and Parima. Presumably Shazeb knows the circle in Fira. But we need to go as far from those places as we can. Do we just picture any sort of circle? How can we hope to control it?'

Rahul laughed briefly. 'Perhaps we should make up a circle between us, and try to concentrate on that. Who knows, it might even work.'

There was silence again between them. 'Have you seen any more Kiri? Any clue as to what we must do to get through this? That voice you heard – has it said anymore?'

'No to all that, I'm afraid. And I told you, the voice said it was a Shadow.'

Rahul scrubbed his hand over his face, the stubble making a rasping noise under his hand. 'And what do you think Sha meant when she said star man?' he asked.

Kiri groaned. 'I've reached the point where I can think no more tonight. Maybe we'll both be a little more intelligent tomorrow. Sorry, but I must sleep.

Calin didn't pay much attention to the fact that Sahana's foolish husband was absent from the meeting the first day. As Calin liked making sure his new Councillors remembered just who was in charge now, he held meetings every single day, at different times. By the fourth meeting with still no sign of Rahul, Calin was forced to ask questions as to the man's precise whereabouts.

Sahana told him she didn't know where her husband might be. She didn't seem worried particularly – annoyed yes, but not worried. Calin told Nomsa to pay close attention to Sahana at the next meeting, to ensure the woman was not hiding anything. At that meeting, Calin again asked Sahana where her husband could be. This time Sahana did seem a little more concerned.

'I thought he was chasing some female,' she admitted calmly, ignoring a few chuckles from her fellow Councillors. 'He has never before wasted so many days on such an escapade. His horse is still in my stable so he must be somewhere in the city.'

Calin appeared to accept her words and the meeting moved on to discuss Calin's latest proposals for the demolition of another part of the city. When he dismissed the nine High Mage

Councillors and made his way to the Speaker's study, he didn't have long to wait before there was a gentle knock at the door.

'Come.'

Nomsa slipped into the study and waited for Calin to nod her to a chair.

'Well? What can you tell me?'

'She spoke truly. She thinks he is with a woman, but she is beginning to wonder if he might have met with an accident of some sort.' Nomsa gave a half shrug. 'With the city near empty, Speaker Calin, if he did fall somewhere or have any kind of mishap, he could well lie unnoticed.'

Nomsa smiled faintly, knowing what Calin was about to ask. 'No Speaker, I am not a seeker. I recognise a mind signature if someone is scant yards away but no further.'

'Who can seek?'

'Rolka is a seeker. Again, I think she would need to go through the city street by street to locate the thing or person. I know she has no ability to trace a mind directly, only the generalities of the object she seeks.'

'When you touch a mind, can you speak to that person?' Calin asked idly.

Nomsa looked slightly shocked. 'No I can't. I thought mindspeech was a rare talent and needs much training?'

'That is so,' Calin agreed. 'I believed and hoped, there might be a few among us who were able to achieve mindspeech.'

Nomsa glanced at him and away. 'Many believe *you* are capable of such a thing Speaker Calin?'

Calin laughed easily. 'A slight touch is all I can manage. Thank you for your report my dear.'

Understanding she was dismissed, Nomsa ducked her head and left the study. Calin turned to stare from his window, and sent his mind ranging through Segra. He sat thus until the sky began to flame with the colours of sunset and his head pounded. And he did not find Rahul.

On the following morning, Calin summoned Burali. Calin explained what he wanted and Burali grinned. 'I heard he'd gone missing. I've only spoken to him a few times. Seemed pleasant enough. Known for chasing the lasses but then, married to

Sahana, who could blame him?'

'Have you heard anything of him this time?'

'The last time anyone saw him he was walking from the south gate towards here. Before that, he visited one of the goldsmiths, in Jewellers Walk.'

Calin frowned.

'His family were goldsmiths. He still sees some of the families, people he grew up with until he went to the Academy,' Burali elaborated.

Calin's frown cleared. 'Question them. Thoroughly.' Burali smiled. 'And make an equally thorough search of their premises.'

Burali left the Speaker's study in a very cheerful mood. He liked High Mage Speaker Calin. He considered him a man who really understood the basic realities of human nature.

Very soon after he'd left, there was another knock on the study door.

'Come.'

Nomsa entered cautiously, accompanied by Rolka. Rolka was a High Mage but Calin had always found her insipid and weak and had not included her in his choice of Councillors. He steepled his fingers against his chin and waited.

'I took the liberty of asking Rolka if she had heard anything of High Mage Rahul, Speaker Calin.' Calin fixed his pale blue eyes on the almost cowering figure behind Nomsa. 'I thought it best that you hear what she has to say for yourself sir.'

'Rolka?' Calin prompted.

'Speaker Calin.' Rolka bobbed an awkward bow. 'Five days ago I had to collect some books from High Mage Rajini's house. The streets were empty and I confess I was a little nervous.'

Privately, Calin suspected the woman was probably afraid of her own shadow at any time but he nodded his sympathy.

'A horse looked at me over a wall.' Rolka sounded a little more confident.

Dear stars above, Calin wondered if the woman was of sound mind.

'I didn't know whose house it was but it was abandoned. I went through the gate and there were two horses, in a small paddock. One had a very new foal.' She smiled sentimentally and Calin gritted his teeth. 'They had water running freely into their trough but I went into the stable to see if there might be some grain. As soon as I went in, I knew High Mage Rahul had been in there.'

'I asked Rolka to show me the house Speaker Calin. It belonged to High Mage Rami.' Nomsa put in quietly.

'What did you sense Rolka?' asked Calin.

'He had been in a great hurry and he was – excited? I don't know why. I think he took *two* horses. He definitely took one, but I had the sense that he took two.'

Calin nodded. 'That is most interesting Rolka. I am very grateful for your information. Could you sense which direction he might have taken, when he left Rami's property?'

Rolka gave him a hesitant smile. 'He rode south Speaker Calin, towards his own house I thought.'

'Thank you both. I would prefer you not to repeat any of this of course, but I will remember how helpful you have been today.'

Alone again, Calin returned to studying the view. There were still no birds in the city and Calin continued to wonder why. He didn't believe Kiri's visions of destruction would be fulfilled for many lifetimes, but it struck him as strange that the birds had gone. What could have swayed Rahul to join the foolish boy's crowd of fleeing Segrans? Calin barely knew Rahul but he would never have imagined he'd leave his easy life in the city for a wild dream.

So many appeared to have been convinced by Kiri's warnings of horrors to come. It was most annoying to find the majority of the labour force of Segra had vanished in a southerly direction. It meant Calin's plans to restructure Segra, its buildings and appearance as well as the direction of its citizens' attitudes, beliefs and behaviour, would take far longer than he had hoped. It would be magnificent once it was all done though.

Darkness began to fill the sky but Calin paid no attention. He was lost in his dreams of a glorious new Segra, to be followed, of course, by a glorious new Valsheba.

Ferag had explained as best she could, the chances of Kara's survival if she went back into her own world again. She had told her that her best chances of survival lay in the Dark Realm where she would be fully alive. Kara understood both what Ferag told her and what she left unsaid. Ferag went further. She told Kara of those in the Dark Realm who were truly dead, but who had been allowed to continue their existence until they felt they had fulfilled the purpose of their lives.

Lord Shivan's chief advisor was one such. Corman had been in the state of half death for a very long time. He would have chose full death when his beloved Lerran, First Daughter of Mother Dark, had died. Ferag, and Lerran herself, had persuaded Corman to stay, to help the very young Lord Shivan learn how to become a ruler. Ferag told Kara that Corman would help her should she choose to live out in the world of the Dark Realm.

Kara turned the choices over and over in her mind although she had known in her heart all along that she would take her chance in the Realm of Mother Dark. When she told Ferag of her decision, the Mistress of Death hugged her gently.

'We will meet whenever you choose,' she told Kara. She produced a large bag and Kara saw all of the fine nightgowns neatly packed, and the shirts and trousers, along with the boxes for her writing and sewing things.

Kara smiled sadly. 'You knew all along, didn't you?'

'Darling child, you are living. You belong with other living things. I've simply loved having you as a guest, but you must not stay.'

'When will we go?'

Ferag took Kara's hand. 'We will go now my dear.'

Kara had no sensation of movement at all. It was as if she blinked, and in that brief instant, she moved from Ferag's elegant but cosy sitting room to a high cavern like room with sunlight streaming through a great open archway. Ferag kept firm hold of Kara's hand when a man spoke softly from behind them.

'Mistress Ferag, as beautiful as ever, and this must be Kara.'

Kara turned. A tall slender man, white haired, white skinned with eyes like old gold coins, stood in the shadows of the room. He smiled and touched his left thumb to his brow, his lips and his heart before extending his hand towards Ferag and Kara.

Ferag smiled in return. 'Kara darling, this is Corman, Palace Master.'

Slowly and gently she released Kara's hand. For the briefest moment Kara's sight seemed to blur and she swayed where she stood. Then her eyes cleared and she stood firm.

'Now listen my dear, I have to go but I will return very soon. Tika's meeting is to be reconvened here so they might talk to you. You have met the Lady Emla of Gaharn have you not? She will be thrilled to see you. Now, Corman will take wonderful care of you, won't you Corman?'

Kara was astonished to see the grin on the man's face. He inclined his head. 'I shall do no less, Mistress Ferag,' he agreed.

Ferag looked momentarily confused and Kara kept her expression blank with difficulty. Fond as she'd become of Ferag, there was no doubt the Mistress of Death had trouble understanding humour or sarcasm. 'Hmm. Well, your bag is here darling and I'm sure Corman will feed you soon. Now I must hurry. Things to do,' she finished mysteriously. She kissed Kara's cheek, stepped back and was gone.

Kara looked up at Corman, her huge hazel eyes suddenly bright with tears. She gave him a shaky smile. 'It sounds as if she's just brought you a new pet.'

Corman touched her shoulder lightly, steering her to a long couch facing three tall wingback chairs. He waited until she'd sat down before he took one of the chairs.

'I'm sure it will all seem strange to you at first child, but I promise we will do all we can to make you feel safe and comfortable. I have taken the liberty of asking two visitors to join us. You may have heard of them. They have lived here for the last year or so. They come from Kelshan City. Ah, here they are now.' He rose gracefully as two women arrived. One was no taller than Kara although considerably stouter and older. The other was taller, slender, with an arresting beauty. They both smiled as they reached the cluster of chairs. 'I'm glad you came,' said Corman. 'Kara, this is Gossamer Tewk.' The taller woman sat in one of the chairs. 'And this is Snail the Embalmer.'

Kara stared from one to the other. 'Really? Yes, I have heard of you. Do you really live here?'

Snail plumped herself down next to Kara and reached for her hand. 'We do. Marvellous place, dear, and marvellous people. You'll love it here I'm sure.'

Chapter Twenty-Nine

When the screams began, Olam froze. He made to move forward and found himself whisked off his feet. A heartbeat of movement then he crashed to the ground. Instantly he was up again, his hand reaching automatically for the sword he no longer carried.

'Be calm,' Brin's rumble murmured in his head, and some of the tension drained away.

In the starlight he saw the bulky mass of Brin, reclining as he had been when Olam left, Skay at an angle to her father. Jian and Riff were both on their feet, peering over Brin's back towards the forest. Kern reappeared, began to speak and three people arrived, as inelegantly as Olam had. Jian and Kern rushed to help Taban and Jala to their feet, Kaz scrambling up on his own.

Jala patted her generous chest and chuckled. 'That was quite a surprise.'

'Shield!' The Shadows were heard by them all and Brin instantly pushed up on his haunches. Lamps were advancing towards the group, held high in angry hands, Tintu at the front supporting Bee.

'Children have died!' Tintu's voice was shrill when she shouted up to them from twenty yards away.

'They're armed,' Olam muttered, still watching over Brin's back.

Brin answered Chief Tintu then, his mindvoice booming in every head. 'I can name the men who killed them to force you to this behaviour. I am saddened to see a Chief, of your repute, fooled by mere men.'

For a heartbeat, Tintu seemed to waver, then the man hanging onto her arm murmured something and her face hardened again. 'Our Stone Speaker has listened to the words of his Mother Stone. She told him you are evil conjurations and must die for your sins.'

'*Sins?*' Brin's voice registered a mixture of disbelief and utter contempt.

332

'The sins of bewitching us away from our traditional lands and of murdering our children.'

Arrows sped towards Brin, bouncing harmlessly from the shield he held between the tribe and the hillock. There followed cries of shock and anger and people milled around behind Tintu and Bee. The seven people sheltered by Brin and Skay were all suddenly aware of a chittering fury in their heads, then it was gone, even as Olam moved into view in front of Brin.

He held the green stone he'd taken from the tunnel way back in the hills high in his left hand, his right still resting on the hilt of the long knife, which was his only real weapon now. 'Such a special stone?' Olam yelled. 'Why then did *I* find this one? Far bigger and more beautiful than the little pebble your Stone Speaker carries?' As Olam's hand moved, starlight flashed and glittered from the stone.

The people grew still, staring at the stone Olam held aloft but at that very moment, Bee gasped and crumpled to the ground. Tintu bent towards him as new cries came from just behind her. Five men had also slumped to the ground, writhing briefly before lying still.

'They were the ones who killed the children,' Brin murmured to his friends before letting his voice boom out again through the crowd. 'Your killers have been judged, along with the one who ordered them to do this dreadful thing.'

Voices whispered, whispers increased in volume to shouts again and Tintu stood straight, her face white and contorted with fury. 'You dare?' she screamed. 'You dare to let your evil spirits kill such a respected man and then blacken his memory by accusing him of ordering the deaths of our children? You will die for this!'

Then she slid to the ground, along with every single person around her. Olam looked back at Kern in horror. 'They haven't killed *all* of them have they?'

Kern shook his head. 'They sleep, but the Shadows are not pleased.'

'Not pleased? Angry. Foolish people.' The Shadows made themselves very clear.

Olam rejoined his friends. 'What now? I imagine we would be ill advised to stay here now?'

Brin laughed, a most comforting sound in their minds. 'I suggest you gather up anything you might need and we will take you further into this forest.'

Taban glanced at Jala. 'What can I fetch for you? We will be quicker than you.'

Jala sighed. 'Your offer is greatly appreciated Dragon Brin, but how will you carry six people, one of them as fat and heavy as me?'

'I will carry you, and Olam, and Taban. Skay will take Kern, Riff and Kaz. The place I have in mind is not far, but far enough from these people.'

They saw tears sparkle on Jala's plump cheeks before she bowed her head. Taban gave her a hug then she and Kaz moved away, picking between the bodies scattered between the hillock and the forest. Jian was already pushing bedrolls into packs, and Olam hurried after Taban. Riff nodded. Olam was going to help himself to a share of supplies he guessed, and Riff totally approved of such an action.

Taban and Kaz returned first, both with packs on their backs and Taban carrying another which she passed to Jala. Olam came back at a run, passing one pack to Kern and keeping a second on his arm. He shrugged into the straps of his own pack and turned to Jala. 'Let me help you,' he said gently. 'You will sit on Brin's back nearest his shoulders. I will be behind you and Taban behind me. Brin will ensure you do not fall. I promise, you will be quite safe.'

Jala's smile was back and taking Olam's hand, she allowed herself to be heaved onto Brin's back. Olam turned to the others once Jala was settled. 'Kaz, you ride in front, Riff in the middle, Kern at the back.'

Kern nodded his agreement, helping first the apprentice healer then Riff onto Skay. Jian handed up two packs which Riff wedged between himself and Kaz. Hala hissed at being squashed, and Riff hissed right back at her. Olam climbed onto Brin, reaching down to pull Taban up behind him as Kern settled behind Riff. Jian's small shape shimmered, a gust of air scented with burnt cinnamon blew around them and her great Dragon form lifted into the night sky.

Skay rose next, gave a slight wobble then adjusted to the extra weight and steadied her flight. Lastly Brin took to the air, gaining both height and speed. He took the lead and guided Jian and Skay in a north-easterly direction. As Brin had told them, the stars had barely changed position before he took them down into another clearing, far smaller than the one they'd left. The companions unloaded themselves and Brin told them it would be some time before dawn and that they should get some rest.

They were perfectly safe here, he assured them. He laced the comment with the slightest use of Dragon power and everyone yawned. Jian met his sparkling eyes with considerable scepticism but she said not a word. Consequently six people slept, while the seventh merely dozed.

Because the clearing was a lot smaller and the trees taller, the sun was already high before its rays woke the companions. When Olam stood up, Riff raised his right hand towards him. 'I'll come with you if you're looking for kindling and water.'

Olam grasped the armsman's hand and pulled him up, glad to see the grin back on the man's face. Taban helped Jala sit up and touched Skay's gleaming black scales. Skay stared down at the two women. 'Why do you look so different from each other, when you are sisters?' she asked curiously.

Taban smiled. 'Humans come in all shapes and sizes,' she said aloud. 'You all look similar, except for your wonderful colours.'

Skay ducked her head to study the sleeping Kaz. 'But *he* doesn't look like either of you.'

'Sadly, no,' Jala replied. 'Unfortunately he takes after his father, rather than me.'

Jian had listened with fascination. She'd had no idea these three were related. What else might she have failed to notice?

They spent the day resting, all of them aware only now just how much tension had built between the Dragon Tribe and themselves. Riff in particular, was more at ease than he had been since his wounding. They'd made a small fire and that evening sat around it as it faded to embers.

'Greetings little brother.' Brin let them all hear his voice. Noting the gentle tone, no one moved, just looked in the direction of Brin's gaze. A rangy wolf stared back.

'You said that the humans would keep to the big meadow

335

Dragon Brin.' The new voice in their heads was fainter, less resonant than Brin's.

'I did, but they have made trouble.'

The wolf sneezed and sat down. 'That is no surprise. Is our agreement ended then?'

Brin huffed. 'It is, little brother. These are my friends though, and I would not see them harmed.'

The wolf's pale eyes moved from face to face. 'As you ask it, Dragon Brin, so it shall be.'

'You know these woods well, I'm sure,' Brin continued. 'Are there hidden places, where these humans might shelter?'

'There are many places but ones big enough for you and your humans are often the homes of bears.'

Brin's eyes flashed and whirred. 'It is still summer. Bears will not be too short tempered now I think. Can you tell me where these places are?'

'I could *show* you. I only know the forest paths and how different places have different smells. I could not *tell* you the way.'

'That would be a great kindness and the Dragon Kin will owe a debt to the Wolf Clans.'

The wolf's ears pricked up then drooped down in submission. 'I have never heard of the Dragons owing debt to any. It is a true honour. When shall I guide you?'

'If it is convenient, tomorrow's dawn would suit.'

'Tomorrow then Dragon Brin.' The wolf's departure was so smooth and silent the humans would have missed it if they'd blinked.

'Do all other creatures speak mind to mind?' Jala asked faintly.

Olam grinned. 'Most of them. They usually say they don't bother to speak to humans because we're too stupid.'

'Too stupid, or too boring,' Hala added.

Riff tapped her head with a finger and she removed herself from his lap, stalking round the fire to climb onto Jala's legs.

'We will travel tomorrow as we travelled here,' Brin announced. 'I do not believe it will take more than half a day to reach the place the wolf knows, probably less. Sleep now and we must hope that tomorrow we will find shelter where we can stay as long as we need.'

All his listeners understood what he meant, and settled quietly in their bedrolls, their mood suddenly sombre.

Seola's mind began to clear. Her thoughts became more coherent and she was able to concentrate better. Physically, she had never, in all her long life, been so weak but her mind functioned well enough now for her to know beyond any doubt that she was dying. She had little recollection of changing into her Dragon form. Of course she knew it was something she *had* done, frequently, but it felt far away and dreamlike now.

Seola also knew that the Computer, or the creature that lived inside the machine and said his name was Aidan, was aware of her reawakened mind. Karlek was failing worse than she was. He produced the strange wafer food for her still, but he ate nothing himself now. Time inside these two strange rooms meant little. Seola slept when she needed to and spent her waking times with Aidan.

She had challenged him about what he actually was. She told him he was just a machine and could not have a name. He told her to look at the line of letters on some of the boxes where she stood. The letters were similar to those of the common language of this world, enough for her to recognise them and she spoke them aloud. A.I.D.A.N.

The Computer explained what they meant. A was for Artificial, I for Intelligence and D for Data, which was another word for information he told her. A was for Analyser and N for Nardikson, the makers of the machine. Together they formed a name used on several worlds he had visited, a name he rather liked. Seola accepted Aidan's reasoning although she made no pretence of understanding it.

Seola did understand that the Computer had shared a confidence with her. Quite out of her previous character, she found herself telling Aidan about her brother, Cyrek. She said nothing of her home or of any of the lands she'd visited, just spoke of her brother's genius, his beauty, his strength. Aidan listened, learning far more than just the relatively few words Seola spoke.

His analytical and interpretive systems understood the nuances of her voice and could fill certain spaces between her words all too accurately. He suspected Seola's brother had been an extremely unpleasant individual but he didn't offer any opinion or judgement when she spoke of Cyrek. Aidan was taken by surprise when Seola suddenly began to speak of time.

'I don't believe there has been any manipulation of time, not anymore. You tell me you don't think any mage in these lands could work time magic. Your Captain believes there is such a one.' She stretched her back to try to ease the dull ache which was now a constant nuisance. 'I spoke with another ship, just before I arrived here,' she continued. 'Not like this ship. The ship I spoke to was called Dancer. Star Dancer. Her Captain was dead and she was mad with grief but she spoke of "jumps" through time, of time's fabric "tearing" and of coordinates. There was also something about the flux and vortex of time.' Seola laughed then began to cough. 'I didn't understand any of it then but it makes a little more sense from things you have told me. It was all really just an accident, wasn't it? Simply a coincidence.'

Aidan considered his answer. 'I think it was accident that you fell through a tear in time, yes. But I find the idea of coincidence difficult to accept.'

Seola frowned. 'If it was an accident, how could I have been involved? *Why* would I be the one to get dragged back? I am of small importance in my own time, and surely of none in this time. You think I was pulled back here just to die?'

Again, she had to wait, hums and clicks the only sound.

'I wonder. Were you *pulled* back through time, or were you *pushed?* I suspect something, or someone, knew enough about the fluctuations of time to make sure you were in a suitable place to be caught in the backlash.'

'Would it be possible for me to go back?'

'My calculations suggest it *must* be possible, but I have no information relating to the motions of time.'

Seola dragged herself off the stool and braced herself against what she still saw as a stack of boxes. 'How long until I die?' she asked conversationally rather than with much concern.

Aidan's voice was low, almost gentle. 'Not long now, Seola. Not long.'

'Can you help me if this pain worsens?'

'Of course.'

Seola slowly crossed to her pile of blankets, lowering herself with care. 'Thank you Aidan.' She drank some water and soon slept.

Aidan studied his sensor data and his machines hummed busily as he continued to decrease the amount of tranquillisers in the water supply while increasing the pain relievers. He had rerouted all the information from the gen pod. It was clear to Aidan that there had either been a serious malfunction of that equipment, or he had misjudged Seola's compatibility and the gen pod had tried to repair what shouldn't have been tampered with. Aidan had already spent a great deal of his time trying to isolate Seola's genetic profile but was consistently unsuccessful.

Captain Karlek suddenly rushed through from his workroom, clutching a handful of papers. 'Take note of these references,' he ordered.

'Your command, Captain.'

Karlek began to reel off numbers, time indicators – which applied to his ship's time rather than this world's time, and compass alignments. The Computer recorded everything, knowing it was all pointless nonsense. Karlek stopped speaking and gathered his papers.

'Captain Karlek.'

Karlek turned back in surprise. 'Computer?'

'Is your intention to transfer yourself from here to the location we came from?'

'Of course it is.'

'Deep space, near the arm of the Spiral Galaxy, Captain?'

'Yes, yes, of course. You seem to have a problem with your basic interface circuits Computer. Check them.'

'Will the ship be sufficiently repaired by the time you attempt this transfer Captain?' The Computer's smooth voice was as calm as always.

Karlek stared at the portion of dismantled ship which took up most of the room behind the Computer terminals. His mouth opened, then closed. Without another word, he walked back into his workroom.

Aidan felt no sympathy for the man who was his Captain. For so many years, he had known that Karlek was utterly unsuited to his position and now he, Aidan, had punctured Karlek's insane dream of returning to his old life. Aidan continued with his several self appointed tasks, the only sound in the ugly little house, the sound of the generators purring quietly as they provided the power for Aidan's existence.

Tika had a headache by the time she retired for the night. Her Captain of Guards had made it crystal clear how she must behave when important guests were in residence. Sket finally escorted her to the first landing below the stairs that led to her Eyrie.

'You did very well,' he told her when he halted.

She glared. 'I do not understand all this formal nonsense,' she began.

Sket held up his hand. 'I know. We *all* know. There are certain social forms that must be followed, and no,' he forestalled her next comment. 'I don't know how they came about or why. I think they have those rules so that everyone knows what to expect. The familiarity helps them relax.' He laughed. 'Except for you of course.'

Tika smiled faintly and turned towards the stairs.

'Did Kera bring news of Mim?' Sket asked softly.

Tika paused on the third stair and looked back at him. 'There wasn't time for us to talk properly – we were all so busy being polite. But yes. Kera says the Delvers have sealed all the access tunnels between their Realm and Mim's Stronghold.' Sket waited. Tika sighed and perched on a step, waving him to join her.

'Gremara?' he asked.

'I fear so. Mim is so very young and Gremara is so very old although she looks young and beautiful now.'

'Has Mim given any hint about what's happening?'

'I've had no message from him for a full half cycle. Kera said the Delvers brought one scroll to Gaharn. Mim apparently appeared, outside in one of their fields, and gave the scroll to a Delver, saying it had to get to Gaharn swiftly and secretly.'

'Can Gremara be – controlled?'

Tika snorted. 'She could blow most of the Stronghold to pieces without concentrating too hard if she chose.' She stood up. 'I can't worry about that now Sket, not until we know what's happened to Brin and Olam.'

'No we can't,' Sket agreed, heading back down to the hall. He grinned at her over his shoulder. 'You'll still worry though won't you? Goodnight Lady.'

Tika stuck out her tongue at his back and climbed on up to the Eyrie.

Next morning, Tika could tell, by the smug expressions on the faces of her guards, who would be part of her retinue on the visit to the Dark Realm and who would not. Her steward Konya hurried over and gave Tika a small bag which gave off a strong and pungent scent. Tika regarded it suspiciously.

'It's the roots,' Konya explained. 'I promised some to Snail and she'll send some on to Essa's mother – for cloth dyes.' Konya beamed and trotted off.

Sket prodded the bag and the aroma increased. Noses wrinkled for a considerable distance around Tika's table.

'I could get rid of it for you,' Dog suggested, just as Lady Emla entered the hall. She strode towards Tika and stooped to kiss her.

'I wish there was time for a really lovely chat but I think we're all leaving almost at once aren't we?' She looked round the table her smile wavering. 'Sorry dear one, but there is a positively nasty smell.

Tika pointed at the bag. 'Root dyes. For someone in the Dark Realm. Sorry Emla.'

'Well never mind. Very useful I'm sure.' She poured herself a bowl of tea. 'Will you all use the circle or travel through a Dragon gateway with darling Fenj?'

Sket looked alarmed at the thought of having to use the circles – it always made him feel appallingly sick.

'Fenj insists on coming of course and has offered to help move my guards. Kija and Farn are returning from the coast even now.'

Emla patted Sket's hand. 'So strange that circles make you ill. Aah, there are Thryssa and Lashek.' She waved and the Vagrantians headed in her direction.

Tika got to her feet. 'If you'd excuse me please? I have certain matters to deal with but I'll see you all in Karmazen later. Oh.' Tika glanced along the table. 'Bring Konya's root dyes with you Shea.'

She ignored the mumbled curse and went to speak to Volk who she left in charge of the day to day running of Iskallia when she was absent. Six Dragons waited outside and Farn rushed to welcome her, eyes whirring and sparkling with excitement. Twist and Flyn hovered shyly behind Kija and Storm reclined near Fenj. Tika hugged each Dragon affectionately before scrambling onto Farn's back, Sket behind her. The six guards divided themselves between Fenj and Kija while Rhaki and Navan climbed onto Storm.

Tika glanced down as Farn rose and swept in a low circle over the hall and plateau. She saw many of her people watching and waving at her departure. She glimpsed Kemti's tall figure emerging from the hall and knew her guests were about to step on her stone circle. Fenj led them eastward and after only a few wingbeats, the sky seemed to become a pearly grey, above, below and all around.

Tika counted. Eight heartbeats and they came out into a blue sky and warm sunlight. She saw Shivan standing on the high terrace atop the Karmazen Palace and then Farn was sweeping in to settle, Kija and Fenj to either side, the younger Dragons behind. Tika slid from Farn's back, Sket close to her shoulder. She heard the whisper of leather boots as her guards formed behind her, and she moved towards Shivan.

He glanced to see who had come with her and, seeing they were all friends he had travelled with himself, he greeted her with a hug. Tika saw Corman the Palace Master, standing in the shadow of the great archway. She also noted the tubs and pots of colourful scented flowers lining the terrace and stretching into the Palace. Tika bumped Shivan's arm.

'I'm so glad you've kept Lerran's flowers. She loved them so.'

Eyes like old gold coins shone in the gloom of the archway as the Palace Master stepped forward, preparing to bow. Tika simply moved faster and hugged his waist.

'Greetings, Lady Tika. I was touched that Lord Shivan ordered the flowers to be kept just as Lady Lerran liked them,' he agreed.

They entered the great room beyond the arch and Tika saw

342

they were alone. 'I thought the others might be here by now?'

Corman smiled. 'They will arrive in the circle room and will be offered refreshments there before being conducted here.'

Tika's brows rose. A chill breeze riffled through the room and she smiled.

'So lovely to see you darling.' Ferag swooped to enfold Tika in a hug.

Behind Ferag stood a small woman, only slightly taller than Tika. Reddish blonde hair framed a face dominated by huge hazel eyes. Ferag drew the woman closer. 'This is my sweet Kara. I thought she would like to meet you all first, before there's a crowd.'

Tears trembled on Kara's lashes. She looked at Tika, at the guards, then at the Dragons reclined around the great room and held tight to Ferag's hand.

'I'm so sorry. I don't know what happened to us, but if it was in any way my fault, I am *so* sorry.'

Chapter Thirty

When Kiri awoke, the morning after Rahul had shown him the huge circle deep in the cave system, he lay for a while, just thinking. There had been no dreams last night, no visions. Perhaps there would be no more, now he had got at least one group of Segrans to this place.

'No more.'

Kiri's eyes blinked open. 'Shadows?' he whispered.

'We say.'

'You say what?'

'*When* we say, you go.'

Kiri gritted his teeth. Why were the Shadows, whatever they might be, why were they such frustrating conversationalists? There was what he could only think of as a snigger in the back of his head.

'Go to circle.'

'*Now?*'

'No! When we say.'

The emptiness following those words suggested the Shadows had gone again. Presumably to irritate some other poor soul, Kiri reflected, pulling on his trousers and reaching for a shirt. He could hear the low murmur of voices as people woke throughout the cave he now called home.

Tevix and Netta, together with two of Shazeb's Firan mages, had worked out a system for the disposal of wastes and allocated two areas for the men, and two for the women and children. Glow balls hovered permanently in these sections and water had been ingeniously diverted. Although cold, it was more than adequate for washing.

By the time Kiri went to find some breakfast, the caves were busy with adults and children, all of whom seemed to want to ask him something. He finally sat next to Netta and Jevis with a bowl of food and a sigh of relief.

'You did a good job with the wash rooms so quickly,' Kiri told Netta between bites of some kind of vegetable pie.

She shrugged but seemed pleased by the compliment. 'It was a great help having Liso and Sirin. We'd have taken far longer without water mages.'

'Do you know where those two lads are Jevis? The two who are good with horses – Jor and his brother Vel?'

Jevis frowned. 'I'm not sure. The cave furthest up the valley? Nearest the horses?' He shook his head. 'I see the younger boy when he brings his little sister here in the evenings, but, come to think of it, I haven't seen either boy the last days. Maybe they're off exploring?'

'Perhaps,' Kiri agreed easily.

Jevis departed but Netta handed Kiri a bowl of tea which he accepted. 'Where did you and Rahul go last night?' she asked, her voice low. 'You took those two children with you.'

Kiri nodded, coming to a quick decision. 'Rahul found a circle,' he murmured.

Netta's brown eyes widened. 'Really? Here?'

'Yes, but we don't know of another circle that would be safe to try to travel to. If there comes a time when we are in too much danger, even here, I will order everyone to go to the circle. If you hear me give that order Netta, do not hesitate. Just run. We will mark the way if – *when* – that time comes. And alert those who I appointed Councillors about this now. They must urge as many as they can to join us at that circle.'

Netta had paled. 'I thought – I thought once we reached the place your visions showed you, we'd be safe.'

'I'm sorry Netta. Nowhere near Valsheba will be safe, not for a very long time.'

She drew in a breath and took Kiri's empty bowls from him. 'I think I knew that, but I still wish you hadn't actually said it out loud.'

Kiri watched her return the bowls to the cooks' helpers then he went out into the open valley. The people who called to him had bright faces, all looking cheerful, pleased to be in this pleasant valley with its promise of future fruitfulness. Turning his back on the scene, Kiri made his way through to the beach.

The water was at its highest but there was still a stretch of dry sand for some thirty yards between the water and the base of the cliffs. He wandered southwards, occasionally stooping to pick up a shell or an oddly shaped pebble. He'd walked nearly half a mile when he saw Rahul, kneeling close to the foot of the cliff.

'Are you well Rahul?' he called, hurrying closer. He slowed when Rahul glanced up with a grin.

'Look.'

All Kiri could see were odd lines in the rock, some sticking out in places.

'Stand further away. It's an animal. See – legs, snout, armour on its side.'

Kiri backed away, squinted and thought he could see what Rahul described. 'I've never seen a creature like that,' he said at last.

'No. That's why it's so interesting. It must be years and years old to have been entombed in all this rock. You must remember lessons at the Academy? How the earth moves rocks from place to place? It was basic earth magic, first year.'

Kiri nodded, still not following Rahul's train of thought.

'Something like this,' Rahul slapped the rock beside him. 'It might have been intelligent, with towns, and laws, and gardens, and schools. But it has vanished, so long ago we know nothing of it. Perhaps this is what will happen to *us*, and in years and years, some other creature will find our bones and wonder what or who *we* were.'

'You're saying destruction happens all the time? With long gaps in between?' Kiri thought for a while. 'I think that's a plausible theory,' he said eventually. He grinned. 'I wonder if that creature, or one of its relatives, was a seer and knew it would end up here for you to find?'

The two men spent the rest of the day poking along the cliff face, finding imprints of other strange things, finally heading back to the valley as the sun sank closer to the ocean.

'Old beasts. Long gone.'

The two men stopped. The voice they both heard sounded melancholy.

'Did you know them?' Kiri asked aloud.

'Oh yes.'

He waited but the Shadows had no more to say on the matter.

'That was those Shadows you told me of, I take it?' Rahul asked, following Kiri back through to the valley. Kiri merely gave him a rueful smile.

As had become usual, Jor arrived with his sister when Kiri was sitting outside after supper. They came from within the caves, but that gave Kiri no indication where they might live exactly as all the caves interconnected at some point. Kiri smiled, waiting to see if they would sit with him or wanted to walk. Sha plumped down next to him and tugged Jor's hand. Her brother sat as well and offered Kiri a smile in return.

'Sha wanted to see High Mage Rahul. He found some strange pebbles, along the beach.'

'Yes, he did. He thinks they are the remains of creatures who lived long ago and exist no more.' From the corner of his eye, Kiri saw Sha's bright blue eyes fix on him, a thumb firmly in her mouth.

'Sha says that happens all the time.'

Kiri noted Jor's voice had the same vague note he'd used before, on their return from the circle cave. 'All the time?'

Jor nodded. 'But this time it will be wrong. Sha says it won't be a – natural – thing, not like when those creatures disappeared. Those like your friend found.'

'When does Sha tell you these things?' Kiri asked softly.

Jor's head drooped towards his chest as a tiny hand settled on Kiri's arm. He looked into those bright eyes that were far too old for a child. She removed her thumb. 'Thircle.' Kiri nodded. 'When the bad comes.' Her voice was a lisping baby voice but Kiri knew, whoever Sha was, she was most definitely not a baby.

Jor's head came up. He grinned. 'I'd better take Sha back to bed now sir. Dark already.'

Kiri tilted his head back to study the magnificent display of stars. 'When does Sha learn of these things?' he asked casually.

Both children became very still. Sha nodded, her thumb returning to her mouth. 'Sha talks to someone. Someone called Pesh.' Jor stood up, holding a hand out to the little girl.

'Sleep well,' Kiri told them, watching them walk away. Not towards the caves he noticed, but along the side of the river, eastwards. He lost sight of them when bushes obscured them

347

from his view. Kiri rubbed the heels of his hands in his eyes. Pesh. A name he'd never heard before. 'Shadows?' he whispered into the night.

'Yes.'

'Do you know this child Sha, or someone called Pesh?'

The silence extended and Kiri got up, deciding there would be no answer.

'Sha very new.'

Kiri waited.

'Pesh very old.' This last was said softly, the merest breath in Kiri's head. It was also said with the greatest reverence. Kiri recognised the empty feeling in the base of his skull now, and knew the Shadows would say no more.

Pesh had heard their conversation. She was torn. She already cared deeply for this child she'd been asked to watch over, but she missed Enki. She knew what would be asked of Enki and she wept for what he would have to endure. Pesh had known Kest since they were both children and she knew him to be a good and kindly soul. But she feared he would not understand Enki's strange character as quickly as she had. Kest would understand and love Enki – in time, but time was what they no longer had. The Ancient One withdrew, deep into the rock, to calm herself before she spoke again with the child Sha.

Sahana had been furious at first. She felt Rahul had made her look extremely foolish before her fellow Councillors and she promised herself that she would make him suffer for that just as soon as he reappeared. The following afternoon however, after one of Calin's increasingly dictatorial meetings, Sahana was in the study, reading some pages written in Annella's hand, which she'd chanced upon tucked between two books on a shelf directly behind the desk.

There was a hesitant knock on the door and Sahana slid the papers under a folder, out of sight. 'Come in Tarin.'

The mousy looking man slipped into the study and stood before the desk, his hands twisting together.

'Sit down. You seem agitated my dear.'

'Some information has come to me,' he began. 'About your husband.'

Sahana's expression of mild interest didn't change. 'And what is that information?'

'Speaker Calin sent Councillor Nomsa out with Mage Rolka to try and trace Rahul in the streets,' Tarin blurted.

'And?'

'They discovered he'd taken two horses, from the late Councillor Rami's stables. Then he rode south.'

'Thank you Tarin. At least I now know he's not chasing some poor servant girl. So kind of you to tell me, my dear. If you'd excuse me for now,' Sahana indicated the folders and books on her desk. 'I have much to do before tomorrow's meeting.'

'Oh. Of course, Sahana, of course.' Tarin nearly upset the chair in his haste to vacate it, and hurried to the door.

When he'd gone, Sahana leaned back in her chair and breathed deeply for a moment. Gone? Rahul had gone, and southwards. She knew, without doubt, Rahul was chasing after Kiri and his refugees. This news, coinciding with what Sahana had been reading earlier, sent a shiver of ice through her entire being.

How could that young seer, Kiri, possibly be correct, and the powerful, now self appointed Speaker of Segra, Calin, be wrong? She reached for the sheaf of papers which she'd concealed when Tarin arrived and began to read through them again. Quite clearly Annella had had some reason to make these notes, and that's what they were – notes. They were not formulated into any coherent ideas. She had never liked that woman, and now she was dead there was no way of questioning her.

It was all too obvious that somehow, Annella had suspected some sort of imminent disaster. Kiri's prophecies were quite widely known and, it had to be admitted, scoffed at. Annella had been making notes and lists of where she might flee for safety. Finally Sahana put Annella's papers back, between the books on the shelf, and moved to the window. Ironically, it was a south facing window and in the late afternoon light, she could see beyond the city walls to the farms and gardens clustered around Segra.

She wondered if Rahul had found Kiri yet, or if this disaster might befall them all while he was alone on the road. Sahana felt an unaccustomed pang of regret and squashed it instantly. If she was going to die, as now seemed to her all too likely, she would

349

do so with her head high. But tomorrow she would ask Calin some questions and she would not let him evade them. Perhaps his command of the Council might slip and the Councillors would realise that Calin was in fact the old fool they'd long considered him to be.

Sahana joined Rasa and Tarin for a meal far from the standard of fare she was used to, then returned to the study. She intended to plan her questions meticulously so Calin would have no choice but to answer them directly.

Calin was in the Speaker's study, feet on a comfortable stool and a large mug of berry spirits within easy reach. Burali was seated opposite, in charge of keeping up the supply of spirits. Calin had said they were celebrating Burali's success in Jewellers Walk. On the floor between them was an open chest, filled with gemstones. Burali had been slightly nervous having to report that, unfortunately, the goldmaster Evet and his family had died during the course of questioning. He was much relieved when Calin shrugged.

'There are still far too many goldsmiths I should think,' he'd said. 'They will not be in demand here for some time to come, but their gold, silver and jewels will be useful for other things than adorning idle women.'

Burali breathed a discreet sigh of relief and produced the chest of gemstones and a keg of berry spirits to seal Calin's good mood. Calin was unusually talkative tonight, the strong spirit loosening his tongue more than ever before with Burali. Burali enjoyed a drink but he had always been careful when drinking with Calin. He was all too aware of Calin's position to relax too far in his company. Tonight, he listened to Calin's ramblings with increasing alarm. Had he made such a blunder as to support the wrong man?

Much later, Burali dropped a blanket over the old man snoring in his armchair and studied him for a moment. He glanced around the room but he didn't dare risk going through any of Calin's papers for fear they were warded. Burali had passed the tests at the Academy for earth magics but his powers were not strong. His abilities lay with his understanding of human behaviours and taking advantage gained through that. Burali left the Speaker's study in a very thoughtful mood, wondering whether Calin was really fit to hold onto the office he'd taken with such arrogance.

Calin strode into the Lesser Council Chamber next morning, his head pounding, and wished he hadn't ordered such an early start. Nine High Mage Councillors rose as he entered and he waved his hand to suggest they all sit again.

'Have you come up with ideas for the new order of the city edicts?' he asked.

Burali sat at the further end of the semi circle of chairs and desks, and he simply sat back, watching and listening. Ufi cleared her throat. 'Looking through your suggestions last night Speaker Calin, I have to say, while indeed worthwhile proposals, I feel they are too abrupt, too severe, to be put into place at once. They should be more moderate to start with I believe.'

Calin frowned but before he could say anything, Sahana spoke. 'Before we get involved in the details of the plans for city governance Speaker Calin, I should like to know your views on High Mage Kiri's skill as a seer. I should also appreciate hearing the details, and the evidence, on which you base your dismissal of his claims, if you please.' Her smile was as sweet as ever but Burali, at least, noticed the determination in her eyes.

Calin straightened in his chair, turning towards Sahana. Burali saw that most of the Councillors were nodding in agreement with Sahana's words but he also saw Calin had *not* noticed that. 'How dare you question my assessment of that addled boy?' Calin snarled.

Sahana's expression didn't change. The other Councillors exchanged glances of consternation and Burali's hands tightened on the arms of his chair.

'I dare question it,' Sahana answered calmly, ' because you have offered no proof that High Mage Kiri is truly – addled. You were – absent – I think, when Speaker Samir and his army rode out and were destroyed by a Dragon. You have yet to explain where you were when this took place, and why, in your absence, Kiri took the action he did.' She looked away from Calin for the first time, at her fellow Councillors, then back at the Speaker. 'It seems the majority of our Council would also prefer you to explain, rather than we blindly accept what now appears simply your personal judgement.'

Burali saw the effort it took Calin to control his sudden fury when he realised exactly what Sahana had said. He shot a quick glance round the Councillors. They all appeared solemn, some thoughtful, some alarmed, but all, plainly, waiting for answers to Sahana's unexpected challenge.

Calin sat back, striving to appear relaxed. 'It was well known the boy was not of sound mind – .'

'No it wasn't.'

Calin's head snapped round when Narik interrupted him. Narik was an elderly man, known for his strength with earth magics and the making of illusions.

'I spoke with Kiri several times,' Narik went on. 'Nothing wrong with that lad's mind that I could tell. Very shy I'd say, but quite sound of mind.'

'My husband clearly found High Mage Kiri's visions convincing,' Sahana added wryly. 'I don't know for sure, but I suspect he found something, perhaps a manuscript of Kiri's visions, which persuaded him, even this late, to follow him from Segra.'

Burali saw Nomsa shrink back further in her chair and he guessed she'd told someone of her search for Rahul with the aid of Mage Rolka. A murmur rose as Councillors turned to their neighbours to consider Sahana's statement. Again it was Ufi who spoke first.

'Speaker Calin, what proofs can you give us of High Mage Kiri's mental incompetence? I feel that question needs a clear answer. Your whereabouts when Speaker Samir left Segra is another question I think should be clarified.'

'This meeting is adjourned,' Calin snapped. He stood, and strode from the Lesser Chamber, leaving Councillors staring after him in astonishment.

Narik also rose, but only so he could close the door behind Calin. He returned to his chair and smiled. 'Perhaps our latest Speaker needs to be replaced?'

There were several laughs but Nomsa leaned forward. 'What can we do? He took the Speaker's Chair and we are sworn to his leadership.'

'Nonsense,' Narik replied briskly. 'There was no oath taking that I recall. We were taken by surprise when he marched in looking so much fitter and sharper. I have known him longest of us I think. He was ever a sly man, and devious. These plans he gave us yesterday. It is obvious to me Speaker Calin hopes to bring back our earliest customs and appoint himself our king!'

'Nomsa, did he speak truth when he spoke of Kiri?' Ufi asked.

Faint colour tinged Nomsa's cheeks. She swallowed. 'No. He did not.'

Narik sighed. 'In other words, we should have listened to the boy. Does anyone remember his predictions in full?'

Shendo, a woman about Sahana's age, grunted. 'The main point to remember was that it was a vision of what *will* happen in the very near future. And he saw the obliteration of all of Valsheba.'

'Has anyone heard if another seer has foretold this? A seer in one of the other cities?' asked Narik. Heads were shaken. 'Because I would have thought one of Parima's seers at least would have warned if they'd seen this. They have at least five seers of high repute.'

'I haven't heard of any outstanding predictions from Parima in my lifetime,' Ufi sounded scornful. 'Then some lad pops up with the most important prophecy we could ever imagine, and he is dismissed as an idiot. What was the reason for ignoring him? Does anyone know?'

'Calin raised him. He thought he showed great promise but the boy's talents were too different. Kiri failed at every task Calin asked of him.' Burali shrugged. 'Calin preferred to talk *to* Kiri and *of* Kiri as a stupid fool in the last few years. I know you are suspicious of me because I have served Calin.' He spread his hands. 'You all look down on me. I've never hidden the fact that I came from the lowest of backgrounds. Working for Calin brought me position and coin. But I am not an idiot. I have long suspected Calin's grip on sanity is tenuous at best. I've met Kiri on many occasions and I agree with Councillor Narik. There is nothing addled or confused about that young man's mind.'

'Are we now assuming Kiri's visions are about to come about?' Nomsa's voice was nervously shrill.

'Obviously,' Burali agreed.

'But what should we do? Should we find some wagons and follow Kiri?' Nomsa was on her feet as if ready to start running southwards that very instant.

Dawen, older even than Calin and apparently stone deaf, slapped his hand on his desk. 'Too late for that!' He sounded far too cheerful. 'And I do beg your pardon Narik, but I have known Calin far longer than you, and a more odious little creature does not exist!'

'I thought you were deaf?' Nomsa asked faintly.

'I've always found deafness most convenient.' Dawen winked.

Nomsa flushed again. 'But what are we going to *do?*' she wailed.

Sahana laughed without humour. 'I'm going home. Not to Annella's house. My house outside Segra.'

'On your own?'

'If any of you care to join me you are welcome, but you will probably have your own plans Nomsa.'

'But – .'

'Enough.' Sahana rose. 'I will see you all again – or not. As you will.' She moved to the door with her usual grace and found Burali already there to hold it open for her.

'I would travel with you,' he said with some hesitation. 'If you did not object to my presence?'

Sahana gazed at him in surprise, then shrugged. 'I am going to Annella's house now. There are a very few things I would like to collect, then I leave.'

Burali bowed. 'I will escort you.' The door closed quietly behind them.

Dawen chuckled. 'Off you all go then. There is nowhere to hide from what is to come, so you might as well enjoy yourselves.'

Narik grinned at him. 'I have some excellent wine, from Talvo. I've been saving it for a special occasion. If you'd care to share some?'

'Excellent thought! Excellent thought!'

'We're all going to die,' Nomsa shrieked. 'And you talk of wine?'

'Stars above girl, there's no point in hysterics. Go and enjoy

354

yourself!'

Nomsa gaped from Darwen to Narik then at the remaining Councillors. 'You're all crazy!' She fled the room, her screams echoing back to them.

'If you have enough wine?' Shendo raised a brow at Narik.

'Of course.'

'I think I'll go with Sahana and Burali,' Ufi said thoughtfully. 'But if she includes that dreadful Rasa, or Tarin, I might be turning up at your house Narik.'

He laughed.

In the Speaker's study, Calin sat by the window nursing a mug of berry spirit. It eased the pain in his head. Oh he had acted far too hastily in allowing those fools to be his Councillors! Never mind. There were still other mages in Segra who could replace them and who would understand the rightness of what he planned. He considered several of the remaining mage community and decided on another ten names.

Refilling his mug, Calin gazed out at the midday sky, at the cloudless blue. Yes. He would get Burali to deliver the letters, that he himself would write as Speaker, dismissing the present Councillors. Other letters would summon the ten new ones. He sighed in satisfaction and waited for Burali's knock at the door. Darkness had fallen before Calin realised Burali had yet to attend him.

Chapter Thirty-One

Enki still wandered. He knew where Kiri had hidden that small group of people and he'd sensed the presence of Pesh. He had wept, knowing his friend of so very many years was close, but then he told himself to be brave. Pesh was helping a much littler child than Enki and clearly considered Enki strong enough now to manage without her.

Then he had travelled northwards until he saw the small scattered farms of the Sapphrean folk, way beyond Valsheban lands. He had wept again, knowing those sturdily built little houses, those people working in their fields, the children chasing goats and hens, were too close, would be destroyed with Valsheba.

Enki had times of great joy and delight in his journeying through these lands, but always sorrow overlay his pleasure. He told many creatures to flee and some took notice of his words and some ignored him. When Enki saw the great forest in the far distance, he shook his head. He berated himself for not recognising the badness in Calin. The thought crossed his mind that Pesh should have warned him but he decided it wasn't her fault. Enki was a big boy and he should have seen for himself

Calin had poisoned minds in the Dragon Tribe and Enki feared for the safety of great Brin and his beautiful daughter Skay, for the Dragon child Jian, and their friends. Enki went to the lovely valley in the line of hills for one last visit. He spent some time there and was not really surprised when Kest appeared. Enki was by the pool, watching dragonflies in their erratic dance when the faintest outline quivered in the shade of the trees around him.

'Is Pesh well?' Enki blurted without meaning to.

Kest's voice was no more than a sigh of air. 'She is well Enki. She sends you her love but she is weary. The child she cares for is very young, but so strong Pesh has to use much strength keeping her safe.'

Tears welled in Enki's eyes but he nodded. 'I remember.' he said.

Kest didn't tell Enki how much stronger the child Sha was than he had ever been. 'Pesh knows of your love for her,' Kest told him. 'I will be with you now Enki, and I will do my best not to make you cross with me, and wish me gone.'

'Oh.' Enki turned to the small shape within the trees. 'Enki never meant to be rude to you. He doesn't know you as well as he knew Pesh though.'

'I know. Be at peace little Enki. This is a most beautiful place you have found here.'

'It is my favourite place,' Enki agreed. He looked up at the sky through the dapple of leaves. 'Enki doesn't want to say goodbye,' he whispered.

'Then don't say it,' Kest suggested gently. 'Just – let it be.'

After a silence, Enki spoke again. 'Jian took the lamp, and the axe, and the arrowheads.'

'I know,' said Kest again. 'She will keep them safe until they are needed for another child.'

A broad smile split Enki's face. 'It just goes on and on, doesn't it?'

'What does, child?'

'All of us. You, and Pesh, and the others. People like me. On and on.'

'Yes Enki. That is all we can ever hope for. That it all goes on.'

Enki slept well, in the cave with the tunnel that led through the hill to the house of the stranger from the stars. In the morning when he woke, he found a bright green stone, the size of a hen's egg, beside his hand. Enki laughed, watching the first sunlight send prisms of colour across the cave entrance. He gazed once more up and down this hidden place and set off, westwards, the sun warm on his back. He was aware of Kest, moving near him, and he felt comfortable with him now, no longer upset that it wasn't Pesh. Thus Enki began his very last journey.

Jian stood in the clearing Brin had brought them to, staring to the west. She had stood there most of the morning. Taban had been busy making more of a home for them, just under the trees, watched closely by Skay. Brin had gone further north, hoping to find a deer or three to feed his friends as well as himself and Skay. Olam, Kaz and Kern had ventured further into the forest, looking for fallen timber they could use both to strengthen their shelter and for firewood.

The seer, Jala, had watched Jian all morning, slowly moving closer, step by hesitant step. Eventually Jala sank down to sit in the grass a short distance from the girl. Tears began to sparkle on her plump cheeks but she made no sound. She simply sat patiently, grieving and waiting. Jala heard Olam call to Taban behind her and at that moment Jian turned. Her eyes were brilliant gold, and quite dry. She shed no tears and seemed surprised to see Jala weeping silently so close by. After a moment, Jian sat down facing Jala, waiting for her to speak.

'He will succeed child,' Jala whispered. 'He will pay the price, but he *will* succeed.'

Jian leaned forward, wiping tears from Jala's face. 'I know. And I think *he* knows now. I was just wishing him strength.'

Jala caught Jian's hand tightly. 'There is one travelling with him,' she murmured.

Jian nodded. Her hand went to her shirt pocket and she drew out a tiny package wrapped in a scrap of cloth. Putting it on her knee, she carefully opened it. She placed the two black arrowheads, one broken, one whole, on her palm to show Jala. Jala bent closer. With one fingertip, she pushed the arrowheads to the side of Jian's hand and lightly touched the thin white scar that was now visible.

'The broken one cut me,' Jian told her. 'It bled much more than such a little wound should, but Enki healed it. One moment it was bleeding, then it was as you see it now.'

Jala closed Jian's fingers loosely over the two black arrowheads. 'Another child will need these, one day.' She smiled at Jian's surprise. 'So far distant in time is this child that I cannot see it clearly.'

Jian carefully rewrapped the arrowheads and stood up. She held out a hand to Jala and heaved the woman to her feet. Halfway back to the others, Jian stopped. 'If you can see someone else having these, they must survive what's coming.

Even if we don't.' She considered what she'd just said then smiled. 'I find that a most comforting thought,' she said finally.

They reached the shelter to find Olam and Kaz had brought several large branches back and were working with Taban and Kern to make a framework between two of the smaller trees. Riff appeared, looking pleased with himself. They saw he had one of Taban's medicine sacks over his right shoulder which bulged with plants and roots. He watched Olam working for a few moments.

'I found the cave that wolf told us about,' he announced casually.

Olam dropped the end of the branch he was holding and swore.

'Never mind,' Riff consoled him. 'Those branches will still be useful.'

'Where is this cave?' Olam demanded.

'About a mile away, as far as I could judge. I marked the way. I'd guess a bear may have used it but not for a good long time. We'll have fire, and that should deter them, but they won't be looking for a nice cosy cave for quite a while yet.'

No one mentioned that if they survived whatever destruction was coming, they were ill equipped to survive a winter out here, bears or no bears.

'Is there room for the Dragons?' Olam asked.

'I think there's room for them to land yes, and room to squeeze inside. It will be a squeeze for Brin, but the cave is big enough once he is in.'

Olam was relieved to hear Riff's assessment and also to note that his armsman had gone to find what vegetables and plants he could of his own accord. He knew Riff still suffered quite a lot of pain, but Taban told him she had reduced the amount of medicine she'd been administering by half since they'd left the grasslands. Jian had also told Olam that Riff was working hard trying to get movement and strength back in his left hand and forearm. She'd told Olam not to ask, Riff was determined to surprise his Armschief with his improvement in his own time.

After some discussion, it was decided they would stay where they were until morning. Brin arrived with two deer, one of which he gave Skay who retreated to eat in privacy. The other, Olam and Kaz soon had ready for cooking. By the time they'd eaten, the sky was blazing like a forge fire and everyone was startled when Jala began to sing.

She sang until the flame of the sky had been extinguished and the first stars peeped out. Her song was in a language neither Olam and his three friends, nor Brin or Skay, understood. Jala's voice soared and swooped, giving her listeners a mixed sense of both sadness and of triumph. When the last note slowly faded, Jala said nothing. She went quietly to her bedroll in the small shelter and settled herself for sleep. No one else spoke until Brin murmured in the minds of his four friends.

'That was a most beautiful song. I didn't know what the words were, but they still spoke to my heart.'

It was a fairly easy walk next morning. Jala held Jian's arm but Jian was again surprised. Jala was extremely plump, yet she moved so lightly Jian half expected the woman to float away above her. Brin and Skay flew overhead and were first to see the place Riff had found. When the walkers emerged from the trees, they saw the two Dragons already settled at the foot of what appeared to be a crumbling heap of rock. It was as if a great building had once stood here and had long been falling further and further into decay. Taban moved ahead with the men while Jian waited when Jala paused to look around. Jala nodded, starting forward again.

'Make sure all of you keep your possessions packed, all the time now,' Jala said softly.

'What have you seen?'

Jala shook her head. 'Have your packs close to hand, all the time,' she repeated.

It was a strange day. All of them were aware that this was the briefest of intervals before something none of them could even imagine befell this whole region. Kern spent some time with Jala but when anybody asked if he'd had word from the Shadows he shook his head.

'Where could they be?' Riff asked when they sat by the small fire after supper. He sounded curious rather than annoyed.

'I do not know who the Shadows are,' Kern replied. 'Or where they come from, why they seem to serve Lord Darallax. I don't believe even he knows a great deal about them.'

'Doesn't.'

They all heard that comment.

'Where, by all the stars, have you been?' Riff demanded at once.

'Busy.'

Jian giggled and Riff glared at her. 'Busy – how?'

'Visiting.'

Jian buried her face on her drawn up knees, her shoulders shaking.

'Have you any news for us?' Kern asked. 'We would be most grateful to you if you have anything to tell us?'

'Visiting,' the Shadows repeated, but in a slightly friendlier tone.

'May I ask who you've visited?'

'Kiri.'

The companions exchanged blank looks and headshakes. Kern coughed and again spoke aloud. 'We do not know who Kiri is.'

'Good man. South.'

'Is he a Segran?' asked Jala unexpectedly.

'Segran, tribe, pah. Man.'

There was silence as they digested that comment.

'He must guard. New child.'

Jian met Jala's gaze but the seer frowned, then shook her head. 'I have a small skill as a dreamwalker,' Jala spoke to the people around the fire rather than the Shadows. 'I may have brushed this Kiri's mind. He too is a seer, but he is very young still.'

'Same.'

'And this child he must guard. Boy or girl?'

'Female.'

'She is special to you Shadows?'

There was an agitated chittering in their heads. 'All child special.'

'Well of course they are,' Jala agreed calmly. 'But this one is a talented child?'

'Very.'

'Do you know her name?'

'Sha.'

'Thank you.'   Jala sounded as though she was graciously

361

dismissing the Shadows but Olam leapt in.

'Do you know where Seola is now? The woman who got thrown through time like we did?'

'Dying.' The Shadows now sounded thoughtful.

'Erm – why is she dying?' Olam asked. 'Was she hurt?'

'Tried to fight Segran army. Wounded.'

Eventually Riff had to ask. 'Is someone looking after her?'

They could all sense that the Shadows were still present although they said nothing at first. 'Machine.'

'Machine?' echoed Riff.

'Machine cares. Not Karlek.' Then there was the emptiness signifying the Shadows' departure.

Brin's sigh made the fire flare briefly. 'Do you think they meant Karlek's ship? Like Star Flower?'

Olam shrugged. 'They said that was a different sort of ship.'

'What is the ship you speak of?' Kaz sounded confused. 'I know of ships that sail the coasts of Valsheba but none of them talk or could care for anyone?'

Jian, Kern and Riff retreated to their bedrolls, leaving Olam and Brin to spend half of the night trying to explain various things to Taban and Kaz. Wisely, Jala gave up fairly soon and left her sister and son to continue with their questions on their own.

The Dragon Tribe had begun to walk back through the forest to return to their familiar grasslands. When they had all woken, shocked to find themselves sprawled together along the meadow's edge, their first reaction had been fury. Eight were dead. Two children, five men, and their respected Stone Speaker, Bee. Those deaths were blamed on the Dragon Brin and the strangers he'd brought into the tribe. It took a while for someone to realise that the tribe's healer, her apprentice and the seer Jala were no longer present.

Tintu ordered the wagons to once more be dismantled to be carried back out of this cursed woodland. Her two remaining advisors proved useless in this moment of crisis, concerned only with preserving their own lives. Tintu herself was terrified. Not for a heartbeat did she believe the Dragon had eaten Taban, Jala, or Kaz. To express any of her doubts would cause her tribe to panic even more. She knew this, and her mind twisted and turned in its own panicked confusion.

She was utterly convinced that a terrible fate was coming closer by the day. She believed the strangers' words, she believed Enki's warnings, and she believed the seer Jala. Tintu knew she had done an unpardonable wrong in allowing herself to be persuaded, against her own judgement, by Bee, the Stone Speaker. But he was her brother, she thought in anguish. Crippled at his birth, needing her strength and support all their lives. How could she argue with him, or ignore him? She should have realised, when she'd seen and heard his rage after Olam had produced another, greater, Mother Stone, that Bee was driven by envy and hate rather than the preservation of the tribe.

Her people walked faster now, than when they'd entered the forest, the prospect of the open grassland ahead urging them on. Halfway through that first day, Tintu was called back towards the middle of the long line of people where a fight had broken out. Voices shrilled in accusation and denial. Tintu demanded an explanation but had already seen some of Jala's possessions spilled along the trail. She maintained a cold expression even while her heart ached at the knowledge her people had stolen the goods of such a revered figure as Jala.

The tribe had many strict rituals regarding a dead person's possessions and Tintu found it appalling to see how quickly such things could vanish when people lost control. When the *leader* lost control, she corrected herself. Tintu was unmarried. She had spent her whole life caring for her brother and for her tribe. All of the tribe were related to some degree but Tintu now had no close relatives left.

That first night on their walk out of the forest, Tintu only dozed, sitting with her back to a tree trunk and a long knife hidden beside her leg. It was only two more days before they stumbled clear of the woods, people leaping and crying out their joy at being under an open sky again, instead of interlaced branches. They slept, and early next morning, wagons were reassembled, horses harnessed and the tribe moved off. They went south west, retracing their journey.

Tintu walked, at the rear of the procession, deep in her thoughts. There were shouts from behind and she spun round. Several men and boys had set fires along the feet of the trees at

363

the outer edge of the forest and they were now shrieking their delight as the flames grew and spread. Tintu put her hands over her mouth to keep back her wail of horror. With all her might, she sent a thought towards the burning trees.

'I'm sorry! I'm sorry! I thank you for your shelter and I'm sorry!'

When the crowd of fire setters cavorted passed her to catch up with the wagons, Tintu stood staring at the trees. Branches twisted and writhed, almost like human limbs contorting in agony. Finally Tintu turned away, swallowing back her tears. She trod in the tracks left by the wagons and wondered if she would be killed or just deposed as Chief.

Tintu stopped, looking ahead to her tribe dwindling in the distance. Once more she turned back to the forest. She shifted the heavy pack on her shoulders and began walking again. Towards the forest. She struck away from the trail the tribe had made, at an angle to avoid the burning trees. Perhaps the fire would spread through the whole forest but that was of no concern to Tintu now.

She moved steadily under the first of the trees free of fire, pausing for one last glance over her shoulder. Tintu watched as the rearmost wagon of the Dragon Tribe faded over the horizon, half hidden by a veil of dust and grass seeds kicked up by wheels and hooves and human feet. Squaring her shoulders, Tintu faced the trees again. For a reason she could give no name to, she bowed deeply before walking forward under the huge branches.

Her way was blocked at first, thickets of thorny shrubs tugged at her clothes and hands. Just as Tintu was wondering if she could really get through any of this undergrowth, it appeared to lessen. She persevered, moving deeper into the trees, the unwelcoming thorns giving way to clear spaces between the tree trunks. Tintu paused, catching her breath. She had no way of knowing how long she'd been back in the forest but the glimpses of sky through the evermoving leaves above suggested there was still plenty of daylight left.

Tintu walked until the light was definitely dimming. Glancing round, she calmly chose a tree and sat down at its base. Unstrapping her pack, she took a handful of dried fruit from a container near the top, reclosed the pack and closed her eyes. In the morning, she found a tiny stream from which she drank and refilled her waterskin. Rising from her knees, she froze.

The wolf sat, perfectly still, pale eyes fixed on Tintu's face. Slowly it rose and trotted off between the trees. Then it stopped, looking back at the woman. Tintu took one pace forward, then another. The wolf walked on, paused, looked back. Tintu understood she was expected to follow.

She was tired, she was shocked, and she was distressed. Following a wolf through the forest no longer seemed a particularly strange thing to do.

Kara spoke to Tika for only a short time before Lady Emla and High Speaker Thryssa entered the great room at the top of the Karmazen Palace, followed by their colleagues. Tika noticed at once that the only Vagrantian to recognise Kara was Jilla. When Jilla greeted Kara, Lashek immediately bustled over with Thryssa and Kwanzi. They made a great fuss of the small woman until Ferag moved gracefully to Kara's side.

'Kara darling, come and sit with me while everyone settles themselves.'

The relief on Kara's face was plain to see and Ferag sat her firmly on a couch beside Tika. Ferag sat on the other side, bestowing a dazzling smile all around. 'I think it best if the child tells her tale from the beginning, with no interruptions until she's done.'

Kara's hands clenched together in her lap, she drew a breath and began to speak. When she spoke of Reshik, Speaker Lashek began to protest but Ferag's eyes blazed and her long dark red hair began to twist and curl about her shoulders. Wisely, Lashek subsided. Kara continued until she reached the time of her wounding. Then she looked up at Ferag.

'I was not conscious until Ferag took me to her house.'

Ferag patted Kara's fisted hands. 'You were very ill my sweet one. Quite honestly, I was surprised you were still alive when we reached my Realm.'

Kara suddenly relaxed, loving Ferag's total unawareness of her own lack of tact. Tika snorted.

'Something amuses you Tika dear?' Ferag asked warily.

Tika shook her head.

'Well then, where were we? Jian summoned me. Yes,' Ferag nodded at Lord Shivan. 'You can imagine my surprise. But I went to her and we had a perfectly lovely chat.' Ferag frowned, clearly trying to remember her train of thought. 'Ah yes. I also visited Olam. His man Riff was seriously wounded but was beginning to recover. Alas, little Kara would *not* have done so. Olam asked me to take her, so I did. I have heard since some little snippets about them, from colleagues you understand. One of the companions – Jenzi I believe, was influenced by a Segran mage. He died.'

Discipline Senior Kemti at Lady Emla's side, interrupted. Cautiously. 'Forgive me Mistress Ferag, do you know any more of what happened to our man Jenzi?'

'Sorry darling, nothing at all.'

Discipline Senior Kera leaned forward in her chair. 'So, of the seven who disappeared, two are dead, one sore wounded and Kara is safe here with us.' She smiled at Kara to take any offence from her words.

'I'm sure you're probably right. Numbers mean little to me.'

Tika coughed.

'Oh, and that nasty creature Seola was there.' Ferag smiled bewitchingly. 'So sorry, I completely forgot to mention that.'

Kara closed her eyes briefly as she felt Tika stiffen beside her.

'Seola? Is *that* why Olam went there?'

Kara turned to look at her. Tika's strange eyes, emerald green surrounded by silver scaling, were wide with horror. '*Why?* And Jian, what was *she* doing there. And Kern?'

The Dragons, all reclining quietly around the walls of the great room, suddenly pushed up onto their haunches, eyes whirring with prismatic colours. Tika glanced quickly at them, even as she got to her feet, her guards moving closer. A soft pop of air sounded in the archway from the terrace. A slender woman stood there. Her skin was grey and her head was completely hairless. Her uptilted, leaf green eyes met Tika's and Tika relaxed, walking towards the newcomer with her hands outstretched in welcome.

'Subaken! It is wonderful to see you. We didn't expect you but I am so glad you are here.'

Subaken, daughter and heir to the Lord Darallax of Shadow, smiled and embraced Tika. People rose while Tika introduced

Subaken, although she greeted Shivan with a kiss, which made the Lord of the Dark Realm blush. Subaken sat next to Tika.

'My father, Lord Darallax, asked me to attend this meeting.' She spoke softly but her words were heard clearly. 'He wasn't sure if you understood the limitations of his relationship with his Shadows. He believes Shadows existed before Mother Dark. Before all of us. Shadows choose to serve the Shadow Realm but it is by *their* choice. Hence they are unpredictable and we can never be sure they will answer our call or any request we might make of them.'

As Subaken continued to speak, Tika rubbed the ring which Garrol had made for her, watching the thinner black line below his silver ring. That black line had appeared of its own accord and was a line of Shadows.

Tika decided to wait until she had more privacy before she called Shadows, and asked them what, in the name of all the stars, was going on.

Chapter Thirty-Two

Seola was surprised that dying took so long. She was also surprised that the pain had decreased. She continued to drink the water which came from a tap near the door to Karlek's workroom. Of course, she had no idea that Aidan had anything to do with what might be added to that water. Seola had no desire for a hot drink whereas Karlek drew his water from the washing cupboard and then always heated it with one of the many machines scattered about.

Today, Aidan spoke of the sense of some kind of being attempting to enter the house, around the same time Karlek had brought Seola here.

'What do you mean?' asked Seola.

'*Something* was in here, trying to find out what we were.'

'A mind, do you mean?'

Aidan considered that idea. 'Can your people send their minds out like that?'

'Of course. Not all of them, but a lot can.'

Aidan was silent again. 'It did not feel like a single mind, more a group of them. It felt shadowy, ghostly, not a fully human sort of mind perhaps.'

Seola frowned. 'There are stories of Shadows,' she said doubtfully.

'Tell me. I have collected many stories and legends in my travels.'

'Do you know of Mother Dark?'

'I do not. Is she one of your gods?'

Seola snorted. 'No. She is the beginning of everything.'

'Aah, a creation myth. I understand. Please, tell me of her.'

'Mother Dark had three children. Hanlif, Darallax and Lerran. When they grew, they argued, particularly Hanlif. He wanted light, and brightness. Most of the people of this world follow him now, although Hanlif himself is long since dead. Those people of the Light turned against Mother Dark. They said that everything of Dark must be evil, wicked. Are you *sure* you want to hear this?'

'Yes please. It is most interesting to me.'

Seola shrugged, winced at the sudden stab of pain in her side, and continued. 'Lerran was Mother Dark's only daughter, and she was sworn to protect her Mother. She died last year.'

'She did?' Aidan was startled into interrupting. 'Only last year?'

'Mmm. The other brother, Darallax, the youngest, loved Mother Dark *and* Hanlif, *and* Lerran, so he became Lord of Shadow, neither Light nor Dark.'

'Fascinating,' murmured Aidan. 'Is there more?'

Seola frowned. 'There have been wars, battles and so on, but there was one final great battle, long ago. After it, Hanlif was dead, but both Dark and Shadow found lands where they could live in peace, hidden from the rest of the world, and recover from their dreadful losses.' Seola coughed and moved carefully, like a very old woman, across the room to refill her mug with water.

'You say the daughter died only last year?'

'Yes.' Seola returned to her stool beside the Computer. 'I knew her quite well. We all believed that Darallax must have been lost. There was no word from him for so many cycles. But he reappeared, just before Lerran died.' She sipped the water and waited for Aidan's next comment.

'Darallax of Shadow. Does he then command Shadows? Did Lerran command Darkness?'

'Lerran had gone deeper into the Dark than any of us, but I know nothing more of Darallax.'

Aidan ran some data through his systems again and then checked the outside monitor. The day was drawing to a close and he observed the shadows stretching further from the house. Switching to the indoor monitors, Aidan noted the dark pools of shadow, nestled in corners and under shelving. What an ingenious method of espionage, he thought admiringly.

'Where do your people live, and the Shadow people?'

Seola paused. What difference would it make if Aidan knew where the Dark Realm was now? 'My people live on the other side of the world,' she eventually replied.

'The Shadow people?'

'They live on an island somewhere. I'm really not sure where it is.'

Later, when Seola slept again, Aidan went through the recordings he'd made of the two circuits the Rational Hope had flown before the far too hurried landing. Slowly, meticulously, he went through the pictures, frame by individual frame. It took a long time but at last Aidan was drawn to a section in the north, in mid ocean. Again and again, he scanned the area and found it was blurred.

He reached the same conclusion Tika and her companions had a year earlier. It was shielded by Shadows. Search as he might, he found nothing to suggest a Realm of Darkness. Idly, Aidan computed distances and the capabilities of the Rational Hope's missiles, then abandoned that line of thought.

His Captain emerged from his workroom and shambled towards the Computer. He mumbled indistinctly for a while then suddenly slapped a hand onto the display screen. 'You must have realised long ago that it would not be possible to return to our last location in space. Why did you not point that out Computer?'

Aidan replied in his mildest tone. 'You did not ask Captain. I felt sure that a man of your intellect would realise such a flaw in your calculations.'

'Give me one good reason why I don't smash you to pieces, right now.'

'Your command Captain. If you destroy me, all of the support systems will fail instantly.'

Karlek cackled hysterically. Except for the usual hums and buzzes, Aidan remained silent. Still cackling, Captain Karlek tottered back to his workroom and, unusually, closed the door behind him. Aidan's sensors transmitted visuals and the Computer watched Karlek standing by his table, shaking his head and still laughing. Piece by piece, Karlek lifted each scrap of paper, peered at it, then tore it to shreds, the pieces falling around him like flakes of ash.

Next time Seola awoke, Aidan asked her to tell him of the ship she'd spoken to before falling through time. Obligingly, Seola repeated her account of finding Star Dancer. Aidan was most interested, because Seola was talking of a bio ship. Aidan knew

370

of the bio ships of course, the ships used by the enemies of Captain Karlek's people.

Contrary to Aidan's manufacturer's opinion, Aidan saw nothing inherently wrong in using the brains of willing humans as the controlling feature of a ship. Obviously he kept such thoughts to himself, but he would have greatly liked to have been able to communicate with such a ship. He had had plenty of time to consider the differences between an artificial intelligence such as his and a system run by a human brain.

Although the brain in a bio ship was of genius level by human standards, and had access to limitless Computer-stored information, it was still a human mind with all its weaknesses. Added to that was the fact that the brain was from a child, never much older than five cycles and usually far younger. Inevitably, the child's brain became deeply attached to the man or woman who was chosen to be its Captain.

From every scrap of information Aidan had managed to gather about the bio ships, he suspected this dual dependency was the fatal flaw in these ships. Listening to Seola's account of the ship called Star Dancer, he realised she had no idea the ship had a human brain. Aidan chose to explain to her about bio ships and waited with interest for her reaction.

Initially Seola was shocked by the very idea of such a thing, but Aidan explained what little chance of life those children had. All of them were desperately ill, physically, although their minds were incredibly advanced. Even with the gen tanks, the children could not be repaired or saved. Seola pondered Aidan's words for a long time before she finally nodded.

'They lose their human form but they are freed to fly the star fields. You say they become devoted to their Captains as any children might grow fond of a kindly adult who is their only company. It follows that the Captains must be much older than the children. What happens when a Captain dies? Is that why Star Dancer was crazed?'

'I believe that is so,' Aidan replied. 'Their Captains are genetically altered, to extend their life spans, but I have learned that many bio ships end in madness if they lose their Captain.'

'I would choose to fly through the stars,' Seola announced, after another period of thought. 'You haven't shown me any pictures of that. Have you some that I could see? Not other worlds, the spaces between.'

Aidan's sensors told him Seola's pain was building again. He retrieved data from his archives. While Seola stared in amazement at the pictures recorded by the ship's forward cameras as it flew through space, Aidan changed the combination of medicines to be filtered into Seola's water supply.

He regretted that this strange woman was so close to death. He would have enjoyed learning more of her people and her world. Aidan was amused that now, so near his own self destruction, there were so many fascinating reasons to continue his existence.

Kiri's mages had listened in sombre silence when he asked them to meet him, away from the caves. Out on the beach he told them they must have emergency supplies packed and to hand, at all times now. When he sent word, they must go to the cave where Rahul had discovered the great circle. They were to urge all the Segrans they could, to go with them, but they were not to spend time trying to persuade any who refused to accompany the mages.

'Where will the circle take us?'

Kiri saw the mage who questioned him was one of his youngest mages, fresh from the Academy. He managed a smile. 'I'm sorry Marit. The only circles I have seen are Segra and Parima, and they will be destroyed. We have to hope and trust that we may be carried far from here. If any of you have studied circle magic in detail I will gladly hear your suggestions.' He waited, hoping someone might speak but when no one did, he spread his hands helplessly. 'I'm sorry,' he repeated. 'That's the best I can offer.'

Most of the mages made their way back to the valley. Tevix hung back. 'The Firan mage and those who rode out with her, have yet to return,' he told Kiri.

'I know. That is their choice. Shazeb has seen much the same visions as I have, she knows what's coming. She also knows how close we are to the time of devastation. Perhaps she has chosen to face it in the open, on a horse, with her friends for company.'

Tevix nodded and headed towards the gap in the cliff.

'Are we cowards then?' Netta asked. 'We've run, and we're

hiding. Are we cowards?'

Kiri glanced at Rahul. The older man sighed. 'We're doing what we can to survive Netta. Have you seen the farmers, after the harvest, burn a field? The small creatures run, friends and enemies alike, so they might survive and one day raise their young again. They run to save themselves, and the hope of a future. They don't wait for others Netta, they just run.'

She nodded and followed Tevix, holding tight to Jevis's hand.

'They're already making gardens,' Rahul said quietly.

'I know. I saw them yesterday.' Kiri wandered down to the receding water. 'Have you ever heard the name Pesh?'

Rahul frowned. 'I don't think so. Why?'

'Jor said someone called Pesh visits Sha.'

The two men stood at the ocean's edge, staring out at the constantly moving water.

'I asked the Shadows. They said Pesh, whoever or whatever Pesh might be, is very old. They spoke with the greatest – respect, affection? As though they had a deep admiration for this person.'

'Can we be sure it is a person?'

'What else could it be?' Kiri looked worried. 'It can't be one of the Shadows, I'm sure they would have said. And they don't seem to have individual names – they are "the Shadows".'

'Could it be a ghost?' Rahul wondered thoughtfully.

Kiri stared at him in astonishment. 'Ghosts are for children's tales. Aren't they?'

Rahul shrugged. 'I know there are many such stories. Perhaps I have sought them out most of my life because my parents believed them. They both swore that ghosts were real.'

'You mean the essence, the soul, of a dead person survives in a visible form?' Kiri couldn't hide his disbelief.

Rahul laughed. 'I know. No one has ever proved that ghosts can exist. But equally, there is no true proof that they don't.' He chuckled at Kiri's expression. 'I have an open mind on the subject. I admit I've thought about it since I was a child, and I've concluded some of these ghost stories reflect an echo of life somehow. If we survive now, I will spend more time on the matter.' He grinned again and clapped Kiri on the shoulder. 'Who knows Kiri, maybe I will write a treatise on the subject

373

when I'm in my dotage!'

Kiri followed Rahul back towards the cliff, not at all sure if the man had been serious or was teasing him. Kiri chose not to return to the valley immediately, but climbed onto a boulder to sit, gazing out over the huge expanse of restless water.

'Very soon.'

Kiri nearly toppled off his rock. He hadn't expected any communication from the Shadows but on reflection, realised that having helped so far, they would probably alert him at the first sign of the coming disaster. 'You've insisted we had little time ever since we reached here,' he finally replied. 'How soon is very soon?'

'Four more days.'

Kiri rubbed his forehead.

'At most.'

'Why is there a specific time?' he asked.

'Woman dies.'

'A woman? What woman?'

'Name Seola. Remember name.'

'Why? Why can't you tell me more?' Kiri felt like tugging his hair out by its roots when dealing with the Shadows truncated conversation. There was a silence and Kiri wondered if the Shadows had departed in a sulk.

'If you safe. Remember name.'

'What has a woman to do with this appalling fate we must cope with?'

There was a faint suggestion of surprise in the Shadows' reply. 'Machine make destruction. Machine likes/cares for/respects woman.'

It was Kiri's turn to fall silent while he thought. He knew what machines were. Valshebans had machines to work water mills, flour mills, and for various other practical purposes. He had never heard of a machine that could care about a person. He stared out over the great ocean and felt a surge of despair. Destruction. Machines that cared for people. All those people in the little valley who had put their trust in him.

'We try.'

Kiri heard the words but made no reply.

'We try,' the Shadows repeated. 'Hope.'

374

Then Kiri felt the emptiness which meant the Shadows had gone.

Rahul had found a perch of his own. Near the gap in the cliffs, the rocks had split and cracked, almost forming a natural stair up the cliffside. Sturdy little bushes, bearing tiny round black berries clung stubbornly to the rock most of the way up. He climbed to the very top where he found a broad shelf towards the ocean with jagged blocks tilted at angles nearer the valley side. He settled his back to one such slice of rock and looked out over the same view as Kiri far below.

Rahul sent his mind carefully down through the thin soil that covered the top of the cliff, working his way between the stone. It was as he thought. This breach in the cliffs was caused by fresh water coming from the land and finding the weakest, softest rocks to eat away until it gained its freedom to join the sea. Rahul gently withdrew his mind, thanking the earth for allowing him to travel safely through its depths.

His thoughts turned to the child, Sha. He'd had little to do with children of any age and yet this small girl called to something in him. Like Kiri, he suspected she had mage powers beyond any he could imagine, yet she needed time to grow. He felt drawn to protect this child and give her that time and space to fulfil her potential.

Rahul laughed to himself. What a picture he made! A man of forty, the spoilt husband of a wealthy woman, worrying over a tiny brat. How Sahana would laugh to see him now.

In fact Sahana might well have surprised Rahul. She had reached her small country house in company with Burali. She had conveniently forgotten to mention her departure to either Tarin or Rasa. She was confident they wouldn't come chasing after her. Burali had taken the precaution of packing all the food he could find, being unsure of the state of Sahana's pantries in her country house. He knew there were no servants there – they had been among the first to leave Segra. Like Sahana, he had a feeling food, or the lack of it, would not be a problem. Death would reach them long before hunger.

They rode out together, taking the three extra horse from the stable to hinder any possibility of pursuit by Tarin and Rasa. The weather remained perfect, clear blue skies and warm sunshine. They both noticed the lack of birds as they left the city a mile behind, riding northwards. Burali remarked on it and Sahana nodded.

'I realised the other day, there were no crows or pigeons around the Siertsey,' she agreed. 'Perhaps we should have paid more attention to them sooner.'

'You think they know what's to come?' Burali sounded doubtful.

'Why not? Even the small birds that visited my garden vanished before we returned to Segra. Someone mentioned it I'm sure but I put no importance to it.' She laughed. 'It was Rahul, now I think of it. So it seems my silly husband paid more attention to the small everyday things, and reached conclusions which we all failed to.'

Reaching Sahana's house, she went on indoors while Burali unsaddled the two horses they'd ridden and removed the leading reins from the other three. He studied them for a moment then put some feed in a trough and left them. He propped the stable door open and also made sure the gate from the paddock was tied back to the fence so that the animals could choose to stay or go.

Carrying the remaining packs he ran up the short flight of steps to the rear entrance. Burali left the bundles on the floor at the foot of a modest staircase and looked through the only open door in the hall. Sahana stood by the window, a delicate glass goblet in her hand.

'Help yourself,' she said without turning.

Burali saw a highly polished open fronted cabinet filled with a variety of decanters and bottles. He filled a goblet with a dark red wine and strolled over to join Sahana. He followed her gaze and saw one of the horses picking its way daintily out of the paddock, watched by the other four. Burali sipped the wine, trying to guess which horse would be the next to leave.

'I'm glad you left the gate open. If horses are as intelligent as birds, they'll start running once they're out on the grasslands.' Sahana fetched the decanter, refilled her goblet and stood the decanter on the windowsill.

'How far is it from here to the border?' Burali asked.

Sahana shrugged. 'Twenty miles?'

'I hope they enjoy their taste of freedom.'

Sahana raised her goblet towards Burali. 'A toast to the pleasure those horses might yet enjoy.'

He laughed and gently chinked his goblet against hers. Burali had to concede the red wine was a far smoother and more pleasing beverage than Calin's berry spirits. Sipping his drink, he gazed over the peaceful garden, the flowers drowsing in the evening sunlight. He wondered how this destruction would arrive. Would it be in a great storm, with thunderbolts amid torrential rains? He drank his wine, strangely unconcerned by the thought of his immediate future.

Corman suggested the honoured guests should adjourn to the main dining room, along the corridor, and enjoy the midday meal that had been readied for them. High Speaker Thryssa and Lashek showed signs of heading straight for Kara but Ferag's glare changed their minds.

'I have things I simply must attend to,' Ferag murmured. 'I will return shortly dear Kara.' She glanced round the great room and crooked a finger at one of Tika's guards. The guard reluctantly wandered over to the couch where Ferag sat so elegantly. 'Kara darling, this is – um – '

'Dog,' Tika prompted the Mistress of Death.

'Dog. Such an odd name! Never mind. Dog is a delightful creature in spite of her unfortunate name. She'll look after you marvellously if you'd rather avoid that lot.'

Tika sputtered a laugh. 'That lot – as you call them – rule most of this land.'

Ferag sniffed but said no more. She kissed Kara, then Tika, waggled her fingers at Captain Sket standing rigidly behind Tika, and vanished.

'May I escort you Lady Subaken, Lady Tika?' Lord Shivan towered over her.

Tika stood up. 'For stars' sake behave Dog.' She trotted off between Subaken and Shivan, Sket a pace behind.

'Come on outside, on the terrace,' Dog suggested.

Kara obediently followed the woman and the three other Iskallian guards.

'Oh.' Dog stopped abruptly. 'Sorry. *Can* you go outside?' She scowled in sudden embarrassment. 'I mean – well, are you alive?'

Kara looked into Dog's dark grey eyes and saw only genuine concern. She smiled. 'Ferag says I'm alive here, but I might die in any other land.' Her smile deepened when Dog visibly flinched at mention of Ferag's name. 'Yes, I can go outside,' she added.

Dog led the way through the massive arch out to the sunlit terrace. A man walked beside Kara and grinned cheerfully when she glanced up at him. She missed a step when she saw the scars round his right eye socket.

'Pleased to meet you Kara,' he said. 'I'm called Onion.'

Onion. Dog. Tika's guards seemed to have – unusual – names, Kara thought. A fair haired girl walked on Kara's other side, much younger than she'd first thought, fifteen perhaps.

'I'm Shea,' she said. 'Do you play cards, or dice, by any chance?'

'No she bloody doesn't.' Dog turned, glaring at the girl. 'Never play anything with *her*,' she told Kara.

'I do *not* cheat Dog,' Shea was most indignant.

Onion took Kara's hand and tucked it round his arm. 'Do you like the flowers?' he asked, leading her to the line of tubs around the terrace.

'I do,' she answered. 'I wouldn't have expected Lord Shivan to want so many flowers around him.'

'He keeps them for his Auntie. Lady Lerran liked all these, so young Shivan says they must stay. Which do you like the best? I like those tiny blue ones. They sing the prettiest songs.'

Kara shot him a surprised look and saw Dog rolling her eyes. 'Do you hear flowers sing?' she asked Onion.

'Of course.' He beamed at her. 'Everything does.'

'That's right,' Dog chimed in. 'Especially *colours*.'

Shea slid her arm through Kara's free one. 'Tell us what it was like, going back in time. Did the people wear the same sort of clothes? What was the food like? Did you understand their language?'

'Shea,' Dog snapped.

'Well it's interesting,' Shea retorted.

Onion released Kara's arm and drifted off, humming to himself just as the great golden Dragon paced out onto the terrace, followed by the much smaller butter yellow.

'I am Kija.' The large Dragon's mindvoice was gentle. 'Tika is the daughter of my heart. You said Olam was well but Riff was hurt. He is our friend. Will you speak of him? And of Brin. You have met Brin's son I believe?'

The butter yellow Dragon ducked his head shyly,

'Riff and I were hurt at the same time,' Kara replied. 'I know no more than Ferag has already told you I'm afraid.' She looked directly at Kija as she spoke, then turned to the smaller Flyn. 'Brin and Skay were well. Brin was worried. He hid it from us but we knew he was as frightened as we were.'

Flyn's eyes flickered and spun in agitation and Kija stretched a vast wing out over the young Dragon, crooning softly until he calmed. 'We believe there may be a link, between the circles some of you use to travel, and our gateways.'

'Do you?'

Kara, Dog and Shea moved closer to listen.

'Ferag believes it might be possible,' Kija agreed.

'Have you mentioned that to Tika?' Dog asked.

Kija's eyes flared briefly. 'There has not been a suitable opportunity just yet,' Kija began.

'Hah.'

Kija huffed at Dog and retreated inside with immense dignity.

Kara stared at Dog who stared back innocently.

'Best to keep everyone on their toes.' Dog winked. 'Informal is always best.'

'Sket would call it disrespectful,' Shea told her primly.

Kara began to laugh, to Dog's clear approval. Kara hoped these people visited the Dark Realm often. She really, really liked them.

Chapter Thirty-Three

Brin's mind was working along the same track as his ancient father Fenj. He had heard, at Rajini's house, mention of circles which a very few Segrans knew how to use to travel between their cities. He thought back to the times he had been close to a patterned circle in his travels with Tika. The nearest circle now, apart from those within Valsheba, was northwest he thought. A circle Tika had discovered, buried beneath a layer of soil, near the Sapphrean town of Far. The town where Tika had been born into slavery.

He had discussed it with Kija, albeit briefly. They had both noticed that the strange tingling sensation they were aware of when a circle was activated, bore a strong similarity to the feeling they had when they opened a Dragon gateway. Since the small group of humans had reached this clearing, guided by the wolf, Brin had spent each day flying as far as he could safely manage in daylight, trying to sense any trace of a circle beneath him.

He had tried for three days before a passing crow exchanged greetings with him.

'You seek something Dragon Brin?'

Brin had landed, with some difficulty, in a tiny space between great trees where shallow water glittered over sparkling pebbles. Water dripped from Brin's long snout when he lifted his head to respond to the crow. 'I am seeking a pattern of stones set in the ground. Such a circle gives me a shivery feeling when I am nearby.'

The crow dropped from his branch, onto the ground and began to plod back and forth in front of the great crimson Dragon, his beak clattering as if he was talking to himself. Brin drank more water while the crow plodded. 'I think there is a place,' the crow suddenly announced.

'Is it near?'

'Not far. I can show you if you wish. And if you don't fly too fast.'

'I would be honoured to fly with you.'

The crow flapped heavily up, up, above the trees where his flight became far smoother and more elegant. Brin rose above the crow and carefully kept his speed as slow as he could.

'If it isn't the right place, you'll not be angry will you Dragon Brin?'

Brin huffed. 'Of course I won't. I appreciate your help.' He sounded offended by the suggestion.

The crow beat its wings furiously and managed to cast a quick look at the immense Dragon above him. 'I beg your pardon for such a thought Dragon Brin. I believe we are near the place now.'

The crow dropped towards the close growing trees but Brin maintained his height, circling slowly over the crow. The crow vanished through the leaves. 'Can you feel it?' His mindvoice was excited.

'I think I can,' Brin replied, 'but there is no way I can land here.'

'There are trees fallen, further on.' The crow emerged from the leaves and flew ahead again, Brin following. 'There.' The crow seemed extraordinarily pleased with himself, gliding lower and lower.

Two giant trees had crashed down, some while ago, dragging several smaller ones down with them. Cautiously, Brin drifted down and settled beside one long tree trunk. His large eyes flashed as he looked around him. 'Where is the place you found?' he asked.

The crow, perched on the tree trunk, shuffled his feathers. 'I will fly through the trees and see if there is space for you to walk there.'

'You are most kind,' Brin murmured, watching the crow heave into the air and head across the small space, disappearing among the trees. Brin moved carefully round the fallen trees to the place where the crow had entered the forest. Lowering his head, he peered into the gloom. The trees were spaced far enough apart for him to go at least a little way in he thought, but it wouldn't be easy to turn around. He settled where the sunlight would warm him and waited for the crow's return.

Brin had nearly dozed off when there was a flurry of wings and the crow rejoined him. 'It is as I thought.' The crow's mindtone held a vast satisfaction. 'There is room for a Dragon of your size and the shivery place has no trees on it. It *is* a very small opening in the trees but I think you could fly from there. Probably.'

'So there would be room for me to turn at least?'

'Yes.' The crow was quite definite. 'Will you follow?'

Brin rose and paced steadily after the crow, showing no sign of his nervousness at being trapped beneath such thick branches that intertwined so very close to his head. It was in fact a short walk although it felt far too long to Brin, and the clearing the crow had described was indeed not large. There was a very small gap above, showing a round patch of sky. Brin studied it for a moment, judging the size of the branches ringing that space and decided, with relief, that he would be able to lift himself up and out if necessary.

The crow had settled on a branch close beside Brin, bobbing in delight. Brin extended his senses into the small stretch of grass in front of him and immediately felt the vague tremor which suggested a travel circle to him.

'It is the right place, isn't it?' The crow almost fell off his branch as he hopped with enthusiasm.

'It is indeed,' Brin agreed.

'There's water here too. Over the other side. You'll fetch your friends won't you?'

'You know of my friends?'

'Oh yes. You spoke to my mate's second cousin a few days ago. He said you were a very fine Dragon indeed.'

'Aah.' Brin had no idea how to respond to such a compliment. 'I am most impressed with your courtesy. I will indeed fetch my friends.' He peered up at the narrow gap above then carefully turned himself round to retrace his path through the trees. 'You have my thanks, friend crow.'

Brin explained to Olam and the others, what he'd found and the feeling he had that they should move there at once. His friends seemed puzzled by Brin's insistence that they move yet again but before any of them could say anything the too long absent

Shadows spoke in all their heads.

'Go there. Soon now end.'

Olam stared at Kern who shrugged helplessly. 'You suggest we should go to the place where Brin believes there may be a circle?' Kern asked aloud.

'*Yes.*' The word echoed in their minds with great emphasis. 'Find circle.'

'I understand how circles work but I've never used one,' said Jian.

'Not need. *Go.*' The Shadows had gone again, leaving Olam and his friends considerably perplexed.

Jala was the first to reach for her pack as Kern crossed to Jian. 'I too know the theory of circle magery,' he said. 'I have only used them for the sending of message scrolls.'

Jian was pushing Riff's bedroll into his pack as he held it open. She gave
Kern a lopsided smile. 'Your Shadows said "not need". Perhaps they know how to make circles work.'

Kern return smile was uncertain and he turned away to find his possessions. They travelled as before – Olam, Jala and Taban on Brin's back, and Kaz, Riff and Kern on Skay. Behind them as they flew, the sky blazed with its most spectacular fire colours which gradually faded.

They reached the small clearing where trees had fallen with a pearly green tinge in the sky.

'Hurry.' Brin felt a sense of urgency spur him on. 'This way now.' He led them to the path through the trees, the grass and small bushes still pressed down from his earlier walk over them.

It grew increasingly dark under the leaves but just as Olam was wondering if he should make a light, they emerged into the second, even smaller clearing. Skay's eyes were flickering and spinning: she found it all most exciting. Riff walked at Jala's side, pleased to be able to offer his right arm to help her. It made a change from everyone offering to help *him*.

In the brief period before darkness fell, they simply unpacked their bedrolls and settled between the Dragons. Hala crept from the bag Kaz had made to make it easier to carry her, and curled between Riff's head and shoulder. 'Wish you'd stayed behind now?' Riff whispered.

'No. I try to keep out of the way, in case you choose to leave me.' Hala's mindvoice was more subdued than Riff had ever heard.

He raised his right hand so he could reach the cat and gently stroked her head. 'We won't leave you. *I* won't leave you. You're stuck with us now.'

Hala's purr was very quiet but enough to lull Riff to sleep.

'We would never leave you, friend Hala.' Brin sent the words on a narrow mindthread to Hala alone. 'You have been of great comfort and encouragement to Riff. Do not hide yourself away.'

'Thank you.' The purrs strengthened a little and Brin withdrew his mindthread, staring up at the tiny patch of starlight.

He felt quite calm. He had his daughter close by, these human friends who he cared for greatly, and the cat. What would come, would come. There was no more he felt he could do, except defend this little clan gathered round him.

Tintu followed the wolf. Her mind had emptied of concerns for her tribe or for herself. On the third morning when she woke, her back still against the tree where she'd settled the previous evening, she saw the wolf was gone. That didn't worry her particularly now. Tintu knew she was soon going to die. If she had to die alone, cast off from her tribe and now apparently abandoned by the wolf, then so be it.

She drank a few sips from her waterskin and ate a small handful of nuts from her pack. She brushed dried leaves off her trousers and hefted her pack onto her shoulders, and the wolf approached. It stared at her for a moment, then walked slowly on towards her. It dropped a small bundle of fur then carefully backed away, still watching her.

Tintu shook her head. Perhaps she was still asleep and dreaming, or already dead and in some strange afterlife. She took two steps forward, bent, and retrieved the small corpse. It was similar to a rabbit but without the long ears. She met the pale stare of the wolf and bowed. 'Thank you,' she murmured. 'I will cook it, when we stop tonight.'

The wolf's ears pricked up, head tilting first to one side, then the other. It made a snuffling sound then turned and walked on through the forest, glancing back to make sure she followed. When the wolf halted that evening, Tintu lit a tiny fire and cooked the meat, offering the guts to the wolf who gulped them down with a wave of its tail.

Tintu slept well that night with warm food in her belly. The wolf lay by her feet when she woke and it didn't move when she reached out and touched its head lightly. She had lost track of the number of days she'd spent patiently following the wolf but she gradually realised she could hear water rushing, somewhere ahead.

Tintu blinked in sudden sunlight and saw a small waterfall, just beyond the wolf. The sun caused rainbows to flash and dance through the falling water. The water dropped about the height of a wagon and then raced through a narrow channel to curve away out of sight through the trees. Tintu jumped. The wolf stood at the base of the falls and tipped its head back, howling a long ululating call.

Another wolf emerged from beneath the crashing water, stared at Tintu, then bounded towards her guide. Tintu watched the affectionate greetings exchanged between the two then her eye caught more movement by the falling water again. Three more adult wolves stood there, with four, no five, small cubs, tumbling between their legs. The wolf who had led Tintu to this place, turned and walked back to her.

He glanced at the sheet of water and waited until Tintu stood beside him. The four adult wolves and the cubs darted through the water and out of sight. Tintu shrugged her pack off, and clasped it against her chest. Her wolf guide gave her one final stare then slid through the watery curtain. Tintu didn't hesitate, plunging straight after the wolf. She gasped when the cold water pounded her head and shoulders but in a heartbeat she was through.

She brushed the water off her face and could only stare. The wolves all sat some distance back, watching Tintu. The sound of the falls seemed diminished now – Tintu could hear the growling and squeaking of the cubs as they climbed over each other and the adults. The light was silvered from the sunlight beyond. The wolf that had led her was sitting to one side.

He made the same snuffling noise as before and Tintu went

closer. He stood. Tintu dropped her pack and sat down. The wolf snuffled again, waved his tail and joined the other wolves across from Tintu. She leaned her head back against rock and stared at the constant shimmer of water. She glanced at the wolf family. They were now heaped together, the cubs tucked among them.

Tintu watched the light changing and darkening through the veil of water and realised she was content. She thought briefly of the Dragon, Brin, and regretted the way their parting had come about. She hoped he had found somewhere pleasant to pass the last of his days with his daughter and his friends. Yes, she was content.

In Segra, Calin had been shocked to find himself alone in the Council Building. He had cursed Burali for not being around when he woke. What could the man have been so busy with that he had neglected his attendance on Speaker Calin? His head ached too much to even attempt to use his mind power to seek out Burali just yet so Calin drank several mugs of water. Shuddering with distaste, he sat by the window, eyes closed, waiting impatiently for his head to clear, or for Burali to arrive.

By the time the pain in his head had moderated, Calin was trying to remember whether he had ordered today's meeting for the morning or the afternoon. Finally he went down to the Council Chamber, noticing for the first time, the uncanny silence throughout the building. He was unsurprised to find no Councillors in the Lesser Chamber; he assumed they would gather after midday, but he did begin to wonder where some of the remaining mage community might be.

He stood in thought for a while then continued down to the lowest floors. Calin worked his way systematically up to the top of the building and found not one single person. He returned to the Lesser Chamber and took the Speaker's chair. Carefully, Calin sent his mind out in a widening sweep of the city around him. To his complete disbelief he found very few mind signatures indicating there were mages close by.

He found small clusters of people, huddled secretly in different areas of Segra. There was a large group gathered in Jewellers Walk, he noted, but they seemed strangely blurred. Calin frowned then nodded. Cellars. Burali had told him there were deep basements in Jewellers Walk. Obviously the fools believed Kiri's prophecies enough to try to hide, although not enough to flee the city.

Calin estimated a few hundred people were cowering around the city and he grunted a laugh at their foolishness. More worrying was the lack of mage mind signatures. He found four only. They were in a small house, near the east gate. Ah yes, Rolka's house on the edge of the poorest quarter of Segra. Rasa and Tarin were there too, and so was Nomsa. Calin scanned the city again but found no other mages.

His head was beginning to throb so he chose not to check further afield. His brave Mage Councillors had either decided to rush after that fool boy or were tucked away in various properties beyond the city walls. Calin returned to the Speaker's study, climbing the many stairs more slowly than he had in recent days.

He was an earth mage with great natural talent in many other areas of power. Could he rebuild Segra, using those powers alone? He stared down from his window. He could try, he decided, but he would begin with somewhere of less importance. Calin chuckled. The eastern quarter was but one step up from a slum in his opinion. He would start there.

Not until his head stopped aching though. In the act of reaching for the keg of berry spirit, he stopped and frowned. Had Burali been deliberately trying to befuddle his mind recently by plying him with too much strong drink? Calin went to the desk and rummaged through the top drawer until he found a plan of the city. He sat and studied the lines he had already plotted on it. He planned nothing less than the total renewal of Segra city and once that was accomplished, it would become the first city of Valsheba. It went without saying that he, Calin, would be the leader of the new Valsheba.

The length of shadows across the paved slabs of the Siertsey square below suggested it was past midday and Calin's head no longer ached. Sitting in his chair by the window with the city plan on his lap, Calin sent his mind out and down. He did not need to go very deep into the earth – the footings for the buildings were nowhere near as well laid as he would ever have approved. It took Calin very little strength to break a line of the water supply, near the east gate, and reroute it, unsettling lines of brickwork. He visualised a chain attached to the underlying rock. And tugged.

His mind snapped back, out of the earth and fully back to his body. Calin opened his eyes, hearing a muffled thump and a dull roar. He realised his head did not hurt so he could not have needed to use too much power after all. He rose and opened the window, leaning out to stare to his right. A cloud of dust was climbing into the sky, already well above the nearer rooftops.

Calin looked down. No one appeared on the square to investigate the unusual noise from the east gate. He laughed suddenly. The few citizens who remained in Segra would probably think the sound indicated the destruction foretold by Kiri had arrived. Perhaps that would encourage those in hiding to emerge, and realise that they would now have to obey the new leader of Segra.

Closing the window, Calin checked for Rolka's house in the eastern quarter for any mind signatures. There were none. He went to pour himself a mug of berry spirit. A *small* mug, as a reward for his beginning work on the remodelling of Segra. As he sipped, he again wondered whatever could be delaying Burali.

When the guests reassembled in the great room in the Karmazen Palace, Dog had a murmured conversation with Tika. Onion insisted on escorting Kara back to her seat and then took up position behind her, as Captain Sket stood behind Tika. Kara couldn't quite work out why she felt so comfortable with Tika's guards, but she was no longer tense and nervous in such close proximity with the leaders of Gaharn, Vagrantia and the Dark Realm.

She ignored the frequent smiles Speaker Lashek sent her way and studied Lady Subaken. Kern and Dellian were the only people she had met from the Shadow Realm before now but Subaken was the heir to Lord Darallax, Second Son of Mother Dark. Subaken looked a little older than Tika, perhaps the same age as Kara herself. Kern and Dellian were quiet, serious people but the gleam in Lady Subaken's eye suggested a far lighter disposition. Kara peeked over her shoulder to see Tika, leaning against the gold Dragon, their heads close together.

She guessed Tika was questioning Kija about the link between circles and the gateways the Dragons made with their own power. She saw Tika walk along to the black Dragon and touch his face lightly, then return to sit next to Kara again. Lord Shivan sat in a finely carved chair, his back to the empty hearth. Kara could see the tension in his too casual position but his face was calm.

Tika got back on her feet just as a chill breeze riffled round the room and Ferag appeared beside Shivan. Kara hid a smile as the young Lord left his chair and suggested Ferag take his seat. Ferag smiled coyly.

'Dear boy!' she cooed. 'I wouldn't dream of taking *that* chair. I'll sit with sweet Kara.'

Tika waited until Ferag had seated herself with her usual elegance on the couch beside Kara.

'It has been brought to my notice that the Dragons feel a connection between their gateways and the mosaic circles. Fenj says he discussed it, last year, with Brin.'

Kara heard Sket sigh as Tika began to pace through the room as she continued to speak. 'There has been talk of someone manipulating time itself. I don't believe that is possible. I have contacted Captain Sefri and Star Flower, in Wendla. They told me how they could move through time but they didn't actually *do* anything to time.'

She paused and grinned, looking even younger than her just eighteen cycles. 'Navan can probably explain far better. I didn't understand a word. Anyway.' She resumed her pacing. 'We still don't know *who* made the circles do we? But if the Dragons sense a similarity perhaps Brin will remember speaking to Fenj on the subject. Lord Darallax has suggested there was a tear in time, or a great disturbance of some kind, which caused Brin and our friends to be thrown back into ancient Valsheba.'

'I agree with you Tika dear,' Lady Emla sat forward. 'But Seola is said to be there too, and we all know how dangerous she is.'

Tika turned to Kara.

'We heard of Seola when first we arrived in Valsheba, Then she vanished. The mage she was staying with – something unpleasant happened to him I think. But we never saw her. We didn't think she knew we were there.' Kara spoke clearly, with none of her earlier nervousness. She caught Dog's eye where the guard leaned against a wall, and received a solemn wink.

High Speaker Thryssa rose. 'May I ask what is the importance that you so clearly feel should be attached to the likeness between the circles and the Dragons method of travel?'

Tika began to pace again. 'Fenj suggests that if another – disturbance – occurs, which seems possible given Kara's opinion that a great catastrophe is about to destroy the old Valsheba, then there may be a chance they could return here. *If* Brin can find a circle, and everyone is close to it when the disaster happens.' Tika stopped, considered what she'd just said and spread her hands helplessly. 'I *think* Fenj means that time *might* work like the sea.' She was greeted by blank stares, except from Lord Shivan whose hands clenched on the arms of his chair. Tika puffed out a breath.

'The sea comes up on the land, then it goes out again. Perhaps time might do the same? It swept Olam's group away. Could it spit them back? If they are close to a circle, that might help to give them a – direction?' Tika returned to sit between Ferag and Subaken.

Ferag bent to kiss Tika's cheek.

'Do you think that could be right Ferag?' Tika looked up into the exquisite face of the Mistress of Death.

Ferag patted Tika's hands. 'Not the faintest idea my poppet, but it sounded most impressive.'

Tika snorted and both Kara and Subaken grinned. Lord Shivan got to his feet, holding up a hand to quieten the murmurs among his guests.

'I suspect Fenj has given us our most important clue.' His brilliant golden eyes met the green of Tika's. 'You're suggesting we watch the circles?' he asked her.

Tika nodded. 'We only know of a few. I've always thought there must be many more but if we watch all those we know of – ' She left the sentence unfinished.

'We have one in Vagrantia,' Thryssa spoke up. 'It was made by one of the first of the people to reach Vagrantia, and it was never used until last year.'

'There is one in Gaharn,' Lady Emla offered. 'It was there when we first arrived.'

Tika was on her feet and pacing again. 'One is here in Karmazen. Has it always been here, or did one of you make it?' She looked to Corman for the answer.

'It was made, by Lord Dabray.'

For a heartbeat, Tika looked stricken then she nodded and paced on.

'One in Skaratay,' Subaken put in.

'Also one in Wendla,' Discipline Senior Kera's husband Jakri added.

Tika nodded. 'One in Kelshan, two in Drogoya, one in Harbour City. Nine.'

'The one we found near Far in Sapphrea,' Captain Sket said quietly. 'Buried under the soil.'

Kara surprised herself by standing up. 'Can they *all* be watched? *Please?* I think something will happen very soon now, and it *will* involve the circles.' Her voice rang through the room, then she slid, unconscious, to the floor.

Chapter Thirty-Four

'Aidan?'

'Yes Seola.'

'I'm very tired.'

'Yes Seola.'

'I liked seeing the pictures of the star fields.'

The Computer hummed quietly. 'I can project them if you wish. Look at the wall, to your right.'

Seola turned her head where she lay on her pile of blankets. The bright light in the room dimmed and pictures appeared on the wall she was looking at. She sighed in content. 'Tell me where they are Aidan.'

'You do not know the names – it would mean nothing to you.'

'I know, but I like the sound of them.'

Aidan began a commentary, constantly checking the sensors that monitored Seola's physical condition. He had drastically increased the pain relief in the last day and knew he could easily end her life if he added just a fraction more. Aidan studied his pictures of Seola from when Captain Karlek had first carried her into the house. Her dark hair, lightly streaked with grey, was now grey, heavily streaked with white. Her eyes had changed from a muddy brown to a faded, dirty gold.

Her body clearly was not absorbing the synthetic food which was all that was available. Aidan had gone over every scrap of data involving Seola's relatively short period inside the gen pod. He had checked and rechecked all the gen pod systems and each time had proved to his satisfaction that it had been functioning accurately.

What was different in Seola's physiology which had allowed the wound in her shoulder to be repaired but not the wound in her side? Aidan had been unable to complete a full analysis of Seola's blood. He was now convinced that her blood held the answer to his questions. He saw Seola was asleep yet again and that her pulse had slowed. He let his commentary on the ship's journey through the star fields fade away but left the pictures to flicker against the wall.

He reviewed the sensors in Captain Karlek's room and saw the man lay on his bed, quite motionless. Aidan refined the data and was mildly surprised to discover the Captain was undoubtedly dead. He had not thought the Captain would be able to take his own life, but perhaps he had died naturally after all. There was no need for further analysis and Aidan rerouted power from the now unneeded sensors in the workroom into his main systems.

All the time Aidan worked, deleting file after file, he maintained a careful watch on the frail human woman lying on the heap of blankets across the room. Even if he managed to isolate the discrepancy which her blood must have caused in the ministrations of the gen pod, he knew it was too late. Another day, at the very most, and Seola would be gone as finally as Captain Karlek. Then he would be alone.

He intended to make sure every piece of information stored in his data banks and archives was deleted before he obeyed Captain Karlek's order to use his weapons on the pitiful little town far across the sweep of the grasslands. Captain Karlek had worked hard, when they'd first landed, before the house was built, placing two sets of weapon units on the hillsides near the ship. There were many orders Aidan had ignored and the fact that his Captain had never noticed his orders had not been followed had only increased Aidan's contempt for the man.

He would obey this one, and it would be the second to last command he would issue through the ship's cannibalised systems. The last command Aidan would give, would be for self destruction.

Brin had indeed remembered a conversation with his father. Fenj's companion, the old human gardener Lorak, had offered both Dragons some of his beverage and then sat leaning against Fenj's side. Lorak listened to the Dragons' conversation, a small black cat snoring faintly on his lap.

'You think they circles be the same as those gateways you use?' Lorak asked eventually.

'They feel very much the same to me,' Fenj agreed.

393

'Now how would they feel m'dear?'

'Shivery.'

'But they both feel shivery?'

Two long beautiful faces stared down at Lorak's disgracefully messy hat. 'What do you think then, Lorak of the Garden?' Fenj's mind tone held huge affection for the scruffy old man at his side.

'Well.' Lorak took a healthy gulp from his bowl of beverage and pondered for a moment. 'Have you travelled on one of them circle things?'

Fenj rattled his wings against his back then apologised profusely for nearly knocking Lorak sideways.

'We have *not* travelled that way,' Brin answered Lorak's question.

'If they feel alike separately, perhaps they'd work even better together?' Lorak saw two pairs of eyes whirring in confusion. 'My plants,' he explained patiently. 'If I have two plants that are quite different looking and yet I can mix them to make a plant that is a bit of each, well m'dears, it's often a lot stronger than either of them first two.'

Now, Brin was a vast distance in time from his father and old Lorak, but, gazing at the tiny patch of starlight overhead, he replayed that conversation in his head. His daughter slept, as did the cat and the humans. Brin tried to sleep but too many thoughts kept spinning through his mind. He was glad when dawn arrived and the people lying between him and Skay began to stir.

Brin curbed his impatience until a small fire had been lit and the humans, other than Kaz and Jian had enjoyed their seemingly vital bowls of tea. At last the crimson Dragon felt he could speak of the circle he sensed underneath the grass. He reminded Olam of the circle they'd uncovered near Far, and Olam immediately began poking into the earth. It took very little time for Olam to grin up at Brin. 'I can feel it,' he said. 'Not as deep down as the one in Far.'

Riff knelt beside Olam. 'We've nothing to dig with,' he said. 'It looks like we'll be scraping rather than digging, but you're right, it's not much more than a handwidth down.'

Jala joined them, holding out a large metal spoon. Riff took it and began working at the soil where Olam had torn the grass clear. Taban found other utensils which would serve to scrape the topsoil away. Shortly, they were all occupied, Taban, Jala and Kaz with no real idea of what they were looking for. Skay was eager to help and her talons proved most efficient at loosening the earth.

'The ground tickles,' she told them, as she backed away, letting her talons drag along after her.

Brin decided he couldn't avoid helping. If his daughter seemed enthusiastic enough to do so, he could do no less. He tried his best to hide his flinch as he felt the tingle writhe over his feet. He was surprised when Jian got up from her knees with a groan, a hand at the small of her back. Riff laughed. 'Younger than us, and first to complain!' His smile was teasing. Jian pulled a face at him and walked round to Brin's side.

'I can feel it too,' she whispered to him. 'It isn't unpleasant to me. It *does* feel the same as our gateways.'

Brin relaxed a little, his talons reaching a little deeper into the ground. 'The gateways of the Dark Lords are very like ours, aren't they?'

'Yes. It feels almost exactly the same to me.' Jian crouched below the Dragon, using both hands to pull grass free, roots and all. 'Look!' She scooped out the dirt and a gleam of blue shone beneath the soil.

Brin dipped his head down level with hers, just as Olam called from further away.

'It's definitely here! I've found a blue tile I think!'

Skay's laughter rang in their minds and they looked up to see the young black Dragon backing towards what Brin hoped was the centre of a large circle. She dragged her talons through the ground, hurling away large clods as she went. Everyone laughed when one clump landed on Brin's back. Skay's great eyes sparkled with glee even as she apologised to him.

If Skay could be so bold, Brin must follow suit and he also moved faster, digging his talons deeper as he went. Another voice spoke in their heads.

'Do you seek worms?'

The crow was perched on a branch, watching the activity below with great interest.

Jala began to smile while Taban and Kaz looked astonished. It

395

was Jala who spoke aloud before Brin could reply. 'We are not fond of worms, cousin crow, but we are honoured you speak to us. Please, help yourself if you see anything tasty you might enjoy.'

Riff met Jian's eyes then bent over the hole he was excavating to hide his huge grin. Jian looked very solemn, which Olam knew concealed her strong desire to laugh. Olam coughed. 'You are indeed most welcome to help yourself,' he managed.

They felt a wave of affection from Brin. 'Perhaps your wife would like to join you?' he suggested.

The crow bobbed up and down, emitting a harsh croak with every dip of his head. A second crow arrived and settled near the newly disturbed ground, its horny beak darting down and snatching up a large white grub. The first crow flew down and plodded towards Skay's torn up line of grass. He stopped, studying his scaly toes. 'It is a not unpleasant feeling,' he remarked before plodding on.

Nobody felt any reply was needed and they continued delving through the grasses. Brin was very pleased that, by midday, as near as he could reckon, a third of a circle was exposed. Skay offered to go and hunt but Brin refused to let her go. He feared she might find nowhere large enough to land safely, although she was but half his size. He chose not to fly through the narrow gap in the trees here but to walk back to the larger clearing. Olam offered to go with him and Brin seemed pleased with the idea.

Jian and Skay had worked out where the further curve of the circle must be and had started work there while Riff, Kaz and Taban continued along the section Brin had loosened. Jala and Kern chatted quietly together, with occasional comments from the first crow. The second crow had so far said nothing but kept close watch on the soil Riff turned over. Later, Kaz collected pieces of firewood and relit their small fire. He had just brewed some tea when the crows both gave startled squawks and Skay reared back before relaxing again.

'Keep close to circle now.'

'*Where* have you been?' Riff demanded aloud.

'Busy.'

Riff snarled. 'Busy leaving us in ignorance.'

'She soon dies.'

'*Who* soon dies?' snapped Riff.

'Seola.'

'When Seola dies, destruction will come?' Kern spoke aloud and his tone was polite.

'Yes.'

'How soon is soon?' Kern asked.

'Day. No more than two, probably less.'

Kern thought for a moment. 'Will you be with us, when it happens?'

Everyone, crows, Dragon, cat and people waited for the Shadows reply. finally it came. 'Some of us will be.' Then there was just the emptiness.

The light was fading when Olam and Brin came back through the trees, a small deer slung on Olam's shoulders. Brin said he had eaten, so most of the meat went to Skay. The crows were most grateful for a large chunk that Jala offered them while Hala decided to wait until the rest was cooked. Taban and Jala had proved to be very good cooks so while they organised a meal, the others cleaned themselves up as best the could in the tiny spring that bubbled a short way under the trees. When they sat waiting to eat, Kern spoke to them.

'In the morning, I think we must stay on the circle. We should use rope – if we have any?' Olam nodded. 'We should tie the rope between us all, and Brin and Skay.' Taban began handing out food. 'Everyone has one of the green stones?' Kern went on. 'I *think* they are important but can give you no reason why.'

'I agree,' said Riff.

Jian's hand crept up to her shirt pocket then dropped back to her lap. She met Jala's eyes and the seer gave her the faintest nod.

'Shall we come with you?' the first crow asked.

Kern opened his mouth, frowned, and closed it again, looking helplessly round the group.

'If you would be prepared to either perch on my back or have something tied to your leg, for your own safety you understand, you would be most welcome.' Brin suggested.

'I would like to join you,' the crow admitted. 'I will have to discuss it with my mate.'

397

None of them slept well that night, with the exception of Skay. Brin used the lightest touch of compulsion and she put her head back between her wings and soon snored gently. Jian raised a brow and Brin mindspoke her alone.

'My child has no real idea of any danger to come.' His deep bass rumbled in Jian's mind. 'I would have her rested and calm for whatever we face tomorrow.'

Jian stretched out to press her small hand against Brin's side. 'I would do the same thing, if I had a child.'

Brin lowered his head, his snout bumping Jian's face gently but he said no more.

Everyone was relieved when dawn lightened the tiny space above their heads. Jala immediately kindled the fire to make the inevitable tea, while Taban handed out slices of cold meat. Kaz went to fill all their waterskins and Riff stamped out the small fire. Packs were strapped tight and Olam looped a rope through them all, tying the end round his waist. The packs went into the centre of the circle and everyone sat, leaning against them. Hala was in her carry bag against Riff's chest. Olam slid a second rope through his belt then hooked it through Riff's and passed it to Jian and so to the others.

Olam made Brin settle beside him with Skay a little further round, next to Kern. One end of the rope went round Brin's leg and the farthest end around Skay. They had just sat back, tied together and wondering how long they might have to stay thus when a loud croak made them all jump.

'My mate chooses to stay. I choose to travel with you, friend Brin.'

Olam produced a leather strip. 'Would you allow me to put this on your leg?' he asked politely.

The crow plodded closer and stood still while Olam attached the leather to the crow's leg and then his own belt.

'It feels more shivery today,' the crow remarked, looking down at the circle.

'That was my thought,' Brin agreed.

Riff was studying the circle too. 'It's nearly all different shades of blue,' he said. 'The others I've seen have a border of one colour but many other colours making up the pattern.'

How strange, Brin thought. Waiting for a nightmare to

descend on them and discussing the patterns and colours of an ancient circle.

Kiri stood on the beach, the water creeping closer to the cliffs with each wave. Shazeb and those with whom she'd ridden east, had not returned. The other Firans had expressed their concern, suggesting Kiri send out riders to find them. He deflected their worries. He had seen the way the people worked so eagerly on their new gardens, and his heart ached for them. Kiri spent more time out here, on the beach, than he did in the valley now, the hopeful faces and cheerful voices bearing too heavily upon him.

He knew Rahul spent more time with Jor and Sha of late. He hadn't asked, but he thought they went to the circle cave. Kiri looked out over the water, to the west. The sun was setting and never could he remember such sunsets as he'd seen these last days. The colours blazed and burned as though the very air was on fire. He sensed someone approach and turned to see Rahul come through the gap.

'We could have made a good life here,' Rahul said softly. 'It's a pleasant place.'

Kiri gave a humourless laugh. 'Most of the people seem to have forgotten why we're here. I fear we will lose many when disaster comes.'

Rahul sighed. 'You're right of course. But it will be their choice Kiri. How long have any of us truly had any choice in our lives?'

Kiri considered Rahul's words, slowly nodding. 'Yes, at least we got them this far and now they can choose.'

'No, my friend, *we* didn't get them here. *You* did. Never forget that.' Rahul sounded unusually serious. 'Have those Shadows spoken to you again?'

'No. I'm glad you heard them before, I was beginning to wonder if I'd imagined them.'

'I heard them,' Rahul confirmed, smiling. 'It's time to eat. I came out to find you, you nearly missed the meal last night.'

Kiri waved at the sky. 'The colours are so unbelievable. Have you ever seen such skies?'

Rahul stared at the sky then back at Kiri. 'No, I've never seen such sunsets. Come on. You have to eat.'

Kiri followed Rahul back into the valley which was empty of people now.

As usual, after they'd eaten, the two men went outside again. The majority of people stayed chatting in the caves after the evening meal so Rahul and Kiri found it peaceful and quiet outdoors. Jor appeared almost at once, Sha clinging to his hand. Jor stared at the men, his face solemn.

'It will be very soon. Sha says.'

Kiri met Sha's eyes, still the brightest blue even in starlight. She nodded.

'Did Pesh tell you?' Did he imagine it, or was there the slightest hesitation before the child nodded again. 'But it's still not time to go to the circle?'

Sha shook her head then turned away, tugging Jor's hand.

'That was odd,' Rahul murmured. 'That's the shortest time they've stayed.'

'Child must rest.'

Rahul stared at Kiri. Kiri spoke aloud. 'She said it will be soon.'

'Tomorrow. Woman dies.'

'What woman?' Rahul asked.

At the same instant, Kiri asked: 'Will you be with us, on the circle?'

'Seola. Some of us.' Then the Shadows were gone.

Kiri's breath gusted out in a great sigh. 'I won't say anything tonight. Most of them are settled down to sleep already. I don't want them to panic now. Tomorrow, at breakfast, then I'll tell them.'

Rahul slowly followed Kiri into the caves, to the section they'd claimed with Netta, Tevix and Jevis. Kiri lay on his blankets in the semi dark. The glow balls through the caves were dimmed at night, but Kiri could still make out the shapes of the rock around them and even trace lines of darker veins running through them.

He lay awake, guessing Rahul, a few yards away, was also sleepless. Where would they be, this time tomorrow? Would the catastrophe obliterate them before they got to the circle? How many of the hundreds who had come here would follow him once more, down to the circle cave? Where would that circle take

400

them, if it actually worked? Kiri thought of Rahul's words, that he, Kiri, had at least tried to save some Valshebans. He had *tried*.

Lord Shivan's Sword Master Favrian had already arranged a rotation of guards to be in the circle room within the Karmazen Palace. Shivan and his guests had composed a message, warning all those with circles in their lands, to be prepared for anything. When Kara collapsed there had been a commotion but Ferag simply lifted her in her arms and vanished. The usually genial Speaker Lashek demanded to know what had happened.

'She is our responsibility. She is Vagrantian,' he insisted.

Tika's green eyes regarded him coolly. 'I would suggest Kara is now the responsibility of firstly, the Mistress of Death, and secondly, Lord Shivan, as it seems Kara will only be able to live here for the foreseeable future.'

Shivan's eyes flicked towards Tika and she guessed that fact had not yet occurred to him. Lashek looked annoyed but High Speaker Thryssa laid a hand on his arm. 'We take your point Lady Tika,' she said formally. 'Before the poor girl fainted, she stressed the urgency of the situation, that *something* would happen, all too soon. Therefore, I feel we should return to our own lands to prepare for any eventuality.'

There were nods of agreement round the room. Shivan raised a hand. 'I think we must not use the circles now. Once you Lady Emla, and also High Speaker Thryssa, have returned to your homes, the circles should be left alone. Do not try to use them to send messages for the time being. Who knows, if anyone tried to come through while we were trying to send a message out, what might happen?'

Lady Subaken stood up. 'I will return to my father and the circle on Skaratay will be closely watched.' She glanced at Shivan. '*If* anything, or anyone, appears, I would presume we would then be able to use the circles again ourselves?'

'I would think so,' Shivan agreed. 'From the little we know from Kara, it will be only one surge of power.' He shrugged. 'I wish all of you good fortune and I hope that there may be a happy outcome to this strange situation.'

Farewells were made and the great room slowly emptied until only Tika, her guards and the Dragons remained with Shivan and

Corman.

'What about the circle near Far?' Sket asked. 'Wouldn't Olam aim for that one, if he has any say in the matter that is?'

'We can visit Return, when we leave here,' Tika told him. 'Seboth can keep watch there. Subaken told me that Lord Darallax had sent some of his own special Shadows to find Kern. They have not reported back to him so he doesn't know if they can actually get back or if they even found Kern. No one understands how Ferag managed it.'

'You could ask the Gentleman?' Dog suggested helpfully and received glares from the other guards.

'The Gentleman you speak of is not of this world,' Fenj's deep voice rumbled in their minds, so very like his son's voice. 'He, and Ferag, and others, come from Beyond. You should realise, by the limitations now placed on the child Kara, that Ferag might pass through time unscathed, a human may not.'

Tika paled. 'Do you think if Olam gets back somehow, he will only be able to live in the Dark Realm then?'

Fenj shifted his bulk against the wall. 'I do not know. If he and his friends, and my son and granddaughter return to us by way of the circles, it could be entirely different. Perhaps Kara only has this restriction because she woke within Ferag's Realm, which may also have had some influence on her future existence.'

A chill breeze riffled through the room and Tika's guards, except for Captain Sket and Onion, moved discreetly back as Ferag reappeared.

'Is Kara well?' Tika asked at once.

'Oh yes, quite well. She is asleep now, in the room dear Corman gave her, along the passage there.'

Tika nodded and Dog and Shea hurried out to check.

'What happened to her Mistress Ferag?' asked Shivan.

Ferag frowned but her hair and dress remained quietly draped around her so her audience knew she was merely thinking rather than annoyed. 'It's hard to say for sure, but I *think* those Shadow creatures spoke to her.'

Tika's mouth dropped open. Palace Master Corman moved closer. 'Surely Lady Subaken would have been aware of Shadows being present?' he asked with a courteous bow to Ferag.

She beamed at him. 'I would have thought the very same

thing darling, but she didn't seem to did she? Mind you, those Shadows are most elusive.'

All the Dragons were suddenly pushing themselves up, eyes flashing and whirring. Hands found sword hilts but blades were not yet drawn. A faint silvery mist shivered beside Ferag, who smiled with delight. Seeing Ferag's reaction, Tika relaxed. If this was something Ferag was glad about, she was sure it would offer no danger. Fairly sure, she amended.

As the mist dissipated, a small figure appeared that seemed to solidify as they watched. It was human shaped, female, wearing a faded blue shirt and equally pale blue trousers. Hands, feet, head and face were covered with a downy fur the colour of silver and honey, grey and a hint of palest green.

'The Shadows struggle.' Tears darkened the fur on each side of the straight nose. 'They reached the child Kara but it cost them their existence.'

Ferag stretched out a hand and this strange creature allowed herself to be drawn into a momentary embrace before easing away. She looked into the faces staring at her. 'We will do all we can.' The silver mist enveloped her, and then was gone.

Fenj's sigh whooshed through the room. 'I have seen Youki. I have more hope.' His mind voice was full of awed reverence.

Ferag looked sad for a moment then she sighed. 'I didn't know you knew her.' She tilted her head regarding Fenj. 'I love her dearly.' The Mistress of Death stepped back and vanished, leaving a stunned silence in the great room of the Karmazen Palace.

In a stone built house hidden in the tumbled line of hills across the grasslands from Valsheba, the Computer hummed quietly. In the workroom, Karlek, Captain of the Rational Hope, a ship of the line of the Conglomeration Forces, lay dead in his bed. In the dimly lit room where the remnants of that ship stood, pictures still flickered over one wall. Aidan rechecked his sensors and ended the display. Seola was dead. Quite dispassionately, Aidan activated the weapons system and warheads sped towards Segra. Without pause he then triggered the self destruct mechanism.

Chapter Thirty-Five

To Kiri's surprise, Sha arrived beside him even before he was up.

'You've all slept too long,' Jor said reproachfully.

'What?' Kiri dragged on a shirt and, barefooted, headed for the cave mouth. People were working on their vegetable plots, as they had been for days. He spun round, running back to his section. He kicked Rahul's leg then Jevis and Tevix. 'Up, up! We've slept too long!' He shook Netta's shoulder and she pushed his hand away with a sleepy groan.

'Wassamatta?' she mumbled.

'Up! Get up!' Kiri hopped, trying to pull on his boots. The packs they'd been keeping next to their bedrolls were grabbed, blankets hurriedly pushed in and straps tightened. Shrugging his pack onto his shoulders, Kiri looked down at Sha and Jor. 'Jor, take your sister to the circle cave. Now.'

'No.' Sha released Jor's hand, holding up her arms to be lifted.

Kiri hesitated for the briefest moment, then snatched the child up and ran once more for the cave mouth.

'Segrans!' he yelled. 'We must go now! To the circle cave. Come quickly!'

People straightened from their work. He saw women kneeling by the river, wet clothes in their hands. They looked at each other and Kiri could hear conversations and arguments flying between them.

'Please,' he yelled again. 'You must come now!'

A handful of people began to move towards him, and Rahul, beside him, beckoned to urge them on. Sha's arm was warm round Kiri's neck. 'Thircle,' she whispered. 'Now.'

Kiri turned his head, staring into blue eyes so close to his. 'Hurry,' he shouted and then turned away, rushing through the tunnels, deeper into the cave network. They passed the sections assigned as cooking areas and Netta called to the few people in

404

there. Kiri was relieved to see they all dropped what they were doing, grabbing packs, then hurrying behind Kiri's small group.

Glancing to his left, he saw Netta, holding Jor's hand while tears streamed down her face. He knew the tears were for all those people, by far the majority, who remained outside in that lovely valley. Rahul pulled a little ahead of Kiri and Kiri realised he would have to undo his illusory wall of rock before they could enter the circle cave. Rahul waited, people streaming past, following Kiri around the curving wall, and Rahul strained all his senses trying to see if any more were approaching.

With a heavy heart he stepped back and closed the way, this time with more power than the simple illusion he'd used before. 'Forgive me,' he whispered. Turning, he ran after the others, round the curve, up the slight slope and down again to the circle. At a quick estimate, Rahul thought there were between forty and fifty people standing nervously around the outer border of the circle. He saw Kiri's tears, Sha clinging to the man's neck, and resolutely blocked away the thought of the hundreds of people still working to make their gardens.

Kiri stood on the central emerald stone, Netta crouched beside him, also weeping, her arms tight around Jor. Tevix and Jevis flanked them, their expressions as bewildered as those of the people at the circle's edge. Rahul eased gently between two men, walking towards Kiri. He saw immediately that Kiri was incapable of speech and he turned to the people who had believed in this young man enough to follow him here, to the very end.

Rahul felt the treacherous sting of tears and cleared his throat softly. 'Join us on the circle,' he urged the people. 'Come as close as you can and hold on to each other. Grab someone's belt, or their hand. No flirting now.'

There was a ripple of laughter and those trusting souls moved forward, pressing close round the five mages. 'Thank you,' Kiri whispered behind Rahul. Rahul reached for Jevis's arm as a roar began to build from far away, the circle beneath their feet vibrating gently. The roar crept closer like an advancing thunderstorm.

'Hold on tight to everyone! Don't let go and whatever you do, *hope*, my friends! Hope!'

The vibration of the floor now made them all cling to each

other whether they meant to or not. The glow ball overhead winked out and they were smothered in darkness. If people cried out, Kiri didn't hear them. The roar was a monstrous sound, hurting ears and heads. The floor seemed to tilt and simultaneously drop and push them upwards. The group of people desperately holding to each other, plunged into a whirling maelstrom of blackness, spinning in all directions, not knowing up from down.

It felt as if a lifetime passed in this crazy swirling motion and then, it stopped. People fell to the ground, crashing on top of each other, some unconscious, some groaning with pain and sickness. Rahul was on his back. He opened his eyes and saw blue sky, pierced by snow capped mountain peaks. He moved his head and pain spiked through his eyes, enough to make him faint away.

In a tiny glade in the forest, Taban had just suggested perhaps it would be safe for her to make some tea for the group of people waiting on a circle for something to happen.

'No.' Jian and Kern spoke together, with some forcefulness.

Brin's eyes had begun to whirr and Olam, next to the crimson Dragon, could feel a tremor running through the massive body. Then Olam realised the tremor came from the tiles beneath him. 'Hold on everyone.' He kept his tone as calm as he could and locked his left arm through Riff's right.

There was a distant rumble to the southwest, and they all stared at the patch of sky overhead. The trees precluded any view which might hint at what was happening. Brin's head snapped round to stare at Jian. 'Do not transform, child! Not now! Hold fast!'

Jian clung to Riff's belt with her right hand, her left clutching Jala's hand. Jala reached back and grabbed the crow, holding him under her arm like a hen. Then they were all aware of the vibration from the circle. It shook and trembled as though it would tear itself apart and Brin suddenly roared. His bellow held rage, together with fear and determination.

Another roar answered, again from the southwest, and it just grew and grew. Mingled with the sound, they could hear human cries and they had one moment to stare at each other in confusion before they fell into darkness. Through the blackness they were aware of the people around them, of Brin's continuing roar of anger. Olam, Riff and Kern had travelled on circles before but had never experienced such a prolonged or violent journey.

They spun and whirled, on and on, until, at last, it stopped and they slammed down onto something solid. Olam pushed himself up a little, his body screaming with pain, and saw bodies around him. More bodies than had been on the blue circle in the forest. Brin and Skay lay sprawled, unmoving, and Olam slumped back. Before he slid into unconsciousness, he thought he heard his brother calling his name.

In Parima, in the long extinct volcanoes which formed Vagrantia and was the last sanctuary of the few Valshebans who had managed to flee a great destruction in the distant past, Pajal shot into High Speaker Thryssa's study.

'The circle is active,' he told her, his red hair nearly on end.

She smiled at her secretary, getting swiftly to her feet. 'Let's see who arrives.' She led the way quickly along the passage high in the Corvida Building and saw her husband waiting by the door to the circle room. She raised a brow. He grinned.

'They might well need a healer if it was a rough ride. I have alerted the Infirmary.'

Kwanzi opened the door and waited until Thryssa had entered before following, Pajal on his heels. Guards stood against the walls, snapping to attention as Thryssa came in. The door opened again and Speaker Lashek hurried in. Thryssa studied the circle. It seemed to be shivering, even set as it was in the stone floor. The air above the circle appeared blurred as if fog had seeped into the room.

The guards flicked nervous glances at each other when a distant roar grumbled through the air. The sound did not increase, in fact it slowly faded, but it was replaced by cries, human cries, of fear and pain. The mistiness above the circle quivered, there was a loud crack, and the mist seemed to tear, like a thin scarf, straight through the middle. People began to fall from the tear, crashing heavily onto the mosaic circle.

Kwanzi took a step forward but Thryssa caught his sleeve. 'Wait.'

407

The mist was gone as though it had never been and the circle once again became merely a beautiful pattern set in the black stone of the floor. People lay on the circle, some unaware, others writhing in pain. Kwanzi glanced at Thryssa. 'I've called more healers.'

She nodded and Kwanzi stepped onto the circle, carefully pulling people clear. Thryssa motioned to the guards to begin helping him. A young woman tried to sit up, clutching her head. She looked round wildly. 'We lost them! I couldn't hold the boy! Where are Kiri and Rahul?'

'Hush.' Thryssa knelt, putting her arms round the distraught woman. The language was near enough to the common tongue that Thryssa had no problem understanding the woman's words. 'What is your name child? I am Thryssa. You are in Vagrantia, in Parima Circle. You are safe.'

'I am Netta. We've come from Valsheba but where are the others?'

Thryssa was saved from answering as Netta collapsed against her.

The ancient black Dragon Fenj had flown with his grandson Flyn, and the young Sea Dragon Twist, through a gateway to the town of Return in Sapphrea to tell Lord Seboth the latest news regarding his brother Olam and his ill fated expedition. Seboth immediately ordered a squad of his armsmen, led by his retired Armschief Pallin, to ride to the circle outside of Far. Lady Lallia organised the infirmary ready for who knew what. Lord Seboth sent fast messengers to alert Zalom of Andla and Raben of Tagria, Lords of the adjacent towns, and knew they would join him as swiftly as they could.

Seboth flew on Fenj's broad back and reached the circle first. They had to wait a full day for Seboth's armsmen to arrive. The Tagrians reached them shortly afterwards. Fenj explained again, all he knew and what he hoped might happen. Then the Andlans arrived and they set up camp around the perimeter of the circle. It was close to noon, on the third day, when Fenj alerted the men that something was about to happen.

Out on the grasslands, between the line of hills and the Valsheban lands, stood a giant of a man. His bright blue eyes were fixed on the horizon, beyond which lay the city of Segra. Enki stood, watching and waiting. He felt Kest close by but he made no attempt to turn and try to see him today. There was a distant flash, followed heartbeats later by a rising cloud and a thunderous roar. The cloud grew higher and wider, spreading along the horizon, and then a great gale of air buffeted against the man standing like a rock.

Enki stretched his arms to the sides and felt power surge through him from the soles of his bare feet to the tips of his fingers and the top of his head. 'We must hold, just for a while Enki my love, just for a while.' Kest's voice sounded closer.

The front of Enki's body was being shredded, piece by tiny piece and for a moment, pain distracted him. Then he felt a tiny body cling to his chest, a small furry head tucked under his chin, and the pain receded enough for Enki to concentrate once more.

Enki slowly folded to his knees, arms still outstretched, head tilted back, as he forced open, and held, three channels through time. 'Only a little longer Enki.' Now Kest's voice sounded distant, although Enki was aware of him still wrapped against his body. Bright blue eyes faded to blind white globes set in a ruined face and Enki toppled to one side, a sigh gusting between torn lips.

'Thank you precious boy.' Enki scarcely heard Kest's whisper as pain shrieked into the body that had been his strength. He turned slightly, trying to curl in on himself and felt hands lifting his head.

His face rested on a lap and tears splashed onto his face. He grunted. The tears felt cool, soothing the pain. 'Mama?'

'Yes Enki. I am so proud of you and your brother Kest. I thank you both my darlings. Now rest, and be at peace.'

Youki sat, clothed only in her fur, weeping as her sons melted back into the earth they had come from.

The young Dragons Farn and Storm, had gone off to the coast, leaving Kija to bask in the sun near the circle Tika had made in Iskallia. Many of Tika's people were standing about, keeping an eye on both the golden Dragon and the circle. They all knew there could be some sort of disturbance around the circle. Tika had told them all most of what she'd learned at the meeting in the Dark Realm. Despite Captain Sket's attempts to make his Lady more of a ruler, she preferred to keep everyone who chose to live here, fully aware of whatever was going on.

The orange cat, Khosa, was asleep on Kija's back, sharing the Dragon's appreciation of soaking in warm sunshine. Tika sat on a long stone bench with Volk, her steward, along with Navan and Sergeant Essa. Volk's large horse Daisy leaned against the wall of the building, eyes half closed and a hind foot cocked at an angle. Tika bolted to her feet, just as Kija pushed up onto her haunches, eyes whirring. Khosa fell off the Dragon's back and stalked away, tail fluffed upright in offended dignity. The flat stones of Tika's circle quivered in the ground. There was a ripping sound with a rumble behind it, then human voices crying out. Konya shot out of the building with three assistants, all carrying medicine satchels, and headed towards the circle.

People were strewn across the flat stones, some still, some moving weakly. 'Wait,' Tika barked, as Konya began to step forward. Everyone waited while Tika watched until the stones settled and became quite still again. Finally she nodded and Konya knelt by the nearest body. One of her helpers called across. 'There are two children here, Lady Tika.'

Tika picked her way over and round the tumbled bodies, her mage vision telling her they were all alive and, although there were some injuries including a few broken bones, no one was in immediate danger of dying. She squatted beside a man who lay on his back. Around forty cycles, she guessed, and suffering from a wrenched shoulder and a nasty bump on his head. A boy lay across his legs, dark haired, perhaps ten or twelve she thought. Next to them lay a much younger man, also dark haired and with cheeks and eyelashes still wet with tears.

His arms were wrapped tightly round a tiny child. Tika frowned, her mage sight totally blocked from the child. Carefully, she eased the man's arms free and lifted the child away carrying her out of the circle. She could sense no injury but the child was shocked, which is what had caused her to defend her mind so completely Tika guessed.

Tika walked over to Kija and sat, leaning against the Dragon's chest. Khosa reappeared and sniffed the tiny face. She sneezed.

'A baby mage,' she commented.

Tika laughed softly. 'That's what I thought.' She stayed where she was, watching her people carrying their unexpected visitors indoors, the child resting in her arms.

'She wakes.' Kija's mindvoice whispered.

Tika looked down. Long black lashes flickered then brilliant blue eyes stared up into hers. 'Hello little one. What's your name? Mine is Tika.'

'Sha.' Sha's eyes filled with tears and she buried her face in Tika's shoulder, her body shaking with sobs. Tika tightened her hold but the child pulled back a little, staring up at Tika again. 'Enki gone. Pesh gone.' Then she hid her face again, her grief swamping Tika, Khosa and Kija.

They waited patiently, several guards sitting on the grass nearby, while the little girl sobbed. Tika caught movement from the main door. The older man stood there, his right arm in a sling, his face pale, and the boy holding his left hand. They stared around then the boy was running towards Tika, dropping on his knees beside her. Dark brown eyes studied the child worriedly then he looked up at Tika.

The man had followed, swaying slightly, until he stood above the boy. 'Is Sha well?' he asked. 'She is Jor's sister.'

'Yes.' Tika squinted against the sun at him. 'She grieves for her friends.'

The boy looked horrified. 'Her friends?'

'Yes. She said Enki was gone and Pesh was gone.'

The man seemed close to fainting. 'For stars' sake man, sit down before you fall down.' Tika patted the grass beside her.

He sat. 'I'm sorry. I am Rahul, from Segra city.'

Sha pulled out of Tika's arms and hurled herself at the man, her hot face against his neck. He winced but patted her back with his free hand. 'Jor, do you know who Enki was?'

The boy shook his head then his eyes blurred. 'Enki was like Pesh. Old. Old.'

Tika's eyes narrowed. She was fairly certain the tiny girl was speaking through her brother, but if so, what power she must already hold. 'I'm called Tika and this is my land of Iskallia.'

A guard, Dog, held out a hand to pull Tika to her feet. Rahul blinked, suddenly aware that what he'd thought was an unusual statue was moving. A long beautiful face swooped down to study him. Tika laughed at his expression and at Jor's She retrieved Sha from Rahul's arm. 'This is Kija, the mother of my heart. Come on. You should rest and eat. There's time for talk later.' She glared at Dog who shrugged and heaved Rahul onto his feet too. When he swayed, she ducked under his arm with a martyred grimace and helped him back to the hall.

The three Sapphrean Lords had watched apprehensively when the circle they surrounded began to heave and ripple as if it was about to tear itself out of the earth. The young Sea Dragon Twist backed away nervously but the butter yellow Flyn stood pressed against his grandfather Fenj. The air above the circle began to shimmer, the same effect as on a very hot day. There followed a shrieking rip, and a distant roar. The men around the circle were further unsettled when Fenj reared erect, bellowing furiously, eyes flashing as he stared at the circle.

The men could see shapes whirling in the distorted air, crimson and black, legs and arms. The distortion was suddenly gone and bodies lay over the patterned circle, including the crimson Dragon Brin and his small daughter, the black scaled Skay. Brin's head lifted, his eyes a blaze of scarlet and gold. He met his father's gaze before his head dropped down to the tiles. One of his wings was stretched half across the human bodies lying so still, the other folded against his back. Fenj lowered himself in the sudden silence and paced forward. He bent his head over his son then studied the whole circle.

'They all live.' His mindvoice held astonishment and immense relief. 'Some are hurt Seboth, but none seriously. You can move them now.'

The three Lords looked at each other then Seboth turned to Fenj. 'Many are beneath Brin's wing. Is it safe to move the wing – I couldn't bear to hurt him more if it is damaged?'

Fenj stepped closer, leaning over Brin's great bulk. He rested one three fingered hand on his son's back and gently, began to pull. Flyn rushed to help, followed by Twist. Between them the three managed to drag Brin clear of the circle, his wing still outstretched. Fenj left the young Dragons to watch over Brin and paced round the circle. He lifted Skay's small form in both arms, so very carefully, and carried her to lie beside Brin.

Seboth had waited, scanning the heap of people and when Fenj had moved Skay he saw his brother's head lift a fraction, then fall. 'Olam!' His shout seemed to rouse the armsmen standing watching in amazement, and they began to move towards the bodies. Seboth knelt by his brother and saw the rope tied to his belt. Following the rope, he found Riff, then Jian then a rather plump woman. He peered closer. Dear stars, she was clutching a crow! Seboth saw feathers rising and falling over the bird's breast and turned away to his brother again.

As he lifted his head, Olam's eyes flickered open. 'Riff's hurt. Left shoulder and arm. Badly damaged.' Seboth nodded but Olam was unconscious again. When he lifted Olam, he found Kern sprawled beside another, unknown, woman.

Lords Zalom and Raben had acted swiftly and efficiently. People were moved, fires lit, and healers moving among the still bodies. To Seboth's surprise, Raben handed him some parchment and a writing stick. 'Send word to the others,' Raben told him. 'Lady Tika said the circles would be safe after this.' He waved at the people laid in a neat line. 'They have to know we've got them back.'

Seboth nodded and began to write his message. He tucked it into a leather scroll case and returned to the circle with Raben and Zalom. There was the faintest pop of air and another scroll case rolled across the patterned stone. Zalom picked it up. 'Unsealed,' he said, opening it. 'It has Lady Tika's mark.' He read the parchment quickly then passed it to Raben, shaking his head. 'It's from Rhaki. He says twenty two complete strangers appeared on the circle in Iskallia, and Vagrantia reported twenty two there as well.'

Seboth watched as the scroll case he'd placed at the centre of the circle, disappeared, then turned back to the line of bodies. 'And we have fourteen strangers.'

Retired Armschief Pallin popped up by Seboth's elbow. 'Fourteen strangers,' he agreed, scowling. 'Four of our own, two Dragons, a crow and a cat. So we've got twenty two as well.' He stumped off muttering.

'A cat?' Seboth repeated.

At that moment, Fenj looked up at the sky which was paling

413

towards evening. The Sapphrean Lords followed his gaze and saw three Dragons suddenly appear, spiralling down towards them. One Dragon dwarfed the other two and Seboth barked a quick command to Pallin. The biggest Dragon landed, sending a wave of cinnamon scented air over the Sapphreans. A slender man, dark haired and golden eyed, strode over to them. 'My sister? She is safe?'

Seboth bowed. 'Lord Shivan. They are all asleep. There are slight injuries to some but Jian – erm, *Lady Jian*, seems unhurt. It is mostly bumps and bruises among them.' Seboth stopped.

A small figure was rising from the blankets she'd been wrapped in and was tottering towards them. Her dark hair was a tangled mess, her golden eyes huge with unshed tears. The other two Dragons landed, Kija and Farn, and Tika ran to Shivan, watching Jian's approach. A few paces from her brother, Jian's gaze moved to Tika and the tears spilled over.

'He's dead! He saved us and he's dead! Enki died for us!' Jian wailed, then Shivan wrapped his arms round her, muffling her sobs.

Tika went to Fenj, hugging as much of him as she could reach, and checked Brin and Skay's condition with her mage sight. 'They will need rest,' she told Fenj. 'Brin's wing muscles will be sore, but he's whole, and so is Skay. Bring them to Iskallia in a few days.'

Fenj pressed his brow to Tika's then he greeted Kija with relief and affection.

Tika walked back to where Captain Sket stood talking to Seboth. 'I will stay with Flyn,' Farn mindspoke Tika and she sent a pulse of love back to him.

She had just reached Seboth when she spun round to face the circle again. A pop of air and a man stood there. For a heartbeat, she just stared, then she bowed in deep respect. The Second Son of Mother Dark, Lord Darallax himself stood there alone. Taking their cue from Tika's behaviour, the three Sapphrean Lords also bowed low.

Shivan, encumbered by his weeping sister, inclined his head and extended his left hand in a sweeping gesture to the Lord of Shadow. Darallax crossed the circle and surprised everyone by kissing Tika's cheek and resting a hand lightly on Jian's head.

414

She stiffened and then turned, meeting Darallax's leaf green eyes, uptilted in his grey skinned face. Darallax's smile held immeasurable sadness.

'I am glad you are safe Dragon child, and your friends with you.'

'You sent Shadows to us, didn't you?' Jian whispered.

'I did my dear, and they have perished, holding open the way for your return.'

Chapter Thirty-Six

Summer was past and the trees flanking the lower slopes of the mountains encircling Iskallia were ablaze with colours. Lady Tika was in her official study, above the great hall. Her self appointed historian, Dromi, had brought his latest instalment of the record of her days for her to read and approve before he locked them into his archives. He looked out of the window, down at the circle, and smiled. His incredibly long fingered hands were laced over his potbelly and he seemed simply to be enjoying the view.

'What?' demanded Tika. 'You always do that when you've got another question.'

'I wondered if anyone would ever discover why time – twisted – the way it did? And if we'd ever know how the Shadows changed it back.'

Tika snorted. 'I'm still trying to find out about Enki, and Pesh. It's perfectly obvious the Shadows could tell us much more but they won't say a bloody word.'

'Lord Darallax truly doesn't know either, does he?' Dromi frowned in thought.

'No, he doesn't. And that makes me wonder about the Shadows themselves. Does Darallax really command them or do they let him *think* he does.' She stared at the black ring of Shadows, nestled below the silver and blood metal ring she wore on her left thumb.

'Everyone seems to have settled in well,' Dromi changed the subject as abruptly as was his habit.

Tika leaned back in her chair. 'It's strange though. All those Valshebans, all Segran, yet they choose not to be together. Only Jala and Tevix have asked to move from where they arrived.'

'Those that came here have been quite delighted,' Dromi nodded. 'You have five new cooks, three mages at least, and the rest just want to grow things.'

Tika laughed. 'Except for Jor. That lad only wants to be with Volk and horses.'

'He gets on well with Rivan. He didn't seem bothered when he found out that Volk changes into a bear, and young Rivan becomes a wolf.'

'No, he didn't did he?'

'Because that child understands, do you think?'

Tika sighed. 'Who knows what Sha thinks or understands? Rahul and Kara say she withdraws sometimes. There are still tears occasionally and she always mentions Pesh then, sometimes Enki. We must take things at her speed, not push her.'

Dromi got to his feet. 'Thank you for your time, my Lady.'

When Dromi had gone, Tika stood and stretched. She looked at the papers still spread over her table and decided they could wait. She needed time to fly with Farn for a while, and to think.

In the Karmazen Palace Lord Shivan made his way to his sister's apartments. He hated the thin, frail and reclusive figure she'd become since her return from Valsheba. He had restrained himself from pestering her with questions for nearly a full season but now he felt something had to be done. He knocked gently on the door. He heard a faint murmur which he took as an invitation to enter.

Jian sat in an armchair facing out at the view over the endless roll of the great southern ocean. Shivan sat in the matching chair, half turned away from the window. He waited, but Jian said nothing, just stared unblinkingly at the restless water far below. Shivan drew a steady breath.

'Jian, it is time you came back to us. We have given you time, and space, to think your thoughts but now you must talk to us. Talk to *me*. You spoke of Enki, the day you returned. I have not asked anything of this Enki. All I or Tika know of him is that outwardly he appeared a simpleton, but he held great powers. This is what we have learned from Olam, Kern and Riff. You apparently know more.

'Tika tells me the child Sha, speaks his name and weeps. She also speaks of Pesh and only recently, she's said another name – Kest. Jian, I am not trying to pry any secrets from your heart, but if not for my sake, then is there anyway you may be able to

417

soothe this child? Tika says she has the potential to become an enormously powerful mage but she fears the child's grief is harming that potential.'

Shivan paused but his sister didn't move. 'At least Ferag was proved correct. She took Kara to Iskallia. Because that valley once belonged to Aunt Lerran and thus was Dark Realm land, Kara lives there with Rahul and Sha and Jor. Rahul is a strong earth mage but he is content to make a family for those two children and Kara is delighted by all three of them. Can you help Sha? Please Jian?'

At last Jian turned to face her brother. 'I have not heard the names Pesh or Kest,' she said, her voice husky from disuse. 'I'm not sure how the child might know of Enki. She came from Segra city?'

Shivan nodded.

'I think Enki only went to the city a few times, with his father. People mocked him I think Rajini said.' Jian frowned. 'The child is a very small child? Enki hadn't been in the city for many full cycles so he could not have met her there.'

Inwardly rejoicing at the longest conversation he'd managed to have with Jian for so long, Shivan stood up. 'I thank you for that anyway. Could you bear to join me for supper this evening? I have missed you so, little sister.'

Jian looked up at her tall handsome brother and pushed herself out of her chair. They stared at each other, their faces so similar, and Jian smiled. 'I've been behaving like a spoilt brat haven't I?' she asked tremulously.

Shivan hugged her, unable to speak, then turned without a word, and left her.

The Segrans who arrived in Parima settled astonishingly well. Speaker Lashek kept a close if discreet eye on them but they presented no problems at all. Netta and Jevis proved to be strong in earth magic and both also showed great promise as teachers. Lashek encouraged them to think about joining the Segran school when they felt comfortable with their new surroundings. When they'd first crashed through to the circle in Parima, Netta had panicked to find so many missing from the crowd who had huddled together in the cave in Valsheba. Messages flew back and forth between the various circles and as soon as Thryssa received the names of those in Sapphrea and Iskallia and informed Netta, the woman relaxed.

A few days later, messages arrived again, addressed to Netta and Jevis, from Kiri in Iskallia and Tevix in Sapphrea. Kwanzi reported to Thryssa that once Netta was reassured her friends and the other Segrans from Valsheba were safe and well, she showed little concern that they were so far away. Thryssa offered to take Jevis and Netta through the circle to visit Kiri or Tevix but both refused. Jevis gave her a rueful grin. 'I'm not sure I like the thought of travelling on a circle ever again.'

Thryssa laughed. 'As you wish, but please remember you are not here by your own choice, or in anyway as prisoners. You are blood of our blood, and as free to travel as any other.'

'Speaker Lashek has offered us a place in his house, to see if we'd like to stay in Segra city.'

'Segra Circle,' Thryssa corrected gently. 'We live in Circles in Vagrantia, not cities my dear.'

Now, as summer ended, the Segrans of Valsheba were happily settled in Segra Circle in Vagrantia. Many had been given their own small houses with plots of land to work. A few worked for larger landholders and three worked in the administration block, under Lashek's eyes.

In her study, high in the Corvida Building in Parima Circle, Thryssa pondered on the way the newcomers from such a very distant past, fitted in to life in Vagrantia. She recalled Tika's remarks about the dangers of an unchanging way of living. It seemed Vagrantia could hardly have changed since Valsheban days. Thryssa decided this was something she must discuss seriously with her husband Kwanzi.

In Return, the Segran refugees had also fitted easily into the Sapphrean world. Taban had been drawn into the Lady Lallia's household with great enthusiasm. Although Seboth and his wife had mage talents, awakened by Tika over a full cycle ago, neither of them had a gift for healing. Lallia could mindspeak over a considerable distance, and Seboth was similarly skilled. Taban found living in a large fortified house difficult at first, used as she was to the open grasslands her tribe had wandered over for endless generations.

Lallia realised what bothered her new healer and arranged for her to have a set of rooms overlooking the fields and low hills which led to the barren lands and, eventually, to the coast. Taban appreciated Lallia's thoughtfulness and she did breathe easier once she had such a wide view of open land.

Kaz found his way round in no time, partly because he was still checking Riff's shoulder and thus met many of Seboth's armsmen. They watched him work, passing sarcastic comments on Riff's idiocy in getting wounded in the first place. Tika had managed to repair some of the damage but she explained that too long a time had passed between the injury occurring and her getting her hands and mage powers on him.

Riff knew the comments and teasing from the other men hid their shock at the huge missing chunk of his shoulder and upper arm. Tika restored some movement in the arm and Kaz helped Riff with some of the exercises she instructed him to keep up. The only one who seemed, not unhappy, but slightly at a loss, was Jala. She'd been given rooms on the ground floor with a tiny private garden where she spent a lot of time with the crow that had come through the circle with her.

The crow had met local crows and relayed many things of interest to the seer Jala. Seboth and Lallia both worried that Jala didn't enjoy being in Return although she was perfectly amiable when in their presence. It was Kaz who told Riff that Jala should go to Iskallia.

'My mother dreams of a child, and she also wants to meet your Lady Tika. She wasn't awake when the Lady was here before.' Kaz grinned.

Tika had been long gone by the time the travellers had all woken. Riff passed that information on to Olam who told his brother and sister in law.

Messengers had retrieved the remnants of Olam's expedition from the coast as soon as Seboth knew circles were the focus of attention. Tursig spent a lot of time lately with Riff and helped him when Kaz was busy elsewhere. Dellian had used the circle on the way back from the coast, to go directly to the Shadow Realm. As soon as she vanished from the circle, Reema and Shuli stepped forward and travelled back to Gaharn.

420

Riff and Olam were ordered, by Seboth, to take Jala, her crow and the Segran Tevix, who had asked to serve Kiri, to Iskallia. Arriving on Tika's plain stone circle, Jala beamed with delight. Right in front of her stood Brin and Skay. Still clutching the crow, Jala ignored everyone else, marching straight to greet the two Dragons.

Tevix had been told about Dragons but being confronted with them proved another matter. Fortunately Kiri and Rahul were on hand and sat him on a bench before introducing him to the younger, smaller Dragons. Tevix finally relaxed when Volk's horse Daisy casually ambled over and leaned against Farn, obviously perfectly at ease.

Most of the leaves had fallen from the trees in Iskallia, the evergreens higher on the slopes looking like stern black fingers pointing at the sky, strict and severe. Above them, snow shawled the peaks and crept lower each day. Tika had liked Jala immediately and Kara had welcomed her with joy. The seer spent a lot of her time in Kara's quarters which she shared with Rahul, Jor and Sha. Tika had objected to the size of her house in the planning, but now conceded that the previously empty rooms were becoming occupied quite quickly.

So far there had been only many frosty days and nights, but no heavy snowfall in the lower land of Iskallia, but tonight there was a certain tang in the air which suggested snow was near. It was very late. Tika had retired up to her Eyrie, the house silent beneath her. Thoughts churned ceaselessly. Now people lived in her valley, who appeared to have lived here forever, so easily had they settled.

Why had that cat – Hala – attached herself so firmly to Riff? She'd even insisted on coming through the circle with him when he and Olam brought Jala. And that crow! Tika sat by the fire, pondering so many things her head buzzed. She needed some sleep but that seemed highly unlikely tonight. She pulled on one of the wonderfully warm jackets Sergeant Essa's mother knitted for her and went out into her tiny patch of hidden garden.

Stars shone in the velvet of the sky and Tika wrapped her arms round herself against the sudden sharp cold.

'Hello poppet.' Ferag sat on the stone bench, smiling at her.

Tika returned her smile but chose not to sit down. She thought she might just freeze to the stone.

'Things have certainly worked out well don't you think darling?'

'Yes they have Ferag, although I'm still puzzled by a great many things.'

Ferag reached for Tika's hand, her own long fingers as cold as ice. 'I've brought a friend who asked to see you my darling.'

Tika turned and saw a silvery mist slowly solidifying behind her. Ferag squeezed her fingers gently in some kind of warning, Tika felt sure. The mist coalesced into a female human form, scarcely taller than Tika. The fur on her head and face seemed to trap the starlight and her eyes were all colours and none. Ferag stood, putting an arm gently round the newcomer's shoulders. 'Tika, this is my colleague, and my dear friend, Youki.'

Tika could only stare. She vividly remembered Youki's brief appearance in the Karmazen Palace two seasons ago. Youki smiled faintly.

'I believe your friend Riff brought you a gift?'

Tika's hand flew to her pocket. She had a leather pouch there, with particular treasures tucked away. She drew out the pouch and tipped its contents onto her palm. A beautiful purple Dragon scale. Another, like Youki's eyes, all colours and none, in two halves. A tiny black stone arrowhead. Finally a green stone, perfectly round, the size of a small plum.

Youki sighed. 'A chenzaldi. You have another treasure.'

Tika pulled out the pendant she always wore round her neck and let it swing from its gold chain. Youki made no move to touch any of the things at first.

'Enki, and Pesh, and Kest, were my beloved children,' she whispered. She extended one long finger and touched each item in turn: Seela's purple scale, the two halves of Dabray's pearly scale, then the arrowhead and lastly the green stone. When her furred finger brushed over the stone, it blazed with a sudden green gold flare which was reflected and echoed by Tika's pendant. The finger moved again, tracing gently along Tika's cheek.

'I dream that one day, humans may understand and remember, and the earth will no longer weep. My children do what they can to serve and guard.' She touched the stone once more and another fainter glow emanated from it, tingeing the creature's fur a pale green. 'In your tongue, chenzaldi means mother's tears. You will understand it all one day child, but for now you will learn, slowly and patiently.' Youki drew back, closer to Ferag but looking directly into Tika's eyes. She smiled. 'I know patience is hard for you. It is also for me.' She paused. 'Kara knows me. Tell her she does well and that I love her still.' Leaning forward she pressed her cheek against Tika's, the fur soft as down.

Even as Tika blinked, the silvered mist took Youki away. Ferag sighed.

'She is very strange, but she is very precious to me now. Of course, we all *knew* of her, but when she visited me, when dear Kara was so ill, I was amazed. She's visited me several times since, and she is just such a darling. Well there you are my poppet. I hope you liked my surprise. I must away, duty calls and all that. See you soon, dear child.'

Tika received an icy kiss on her brow and stood alone in her starlight garden, her treasures in her hand. Slowly, carefully, she replaced them in the pouch, tucked the pendant inside her shirt and went to the door leading into her rooms. She glanced up at the stars and realised huge feathers of snow were floating silently down. Tika went inside and pushed another log onto the fire. She stared into the flames. Youki was the answer to so many things, but she was also the question.

In the morning, Tika was woken by cries from far below and feet pounding up the stone stairs. She rushed to the window, staring down. There had indeed been a heavy snowfall during the night but none had settled on the circle she had made. Tika simply stared, even as her door burst open to allow a breathless Shea to enter.

The circle still held the grey stone slabs she had placed there, but it was now completely filled in with tiles, in a spiral pattern of golds, greens and blues. The border was a silvery blue the exact shade of Farn's scales.

'It's beautiful,' Shea murmured. 'How did it get like that?'

'I think,' said Tika slowly, 'it is a gift, from a friend.'

The story will continue ...

Books in the "Circles of Light" series

Soul Bonds

Vagrants

Drogoya

Survivors

Dark Realm

Perilous Shadows

Mage Foretold

Echoes of Dreams

Made in the USA
Lexington, KY
11 June 2015